ARTEMIS FOWL

aurum potestas est

ARTEMIS FOWL is a child genius from Ireland who has dedicated his brilliant mind to criminal activities. When Artemis discovers that there are fairies living below ground, he sees it as a golden opportunity. Now there is a whole new species to trick and cheat with his ingenious schemes. But Artemis doesn't know as much as he thinks about the fairy People. And what he doesn't know could hurt him . . .

PRAISE FOR

ARTEMIS FOWL

Shortlisted for the Whitbread Children's Book of the Year, winner of the WHSmith 'People's Choice' Children's Book of the Year and winner of the British Book Awards Children's Book of the Year

'Fast-paced, tongue-in-cheek' *Sunday Times*

'Smart, amusing. It flashes with high-tech invention' *Observer*

'Funny, fast, cinematic adventure' *Financial Times*

'Brilliant fantasy' *Independent*

'A huge hit' *Guardian*

'It reads like the fastest, punchiest comic strip you've ever come across' *Daily Telegraph*

'A fast and furious ride, jam-packed with wit, invention and magic' *Elle*

'Colfer has done enormously, explosively well'
New York Times Book Review

BOOKS BY EOIN COLFER

ARTEMIS FOWL
ARTEMIS FOWL AND THE ARCTIC INCIDENT
ARTEMIS FOWL AND THE ETERNITY CODE
ARTEMIS FOWL AND THE OPAL DECEPTION
ARTEMIS FOWL AND THE LOST COLONY
ARTEMIS FOWL AND THE TIME PARADOX
ARTEMIS FOWL AND THE ATLANTIS COMPLEX
ARTEMIS FOWL AND THE LAST GUARDIAN

W.A.R.P.: THE RELUCTANT ASSASSIN
W.A.R.P.: THE HANGMAN'S REVOLUTION
W.A.R.P.: THE FOREVER MAN

AIRMAN
BENNY AND BABE
BENNY AND OMAR
HALF MOON INVESTIGATIONS
THE SUPERNATURALIST
THE WISH LIST

GRAPHIC NOVELS
ARTEMIS FOWL: THE GRAPHIC NOVEL
ARTEMIS FOWL AND THE ARCTIC INCIDENT: THE GRAPHIC NOVEL
ARTEMIS FOWL AND THE ETERNITY CODE: THE GRAPHIC NOVEL
ARTEMIS FOWL AND THE OPAL DECEPTION: THE GRAPHIC NOVEL

FOR YOUNGER READERS
THE LEGEND OF SPUD MURPHY
THE LEGEND OF CAPTAIN CROW'S TEETH
THE LEGEND OF THE WORST BOY IN THE WORLD

EOIN COLFER

ARTEMIS FOWL

AND THE
TIME PARADOX

PUFFIN

PUFFIN BOOKS

UK | USA | Canada | Ireland | Australia
India | New Zealand | South Africa

Puffin Books is part of the Penguin Random House group of companies
whose addresses can be found at global.penguinrandomhouse.com.

www.penguin.co.uk
www.puffin.co.uk
www.ladybird.co.uk

Penguin
Random House
UK

First published in hardback 2008
Published in paperback 2009
This edition published 2011
Reissued 2019

006

'LEPrecon' first published in *The Artemis Fowl Files* 2004

Text copyright © Eoin Colfer, Artemis Fowl Ltd, 2004, 2008
Artemis Fowl and the Atlantis Complex text copyright © Eoin Colfer, Artemis Fowl Ltd, 2010
Map by Kev Walker

The moral right of the author and illustrator has been asserted

Typeset in Perpetua by Palimpsest Book Production Ltd, Falkirk, Stirlingshire
Printed in Great Britain by Clays Ltd, Elcograf S.p.A.

A CIP catalogue record for this book is available from the British Library

ISBN: 978-0-141-33912-2

All correspondence to:
Puffin Books
Penguin Random House Children's
80 Strand, London WC2R ORL

For Grace.
A new daughter, granddaughter,
niece and cousin

Hard Drive
8TB Drive

Cloud Files
My Files
Images
Apps
Downloaded
Music

❶ Fowl Manor

Haven City

2 Fez, Morocco

USER NAME ●●●●●●●●●●●●●●●●●● ✓ Password ●●●●●●●●●●●●●●●●●● ✓

CONTENTS

PROLOGUE

BARELY an hour north of Dublin's fair city lies the Fowl estate, where the boundaries have changed little in the past five hundred years.

The manor house is not visible from the main road, shrouded by a fan of oak trees and a parallelogram of high stone walls. The gates are reinforced steel with cameras perched upon their pillars. Were you allowed to pass through these discreetly electrified portals, you would find yourself on a pea-gravel avenue, meandering gently through what was once a manicured lawn, but which has now been encouraged to evolve into a wild garden.

The trees grow dense as you approach the manor itself, soaring oak and horse chestnut, intermingled with more delicate ash and willow. The only signs of cultivation are a driveway free of weeds, and the glowing lamps that float overhead seemingly without tether or cable.

Fowl Manor has been the site of many grand adventures over the centuries. In recent years, the adventures have had more of a magical bent, though most of the Fowl family have been kept in the dark about this fact. They have no idea that the main lobby was completely destroyed when the fairy folk sent a troll to do battle with Artemis, the family's eldest son and a criminal mastermind. He was twelve years old at the time. Today, however, Fowl activity in the manor is entirely legal. There are no fairy special forces storming the battlements. No elfin police officers held captive in the cellar. Nor any sign of a centaur fine-tuning his listening devices or running thermal scans. Artemis has made peace with the fairy People, and formed solid friendships among their ranks.

Though his criminal activities earned Artemis much, they cost him more. People he loves have been distraught, injured and even abducted because of his schemes. For the past three years his parents thought him dead, while he fought demons in Limbo. And on his return he was flabbergasted to find that the world had moved on without him, and he was now the older brother to two-year-old twin boys, Beckett and Myles.

CHAPTER 1: ESPRESSO AND TREACLE

 ARTEMIS sat on an ox-blood leather armchair, facing Beckett and Myles. His mother was in bed with a slight case of the flu, his father was with the doctor in her room, and so Artemis was lending a hand in entertaining the toddlers. And what better entertainment for youngsters than some lessons.

He had decided to dress casually in a sky-blue silk shirt, light grey woollen trousers and Gucci loafers. His black hair was swept back from his forehead, and he was putting on a jolly expression, which he had heard appealed to children.

'Artemis need toilet?' wondered Beckett, who squatted on the Tunisian rug, wearing only a grass-stained vest, which he had pulled down over his knees.

'No, Beckett,' said Artemis brightly. 'I am trying to look jolly. And shouldn't you be wearing a nappy?'

'Nappy,' snorted Myles, who had potty-trained himself

at the age of fourteen months, building a stepladder of encyclopedias to reach the toilet seat.

'No nappy,' pouted Beckett, slapping at a still-buzzing fly trapped in his sticky blond curls. 'Beckett hates nappy.'

Artemis doubted if the nanny had neglected to put a nappy on Beckett, and he wondered briefly where that nappy was now.

'Very well, Beckett,' continued Artemis. 'Let's shelve the nappy issue for now, and move on to today's lesson.'

'Chocolate on shelves,' said Beckett, stretching his fingers high to reach imaginary chocolate.

'Yes, good. There is sometimes chocolate on the shelves.'

'And espresso,' added Beckett, who had a strange set of favourite tastes, which included espresso sachets and treacle. In the same cup, if he could manage it. Once Beckett had managed to down several spoons of this concoction before it was wrestled away from him. The toddler hadn't slept for twenty-eight hours.

'Can we learn the new words, Artemis?' asked Myles, who wanted to get back to a mould jar in his bedroom. 'I am doing speriments with Professor Primate.'

Professor Primate was a stuffed monkey, and Myles's occasional lab partner. The cuddly toy spent most of his time stuffed into a borosilicate glass beaker on the *speriment* table. Artemis had reprogrammed the monkey's voice box to respond to Myles's voice with twelve phrases, including *It's alive! It's alive!* and *History will remember this day, Professor Myles.*

'You can go back to your *laboratory* soon,' said Artemis

approvingly. Myles was cut from the same cloth as himself, a natural-born scientist. 'Now, boys. I thought today we might tackle some restaurant terms.'

'Sneezes look like worms,' said Beckett, who wasn't one for staying on topic.

Artemis was nearly thrown by this remark. *Worms* were most definitely not on the menu, though snails might well be. 'Forget about worms.'

'Forget worms!' said Beckett, horrified.

'Just for the moment,' said Artemis reassuringly. 'As soon as we have finished our word game, you may think on whatever pleases you. And, if you are really good, then I may take you to see the horses.'

Riding was the only form of exercise that Artemis had taken to. This was mainly because the horse did most of the work.

Beckett pointed to himself. 'Beckett,' he said proudly, worms already a distant memory.

Myles sighed. 'Simple-toon.'

Artemis was beginning to regret scheduling this lesson, but having begun he was determined to forge ahead.

'Myles, don't call your brother a simpleton.'

''S OK, Artemis. He likes it. You're a simple-toon, aren't you, Beckett?'

'Beckett simple-toon,' agreed the small boy happily.

Artemis rubbed his hands together. 'Right, brothers. Onwards. Imagine yourself seated at a café table in Montmartre.'

⊗⊕⋇⊞⊗⊙⫞•⫶⋇⏁⊙⫶⏁⫶•⫞⊌⫝⫞⊙⊕⊞⫝•⫶⫝

'In Paris,' said Myles, smugly straightening the cravat he had borrowed from his father.

'Yes, Paris. And, try as you will, you cannot attract the waiter's attention. What do you do?'

The infants stared at him blankly, and Artemis began to wonder if he wasn't pitching his lesson a little high. He was relieved, if a little surprised, to see a spark of comprehension in Beckett's eyes.

'Um . . . tell Butler to jump-jump-jump on his head?'

Myles was impressed. 'I agree with simple-toon.'

'No!' said Artemis. 'You simply raise one finger and say clearly, "*Ici, garçon*."'

'Itchy what?'

'What? No, Beckett, not *itchy*.' Artemis sighed. This was impossible. *Impossible*. And he hadn't even introduced the flashcards yet or his new modified laser pointer, which could either highlight a word or burn through several steel plates, depending on the setting.

'Let's try it together. Raise one finger and say, "*Ici, garçon*."

All together now . . .'

The little boys did as they were told, eager to please their deranged brother.

'*Ici, garçon*,' they chorused, pudgy fingers raised. And then from the corner of his mouth Myles whispered to his twin, 'Artemis simple-toon.'

Artemis raised his hands. 'I surrender. You win – no more lessons. Why don't we paint some pictures?'

'Excellent,' said Myles. 'I shall paint my jar of mould.'

Beckett was suspicious. 'I won't learn?'

'No,' said Artemis, fondly ruffling his brother's hair and immediately regretting it. 'You won't learn a thing.'

'Good. Beckett happy now. See.' The boy pointed to himself once more, specifically to the broad smile on his face.

The three brothers were stretched on the floor, up to their elbows in poster paint, when their father entered the room. He looked tired from his nursing duties, but otherwise fit and strong, moving like a lifelong athlete in spite of his bio-hybrid artificial leg. The leg used lengthened bone, titanium prosthetics and implantable sensors to allow Artemis Senior's brain signals to move it. Occasionally, at the end of the day, he would use a microwaveable gel pouch to ease his stiffness, but otherwise he behaved as if the new leg were his own.

Artemis climbed to his knees, smudged and dripping.

'I abandoned French vocabulary and have joined the twins in play.' He grinned, wiping his hands. 'It's quite liberating, actually. We are finger-painting instead. I did try to sneak in a little lecture on Cubism, but received a splattering for my troubles.'

Artemis noticed then that his father was more than simply tired. He was anxious.

He stepped away from the twins, walking with Artemis Senior to the floor-to-ceiling bookcase.

'What is the matter? Is Mother's influenza worsening?'

Artemis's father rested one hand on the rolling ladder,

lifting his weight from the artificial limb. His expression was strange, and one that Artemis could not recall ever seeing.

He realized his father was more than anxious. Artemis Fowl Senior was afraid.

'Father?'

Artemis Senior gripped the ladder's rung with such force that the wood creaked. He opened his mouth to speak but then seemed to change his mind.

Now Artemis himself grew worried. 'Father, you must tell me.'

'Of course,' said his father with a start, as if just remembering where he was. 'I must tell you . . .'

Then a tear fell from his eye, dripping on to his shirt, deepening the blue.

'I remember when I first saw your mother,' he said. 'I was in London, at a private party in the Ivy. A room full of scoundrels and I was the biggest one in the bunch. She changed me, Arty. Broke my heart, then put it together again. Angeline saved my life. Now . . .'

Artemis felt weak with nerves. His blood pounded in his ears like the Atlantic surf.

'Is Mother dying, Father? Is this what you are trying to tell me?'

The idea seemed ludicrous. Impossible.

His father blinked, as if waking from a dream.

'Not if the Fowl men have something to say about it, eh, son? It's time for you to earn that reputation of yours.' Artemis

Senior's eyes were bright with desperation. 'Whatever we have to do, son. Whatever it takes.'

Artemis felt panic welling up inside him.

Whatever we have to do?

Be calm, he told himself. *You have the power to fix this.*

Artemis did not yet have all the facts, but nonetheless he was reasonably confident that whatever was wrong with his mother could be healed with a burst of fairy magic. And he was the only human on Earth with that magic running through his system.

'Father,' he said gently, 'has the doctor left?'

For a moment the question seemed to puzzle Artemis Senior, then he remembered.

'Left? No. He is in the lobby. I thought you might talk to him. Just in case there's a question I have missed . . .'

Artemis was only mildly surprised to find Doctor Hans Schalke, Europe's leading expert on rare diseases, in the lobby and not the usual family practitioner. Naturally, his father would have sent for Schalke when Angeline Fowl's condition began to deteriorate. Schalke waited below the filigreed Fowl crest, a hard-skinned Gladstone bag standing sentry by his ankles like a giant beetle. He was belting a grey raincoat across his waist and speaking to his assistant in sharp tones.

Everything about the doctor was sharp, from the arrowhead of his widow's peak, to the razor edges of his cheekbones and nose. Twin ovals of cut glass magnified Schalke's blue eyes and his mouth slashed downwards from left to right, barely moving as he talked.

'All of the symptoms,' he said, his accent muted German. 'On all of the databases, you understand?'

His assistant, a petite young lady in an expensively cut grey suit, nodded several times, tapping the instructions on to the screen of her smartphone.

'Universities too?' she asked.

'*All*,' said Schalke, accompanying the word with an impatient nod. 'Did I not say all? Do you not understand my accent? Is it because I am from Germany coming?'

'Sorry, Doctor,' said the assistant contritely. 'All, of course.'

Artemis approached Doctor Schalke, hand outstretched. The doctor did not return the gesture.

'Contamination, Master Fowl,' he said, without a trace of apology or sympathy. 'We have not determined whether your mother's condition is contagious.'

Artemis curled his fingers into his palm, sliding the hand behind his back. The doctor was right, of course.

'We have never met, Doctor. Would you be so good as to describe my mother's symptoms?'

The doctor huffed, irritated. 'Very well, young man, but I am not accustomed to dealing with children, so there will be no sugar coating.'

Artemis swallowed, his throat suddenly dry.

Sugar coating.

'Your mother's condition is possibly unique,' said Schalke, banishing his assistant to her work with a shake of his fingers. 'From what I can tell, her organs seem to be failing.'

'Which organs?'

'*All* of them,' said Schalke. 'I need to bring equipment here from my laboratory at Trinity College. Obviously your mother cannot be moved. My assistant, Imogen, Miss Book, will monitor her until my return. Miss Book is not only my publicist, but an excellent nurse too. A useful combination, wouldn't you say?'

In his peripheral vision, Artemis saw Miss Book scurry round a corner, stammering into her smartphone. He hoped the publicist/nurse would display more confidence when caring for his mother.

'I suppose. All my mother's organs? *All* of them?'

Schalke was not inclined to repeat himself. 'I am reminded of lupus, but more aggressive, combined with all three stages of Lyme disease. I did observe an Amazonian tribe once with similar symptoms, but not so severe. At this rate of decline, your mother has days left to her. Frankly, I doubt we will have time to complete tests. We need a miracle cure, and in my considerable experience miracle cures do not exist.'

'Perhaps they do,' said Artemis absently.

Schalke picked up his bag. 'Put your faith in science, young man,' advised the doctor. 'Science will serve your mother better than some mysterious force.'

Artemis held the door for Schalke, watching him walk the dozen steps to his vintage Mercedes-Benz. The car was grey, like the bruised clouds overhead.

There is no time for science, thought the Irish teenager. *Magic is my only option.*

When Artemis returned to his study, his father was sitting on the rug with Beckett crawling along his torso like a monkey.

'May I see Mother now?' Artemis asked him.

'Yes,' said Artemis Senior. 'Go now; see what you can find out. Study her symptoms for your search.'

My search? thought Artemis. *There are difficult times ahead.*

Artemis's hulking bodyguard, Butler, waited for him at the foot of the stairs wearing full Kendo armour, the helmet's faceguard folded away from his weathered features.

'I was in the dojo, sparring with the holograph,' he explained. 'Your father called and told me I was needed immediately. What's going on?'

'It's Mother,' said Artemis, passing him. 'She's very ill. I'm going to see what I can do.'

Butler hurried to keep pace, his chest plate clanking. 'Be careful, Artemis. Magic is not science. You can't control it. You wouldn't want to accidentally make Mrs Fowl's condition worse.'

Artemis arrived at the top of the grand stairway, tentatively reaching his hand towards the bedroom door's crystal knob, as though it were electrified.

'I fear that her condition couldn't be worse . . .'

*

Artemis went inside alone, leaving the bodyguard to strip off the Kendo headgear and Hon-nuri breastplate. Underneath he wore a tracksuit instead of the traditional wide-legged trousers. Sweat blossomed across his chest and back, but Butler ignored his desire to go and shower, standing sentry outside the door, knowing that he shouldn't strain too hard to listen, but wishing that he could.

Butler was the only other human who knew the full truth of Artemis's magical escapades. He had been at his young charge's shoulder throughout their various adventures, battling fairies and humans across the continents. But Artemis had made the journey through time to Limbo without him, and he had come back changed. A part of his young charge was magical now, and not just Captain Holly Short's hazel left eye the time stream had given him in place of his own. On the journey from Earth to Limbo and back, Artemis had somehow managed to steal a few strands of magic from the fairies whose atoms were mixed with his in the time stream. When he had returned home from Limbo, Artemis had *suggested* to his parents, in the compelling magical *mesmer*, that they simply not think about where he had been for the past few years. It wasn't a very sophisticated plan, as his disappearance had made the news worldwide, and the subject was raised at every function the Fowls attended. But until Artemis could get hold of some LEP mind-wiping equipment, or indeed develop his own, it would have to suffice. He *suggested* to his parents that if anyone were to ask about him they should simply

14

state it was a family matter and ask that their privacy be respected.

Artemis is a magical human, thought Butler. *The only one.*

And now Butler just knew Artemis was going to use his magic to attempt a healing on his mother. It was a dangerous game; magic was not a natural part of his make-up. The boy could well remove one set of symptoms and replace them with another.

Artemis entered his parents' bedroom slowly. The twins charged in here at all hours of the day and night, flinging themselves on the four-poster bed to wrestle with his protesting mother and father, but Artemis had never experienced that. His childhood had been a time of order and discipline.

Always knock before entering, Artemis, his father had instructed him. *It shows respect.*

But his father had changed. A brush with death seven years earlier had shown him what was really important. Now he was always ready to hug and roll in the covers with his beloved sons.

It's too late for me, thought Artemis. *I am too old for tussles with Father.*

Mother was different. She was never cold, apart from during her bouts of depression when his father was missing. But fairy magic and the return of her beloved husband had saved her from that and now she was herself again. Or she had been until now.

Artemis crossed the room slowly, afraid of what lay before him. He walked cautiously across the carpet, careful to tread between the vine patterns in the weave.

Step on a vine, count to nine.

This was a habit from when he was little, an old superstition whispered lightly by his father. Artemis had never forgotten and always counted to nine to ward off the bad luck should so much as a toe touch the carpet vines.

The four-poster bed stood at the rear of the room, swathed in hanging drapes and sunlight. A breeze slipped into the room, rippling the silks like the sails of a pirate ship.

One of his mother's hands dangled over the side. Pale and thin.

Artemis was horrified. Just yesterday his mother had been fine. A slight sniffle, but still her warm, laughing self.

'Mother,' he blurted on seeing her face, feeling as though the word had been punched out of him.

This was not possible. In twenty-four hours, his mother had deteriorated to little more than a skeleton. Her cheekbones were sharp as flint, her eyes lost in dark sockets.

Don't worry, Artemis told himself. *In a few short seconds Mother will be well, then I can investigate what happened here.*

Angeline Fowl's beautiful hair was frizzed and brittle, broken strands criss-crossing her pillow like a spider's web. And there was an odd smell emanating from her pores.

Lilies, thought Artemis. *Sweet yet tinged with sickness.*

Angeline's eyes opened abruptly, round with panic. Her

back arched as she sucked breath through a constricted windpipe, clutching at the air with clawed hands. Just as suddenly she collapsed, and Artemis thought for a terrible moment that she was gone.

But then her eyelids fluttered and she reached out a hand for him.

'Arty,' she said, her voice no more than a whisper. 'I am having the strangest dream.' A short sentence, but it took an age to complete, with a rasped breath between each word.

Artemis took his mother's hand. How slender it was. A parcel of bones.

'Or perhaps I am awake and my other life is a dream.'

Artemis was pained to hear his mother speak like this; it reminded him of the turns she used to suffer from.

'You're awake, Mother, and I am here. You have a light fever and are a little dehydrated, that's all. Nothing to be concerned about.'

'How can I be awake, Arty,' said Angeline, her eyes calm in black circles, 'when I feel myself dying? How can I be awake when I feel that?'

Artemis's feigned calm was knocked by this.

'I-it's the . . . fever,' he stammered. 'You're seeing things a little strangely. Everything will be fine soon. I promise.'

Angeline closed her eyes. 'And my son keeps his promises, I know. Where have you been these past years, Arty? We were so worried. Why are you not seventeen?'

In her delirium, Angeline Fowl saw through a haze of magic to the truth. She realized that he had been missing for three years and had come home the same age as when he went away.

'I am fourteen, Mother. Almost fifteen now, still a boy for another while. Now close your eyes and when you open them again all will be well.'

'What have you done to my thoughts, Artemis? Where has your power come from?'

Artemis was sweating now. The heat of the room, the sickly smell, his own anxiety.

She knows. Mother knows. If you heal her, will she remember everything?

It didn't matter. That could be dealt with in due course. His priority was to mend his parent.

Artemis squeezed the frail hand in his grip, feeling the bones grind against each other. He was about to use magic on his mother for the second time.

Magic did not belong in Artemis's soul, and gave him lightning-bolt headaches whenever he used it. Though he was human, the fairy rules of magic held a certain sway over him. He was forced to chew motion-sickness tablets before entering a dwelling uninvited, and when the moon was full Artemis could often be found in the library, listening to music at maximum volume to drown out the voices in his head. The great commune of magical creatures. The fairies had powerful race memories and they surfaced like a tidal wave of raw emotion, bringing migraines with them.

Sometimes Artemis wondered if stealing the magic had been a mistake, but recently the symptoms had stopped.

No more migraines or sickness. Perhaps his brain was adapting to the strain of being a magical creature.

Artemis held his mother's fingers gently, closed his eyes and cleared his mind.

Magic. Only magic.

The magic was a wild force and needed to be controlled. If Artemis let his thoughts ramble, the magic would ramble too and he could open his eyes to find his mother still sick but with different-coloured hair.

Heal, he thought. *Be well, Mother.*

The magic responded to his wish, spreading along his limbs, buzzing, tingling. Blue sparks circled his wrists, twitching like shoals of tiny minnows. Almost as if they were alive.

Artemis thought of his mother in better times. He saw her skin radiant, her eyes shining with happiness. Heard her laugh, felt her touch on his neck. Remembered the strength of Angeline Fowl's love for her family.

That is what I want.

The sparks sensed his wishes and flowed into Angeline Fowl, sinking into the skin of her hand and wrist, twisting in ropes round her gaunt arms. Artemis pushed harder and a river of magical flickers flowed from his fingers into his mother.

Heal, he thought. *Drive out the sickness.*

Artemis had used his magic before, but this time was different. There was resistance, as though his mother's body did not wish to be healed and was rejecting the power. Sparks fizzled on her skin, spasmed and winked out.

More, thought Artemis. *More*.

He pushed harder, ignoring the sudden blinding headache and rumbling nausea.

Heal, Mother.

The magic wrapped his mother like an Egyptian mummy, snaking underneath her body, raising her fifteen centimetres from the mattress. She shuddered and moaned, steam venting from her pores, sizzling as it touched the blue sparks.

She is in pain, thought Artemis, opening one eye a slit. *In agony. But I cannot stop now.*

Artemis dug down deep, searching his extremities for the last scraps of magic inside him.

Everything. Give her every last spark.

Magic was not an intrinsic part of Artemis; he had stolen it and now he threw it off again, stuffing all he had into the attempted healing. And yet it wasn't working. No, more than that. Her sickness grew stronger. Repelling each blue wave, robbing the sparks of their colour and power, sending them skittering to the ceiling.

Something is wrong, thought Artemis, bile in his throat, a dagger of pain over his left eye. *It shouldn't be like this.*

The final drop of magic left his body with a jolt and Artemis was thrown from his mother's bedside and sent skidding across the floor, then tumbling head over heels until he came to rest sprawled against a chaise longue. Angeline Fowl spasmed a final time, then collapsed back on to her mattress. Her body was soaked with a strange thick, clear gel. Magical sparks flickered and died in the coating, which steamed off almost as quickly as it had appeared.

Artemis lay with his head in his hands, waiting for the chaos in his brain to stop, unable to move or think. His own breathing seemed to rasp against his skull. Eventually, the pain faded to echoes, and jumbled words formed themselves into sentences.

The magic is gone. Spent. I am entirely human.

Artemis registered the sound of the bedroom door creaking and he opened his eyes to find Butler and his father staring down at him, concern large on their faces.

'We heard a crash. You must have fallen,' said Artemis Senior, lifting his son by the elbow. 'I should never have let you in here alone, but I thought that perhaps you could do something. You have certain talents, I know. I was hoping . . .' He straightened his son's shirt, patted his shoulders. 'It was stupid of me.'

Artemis shrugged his father's hands away, stumbling to his mother's sickbed. It took a mere glance to confirm what he already knew. He had not cured his mother. There was no bloom on her cheeks or ease in her breathing.

She is worse. What have I done?

'What is it?' asked his father. 'What the devil is wrong with her? At this rate of decline, in less than a week my Angeline will be —'

Butler interrupted brusquely. 'No giving up now, gents. We all have contacts from our past that might be able to shed some light on Mrs Fowl's condition. People we might prefer not to associate with otherwise. We find them, and bring them back here as fast as we can. We ignore nuisances like passports or visas and get it done.'

Artemis Senior nodded, slowly at first, then with more vigour.

'Yes. Yes, dammit. She is not finished yet. My Angeline is a fighter – are you not, darling?'

He took her hand gently, as though it were made of finest crystal. She did not respond to his touch or voice. 'We talked to every alternative practitioner in Europe about my phantom-limb pains. Perhaps one of them can help us with this.'

'I know a man in China,' said Butler. 'He worked with Madame Ko at the bodyguard academy. He was a miracle worker with herbs. Lived up the mountains. He has never been outside the province, but he would come for me.'

'Good,' said Artemis Senior. 'The more opinions we can call on the better.' He turned to his son. 'Listen, Arty, if you know someone who might be able to help. Anyone. Perhaps you have some underworld contacts?'

Artemis twisted a rather ostentatious ring on his middle finger so that the front rested against his palm. This *ring* was actually a camouflaged fairy communicator.

'Yes,' he said. 'I have a few underworld contacts.'

CHAPTER 2: **THE WORLD'S BIGGEST**

 THE *giant sea monster that is the kraken sent its finned tentacles spiralling towards the ocean's surface, pulling its bloated body behind. Its single eye rolled manically in its socket and its curved beak, the size of a schooner's prow, was open wide, filtering the rushing water through to its rippling gills.*

The kraken was hungry and there was room for only one thought in its tiny brain as it sped towards the holiday ferry above.

Kill . . . Kill . . . KILL . . .

'That is such dwarf manure,' said Lower Elements Police Captain Holly Short, muting the sound file in her helmet. 'For one thing, the kraken doesn't have tentacles, and as for *kill . . . kill . . . kill . . .*'

'I know,' said Foaly, the voice of mission control in her

communicator. 'I thought you might enjoy that passage. You know, have a laugh. Remember laughing?'

Holly was not amused. 'It's so typical of humans, Foaly, to take something perfectly natural and demonize it. Krakens are gentle creatures, and the humans turn them into some kind of murderous giant squid. *Kill . . . kill . . . kill.* Give me a break.'

'Come on, Holly, it's just sensational fiction. You know those humans and their imaginations. Relax.'

Foaly was right. If she got worked up every time the human media misrepresented a *mythical* creature, she would spend half her life in a rage. Over the centuries Mud Men had caught glimpses of the fairy folk, and had twisted the truth of these glimpses almost beyond recognition.

Let it go. There are decent humans. Remember Artemis and Butler.

'Did you see that human movie with the centaurs?' she asked the centaur on the other end of her helmet communicator. 'They were noble and sporty. *My sword for thee, Majesty, then off for a spot of hunting.* Fit centaurs, now that *did* make me laugh.'

Thousands of miles away, somewhere in the Earth's mantle below Ireland, Foaly, the Lower Elements Police technical adviser, rubbed his paunch.

'Holly, that hurts. Caballine likes my belly.'

Foaly had got married, or *hitched* as centaurs called the ceremony, while Holly had been away with Artemis Fowl rescuing demons in Limbo. A lot had changed in the three years she had been away, and sometimes Holly found it difficult to keep up. Foaly had a new bride to occupy his time. Her old friend Trouble Kelp had been promoted to LEP Commander, and she was back working at Recon with the Kraken Watch task force.

'Apologies, friend. That was mean,' said Holly. 'I like your belly too. I'm sorry that I wasn't there to see a hitching sash round it.'

'Me too. Next time.'

Holly smiled. 'Sure. That's going to happen.'

Traditionally, male centaurs were expected to take more than one bride, but Caballine was a modern fairy and Holly doubted if she would stand for a new filly in the household.

'Don't worry, I'm joking.'

'You'd better be, because I'm meeting Caballine at the spa this weekend.'

'How's the new gear?' said Foaly, hurriedly changing the subject.

Holly spread her arms wide, feeling the wind ripple her fingers, seeing the Baltic Sea flash past below in shards of blue and white.

'It's wonderful,' she said. 'Absolutely wonderful.'

Captain Holly Short of LEPrecon flew in wide, lazy circles above Helsinki, enjoying the brisk Scandinavian air filtering through her helmet. It was just after 5 a.m. local time and the rising sun had set the Uspenski Cathedral's golden onion dome shimmering. Already the city's famed marketplace was strobed with headlights as vendors arrived to open up for the morning trade, or eager politicians' aides made their way towards the blue-grey façade of City Hall.

Holly's target lay away from what would shortly be a bustling centre of commerce. She adjusted her fingers, and the sensors in her armoured gloves translated the movements to commands for the mechanical wings on her back, sending her spiralling down towards the small island of Uunisaari, half a mile from the port.

'The body sensors are nice,' she said. 'Very intuitive.'

'It's as close as it gets to being a bird,' said Foaly. 'Unless you want to integrate?'

'No thank you,' said Holly vehemently. She loved flying, but not enough to have an LEP surgeon sew a few implants into her cerebellum.

'Very well, Captain Short,' said Foaly, switching to business mode. 'Pre-op check. Three Ws please.'

The three Ws were every Reconnaissance officer's checklist before approaching an operation's zone. Wings, weapon and a way home.

Holly checked the transparent readouts on her helmet visor.

'Power cell charged. Weapon on green. Wings and suit fully functional. No red lights.'

'Excellent,' said Foaly. 'Check, check and check. Our screens agree.'

Holly heard keys clicking as Foaly recorded this information in the mission log. The centaur was known for his

26

fondness for old-school keyboards, even though he himself had patented an extremely efficient virtual keyboard – the v-board.

'Remember, Holly, this is just reconnaissance. Go down and check the sensor. Those things are two hundred years old, and the problem is more than likely a simple overheat. All you need to do is go where I tell you and fix what I tell you. No indiscriminate blasting involved. Understand?'

Holly snorted. 'I can see why Caballine fell for you, Foaly. You're such a charmer.'

Foaly snickered. 'I don't rise to jibes any more, Holly. Marriage has mellowed me.'

'Mellow? I'll believe that when you last ten minutes in a room with Mulch without throwing a hoof.'

The dwarf, Mulch Diggums, had been at various times enemy, partner and friend to Holly and Foaly. His greatest pleasure in life was stuffing his face, and not far behind that was irritating his various enemies, partners and friends.

'Perhaps I need a few more years of marriage before I get *that* mellow. A few more centuries, in fact.'

The island was large in Holly's visor now, surrounded by a monk's fringe of foam. Time to stop the chit-chat and proceed with the mission, though Holly was tempted to circle in a holding pattern so she could talk some more with her friend. It seemed as though this was the first real conversation they'd had since her return from Limbo. Foaly had moved on with life in the past three years, but for Holly her absence had only lasted a few hours and, though

she had not aged, Holly felt cheated of those years. The
LEP psychiatrist would have told her she was suffering from
Post-time-travel-displacement Depression, and offered to
prescribe a nice shot to cheer her up. Holly trusted happy-
shots just about as much as she trusted brain implants.

'I'm going in,' she said tersely. This was her first solo
mission since debriefing and she did not want anything less
than a perfect report, even if it was only Kraken Watch.

'Copy,' said Foaly. 'You see the sensor?'

There were four bio-sensors on the island relaying information back to Police Plaza. Three pulsed a gentle green
in Holly's visor display unit. The fourth sensor was red.
Red could mean many things. In this case *every* reading had
risen above normal levels. Temperature, heartbeat, brain
activity. All on the danger line.

'It must be a malfunction,' Foaly had explained. 'If not,
the other sensors would show something.'

'I have it. Strong signal.'

'OK. Shield and approach.'

Holly twisted her chin sharply left until her neck bone
clicked, which was her way of summoning the magic. It
wasn't a necessary movement, since the magic was mostly
a brain function, but fairies developed their own tics. She
let a dribble of power into her limbs and vibrated out of the
visible spectrum. Her shimmer suit picked up her frequency
and amplified it so that a tiny spark of magic went a long
way.

'I'm out of sight and going in,' she confirmed.

'Understood,' said the centaur. 'Be careful, Holly. Commander Kelp will be reviewing this video, so stick to your orders.'

'Are you suggesting that I occasionally stray from the rule book?' said Holly, apparently horrified by the very notion.

Foaly sniggered. 'I am suggesting that you may not own a copy of the rule book, and, if you do possess one, you certainly have never opened it.'

Fair point, thought Holly, swooping down towards the surface of Uunisaari.

Whales are thought to be the world's largest mammals. They are not. The kraken can stretch to five kilometres in length and have been a staple of Scandinavian legend since the thirteenth century, when they appeared in the Orvar-Odd saga as the fearsome *lyngbakr*. Early descriptions of the kraken are the most accurate, describing the sea creature as an animal the size of a floating island whose real danger to ships was not the creature itself, but the whirlpool it created when it sank into the ocean. But by the Middle Ages the legend of the kraken had been confused with that of the giant squid, and each was credited with the most fearsome attributes of the other. The squid was pictured big as a mountain, while the peaceful kraken grew tentacles and developed a bloodlust to rival that of the deadliest shark.

Nothing could be further from the truth. The kraken is a docile creature whose main defences are its sheer size and the bulk of shell, gas and fat cells enclosing a melon-sized brain which provides it with just enough intelligence to feed itself and shed its shell. Underneath the crust of rock, weed and coral, the kraken resembles nothing more than the common acorn barnacle, albeit a barnacle that could easily house an Olympic stadium or two.

The kraken enjoy a lifespan of several thousand years, thanks to an incredibly slow metabolism and a huge network of support systems surrounding their soft centres. They tend to settle in a food-rich or magical environment and remain there until the food or energy residue runs out. Nestling in the middle of an archipelago near a human port provides not only camouflage but an abundant source of edible material. And so this is where the kraken are found, anchored to the seabed like gigantic limpets, vacuuming city waste through their gills and fermenting it to methane in their vast stomachs. But, if human garbage is their salvation, it is also their damnation, for increasingly high toxin levels have rendered the kraken sterile, and now there are only half a dozen or so of the ancient creatures left in the oceans.

This particular kraken was the oldest of the bunch. According to shell scrapings, old Shelly, as the small, dedicated Kraken Watch referred to it, was over ten thousand years old, and had been masquerading as an island in Helsinki harbour since the sixteenth century, when the town was known as Helsingfors.

In all that time, Shelly had done little but feed and sleep, feeling no urge to migrate. Any need he may have felt to move on was dulled by the seepings of a paint factory built on his back more than a hundred years previously. To all intents and purposes, Shelly was catatonic, having emitted no more than a couple of methane flashes in over fifty years, so there was no reason to believe that this red light on his sensor was anything more than a crossed wire, and it was Holly's job to uncross it. It was a standard *first day back on the job* kind of mission. No danger, no deadline and little chance of discovery.

Holly turned her palms into the wind, descending till her boots scraped the roof of the island's small restaurant. Actually, there were two islands, separated by a small bridge. One was a genuine island, and the other, larger section was Shelly nestled into the rock. Holly ran a quick thermal sweep, finding nothing but a few rodents and a blotch of heat from the sauna, which was probably on a timer.

She consulted her visor for the sensor's exact location. It was four metres underwater, tucked below a rocky ledge.

Underwater. Of course.

She stowed her wings mid-air, then plunged feet first into the Baltic Sea, corkscrewing to minimize the splash. Not that there were any humans close enough to hear. The sauna and restaurant did not open until eight, and the nearest fishermen were on the mainland, their rods swaying gently like rows of bare flagpoles.

Holly vented the gas bags in her helmet to reduce buoyancy and sank below the waves. Her visor informed her that the water temperature was a little over ten degrees, but the shimmer suit insulated her from cold shock and even flexed to compensate for the slight pressure increase.

'Use the Critters,' said Foaly, his voice crystal clear through the vibration nodes over her ears.

'Get out of my head, centaur.'

'Go on. Use the Critters.'

'I don't need a tracer. It's right there.'

Foaly sighed. 'Then they shall die unfulfilled.'

The Coded Radiation Tracers were micro-organisms bathed in radiation of the same frequency as the object being located. If you knew what you were looking for before leaving Foaly's workshop, then the Critters would bring you right to it. Though they were a little redundant when the sensor was a few metres away and beeping on your screen.

'OK,' moaned Holly. 'I wish you would stop using me as a guinea pig.'

She pulled back a watertight flap on her glove, releasing a cloud of glowing orange mites into the water. They bunched for a moment, then sped off in a ragged arrow towards the sensor.

'They swim, they fly, they burrow,' said Foaly, awed by his own achievement. 'God bless their tiny hearts.'

The Critters left a glowing orange wake for Holly to follow. She pulled herself below a sharp ledge to find the Critters already excavating the growths covering the sensor.

'Now, come on. That is handy. Tell me that's not useful to a field officer.'

⊕⊙෴•⚖⚖•✶)⊕•⧈⊙෴•◻⚥⧖⊕•⚥⊎

It was very useful, especially since Holly only had ten minutes of air left, but Foaly's head was big enough as it was.

'A gill helmet would have been more useful, especially since you *knew* the sensor was underwater.'

'You have more than enough air,' argued Foaly. 'Especially since the Critters are clearing the surrounding area.'

The Critters ate away the rock and moss covering the sensor until it gleamed like the day it had come off the assembly line. Once their mission was completed, the Critters flickered and died, dissolving in the water with a gentle fizz. Holly switched on her helmet lights, focusing both beams on the alloy instrument. The sensor was the size and shape of a banana and covered with an electrolytic gel.

'The water is pretty clean, thanks to Shelly. I'm getting a decent picture.'

Holly topped up her suit buoyancy a few notches until she was at neutral, and hung in the water as still as she could.

'Well, what do you see?'

'The same as you,' replied the centaur. 'A sensor with a flashing red light. I need to take a few readings, if you wouldn't mind touching the screen.'

Holly laid her palm on the gel so that the omni-sensor on her glove could sync with the ancient instrument.

'Nine and a half minutes, Foaly, don't forget.'

'Please,' snickered the centaur. 'I could recalibrate a fleet of satellites in nine and a half minutes.'

It was probably true, thought Holly as her helmet ran a systems check on the sensor.

'Hmm,' sighed Foaly, thirty seconds later.

'Hmm?' repeated Holly nervously. 'Don't hmm, Foaly. Dazzle me with science, but don't hmm.'

'There doesn't seem to be anything wrong with this sensor. It is remarkably functional. Which means . . .'

'That the other three sensors are malfunctioning,' concluded Holly. 'So much for your genius.'

'I did not design these sensors,' said Foaly, wounded. 'They're old Koboi gear.'

Holly shuddered, her body jerking in the water. Her old enemy Opal Koboi had been one of the People's leading innovators, until she'd decided that she would prefer to pursue all criminal avenues to crown herself queen of the world instead. Now she was housed in a specially constructed isolation prison cube suspended in Atlantis, and spent her time shooting off mails to politicians pleading for early release.

'Apologies, old friend, for doubting your wonderful-ness. I suppose I should check the other sensors. Above sea level, I do hope.'

'Hmm,' said Foaly again.

'Please stop that. Surely, now I am here, I should check the remaining sensors?'

Silence for a moment while Foaly accessed a few files, then he spoke in hitched phrases as the information opened before him. 'The other sensors . . . are not the pressing issue . . . right now. What we really need to know . . . is why would Shelly be red-lining on *this* sensor. Let

34

me just see . . . if we have ever had these kinds of readings before.'

Holly had no choice but to maintain contact with the sensor, legs swaying underneath her, watching the air clock on her visor run down.

'OK,' said Foaly finally. 'Two reasons for a kraken's readings to red-line. One, Shelly is having a baby kraken, which is impossible since he's a sterile male.'

'That leaves two,' said Holly, who was certain that she would not like the second reason.

'And two, he's shedding.'

Holly rolled her eyes in relief. 'Shedding. That doesn't sound so bad.'

'Weeeellll, it's a little worse than it sounds.'

'What do you mean, a little?'

'Why don't I explain as you fly away, as fast as you can.'

Holly did not need to be told twice. When Foaly advised an officer to leave *before* he delivered one of his beloved lectures, then the situation was serious. She spread her arms wide and the action was mimicked by the wings on her back.

'Engage,' she said, pointing both arms to the surface, and the engines ignited, blasting her clear of the Baltic, boiling the water wake as it hung in the air. Her suit was instantly dry as moisture slipped from its non-stick material and air resistance tugged at any remaining drops. In seconds she had climbed to a hundred metres, the anxiety in Foaly's voice hurrying her along.

'A kraken sheds its shell once, and records show that

Shelly dumped his three thousand years ago, so we presumed that was that.'

'But now?'

'Now it seems as though Shelly has lived long enough to do it again.'

'And why are we concerned about this?'

'We are concerned about this because kraken shed very explosively. The new shell has already grown and Shelly will get rid of the old one by igniting a layer of methane cells and blasting it off.'

Holly wanted to be sure she understood what was being said. 'So you're saying that Shelly is going to light a fart?'

'No, Shelly is going to light *the* fart. He has stored enough methane to power Haven for a year. There hasn't been a fart like this since the last dwarf tribal gathering.'

A computer representation of the explosion appeared in her visor. To most fairies the image would be little more than a blur, but LEP officers were forced to develop the double focus necessary to read their screens and watch where they were going at the same time.

When the simulation put Holly clear of the projected blast radius, she dropped her boots, swinging in a loose ascending arc to face the kraken.

'Isn't there something we can do?'

'Besides take a couple of pictures, nope. Too late for that. Only a few minutes to go. Shelly's inner shell is already at ignition temperature, so put your glare filter down and watch the show.'

Holly lowered her shade. 'This is going to make the news all over the world. Islands don't just explode.'

'Yes, they do. Volcanic activity, gas leaks, chemical accidents. Believe me, if there's one thing the Mud Men *do* know, it's how to explain away an explosion. The Americans invented Area Fifty-one just because a senator crashed a jet into a mountain.'

'The mainland is safe?'

'Should be. A little shrapnel maybe.'

Holly relaxed, hanging from her wings. There was nothing she could do, nothing she *should* do. This was a natural process and the kraken had every right to shed its shell.

Methane explosions. Mulch would love this.

Mulch Diggums was currently running a private investigations office in Haven with the pixie wheel-fairy, Doodah Day. Mulch had, in his time, caused some methane disturbances himself.

Something pulsed gently in Holly's visor. A plasma splodge of red in the thermal-sweep windows. There was life on the island, and not just insect or rodent. Multiple humans.

'Foaly. I have something.'

Holly resized the window with a series of blink commands to track down the source. There were four hot bodies inside the sauna.

'*Inside* the sauna, Foaly. How did we miss them?'

'Their bodies were at the same temperature as the brick walls,' replied the centaur. 'I'm guessing that one of the Mud Men opened the door.'

Holly magnified her visor to plus six and saw that the sauna door was open a crack, a wedge of steam pushing through the gap. The building was cooling faster than the humans, and so now they showed up separately on her scanner.

'What are those Mud Men doing here? You said nothing opens until eight.'

'I don't know, Holly. How would I know? They're humans. About as reliable as moon-mad demons.'

It didn't matter *why* the humans were there – and wondering about it was a waste of time.

'I have to go back, Foaly.'

Foaly put a camera on himself, broadcasting his live image to Holly's helmet.

'Look at my face, Holly. Do you see this expression? That's my *stern* face. Do not do it, Holly. Do not return to the island. Humans die every day and we do not interfere. The LEP *never* interferes.'

'I know the rules,' said Holly, muting the growling centaur.

There goes my career – again, she thought, angling her wings for a steep dive.

Four men sat in the sauna's outer room, feeling very smug that they had once again outwitted island authorities and managed to sneak a free sauna before work. It did help that one of the men was Uunisaari's security guard and had access to the keys and a little five-horsepower punt that accommodated the four friends and a bucket of Karjala beer.

'Good temperature in the sauna today,' said one.

᠉᠐᠌᠑᠎᠊᠌᠑᠐᠎᠊᠎᠌᠑᠐᠌᠐᠌᠑᠐᠌᠎᠌

A second wiped the steam from his glasses. 'A little hot, I thought. In fact, even here it feels hot underfoot.'

'Go jump in the Baltic, then,' said the guard, miffed at this lack of appreciation for his efforts. 'That will cool down your poor pinkies.'

'Don't pay any attention to him,' said the fourth man, fastening his watch. 'He has sensitive feet. Always some temperature problem.'

The men, friends since childhood, laughed and swigged their beers. The laughing and swigging ceased abruptly when a section of the roof suddenly caught fire and disintegrated.

The guard coughed out a mouthful of beer. 'Was someone smoking? I said no smoking!'

Even if one of his sauna buddies had answered, the guard would not have heard, as he had somehow managed to fly through the hole in the roof.

'My toes are really hot,' said the bespectacled man, as if hanging on to old topics of conversation might make new ones go away.

The others ignored him, busy doing what men generally do in dangerous times – putting on their trousers.

There was no time for introductions or doors, so Holly drew her Neutrino sidearm, carved a two-metre hole in the roof and was treated to the sight of four pale, semi-dressed Mud Men quivering in sudden fright.

I'm not surprised they're quivering, she thought. *And that's only the beginning.*

As she flew, she worked on her problem: how to get four humans out of the blast zone in as many minutes.

Until recently she would have had a second problem: the building itself. According to the fairy Book, fairies were forbidden to enter human buildings without an invitation. This was a ten-thousand-year-old hex that still had a little sting, causing nausea and loss of power to anyone who defied it. The law was an anachronism and a serious impediment to LEP operations, so after a series of public debates and a referendum the hex had been lifted by demon warlock Nº1. It had taken the little demon five minutes to unravel a hex that had stumped elfin warlocks for centuries.

Back to the original problem. Four large humans. Big explosion imminent.

The first one was easy enough and the obvious choice. He was blocking the others and wore nothing but a towel and a tiny security guard's cap, which perched on top of his skull like a nut shell on the head of a bear.

Holly grimaced. *I have to get him out of my sight as soon as possible, or I may never forget this image. That Mud Man has more muscles than a troll.*

Troll! Of course.

There had been several additions to the Recon kit while Holly had been in Limbo, most invented and patented by Foaly, naturally. One such addition was a new clip of darts for her Neutrino. The centaur called them anti-gravity darts, but the officers called them Floaters.

The darts were based on Foaly's own Moonbelt, which

generated a field around whatever was attached to it, reducing the Earth's gravitational pull to one-fifth of normal. The Moonbelt was useful for transporting heavy equipment. Field officers quickly adapted the belt to their own specialized needs, attaching their prisoners to the pitons, which made them much easier to handle.

Foaly had then developed a dart that had the same effect as his Moonbelt. The dart used the fugitive's own flesh to conduct the charge that rendered him almost weightless. Even a troll seems less threatening when it is bobbing in the breeze like a balloon.

Holly slipped the clip from her belt, using the heel of one hand to ram it into the Neutrino.

Darts, she thought. *Back to the Stone Age.*

The big security guard was square in her sights, his lip wobbling petulantly.

No need for laser sights with this Mud Man, she thought. *I could hardly miss.*

And she didn't. The tiny dart pricked the man's shoulder and he quivered for a moment until the anti-gravity field encircled him.

'Ooh,' he said. 'That's a little –'

Then Holly had landed beside him, grasped his pale thigh and hurled him into the sky. He went, faster than a popped balloon, leaving a trail of surprised o's in his wake.

The remaining men hurriedly finished pulling on their trousers. Two tripped in their haste, banging heads before crashing to the ground. Plates of tomato-and-mozzarella rolls were batted aside; bottles of beer went spinning across the tiles.

'My sandwiches,' said one man, even as he struggled with his purple jeans.

No time for panic, thought Holly, silent and invisible among them. She ducked low, avoiding pale swinging limbs, and quickly loosed off three more darts.

A strange calm descended on the sauna as three grown men found themselves floating towards a hole in the roof.

'My feet are –' began the bespectacled man.

'Shut up about your feet!' shouted sandwich man, swiping at him with a fist. The motion sent him spinning and bouncing like a pinball.

Foaly overrode Holly's mute.

'D'Arvit, Holly. You have seconds. *Seconds!* Get out of there now! Even your suit armour will not stop an explosion of this magnitude.'

Holly's face was red and sweating in spite of her helmet's climate control.

Seconds left. How many times have I heard that?

No time for subtleties. She lay flat on her back, tapping the readout on her Neutrino to select concussion beams, and fired a wide pattern blast straight up.

The beam bore the men aloft, as a fast-flowing river would bear bubbles, bouncing them off the walls and each other before finally popping them through the still-sparking circle in the roof.

*

The last man out looked down as he left, wondering absently why he was not gibbering in panic. Surely flying was grounds for hysteria?

That will probably come later, he decided. *If there is a later for me.*

In the steam of the sauna, it seemed to him that there was a small humanoid shape lying on the floor. A diminutive figure with wings that leaped to its feet, then sped towards the flying men.

It's all true, thought the man. *Just like* Lord of the Rings. *Fantasy creatures. All true.*

Then the island exploded, and the man stopped worrying about fantasy creatures and began worrying about his trousers, which had just caught fire.

With all four men in the air, Holly decided that it was time to get herself as far from the supposed island as possible. She jumped from a squatting position, engaged her wings in the air and shot into the morning sky.

'Very nice,' said Foaly. 'You know they're calling that move the *Hollycopter*, don't you?'

Holly drew her weapon, urging the weightless men further away from the island with short bursts.

'Busy staying alive, Foaly. Talk later.'

Foaly said, 'Sorry, friend. I'm worried. I talk when I'm worried. Caballine thinks it's a defence mechanism. Anyway, the *Hollycopter*. You did the same take-off during that rooftop shoot-out in Darmstadt. Major – I mean, *Commander* Kelp caught it on video. They're using the footage in the Academy now. You wouldn't believe how many cadets have broken their ankles trying the same trick.'

Holly was about to insist that her friend please shut up, when Shelly ignited his methane cells, decimating his old shell and sending tons of debris hurtling skywards. The shockwave took Holly from below, like a giant's punch, sending her pinwheeling. She felt her suit flex to avoid the shock, the tiny scales closing ranks against the impact like the shields of a demon battalion. There was a slight hiss as her helmet plumped the safety bags protecting her brain and spinal cord. The screens in her visor flickered, jumped, then settled.

The world spun by her visor in a series of blues and greys. The artificial horizon in her helmet did several revolutions, end over end, though Holly realized that in actuality she was the one revolving and not the display.

Alive. Still alive. My odds must be getting short.

Foaly broke in on her thoughts. '. . . heart rate is up, though I don't know why. One would think you'd be used to these situations by now. The four humans made it, you will be delighted to know, since you risked your life and my technology to save them. What if one of my Floaters had fallen into human hands?'

Holly used a combination of gestures and blinks to fire short bursts from several of her wings' twelve engines, wrestling back control of her rig.

She opened her visor to cough and spit, then answered his accusation.

'I'm fine, thanks for asking. And all LEP equipment is fitted with remote destruct. Even me! So the only way your precious Floaters were ever going to fall into human hands was if *your* technology failed.'

'Which reminds me,' said Foaly. 'I need to get rid of those darts.'

Below was pandemonium. It seemed as though half of Helsinki's inhabitants had already managed to launch themselves in various crafts, and a veritable flotilla was heading towards the explosion site, led by a coastguard vessel, two powerful outboards churning at its stern, nose up for speed. The kraken itself was obscured by smoke and dust, but charred fragments of its shell rained down like volcanic ash, coating the decks of the boats below and draping a dark blanket over the Baltic Sea.

Twenty metres to Holly's left, the floating men bobbed happily through the air, riding the last ripples of explosive shock, trousers hanging in tattered ruins from their waists.

'I am surprised,' said Holly, zooming in on the men. 'No screaming or wetting themselves.'

'A little drop of relaxant in the dart,' chuckled Foaly. 'Well, I say a little drop. Enough to have a troll missing his mummy.'

'Trolls occasionally eat their mothers,' commented Holly.

'Exactly.'

Foaly waited until the men had dropped to within three metres of the ocean's surface, then remote detonated the tiny charge in each dart. Four small pops were followed by four loud splashes. The men were in the water no more than a few seconds before the coastguard reached them.

'OK,' said the centaur, obviously relieved. 'Potential disaster averted and our good deed done for the day. Kick up your boots and head back for the shuttle station. I have no doubt that Commander Kelp will want a detailed report.'

'Just a second – I have mail.'

'Mail! Mail! Do you really think this is the time? Your power levels are down, and the rear panels of your suit have taken a severe pasting. You need to get out of there, before your shield fails altogether.'

'I have to read this one, Foaly. It's important.'

The mail icon flashing in Holly's visor was tagged with Artemis's signature. Artemis and Holly colour-coded their mail icons. Green was social, blue was business and red was urgent. The mail icon in Holly's visor pulsed a bright red. She blinked at the icon, opening the short message.

Mother dying, it read. *Please come at once. Bring Nº1.*

Holly felt a cold dread in her stomach and the world seemed to lurch before her eyes.

Mother dying. Bring Nº1.

The situation must be desperate if Artemis was asking her to bring the powerful demon warlock.

She flashed back to the day, eighteen years ago, when her own mother had passed away. Almost two decades now, and the loss was still as painful as a raw wound. A thought struck her.

It's not eighteen years. It's twenty-one. I've been away for three.

Coral Short had been a doctor with LEPmarine, which

patrolled the Atlantic, cleaning up after humans, protecting endangered species. She had been mortally injured when a particularly rancid-looking tanker they were shadowing accidentally doused their submarine with radioactive waste. Dirty radiation is poison to fairies and it had taken her mother a week to die.

'I will make them pay,' Holly had vowed, crying at her mother's bedside in Haven Clinic. 'I will hunt down every last one of those Mud Men.'

'No,' her mother had said with surprising force. 'I spent my career *saving* creatures. You must do the same. *Destruction* cannot be my legacy.'

It was one of the last things she would ever say. Three days later, Holly stood stony-faced at her mother's recycling ceremony, her green dress uniform buttoned to the chin. The Omnitool that her mother had given her as a graduation present in its holster on her belt.

Saving creatures. So Holly applied to Recon.

And now Artemis's mother was dying. Holly realized that she didn't think of Artemis as a human any more, just as a friend.

'I need to go to Ireland,' she said.

Foaly did not bother to argue: he had sneaked a peek at the *urgent* mail on Holly's screen.

'Go. I can cover for you here for a few hours. I could say you're completing the Ritual. As it happens there's a full moon tonight and we still have a few magical sites near Dublin. I'll send a message to Section Eight. Maybe

Qwan will let Number One out of the magi-lab for a few hours.'

'Thanks, old friend.'

'You're welcome. Now go. I'm going to get out of your head for a while and monitor the chatter here. Maybe I can plant a few ideas in the human media. I like the idea of an underground natural gas pocket. It's almost the truth.'

Almost the truth.

Holly couldn't help applying the phrase to Artemis's mail. So often the Irish boy manipulated people by telling them *almost the truth*.

She chided herself silently. Surely not. Even Artemis Fowl would not lie about something this serious.

Everyone had their limits.

Didn't they?

CHAPTER 3: ECHOES OF MAGIC

 ARTEMIS Senior assembled his troops in Fowl Manor's conference room, which had originally been a banqueting hall. Until recently the soaring Gothic arches were hidden by a false ceiling, but Angeline Fowl had ordered the ceiling to be removed and the hall restored to its original double-height glory.

Artemis, his father and Butler sat in black leather Marcel Breuer chairs round a glass-topped table with space for ten more people.

Not so long ago there were smugglers seated at this table, thought Artemis. *Not to mention crime lords, hackers, insider traders, counterfeiters, black marketeers and cat burglars. The old family businesses.*

Artemis Senior closed his laptop. He was pale and obviously exhausted, but the old determination shone brightly in his eyes.

'The plan is a simple one. We must seek out not just a

second opinion, but as many opinions as possible. Butler will take the jet and go to China. No time for official channels, so perhaps you could find a strip where immigration is a little lax.'

Butler nodded. 'I know just the place. I can be there and back in two days, all going well.'

Artemis Senior was satisfied. 'Good. The jet is fuelled and ready. I have already organized a full crew and an extra pilot.'

'I just need to pack a few things, then I can be on my way.'

Artemis could imagine what kinds of things Butler would pack, especially if there were no officials at the airstrip.

'What will you do, Father?' he asked.

'I am going to England,' said Artemis Senior. 'I can take the helicopter to London City Airport and from there a limousine to Harley Street. There are several specialists I can talk to, and it will be far more efficient to send *me* there than bring *them* all here. If any of them can shed even the most feeble ray of light on your mother's situation, then I will pay them whatever it takes to get them back here. Buy out their practices if necessary.'

Artemis nodded. Wise tactics. Still, he would expect no less from the man who had successfully run a criminal empire for over two decades, and a humanitarian one for the past few years.

Everything Artemis Senior did now was ethical. From his fair-trade clothes company to his shares in Earthpower, a consortium of like-minded businessmen who were building everything from renewable-fuel cars to geothermal rods and solar panels. He'd even had the Fowl cars, jet and helicopter fitted with advanced emission filters to lighten the family's carbon footprint.

'I shall remain here,' announced Artemis, without waiting to be told. 'I can coordinate your efforts, set up a web cam so that the Harley Street specialists can see Mother, supervise Doctor Schalke and Miss Book, and also conduct my own Internet search for possible cures.'

Artemis Senior half smiled. 'Exactly, son. I hadn't thought of the web cam.'

Butler was anxious to depart, but he had a point to make before going. 'I am not comfortable about leaving Artemis alone. A genius he may be, but he is still a habitual meddler and a magnet for trouble.' The bodyguard winked at Artemis. 'No offence, young sir, but you could turn a Sunday picnic into an international incident.'

Artemis accepted the accusation graciously. 'None taken.'

'That thought has occurred to me,' said Artemis Senior, scratching his chin. 'But there is nothing for it. The nanny has agreed to take the twins to her cottage in Howth for a couple of days, but Arty is needed here and so he will have to fend for himself.'

'Which will not be a problem,' said Artemis. 'Have a little faith, please.'

Artemis Senior reached across the table, covering his son's hand with his own. 'Faith in each other is all we have now. We have to believe that saving your mother is possible. Do you believe it?'

Artemis noticed one of the upper windows swinging slowly ajar A leaf curled into the room, riding a swirling breeze, then the window seemed to close itself.

'I absolutely believe it, Father. More with every minute.'

Holly did not reveal herself until Artemis Senior's modified Sikorsky S-76C had lifted off from the rooftop heliport. Artemis was busy rigging a web cam at the foot of his mother's bed when the elf shimmered into view with her hand on his shoulder.

'Artemis, I am so sorry,' she said softly.

'Thanks for coming, Holly,' said Artemis. 'You got here quickly.'

'I was above ground in Finland, chasing a kraken.'

'Ah yes, Tennyson's beast,' said Artemis, closing his eyes, remembering a few lines from the famous poem.

> *Below the thunders of the upper deep;*
> *Far far beneath in the abysmal sea,*
> *His ancient, dreamless, uninvaded sleep,*
> *The kraken sleepeth.'*

'Sleepeth? Not any more. Watch the news headlines later. There was a natural gas explosion apparently.'

'I would guess that Foaly is up to his old spin-doctoring tricks.'

⟨◌⟩ symbols

'Yes.'

'Not many kraken left now,' commented Artemis. 'Seven by my reckoning.'

'Seven?' said Holly, surprised. 'We're only tracking six.'

'Ah yes, six. I meant six. New suit?' he asked, changing the subject a little too quickly.

'Three years more advanced than the last one,' replied Holly, filing the kraken titbit for investigation at a later time. 'It has auto-armour. If the sensors feel something big coming, the entire suit flexes to cushion the blow. It's saved my life once today already.'

A message icon beeped in Holly's helmet, and she took a moment to read the short text.

'Number One is on the way. They're sending the Section Eight shuttle. No way to contain this now, so whatever we need to do has to be done fast.'

'Good. I need all the help I can get.'

Their conversation petered out as Angeline Fowl's deathly illness completely occupied their thoughts. She radiated pallor and the smell of lilies hung yellow in the air.

Artemis fumbled with the web cam and it rolled under the bed.

'Hellfire,' he swore, kneeling to reach an arm into the dark space. 'I can't . . . I just can't . . .'

And suddenly the enormity of the situation struck him hard.

'What kind of son am I?' he whispered. 'A liar and a

thief. All my mother has ever done was love me and try to protect me and now she may die.'

Holly helped Artemis to his feet. 'You're not that person any more, Artemis, and you love your mother, don't you?'

Artemis huffed, embarrassed. 'Yes. Of course.'

'Then you are a good son. And your mother will see that as soon as I cure her.'

Holly clicked her neck and magical sparks leaped from her fingertips, spinning in an inverted cone.

'No,' blurted Artemis. 'Wouldn't it be wise to check the symptoms first?'

Holly closed her fist, smothering the sparks. Suspicious.

She took off her helmet and stepped close to Artemis, closer than he liked people to be, staring hard into his mismatched eyes. It was strange to see her own eye looking back at her.

'Have you done something, Artemis?'

Artemis met her gaze steadily. It seemed that there was nothing in his eyes but sadness.

'No. I am more cautious with my mother than I would be with myself, that is all.'

Holly's suspicion was born of years of experience with Artemis and so she wondered why he would be reluctant to allow her to use magic now when it had never bothered him before. Perhaps he had already tried this route himself. Perhaps the time stream had not stripped him of his stolen magic, as he had claimed.

She clamped her hands to the side of Artemis's head, then laid her forehead against his.

'Stop this, Holly,' objected Artemis. 'We have no time.'

Holly did not answer, closing her eyes, concentrating. Artemis felt heat spread across his skull and the familiar buzz of magic. Holly was probing him. It lasted barely a second.

'Nothing' she said, releasing him. 'Echoes of magic. But no power.'

Artemis stumbled backwards, dizzy.

'I understand your suspicion, Holly. I have earned it repeatedly. Now would you please examine my mother?'

Holly realized that up to this point she had avoided doing anything more than take a cursory glance at Angeline Fowl. This entire situation brought back too many painful memories.

'Of course, Artemis. I'm sorry about the probe. I had to be sure that I could take all of this on face value.'

'My feelings are not important,' said Artemis, leading Holly by the elbow. 'Now, my mother. Please.'

Holly had to force herself to examine Angeline Fowl properly, and, the moment she did, a deep-rooted dread sent pins and needles fluttering up and down her limbs.

'I know this,' she whispered. 'I know it.'

'This condition is familiar to you?' asked Artemis.

His mother's face and arms were coated with a clear gel that oozed from her pores and then steamed away. Angeline's eyes were wide but only the whites were visible and her fingers clutched the sheets as though hanging on to life.

Holly took a medi-kit from her belt, placed it on the bedside table and used a swab to take a sample of the gel. 'This gel. That smell. It can't be. It can't.'

'It can't be what?' asked Artemis, his fingers tight on her forearm.

Holly ignored him, slipping her helmet on and opening a channel to Police Plaza.

'Foaly? Are you there?'

The centaur responded on the second buzz. 'Right here, Holly. Chained to the desk. Commander Kelp has sent me a couple of mails asking where you are. I fobbed him off with the Ritual story. I reckon you have about –'

Holly interrupted his chatter. 'Foaly, listen to me. Artemis's mother. I think we have something . . . I think it's bad.'

The centaur's mood changed instantly. Holly suspected that he had been waffling to hide his anxiety. After all, Artemis's message had been very grim.

'OK. I'll sync with the manor systems. Ask Artemis for his password.'

Holly lifted her visor to look Artemis in the eye. 'Foaly wants your security password.'

'Of course, of course.' Artemis was drifting and it took him a moment to remember his own secret word. 'It's CENTAUR. All caps.'

Below the Earth's crust, Foaly stored the compliment in the corner of his brain that held treasured memories.

꩜𐤟𐌏𐌁𐌅•◉𐊠𐌀𐌔•𐌉𐊢•◉𐊢𐌉𐊨𐌵𐊣𐌰𐊱•𐌉𐊾𐊨•𐌰𐌊𐌁𐌀

He would take that one out later and gloat over a glass of sim-wine.

'Centaur. Right. I'm in.'

A large plasma television on the wall flickered on and Foaly's face appeared, first in blurred bubbles, then in sharp focus. The web cam in Artemis's hand whirred as the centaur remotely fiddled with its focus motor.

'The more points of view the better, eh?' he said, his voice pulsing from the television speakers in surround sound.

Artemis held the camera before his mother's face, holding it as still as possible.

'I take it, from Holly's reaction, that this condition *is* familiar to you?'

Holly pointed to the sheen covering Angeline's face. 'See the gel, Foaly, from the pores. And the smell of lilies too; there can't be any doubt.'

'It's impossible,' muttered the centaur. 'We eradicated this years ago.'

Artemis was growing weary of these vague references.

'*What* is impossible? Eradicated *what*?'

'No diagnosis just yet, Artemis; it would be premature. Holly, I need to run a scan.'

Holly positioned the palm of her hand over Angeline Fowl's forehead and the omni-sensor in her glove bathed Artemis's mother in a matrix of lasers.

Foaly's finger swished like a metronome as the information was fed to his system. It was an unconscious movement that seemed too jolly for the situation.

'OK,' he said, after half a minute. 'I have what I need.'

Holly closed her fist on the sensor, then stood with Artemis, clasping his hand in hers, silently awaiting the results. It did not take long, especially when Foaly had a good idea of his search parameters.

His face was grim as he read the results. 'The computer has analysed the gel. I am afraid it's Spelltropy.'

Artemis noticed Holly's grip tightening. Whatever this *Spelltropy* was, it was bad.

He broke free from Holly, striding to the wall-mounted television. 'I need an explanation, Foaly. Now, please.'

Foaly sighed, then nodded. 'Very well, Artemis. Spelltropy was a plague among the fairy People. Once contracted, it was invariably fatal, and progressed to terminal stages in three months. From that point the patient has less than a week. This disease has everything. Neurotoxins, cell destruction, resistance to all conventional therapies, incredibly aggressive. It's amazing, really.'

Artemis's teeth were clenched. 'That's fabulous, Foaly. At last, something even you can admire.'

Foaly wiped a bead of sweat from his nose, pausing before he spoke. 'There is no cure, Artemis. Not any more. I'm afraid your mother is dying. Judging by the concentration in the gel, I would say she has twenty-four hours, thirty-six if she fights. If it's any consolation, she won't suffer at the end.'

Holly crossed the room, reaching up to grasp Artemis's shoulder, noticing how tall her human friend was becoming.

'Artemis, there are things we can do to make her comfortable.'

Artemis shrugged her off, almost violently. 'No. I can achieve wonders. I have talents. Information is my weapon.' He returned his attention to the screen. 'Foaly, forgive my outburst. I am myself now. You said that this Spelltropy was a plague; where did it begin?'

'Magic,' said Foaly simply, then elaborated: 'Magic is fuelled by the Earth and when the Earth could no longer absorb the sheer bulk of pollutants the magic became tainted also. Spelltropy first appeared about twenty years ago in Linfen, China.'

Artemis nodded. It made sense. Linfen was infamous for its high pollution levels. As the centre of China's coal industry, the city's air was laden with fly ash, carbon monoxide, nitrogen oxides, volatile organic compounds, arsenic and lead. There was a joke among Chinese employers: if you hold a grudge against an employee, send him to work in Linfen.

'It is passed on through magic, and thus is completely impervious to magic. In ten years, it had almost decimated the fairy population. We lost twenty-five per cent of our numbers. Atlantis was worst hit.'

'But you stopped it,' Artemis insisted. 'You must have found a cure.'

'Not me,' said Foaly. 'Our old friend Opal Koboi found the antidote. It took her ten years, then she tried to charge through the nose for it. We had to get a court order to confiscate the supply of antidote.'

Artemis was growing impatient. 'I don't care about the politics, Foaly. I want to know what the cure was, and why we can't administer it to my mother.'

'It's a long story.'

'Abbreviate,' snapped Artemis.

Foaly's eyes dipped, unable to meet Artemis's. 'The cure occurred naturally. Many creatures contain an important pharmacopoeia and act as natural magic enhancers, but because of human activities more than twenty thousand of these potentially life-saving species become extinct every year. Opal developed a simple syringe gun to extract the cure for Spelltropy without killing the donor animal.'

Artemis suddenly realized why Foaly couldn't look him in the eye. He cradled his head in his hands.

'Oh no. Don't say it.'

'Opal Koboi found the antidote in the brain fluid of the silky sifaka lemur of Madagascar.'

'I always knew,' moaned Artemis, 'that this would come back.'

'Unfortunately the silky sifaka is now extinct. The last one died almost eight years ago.'

Artemis's eyes were haunted by guilt.

'I know,' he whispered. 'I killed it.'

CHAPTER 4: MONKEY'S UNCLE

FOWL MANOR, ALMOST EIGHT YEARS AGO

 TEN-year-old Artemis Fowl closed the file he was working on, put his monitor to sleep, then rose from his study desk. His father would arrive in a moment for their meeting. Artemis Senior had confirmed the appointment that morning by internal mail and he was never late. His time was precious, and he expected his son to be ready for their morning talk. Artemis's father arrived promptly at ten, leather greatcoat swishing around his knees.

'Minus fifteen in Murmansk,' he explained, formally shaking his son's hand.

Artemis was standing on a specific flagstone before the fireplace. He was not actually required to stand in this spot, but he knew his father would sit in the Louis XV chair by the hearth and Artemis Senior did not like to crane his neck as he spoke.

His father lowered himself into the period chair and Artemis enjoyed a quiet moment of satisfaction.

'The ship is ready, I take it?'

'Ready to sail,' said his father, excitement flashing in his blue eyes. 'This is a new market, Arty, my boy. Moscow is already one of the most commercial cities in the world. Northern Russia will inevitably follow.'

'I gather Mother is not very pleased with your latest venture.'

Recently, Artemis's parents had been arguing late into the night. The conflict in their otherwise happy marriage was over Artemis Senior's business interests. He controlled a criminal empire that had tentacles from the silver mines of Alaska to the shipyards of New Zealand. Angeline was a dedicated conservationist and humanitarian, and believed that Artemis Senior's criminal activities and ruthless exploitation of natural resources set a terrible example to their son.

'He will grow up just like his father,' Artemis had heard her say one evening, through a little radio bug he'd planted in the aquarium.

'I thought you loved his father.'

Artemis heard a rustling of material as his parents embraced. 'I do. I love you more than life. But I love this planet too.'

'My love,' said Artemis Senior, so gently that it was difficult for the bug to pick up his voice, 'the Fowl finances are in a delicate state right now. What capital we have is locked up in illegal ventures. I need one big deal so that I can begin the transition to completely legitimate businesses. Once we have some blue-chip stock under our belts, then we can save the world.'

Artemis heard his mother kiss his father. 'Very well, my pirate prince. One big deal, then we save the world.'

One big deal. A shipload of tax-free cola for the Russians. But more importantly a pipeline of trade into the Arctic. Artemis suspected that his father would find it hard to abandon this pipeline after a single deal. There were billions to be made.

'The *Fowl Star* is fully loaded and ready for her voyage,' Artemis's father informed his son later during their sched-uled meeting in his study. 'Remember, the world cannot be saved with good intentions alone. Leverage is needed, and gold is leverage.'

Artemis Senior pointed to the Fowl crest and motto, carved into a wooden shield above the fireplace.

'*Aurum potestas est*. Gold is power: never forget that, Arty. Until the greens have wealth behind them, no one will listen.'

Young Artemis was torn between his parents. His father embodied everything the family stood for. The Fowl dynasty had flourished for centuries because of their dedication to wealth, and Artemis had no doubt that his father would find a way first to increase their fortunes and then turn his attention to the environment. He loved his mother, but the Fowls' finances must be saved.

'Some day control of the family business will fall to you,'

Artemis Senior told his son, standing to button his great-coat. 'And, when that day comes, I will rest easy, because I know you will put the Fowls first.'

'Absolutely, Father,' said Artemis. 'Fowls first. But that day will not come for decades.'

Artemis Senior laughed. 'Let's hope not, son. Now, I must be off. Look after your mother while I am gone. And don't let her squander the family fortune, eh?'

The words were said in a light-hearted way, but a week later Artemis Fowl Senior was missing, presumed dead, and those words became the code his son would live by.

Look after your mother, but don't let her squander the family fortune.

Two months later and Artemis was back at his desk, staring at the computer display in his study. On screen were the gloomy details of the family finances, which had dwindled rapidly since the disappearance of his father. He was the man of the house now, custodian of the Fowl empire, and must behave as such.

No sooner had Artemis Senior's ship been claimed by the black Arctic waters than his debtors unanimously defaulted, and his cells of forgers, musclemen, thieves and smugglers allied themselves to other organizations.

Honour among thieves? reflected Artemis bitterly. *I think not.*

Most of the Fowl money simply disappeared overnight, and Artemis was left with an estate to run and a mother who was heading rapidly towards nervous breakdown.

64

It wasn't long before the creditors were closing in, eager to claim their slice of the pie before only crumbs were left. Artemis had been forced to auction a Rembrandt sketch just to pay the mortgage on the manor and settle various other debts.

Mother was not making things any easier. She refused to believe that Artemis Senior was missing and forged ahead with her mission to save the world, hang the expense.

Artemis meanwhile was trying to mount expeditions to find his father. This was difficult when you are ten years old and not taken seriously by the adult world in general, in spite of various international art and music prizes, not to mention over a dozen lucrative patents and copyrights filed worldwide. In time Artemis would build a fortune of his own, but *in time* was not soon enough. Money was needed now.

Artemis wanted to put together a proper situations room to monitor the Internet and world news channels. That would take twenty computers at least. Also there was the team of Arctic explorers waiting in their Moscow hotel for him to wire the next portion of their payment. A payment that he didn't have.

Artemis tapped the screen with an elegant finger.

Something must be done, he thought.

Angeline Fowl was crying on her bed when Artemis entered the bedroom. His heart lurched at the sight, but he clenched his fists and told himself to be strong.

•🜊🜋🜌🜍•🜎🜏🜐•🜑🜒•🜓🜔🜕🜖•🜗🜘🜙•🜚

'Mother,' he said, waving a bank account statement. 'What is this?'

Angeline dried her eyes on a handkerchief, then rose to her elbows, slowly focusing on her son.

'Arty, little Arty. Come and sit with me.'

Angeline's eyes were ringed by black mascara tears, and her complexion had faded to a white that was almost translucent. *Be strong.*

'No, Mother. No sitting and talking. I want you to explain this fifty-thousand-euro cheque to a wildlife centre in South Africa.'

Angeline was bewildered. 'South Africa, darling? Who's gone to South Africa?'

'You sent a cheque for fifty thousand euro to South Africa, Mother. I had that money put aside for the Arctic expedition.'

'Fifty thousand. That figure is familiar. I'll ask your father when he gets in. He had better not be late for dinner again today, or I'll —'

Artemis lost his patience. 'Mother, please. Try to think. We do not have spare funds for South African charities. All the staff have been let go except Butler and he hasn't been paid in a month.'

'Lemur!' shouted Angeline triumphantly. 'I remember now. I bought a silky sifaka lemur.'

'Impossible,' snapped Artemis. 'The *Propithecus candidus* is extinct.'

His mother was suddenly passionate. 'No. No, they found little silky in South Africa. They don't know how it managed to get there from Madagascar – probably on a poacher's boat. So I had to save it. It's the last one, Arty.'

'In a year or two it will die,' said Artemis coldly. 'Then our money will have been wasted.'

Angeline was horrified. 'You sound just like –'

'Father? Good. Someone has to be rational.'

Artemis's face was stern, but inside he quailed. How could he speak to his mother like this when she was literally driven demented by grief?

Why have I not fallen to pieces? he wondered, and the answer came to him quickly: *I am a Fowl, and Fowls have always triumphed in the face of adversity.*

'But fifty thousand, Mother? For a lemur?'

'They may find a female,' argued Angeline. 'Then we will have saved a species.'

There is no point in arguing, thought Artemis. *Logic cannot prevail here.*

'And where is lucky silky now?' he asked innocently, smiling as a ten-year-old should, when discussing a small furry animal.

'He is safe in Rathdown Park. Living like a king. Tomorrow he is being flown to a special artificial habitat in Florida.'

Artemis nodded. Rathdown Park was a privately funded nature reserve in Wicklow, specially constructed to protect endangered species. It had tighter security than the average Swiss bank.

'That's wonderful. Perhaps I will visit the fifty-thousand-euro monkey.'

'Now, now, Artemis,' his mother chided. 'Silky is a lemur, they predate monkeys, as you well know.'

I know but do not care! Artemis wanted to scream. *Father is missing and you have spent the expedition money on a lemur!*

But he held his tongue. Mother was delicate at the moment and he did not want to contribute to her instability.

'Rathdown don't usually accept visitors,' continued Angeline. 'But I am sure if I made a call they would make an exception for you. The Fowls did pay for the primate village, after all.'

Artemis appeared delighted. 'Thank you, Mother. That would be a real treat for me, and Butler too. You know how he likes small furry creatures. I would love to see the species we have saved.'

Angeline smiled with a degree of madness that scared her son terribly.

'Well done, Artemis. This is one in the eye for the big-business men. Mother and son, united, we shall save the world. I shall tease your father terribly when he gets home.'

Artemis backed slowly towards the door, his heart in his shoes.

'Yes, Mother. United, we shall save the world.'

Once the door had closed behind him, Artemis stepped briskly downstairs, fingers conducting imaginary music as he plotted. He detoured to his bedroom and dressed quickly for a trip, then continued to the kitchen, where he found Butler slicing vegetables with a Japanese kodachi short sword. He was now chef and gardener as well as protector.

The huge bodyguard was making quick work of a cucumber.

'A summer salad,' he explained. 'Just greens, hard-boiled egg and some chicken. I thought crème brûlée for dessert. It will give me a chance to try out my flamethrower.' He glanced across at Artemis and was surprised to see him dressed in one of his two suits, the dark blue one he had worn recently to the opera in Covent Garden. Artemis had always been a neat dresser, but a suit and tie was unusual, even for him.

'Are we going somewhere formal, Artemis?'

'Nowhere formal,' said Artemis, with a coldness in his tone that the bodyguard had not heard before, but would come to know well. 'Just business. I am in charge of the family affairs now, and so I should dress accordingly.'

'Ah . . . I detect a distinct echo of your father.' Butler wiped the sword carefully, then pulled off his apron. 'We have some typical Fowl family business to conduct, do we?'

'Yes,' replied Artemis. 'With a monkey's uncle.'

FOWL MANOR, PRESENT DAY

Holly was aghast.

'So, in a fit of childish pique, you murdered the lemur.'

Artemis had composed himself and sat on a bedside chair, holding his mother's hand gently as though it were a bird.

'No. I used to suffer from the occasional fit of pique, as

you well know, but they generally did not last. An intellect such as mine cannot be overpowered by emotions for long.'

'But you said that you killed the animal.'

Artemis rubbed his temple. 'Yes, I did. I didn't wield the knife, but I killed it, make no mistake.'

'How exactly?'

'I was young . . . younger,' mumbled Artemis, uncomfortable with the topic. 'A different person in many ways.'

'We know what you were like, Artemis,' said Foaly in rueful tones. 'You have no idea how much of my budget the Fowl Manor siege ate up.'

Holly pressed for an answer. 'How did you kill the lemur? How did you even get hold of it?'

'It was ridiculously easy,' admitted Artemis. 'Butler and I visited Rathdown Park and simply disabled the security while we were there. Later that evening we both popped back and picked up the lemur.'

'So Butler killed it. I am surprised; it's not his style.'

Artemis's eyes were downcast. 'No, Butler didn't do it. I sold the lemur to a group of Extinctionists.'

Holly was horrified. 'Extinctionists! Artemis, you didn't. That's horrible.'

'It was my first big deal,' said Artemis. 'I delivered it to them in Morocco and they paid me a hundred thousand euro. It funded the entire Arctic expedition.'

Holly and Foaly were speechless. Artemis had effectively put a price on life. Holly backed away from the human she had only moments ago considered a friend.

'I rationalized the whole thing. My father for a lemur. How could I not go through with it?' Artemis had real regret in his eyes. 'I know. It was a terrible thing to do. If I could turn back the clock –'

And suddenly he stopped. *He* couldn't turn back the clock, but he knew a demon warlock who could. It was a chance. *A chance.*

He laid his mother's hand gently on the bed, then stood to pace.

Plotting music, he thought. *I need plotting music.*

He selected Beethoven's Symphony N°7 from his vast selection of mental music and listened to it as he thought.

Good choice. Sombre yet uplifting. Inspiring stuff.

Artemis paced the carpet, almost unaware of his surroundings, lost in ideas and possibilities.

Holly recognized this mood.

'He has a plan,' she said to Foaly.

The centaur pulled a long face, which wasn't difficult. 'Why am I not surprised?'

Holly took advantage of Artemis's distraction to seal her helmet and speak privately to Foaly. She walked to the window and peered out at the estate through a gap in the curtains. The sinking sun wavered behind tree branches, and clumps of dahlias flashed red and white like fireworks.

Holly allowed herself time for a sigh of longing, then focused on the situation.

'There's more at stake here than Artemis's mother,' she said.

Foaly switched off the television so that Artemis could not hear him.

'I know. If there is an outbreak, it could be disaster for fairies. We don't have any antidote left, remember.'

'We need to interview Opal Koboi. She must have kept records somewhere.'

'Opal always kept her most valuable formulae in her head. I think she was caught off-guard by the jungle fire – she lost all her donors in one fell swoop.'

Koboi Industries had attracted the Madagascan lemurs by setting a sonix box in the Tsingy de Bemaraha. Virtually every lemur in the island had responded to the box's call and they had all been wiped out by an unfortunate lightning fire. Luckily, they had already treated most of the infected, but fifteen more fairies had died in quarantine wards.

Artemis stopped pacing and cleared his throat loudly. He was ready to share his plan and he wanted the fairies' complete attention.

'There is a relatively simple solution to our problem,' he said.

Foaly reactivated the television, his face filling the flat screen.

'*Our* problem?'

'Come, Foaly, don't pretend to be obtuse. This is a fairy plague that has mutated and spread to humans. You have no antidote and no time to synthesize one. Who knows how many cases of Spelltropy are incubating right now.'

Including my own, thought Artemis. *I used magic on my mother, so therefore I probably have the disease.*

'We will quarantine the manor,' responded Foaly. 'So long as no one uses magic on your mother we can contain this.'

'I seriously doubt that my mother is patient zero. That is simply too much of a coincidence. There are other cases out there who knows how far along.'

Foaly grunted – his version of conceding a point. 'So, tell me, Artemis, what is this *relatively simple solution*?'

'I go back in time and save the lemur,' said Artemis, smiling brightly as though he had suggested a pleasant summer dip.

Silence. Complete silence for several moments, broken eventually by a strangled whinny from Foaly.

'Go back . . .'

'In time . . .' completed Holly incredulously.

Artemis sat in a comfortable armchair, steepled his fingers and nodded once.

'Present your arguments, please. I am ready.'

'How can you be so smug?' wondered Holly. 'After all the tragedy we have seen, after all the havoc your plans have wreaked.'

'I am determined, not smug,' corrected Artemis. 'There is no time for prudence here. My mother has hours left, and the fairy People don't have much more.'

Foaly was still gaping. 'Do you have any idea how many constitution committee meetings we would have to sit through just to allow us to bring this issue to a Council meeting?'

Artemis wagged a finger dismissively. 'Irrelevant. I have read the People's constitution. It does not govern humans or demons. If Number One decides to help me, technically you have no legal power to stop him.'

Holly joined the discussion. 'Artemis, this is lunacy. Time travel was outlawed for a reason. The potential repercussions from the slightest interference could be catastrophic.'

Artemis smiled mirthlessly. 'Ah yes, the trusty *time paradox*. If I go back in time and kill my grandfather, then shall I cease to exist? I believe, as Gorben and Berndt did, that any repercussions are already being felt. We can only change the future, not the past or present. If I go back, then I have already been back.'

Holly spoke kindly; she felt sorry for Artemis. Angeline's illness reminded her painfully of her own mother's final days.

'We cannot interfere, Artemis. Humans must be allowed to live their lives.'

Artemis knew that to ram home his next argument he should stand and theatrically deliver the accusation, but he could not. He was about to play the cruellest trick of his life on one of his closest friends, and the guilt was almost unbearable.

'You have already interfered, Holly,' he said, forcing himself to meet her eyes.

The words made Holly shiver. She buzzed up her visor. 'What do you mean?'

'You healed my mother. Healed her and damned her.'

Holly took a step back, raising her palms as though to ward off blows.

'Me? I . . . What are you saying?'

Artemis was committed to the lie now, and covered his guilt with a sudden burst of anger.

'You healed my mother after the siege. *You* must have given her Spelltropy.'

Foaly came to his friend's defence. 'Not possible, that healing was years ago. Spelltropy has a three-month incubation period and it never varies by more than a few days.'

'And it *never* affects humans,' Artemis countered. 'This is a new strain. You have no idea what you're dealing with.'

Holly's face was slack with shock and guilt. She believed Artemis's words, though Artemis himself knew that he must have given his mother the disease when he adjusted her memory.

Father must have it too. Who gave it to me? And why am I not sick?

There were so many puzzles but *now* was not the time to unravel them. *Now* he needed to find the antidote and, to ensure fairy aid, he must play on their supposed guilt in this matter.

'But I'm clean,' protested Holly. 'I was tested.'

'Then you must be a carrier,' said Artemis flatly. He turned his gaze on the centaur's image. 'That's possible, isn't it?'

Foaly was taken aback by Artemis's bluntness. 'If this truly is a new strain, then, yes, it's possible,' he admitted. 'But you can't draw any conclusions from supposition . . .'

'Normally, I would agree. *Normally*, I would have the luxuries of time and objectivity. But my mother is dying and so I have neither. I must go back to save the lemur, and you are honour bound to help me, and if you won't help, then at least you must promise not to hinder my efforts.'

The fairies were silent. Holly was lost in thought about what she might have done. Foaly was wracking his considerable brain for responses to Artemis's arguments. He found none.

Holly removed her helmet, walking awkwardly to Angeline Fowl's bedside. Her legs felt strangely numb and the feeling was spreading.

'My mother died – poisoned by humans. It was an accident, but that didn't keep her alive.' Tears dripped from her eyes. 'I wanted to hunt those men down. I hated them.' Holly wrung her hands. 'I'm sorry, Artemis. I didn't know. How many others have I infected? You must hate me.'

Take it back, thought Artemis. *Tell the truth now or your friendship can never be the same.* Then, *No. Be strong. Mother must live.*

'I don't hate you, Holly,' said Artemis softly. *I hate myself, but the deception must continue.* 'Of course none of this is your fault, but you *must* let me go back.'

Holly nodded, then wiped her brimming eyelids. 'I will do more than let you go, I will escort you. A sharp pair of eyes and a quick gun hand will prove useful.'

'No, no, no,' shouted Foaly, increasing the screen's volume with each negative. 'We can't simply alter the past whenever we feel like it. Perhaps Holly should save her mother, or bring Commander Julius Root back from the dead! This is totally unacceptable.'

Artemis pointed a finger at him. 'This is a unique situation,' he said. 'You have a plague about to erupt and we can stop it here. Not only that but you can reintroduce a species that was thought to be extinct. I may have caused one lemur to die, but Opal Koboi gathered the rest together for the lightning fire. The People are as guilty as I am. You harvested a living creature's brain fluid to save yourselves.'

'W-we were desperate,' argued Foaly, horrified that he would actually stutter.

'Exactly,' said Artemis triumphantly. 'You were willing to do anything. Remember how *that* felt and ask yourself if you want to go through it again.'

Foaly dropped his gaze, thinking back. That time had been a waking nightmare for the fairies. The use of magic had been suspended and the lemurs were already extinct by the time a court order forced Opal to reveal the source of her antidote. He had worked sleeplessly to develop an alternative cure, but without success.

'We thought we were invincible. The only disease left was man.' The centaur made up his mind. 'The lemur must be alive,' he stated. 'The brain fluid can be stored for brief periods, but once it becomes inert, the fluid is useless. I was developing a charged container but . . .'

'This time you will succeed,' Artemis assured him. 'You will have a live subject and laboratory conditions. You can clone a female.'

'Cloning is illegal generally,' mused Foaly. 'But in extinction cases exceptions have been made . . .'

Holly's helmet beeped, drawing her attention to a craft landing in the driveway. She hurried to the window in time to see a slight shimmer cast a shadow on the moonlit driveway.

It must be a rookie pilot, thought Holly crossly. *He hasn't activated his shadow-lights.*

'The shuttle's here,' she informed Artemis.

'Tell the pilot to park round the back, in one of the stables. The doctor's assistant is making calls from my father's office. I don't want her going for a walk and bumping into a shielded fairy craft.'

Holly relayed the instructions, and they waited tensely for the shuttle to manoeuvre to the back of the house. It seemed like a long wait, silent but for the rasp of Angeline's laboured breathing.

'Number One might not be able to do it,' said Foaly almost to himself. 'He is a young warlock, with barely any training. Time travel is the most difficult of magics.'

Artemis did not offer a comment. There was no point. All his hopes rested on Nº1.

He does it, or Mother dies.

He took Angeline's hand, stroking the rough parchment skin with his thumb.

'Hold on, Mother,' he whispered. 'I will only be a second.'

CHAPTER 5: I NOW PRONOUNCE YOU

 THE little demon known as Nº1 cut a strange figure waddling down the LEP shuttle's gangplank. A small, stocky individual with grey armoured plates and short limbs, he looked a little like a miniature upright rhinoceros with fingers and toes, except for the head. The head was pure gargoyle.

I wish I had a tail, thought Nº1.

In actual fact, he did have a tail, but it was stubby and not good for much except making snow fans in Haven City's artificial weather park.

Nº1 consoled himself with the observation that at least his tail didn't dangle down the toilet. Some of the Hybras demons had trouble adjusting to the newfangled seats on the recycling lounges in Haven. He had heard horror stories. Apparently there had been three emergency reattachments this month alone.

The transition from Limbo to normal time had been difficult for all demons, but there were many more positives than negatives. Restrictions imposed under the old tribal leader were now being lifted. Demons could eat cooked food if they felt like it. Family units were taking hold again. Even the most belligerent demons were a lot more relaxed with their mothers around. It was difficult to shake off ten millennia of human-hating, and many of the buck demons were undergoing therapy or were on mood pills to stop them hopping a shuttle to the surface and chomping on the first human limb they saw.

Not N°1, though, who had no limb-chomping ambitions whatsoever. He was something of an anomaly among demons. N°1 loved everyone, even humans, especially Artemis Fowl, who had saved them all from the deathly dreariness of Limbo, not to mention Leon Abbot, the psychopathic ex-tribe leader.

So when the call came through to Section Eight that Artemis needed him, N°1 had strapped himself into the division's shuttle and demanded to be taken above ground. Wing Commander Vinyáya had agreed, because *disagreeing* could lead to all sorts of magical tantrums from the fledgling warlock. Once, in a fit of frustration, N°1 had accidentally shattered the magnifying wall of the city's huge aquarium. Fairies were still finding minnows in their toilet ponds.

You can go, Vinyáya had told him, *but only if you take a squad of guards to hold your hand every step of the way.*

Which did not literally mean *hold his hand*, as N°1 had found out when he tried to link with the captain of the guard.

'But Commander Vinyáya said,' he'd objected.

'Stow the hand, demon,' ordered the captain. 'There'll be no hand-holding on my watch.'

And so Nº1 appeared to approach Fowl Manor alone, though he was flanked by a dozen shielded fairies. Halfway up the avenue he remembered to shroud his real appearance with a shape-shifting spell. Any human who happened to be looking down the driveway would now see a small boy in flowing flowered robes strolling towards the front door. This was an image Nº1 had seen in a human movie from the last century, and he thought it was appropriately non-threatening.

Miss Book happened to appear at the doorway just as Nº1 reached it. The sight of him stopped the nurse/publicist in her tracks. She tugged off her glasses as though they were feeding false information to her eyes.

'Hello there, little boy,' she said, smiling, though she probably would not have been so jolly had she been aware of the twelve plasma rifles pointed at her head.

'Hi,' said Nº1 cheerily. 'I love everyone, so no need to feel threatened.'

Miss Book's smiled faltered. 'Threatened? Of course not. Are you looking for someone? Are you playing dress-up?'

Artemis appeared at the doorway, interrupting the conversation.

'Ah . . . Ferdinand, where have you been?' he said, quickly shepherding Nº1 past the nurse. 'This is the gardener's boy, Ferdinand,' he explained. 'A dramatic type. I'll summon his father to collect him.'

⊖•⅋ꞵ•↺⟩◊•⅗ⅉ⟩•⅋ƒᵿ•→•∞⊖Ƀⅈⅈ⅋ⅈⅉ⅋

'Good idea,' said Miss Book doubtfully. 'I know your mother's room is sealed, but don't let him upstairs all the same.'

'Of course not,' said Artemis. 'I'll send him out the back way.'

'Good,' said the nurse. 'I just need a breath of fresh air, then I will come to check on your mother.'

'Take your time,' said Artemis. 'I can read the instruments.'

I designed a few of them, he thought.

As soon as Miss Book disappeared round the corner, Artemis escorted his demon friend up the stairs.

'We're going upstairs,' objected Nº1 mildly. 'Didn't that young lady tell you not to allow me upstairs?'

Artemis sighed. 'How long have you known me, Number One?'

Nº1 nodded craftily. 'Ah, I see. Artemis Fowl *never* does what he is told to do.'

Holly greeted Nº1 on the landing, but refused to hug him until he dropped the shape-shifting spell.

'I hate the feel of those things,' she said. 'It's like hugging a wet sponge.'

Nº1 pouted. 'But I enjoy being Ferdinand. Humans smile at me.'

Artemis assured him that there was no surveillance in his study and so the demon warlock waited until the door was closed behind them, then banished the spell with a click of his fingers. Ferdinand unravelled and fell from Nº1's body in a flurry of sparks, leaving the small grey demon warlock wearing nothing but a wide grin.

Holly hugged him tightly.

'I knew you would come. We need you desperately.'

N°1 stopped smiling. 'Ah, yes. Artemis's mother. Does she want a magical cure?'

'That's the last thing she wants,' said Holly.

Once the situation was explained to N°1, he immediately agreed to help.

'You are in luck, Artemis,' said the little demon, wiggling his eight fingers. 'I did a module on time travel last week on the warlock diploma course I'm taking.'

'Small class, I bet,' commented Artemis drily.

'Just me,' admitted N°1. 'And Qwan, of course, my teacher. Apparently, I am the most powerful warlock Qwan has ever seen.'

'Good,' said Artemis. 'Then transporting us all into the past shouldn't pose any problems for you.'

Foaly had projected himself on to five of Artemis's various monitors. '*All?*' spluttered each image. 'All! You can't take Number One with you.'

Artemis was not in the mood for argument. 'I need him, Foaly. End of discussion.'

Foaly looked as though his head would bulge through the screens. 'It is most certainly not *end of discussion*. Holly is an adult – she can make her own decision – but Number One is little more than a child. You cannot jeopardize him on one of your missions. A lot of hopes rest on that little demon. The future of the fairy families.'

'None of us will have a future if Number One doesn't take us to the past.'

'Please stop,' said N°1. 'All this arguing is making me dizzy. There is no time for it.'

Artemis's face was red, but he held his tongue, unlike Foaly who kept shouting, but at least he muted the screens.

'Foaly needs to vent,' explained Holly, 'or he gets headaches.'

The three waited until the centaur calmed himself, then N°1 spoke: 'In any event, I cannot go with you, Artemis. That's not how it works.'

'But you transported us from Limbo.'

'Qwan did that. He is a master; I am but an apprentice. And, anyway, we had no desire to go *back* to Limbo. If you wish to return *here*, I need to stay as a marker.'

'Explain,' said Artemis tersely.

N°1 spread his arms wide. 'I am a beacon,' he declared. 'A shining supernova of power. Any magic I release into the ether will be attracted back to me. I send you into the past, and you will snap back to me like puppies on a leash.' N°1 frowned, not happy with his simile. 'One of those retractable leashes.'

'Yes, we get it,' said Artemis. 'How long will it take to weave the spell?'

N°1 chewed his lip for a moment. 'About as long as it takes you two to remove your clothing.'

'Hurkk,' said Artemis, half-choking with surprise.

'D'Arvit,' swore Holly.

'I think we all know what D'Arvit means,' said N°1. 'But *hurkk* is not English. Unless you meant *hark*, which means *to listen* or *to remember something from the past*. Which I suppose could be relevant. Or perhaps you were speaking Dutch, and then *hurk* would translate as *squat*.' N°1 paused for a wink. 'Which means squat to me.'

Artemis leaned close to the demon's cornet-shaped ear. 'Why do we need to take our clothes off?'

'That is a very good question,' said Holly into the other ear.

'It's quite simple,' said N°1. 'I am not so skilled as Qwan. And even *with* Qwan overseeing the last transfer, you two managed to switch an eye each, which was probably because someone was focusing on stealing magic. If you take clothes or guns in there, they could become a part of you.' The demon raised a stiff finger. 'Lesson number one of time transfers,' he stated. 'Keep it simple. It's going to take all of your concentration just to reassemble your bodies. *And* you will be thinking for the lemur too.'

N°1 noticed both Artemis and Holly's awkward expressions and took pity on them.

'I suppose you could keep one thing, if you must. A small garment, but make sure it's your colour, because you could be wearing it for a really long time.'

Though they both knew that this was no time for modesty, neither Artemis nor Holly could suppress a blush.

Holly covered her embarrassment by tearing off her shimmer suit as quickly as possible.

'I'm keeping the one-piece,' she said belligerently, daring Nº1 to argue. The *one-piece* looked similar to a swimsuit, but was padded on the shoulders and back to support a wing rig. There were also heat and kinetic panels, which could absorb energy from the wearer to power the suit.

'OK,' said Nº1. 'But I would advise you to remove the pads and any other electronics.'

Holly nodded, tearing the pads from their Velcro strips.

Artemis gathered Holly's things.

'I will put your helmet and suit in the safe, just to be certain they are secure. No need to take chances with the People's technology.'

'Now you're thinking like a centaur,' Foaly piped up.

It took only a minute to hide the fairy gear, and when he returned from the safe room, Artemis took off his shirt and trousers carefully, hanging them in his wardrobe. He placed his loafers on a shoe rack alongside several similar black pairs, and one brown, for casual days.

'Nice underwear,' snickered Foaly from the screen, momentarily forgetting the gravity of the situation.

Artemis was wearing a pair of red Armani boxer shorts, which were pretty much the same colour as his face.

'Can we get on with it?' he snapped. 'Where do you need us to stand?'

'Wherever you need to be,' replied Nº1 simply. 'It's far easier for me if you take off and land at the same point.

It's hard enough shooting you off down a wormhole faster than the speed of light without worrying about location too.'

'We are in the right location,' said Artemis. 'This is where we need to be.'

'You need to know *when* you want to arrive,' added N°1. 'The temporal co-ordinates are as important as the geographical ones.'

'I know when.'

'Very well,' said N°1, rubbing his hands together. 'Time to send you on your way.'

Holly remembered something. 'I haven't completed the Ritual,' she said. 'I'm low on magic, and without weapons that could be a problem. We don't have an acorn.'

'Not to mention a bend in the river,' added Artemis.

N°1 smirked. 'Those things *could* be problems. Unless . . .'

A spiral rune on the demon's forehead glowed red and spun like a Catherine wheel. It was hypnotizing.

'Wow,' said Holly. 'That's really . . .'

Then a pulsing beam of crimson magic blasted from the centre of the rune, enveloping Holly in a cocoon of light.

'Now you're full to the brim,' said N°1, bowing low. 'Thank you very much. I'm here all week. Don't forget to tip your goblins and bury those acorns.'

'Wow,' said Holly again, when her fingertips stopped buzzing. 'That's a neat trick.'

'More than you know. That's my own signature magic.

The Number One cocktail if you like, which makes you a beacon in the time stream.'

Artemis shuffled self-consciously. 'How long do we have?'

Nº1 gazed at the ceiling while he ran some calculations. 'Three hundred years . . . No, no, three days. Holly can bring you back at any point before that simply by making herself open to my power, but after three days the link grows weaker.'

'Is there anything we can do about that?'

'Let's face facts: all-powerful I may be, but I'm a novice at this, so taking off from where you landed is vital. If you go beyond three days, then you are stuck in the past.'

'If we do get separated, couldn't Holly come back and get me?' wondered Artemis.

'No, she could not,' said Nº1. 'It would be impossible for you to meet at a point neither of you had experienced. This is a one-time deal only. It will take everything I have to hold you together for this trip. Any more and your atoms would lose their memory and simply forget where it is they are supposed to go. Both of you have already been in the time stream twice. I can transport objects forever and a day, but living beings break down without a warlock in the stream to shield them.'

Holly asked a very pertinent question. 'Number One, have you done this before?'

'Of course,' said the demon. 'Several times. On a simulator. And two of the holograms survived.'

Artemis's determination barely flickered. 'Two survived. The last two?'

'No,' admitted N°1. 'The last two were trapped in a time wormhole and consumed by quantum zombies.'

Holly felt her pointy ears tingle, always a bad sign. Elfin ears could sense danger.

'Quantum zombies? You're not serious.'

'That's what I said to Qwan. He wrote the program.'

'This is irrelevant,' said Artemis sharply. 'We have no option but to go.'

'Very well,' said N°1, flexing his fingers. He bent his knees, resting his entire body weight on the tip of his tail.

'Power posture,' he explained. 'I do some of my best work in this position.'

'So does Mulch Diggums,' muttered Foaly. 'Quantum zombies. I need to get a copy of *that* program.'

A red haze blossomed around the demon warlock, tiny lightning bolts crackling across his horns.

'He's powering up,' said Foaly from the screens. 'You'll be off any second. Remember, try not to touch anything you don't have to. Don't talk to anyone. Don't contact me in the past. I have no desire not to exist.'

Artemis nodded. 'I know. Make as little impact as possible, in case the time paradox theory has some merit.'

Holly was impatient to get going. 'Enough science. Just blast us into the past. We'll bring the monkey back.'

'Lemur,' said Artemis and Foaly together.

N°1 closed his eyes. When he opened them again, they were pure crimson.

'OK, ready to go,' he said conversationally.

ᴀ♙♙ᴋᴃ☆ᴊ•ꚉꝋᴃᴊᴊᴋᴊᴋ•◻ᴋꚉᴃ•ᵾᴂᴊ

Artemis blinked. He was expecting N°1's voice of power to be a bit less squeaky.

'Are you sure?'

N°1 groaned. 'I know. It's the voice, isn't it? Not enough gravel. Qwan says I should go for less airy and more fairy. Trust me, I'm ready. Now hold hands.'

Artemis and Holly stood together in their underwear, gingerly locking fingers. They had crossed space and time together, weathered rebellions and tangled with demented despots. Coughed blood, lost digits, inhaled dwarf fumes and swapped eyeballs, yet they found holding hands awkward.

N°1 knew he shouldn't, but he couldn't resist a parting crack.

'I now pronounce you . . .'

Neither hand-holder was amused, but before they had time to do more than scowl, twin bolts of red energy crackled from N°1's eyes, blasting his friends into the time stream.

'Man and elf,' he said, finishing his joke, then chuckling delightedly.

On screen, Foaly snorted. 'I'm guessing you're laughing to cover your anxiety?'

'Exactly right,' said N°1.

Where Artemis and Holly had been standing there were flickering copies of them both, mouths open to object to N°1's comment.

'That really freaks me out, the ghost images. It's like they're dead.'

Foaly shuddered. 'Don't say that. If they're dead, we all could be. How soon will they be back?'

'In about ten seconds.'

'And if they're not back in ten seconds?'

'Then never.'

Foaly started counting.

CHAPTER 6: İ TO İ

THERE is a moment of confusion when a land animal enters the water. Beast, human or fairy, it doesn't matter. The surface is broken and every sense is suddenly shocked. The cold stings, motion slows and the eyes are filled with smears of colour and the snap of bursting bubbles. The time stream is like that moment sustained.

That's not to say that travelling through the time stream is a consistent experience. Never the same journey twice. The demon warlock Qwan, who was the planet's most experienced time-travelling fairy, wrote in his bestselling autobiography, *Qwan: My Time is Now*, that 'riding the time stream is like flying through a dwarf's intestine. There are very nice free-flowing stretches, but then you turn a corner to find the thing backed-up and putrid. The problem being that the time stream is largely an emotional construct, and it absorbs ambient feelings from the real time it flows around. If you happen across a stretch of foul-smelling gunk, you can bet that the humans are killing something.'

Artemis and Holly were being dragged through a foul-smelling stretch that corresponded with an entire ecosystem being destroyed in South America. They could sense the animals' terror and even smell the charred wood. Artemis felt, too, that Holly was losing herself in the maelstrom of emotions. Fairies were so much more sensitive to their environments than humans. If Holly lost concentration, her atoms would dissipate and be absorbed by the stream.

Focus, Holly, Artemis broadcast into the stream. *Remember who you are and why we are here.*

It was difficult for them both. Their particle memory had already been weakened by the Limbo journeys and the temptation to meld with the stream was strong.

Artemis conjured a picture of his mother in his consciousness to bolster his determination.

I know when and where I want to be, he thought. *Exactly when and where . . .*

FOWL MANOR, NEARLY EIGHT YEARS AGO

Artemis and Holly exited the time stream and entered ten-year-old Artemis's study. Physically, this was a gentle enough experience, like jumping from a low wall on to thick carpet, but emotionally this particular trip was like a ten-minute blitz of the worst memories of their lives. The time stream: never the same ride twice.

Holly cried for her mother for a minute, but eventually the persistent chiming of a grandfather clock reminded her of where and when she was. She stood shakily and looked around her to find Artemis lurching towards the wardrobe. The sight of him cheered her a little.

'You have really let yourself go,' she said.

Artemis was rummaging through the clothes on the rail.

'Of course nothing will fit,' he muttered. 'All too small.'

Holly elbowed past him. 'Not for me,' she said, pulling a dark suit from its hanger.

'My first suit,' said Artemis fondly. 'For the family Christmas postcard. I had no idea really how to wear it. I remember fidgeting throughout the fitting. It's a Zegna bespoke.'

Holly tore off a protective polythene wrap. 'So long as it fits.'

It was only then that Artemis's emotions settled enough for him to register Holly's comment.

'What do you mean I have let myself go?'

Holly swung the wardrobe's door, so that its mirrored side faced Artemis.

'See for yourself,' she said.

Artemis looked. In the mirror he saw a tall, slender boy, his head all but invisible under a wild mop of shoulder-length hair, and even some bristles on his chin.

'Ah. I see.'

'I'm surprised you do,' said Holly. 'Through all that hair.'

'Accelerated ageing. A side effect of the time stream,' Artemis hypothesized, unconcerned. 'When we return, the effects should be reversed.' He paused, catching sight of

Holly's reflection. 'Perhaps you should check *yourself* in the mirror. I am not the only one who has changed.'

Holly elbowed him aside, certain she was being kidded, but the half-smile died on her lips when she saw the fairy in the looking glass. It was her own face, but different, missing a few scars and a few decades' wear and tear.

'I am young,' she gasped. 'Younger.'

'Don't be upset,' said Artemis briskly. 'It is temporary. All this is nothing more than dress-up. My physical maturity, your youth. In a moment or two we will be back in the stream.'

But Holly *was* upset. She knew how this had happened.

I was thinking of Mother. Of our last hours together. Of how I was then.

And so that was how she had changed.

Look at me. Just out of the Academy. In human terms, barely older than Artemis.

For some reason, this was a disturbing thought.

'Get some trousers on,' she snapped, buttoning a crisp white shirt to her neck. 'Then we can discuss your theories.'

Artemis used his extra inches to reach up and tug a large box from the top of the wardrobe. In it were neatly folded layers of clothes destined for one of Angeline Fowl's charity shops.

He tossed a silver wig to Holly.

'Seventies fancy-dress party,' he explained. 'Mother went as a star-ship trooper, I seem to remember. Now cover those pointy ears.'

'A hat would be easier,' said Holly, pulling the wig over her auburn crew-cut.

'No such luck, I'm afraid,' sighed Artemis, selecting an old tracksuit from the box. 'This is not exactly Harrods; we will have to make do.'

Artemis's old loafers fitted Holly well enough, and there was a pair of his father's trainers in the box that stayed on his feet when the toes were stuffed.

'Always good to be dressed when you're stealing monkeys,' said Holly.

Artemis rolled up the tracksuit sleeves. 'There's no need to dress at all really. We simply wait for a few minutes until my mother almost catches Butler sneaking upstairs with the lemur. I remember him sliding the cage through the doorway, then I brought it back upstairs. The moment that cage comes in here, we grab it, take off these ridiculous clothes and wish our way back to Number One.'

Holly checked herself in the mirror. She looked like a presidential bodyguard from another planet. 'That sounds so simple.'

'It was simple. Will be. Butler never even entered the study. All we need to do is stand here and wait.'

'And how did you find this particular moment?'

Artemis swept a sheaf of black hair back from his brow, revealing mismatched sorrowful eyes.

'Listen,' he said, pointing upwards, towards the ceiling.

Holly tucked strands of silver hair behind one ear, cocking her head to one side to focus her considerable sense of hearing. She heard the grandfather clock, and the time travellers' beating hearts, but above them there was a strident, hysterical voice.

'Mother,' said Artemis, eyes downcast. 'It was the first time that she did not recognize me. She is at this moment threatening to call the police. In a moment she runs downstairs to the phone and discovers Butler.'

Holly understood. How could any son forget a moment like that one? Finding it again must have been easy and painful.

'I remember it clearly. We had just returned from Rathdown Park, the private zoo, and I thought I should check how she was feeling before flying to Morocco. In a month from now she won't be able to look after herself any more.'

Holly squeezed his forearm. 'It's fine, Artemis. This is all in the past. In a few minutes your mother will be back on her feet. She will love you as she always has.'

Artemis nodded glumly. He knew it was probably true, but he also knew that he would never fully escape the spectre of this bad memory.

Upstairs, Angeline Fowl's voice moved from her bedchamber to the upper landing, trailing shrill notes behind her.

Artemis pulled Holly back against the wall.

'Butler will be on the stairs now. We should keep to the shadows just in case.'

Holly couldn't help a flutter of nerves. 'You're sure he stays outside? The last time I faced Butler as an enemy, I had the entire LEP on my side. I don't relish the thought of meeting him armed with nothing more than a silver wig.'

'Calm yourself, Captain,' said Artemis, unconsciously patronizing. 'He stays outside. I saw it with my own eyes.'

'Saw what with your own eyes?' asked Butler, who had appeared in the archway behind them, having let himself in through the adjoining bedroom door.

Artemis felt his pulse throb in his fingertips. How could this be? This was not the way it happened. Artemis had never been on the receiving end of Butler's glare before, and understood for the first time just how terrifying his bodyguard could be.

'You two kids have been helping yourselves to the Fowl wardrobe I see,' continued Butler, without waiting for an answer to his question. 'Now, are you going to cause a fuss or are you going to come quietly? Let me give you a hint, the correct answer is *come quietly.*'

Magic is the only way out, Holly realized.

She twisted her chin sharply to call on her fairy power. If she couldn't stun Butler, she would mesmerize him.

'*Stand down, human*,' she intoned, voice loaded with hypnotic magic. But the *mesmer* is a two-pronged attack, audio and visual. Butler could hear the magical words but eye contact was not consistent in the shadows.

'What?' he said, surprised. 'How did you . . .'

The hulking bodyguard had been drugged enough times to realize that his will was being sapped. Somehow these kids were putting him under. He staggered backwards, his shoulder bashing against the arch.

'*Sleep, Butler,*' said the little one in the star-ship-trooper wig.

She knows me?

This was serious. These two had done some surveillance and decided to break in anyway.

I have to neutralize them before I pass out, thought Butler. *If I go down, Master Artemis and Mrs Fowl are defenceless.*

He had two options: fall on the midget burglars, or shoot them with the tranquillizer pistol he was carrying for the planned animal abduction at Rathdown Park.

He chose the second option. At least tranquillizer darts would not smother these two or crush their bones. Butler felt mildly guilty about his decision to trank a couple of kids, but not overly so; after all, he worked for Artemis Fowl and knew exactly how dangerous children could be.

The star-ship trooper came out of the shadows, and Butler could see her eyes clearly. One blue, one tawny.

'*Sleep, Butler,*' she said again, in that melodious layered voice. '*Aren't your eyelids heavy? Sleep.*'

She's hypnotizing me! Butler realized. He dragged out the pistol with fingers that felt as though they had been dipped in molten rubber, then sprinkled with ball bearings.

'*You* sleep,' he mumbled, then shot the girl in the hip.

Holly stared in disbelief at the hypodermic dart sticking out of her leg.

'Not again,' she moaned, then collapsed to the floor. Butler's head cleared immediately.

The other intruder did not move an inch.

The little girl is the professional of the two, thought Butler, climbing to his feet. *I wonder what this scruffy individual contributes to the partnership.*

Artemis quickly saw that he had no choice but to reveal his identity and enlist Butler as an ally.

This will be difficult. I have nothing more than a passing resemblance to my younger self as proof.

Still, he had to try before his plan unravelled utterly.

'Listen, Butler,' he began. 'I have something to tell you . . .'

Butler didn't entertain another word. 'No, no, no,' he said briskly, shooting Artemis in the shoulder. 'No more talking from either of you.'

Artemis pulled out the dart, but it was too late. The tiny reservoir of sedative was empty.

'Butler!' he gasped, dropping to his knees. 'You shot me.'

'Everyone knows my name,' sighed the bodyguard, bending to sling the intruders over his shoulders.

'I am intrigued,' said ten-year-old Artemis Fowl, studying the two individuals in the Bentley's boot. 'Something extra-ordinary has happened here.'

'Hardly extraordinary,' said Butler, checking the girl's pulse. 'Two thieves somehow broke into the manor.'

'They bypassed all the security. Not so much as a blip on the motion sensors?'

'Nothing. I just happened on them during a routine

sweep. Hiding in the shadows, wearing cast-offs from the wardrobe.'

Artemis tapped his chin. 'Hmm. So, you didn't find their clothes.'

'Not a stitch.'

'Which would mean that they broke in here and bypassed security in their underwear.'

'That is extraordinary,' admitted Butler.

Artemis took a penlight from his jacket pocket, shining it on Holly, setting the strands of her silver wig sparkling like a disco ball. 'There's something about this one. Her bone structure is very unusual. The cheekbones are high – Slavic, perhaps – and the brow is wide and childlike. But the proportion of skull to torso is adult, not infant.'

Butler chuckled low in his throat. 'So, they're aliens?'

'The young man is human, but she's something else,' said Artemis thoughtfully. 'Genetically enhanced, perhaps.' He moved the beam of light along her cheekbone. 'See here. The ears are pointed. Amazing.'

Artemis felt an excitement buzzing on his forehead. Something was happening here. Something important. There were surely serious amounts of money to be earned from this situation.

He rubbed his palms briskly. 'Very well. I cannot be distracted by this now. Long-term, this strange creature could make our fortune, but right now we need to get that lemur.'

Butler was crestfallen, but covered it by slamming the boot. 'I had hoped we could forget the monkey. I was trained in several forms of martial arts, none of them had a monkey defence.'

'It's a lemur, Butler. And I am aware that you believe this operation is beneath us, but my father's life is at stake.'

'Of course, Artemis. Whatever you say.'

'Exactly. So, here is the plan. We will proceed to Rathdown Park as planned and after we have done the deal with the Extinctionists, then I can decide what to do with our two guests. I presume they will be safe in the boot?'

Butler snorted. 'Are you kidding?'

Artemis did not smile. 'Perhaps you have not noticed, Butler. I rarely *kid*.'

'As you say, young master. You are not a kidder. Maybe some day, eh?'

'Perhaps when I find my father.'

'Yes. Perhaps then. Anyway, to answer your question. This is your *father's* car and there have been more prisoners in this boot than you've had birthdays. Mafiya, Triad, Yakuza, Tijuana Cartel, Hell's Angels. You name the gang and a couple of them have spent a night in this boot. In fact, your father had it specially modified. There's air-conditioning, a stay-cool light, soft suspension and even drinking water.'

'Is it secure? Remember our captives already broke into the manor.'

Butler closed the boot. 'Titanium lock, reinforced door. No way out whatsoever. Those two are staying in there until we let them out.'

'Excellent,' said Artemis, sliding into the Bentley's rear

seat. 'Just give me a moment to do this one little thing, then let's forget about them and concentrate on the lemur.'

'Excellent,' echoed Butler, and then under his breath: 'Monkey business. My favourite.'

RATHDOWN PARK, COUNTY WICKLOW, IRELAND

Even though Holly was five kilograms lighter than Artemis, she came to her senses before him. She was glad to be awake, as her dream had been terrible. While asleep, her knees and elbows had struck the metal walls of the Bentley's boot and she'd imagined herself in an LEP submarine.

Holly lay huddled in the dark, swallowing and blinking to conquer the phobia. Her mother had been mortally injured in a metal box, and now she was inside one.

And it was thoughts of her mother that finally calmed Holly. She opened her eyes, and explored the confined space with her vision and fingertips. It didn't take long to find the bubble light set into the steel wall. She snapped it on to find Artemis stretched out beside her and the sloping metal sheeting of a boot door curling down past his arm. Her own borrowed shoes rested on the shining curve of a wheel arch. They were inside a vehicle.

Artemis groaned, twitched and opened his eyes.

'Sell the Phonetix shares,' he blurted, then remembered Butler and the darts. 'Holly. Holly?'

Holly patted his leg. 'It's OK, Artemis,' she said in

Gnommish, in case the car was bugged. 'I'm here. Where else could I be?'

Artemis shifted on to his side, flicking back the dense black hair obscuring his features, and spoke in the fairy tongue.

'We received the same dosage of tranquillizer, and yet you, the lighter person, are awake first. Magic?'

The side of Holly's face was thrown into deep shadow by the bubble light. 'Yes. Number One's signature magic is powerful stuff.'

'Powerful enough to get us out of here?'

Holly spent a minute exploring the boot's surface, running her fingertips along each weld in the metal. Finally, she shook her head, silver wig sparkling. 'Not a weak spot I can find. Even the air-conditioning vent is completely flush. No way out.'

'Of course not,' said Artemis. 'We're inside the Bentley. The boot is a steel box with a titanium lock.' He breathed the cool air deeply. 'How can this have happened? Everything is different. Butler was supposed to have deposited the cage in my study. Instead he creeps in through the bedroom and sedates us both. Now we don't know where we are, or indeed where the lemur is. Do they have it already?'

Holly pressed one ear to the boot door. 'I can tell you where we are.'

Outside, the sounds of snuffling and snoring animals drifted on the air. 'We're close to animals. A park I would guess, or a zoo.'

'Rathdown Park,' exclaimed Artemis. 'And that fact tells

us they do not, in fact, have the lemur. The schedule and situation have changed.'

Holly was thoughtful. 'We are not in control of this situation any more, Artemis. Perhaps it's time to admit defeat and return home when your younger self brings us back to the manor. *Perhaps* you can discover a cure in the future.'

Artemis had been expecting this suggestion. 'I considered that. The lemur is still our best option and we are metres away from it. Just give me five minutes to get us out of here.'

Holly was understandably dubious. 'Five minutes? Even the great Artemis Fowl might have trouble breaking out of a steel box in five minutes.'

Artemis closed his eyes, concentrating. Trying to ignore his cramped surroundings and the sheaves of hair brushing his cheeks, and the itch of bristles on his chin.

'Face it, Artemis,' said Holly impatiently. 'We're stuck. Even Mulch Diggums would probably struggle with a lock like that if he happened to stroll by.'

Artemis's brow flickered, irritated by this interruption, but then a smile spread across his face, made eerie by the stark lighting.

'Mulch Diggums strolling by,' he whispered. 'What are the chances of that?'

'Zero,' said Holly. 'Absolutely none. I would bet my pension on it.'

At that moment something or someone tapped on the boot door, from the outside.

Holly rolled her eyes. 'No. Not even you . . .'

ꞏꝰꞀꝰꞀ⬡•⬡⬡➤•⬮⬩⬥⬩⬡➤•⬡•ꝛꞀ•ꞁꝰꝛꝛ

Artemis's smile was smug beyond belief. 'Just how large is your pension?'

'I do not believe it. I *refuse* to believe it. It is impossible.'

More taps on the door now, followed by a delicate scraping and a muted swear word.

'What a guttural voice,' said Artemis. 'Very like a dwarf's.'

'It could be Butler,' argued Holly, irritated by Artemis's self-satisfied expression.

'Swearing in Gnommish. Hardly.'

More metallic noises from the outside world.

Shhhnick. Chunk. Clackack.

And the boot's lid swung upwards, revealing a slice of starry night with the glinting silhouette of a gigantic pylon behind it. A bedraggled head popped into the space, features smeared with mud and worse. This was a face that only a mother could love, and then perhaps only if her sight were failing. Dark, close-set eyes peered out from above a dense beard that shivered slightly like seaweed in a current. The creature's teeth were large, square and not made any more appealing by the large insect wriggling between two molars.

It was, of course, Mulch Diggums.

The dwarf snagged the unfortunate insect with his tongue, then chewed it delicately.

'Ground beetle,' he said with relish. '*Leistus montanus*. Nice bouquet, solid earthy shell, then, once the carapace cracks, a veritable explosion of flavours on the palate.'

He swallowed the unfortunate creature, then funnelled a mighty burp through his flapping lips.

⊖⊟ᚠ·⊟ᚠⱤ⊕⊕ᚋ·ᚐᚑ⊖⚹⧬⅄ᚱ⊗⊕⊝⅁ᚱᚋ·⊙⌒⅄

'Never burp when you're tunnelling,' he advised Artemis and Holly, as casually as though they were sitting round a café table. 'Dirt coming down, air coming up. Not a good idea.'

Holly knew Mulch well. This chit-chat was simply for distraction while he took a peek around.

'And now, to business,' said the dwarf finally, discarding the dead beard hair he had used to pick the lock. 'I seem to have a human and an elf trapped in a car. So I ask myself, should I let 'em out?'

'And what do you answer yourself?' asked Artemis with barely contained impatience.

Mulch's black pebble eyes danced in the moonlight. 'So, the Mud Boy understands Gnommish. Interesting. Well, understand *this*, human. I let you out as soon as I get my money.'

Ah, thought Holly. *There is money involved. Somehow these two have set up a deal.*

Holly had endured her prison for long enough.

Mulch is not yet my friend, she thought, *so there's no need to be polite.*

She drew a knee to her chin, tugging on it with both hands for an extra pound of elastic force.

Mulch realized what she was about to do. 'Hey, elf. No —'

Which was as far as he got before his face was batted with the boot door. The dwarf tumbled backwards into the hole he had climbed out of, sending up an *oof* of wind and dirt.

Ꭺꮖ•ᏲᏗᎠ⟩•ᏕᎧᏰᎦ•ᏌᏗᎥᎥᎡᏲᏉ⟩→•ᏗᎠᏗ•ᏰᏗ

Holly clambered over Artemis to the fresh air. She gulped down great gasps, chest out, face to the sky.

'Sorry,' she said, between breaths. 'That space is tiny. I don't like tiny.'

'Claustrophobic?' asked Artemis, rolling from the boot.

Holly nodded. 'I used to be. I thought I had overcome it. Lately, though . . .'

There was a commotion in the dwarf hole. A blue riot of swearing and a scuffling in the earth.

Holly quickly recovered herself and leaped into the pit, tackling Mulch before he could unhinge his jaw and disappear.

'He could be useful,' she grunted, bundling the protesting dwarf up the incline. 'And he has already seen us, so the damage has been done.'

'That's a pincer hold,' exclaimed Mulch. 'You're LEP.'

He twisted round, snagging Holly's wig with his beard hair. 'I *know* you. Holly Short. *Captain* Holly Short. One of Julius Root's pet Rottweilers.'

Suddenly the dwarf's already creased brow wrinkled further in confusion.

'But this is impossible.'

Before Artemis could instruct Holly not to ask, she went ahead and did it.

'Why is it impossible, Mulch?'

Mulch did not reply, but his eyes betrayed him, glancing guiltily over his shoulder at a scuffed Tekfab backpack. Holly deftly spun the dwarf round, opening the bag's main compartment.

⊗ • ⚜ • ⚘ ⚛ • ⚙) ◔ ⊌ ☎ • ⊗ ⚛ • ⑧) ⚡ ⌁ ← • ⚑ ⚐

'Quite a treasure trove we have here,' she said, rummaging in the backpack. 'Medi-kit, rations, adhesive com-pads. And look, an old Omnitool.' Then she recognized the inscription laser-etched into the base. 'It's *my* old Omnitool.'

In spite of their years of friendship, Holly turned the full force of her anger on Mulch.

'Where did you get this?' she shouted. 'How did you get it?'

'A present,' offered Mulch lamely. 'From my . . . eh . . .' He squinted to read the writing on the base. 'From my mother. She always called me Holly, because of my, erm, prickly personality.'

Holly was angrier than Artemis had ever seen her. 'Tell me, Diggums. The truth!'

Mulch thought about fighting. It was in the curve of his fingers and the baring of his teeth, but the moment passed quickly and the dwarf's natural passive nature surfaced.

'I stole all this stuff from Tara,' he admitted. 'I'm a thief, aren't I? But, in my defence, I had a difficult childhood, which led to low self-esteem, which I projected on to others, and punished them by stealing their possessions. So, in a very real way, I am the victim here. And *I* forgive *me*.'

Mulch's trademark waffle reminded Holly of the friend he would become and her anger evaporated as quickly as it had appeared. She traced the laser inscription with a fingertip.

'My mother gave me this,' she said quietly. 'Most reliable Omnitool I ever had. Then, one night in Hamburg, my fugitive locked himself in a car. So I reached for my

Omnitool and it was gone. The target was apprehended by humans, I lost my first fugitive and Commander Root had to send in an entire team of techies to clean up. It was a disaster. And all this time it was you.'

Mulch was puzzled. 'All this time? I stole this from a belt in a locker in Tara *an hour ago*. I *saw* you there. What's going on here . . .' Then Mulch blinked and clapped his hairy palms. 'Oh, bless my bum-flap. You're time travellers.'

Holly realized that she had said too much. 'That's ridiculous.'

The dwarf was actually doing a little jig now. 'No. No, it all adds up. You're talking about *future* events in the *past* tense. You sent back a note so that I would come and rescue you here and now.' Mulch clapped his hands to his cheeks in mock horror. 'What you're doing is so much more illegal than anything I could ever do. Imagine the reward I would get for turning you over to Julius Root.'

'Sent back a note?' scoffed Holly. 'That's absurd, isn't it, Artemis?'

'Most certainly,' said Artemis. 'But, if someone were to send back a note from the future, where and when would they send it to?'

Mulch jerked a thumb towards Holly. 'There's a junction box beside her locker. Looked like it hadn't been touched for years. I was checking it out because sometimes they have some valuable tech in 'em. Not this one, though, just an envelope addressed to me. And inside a note asking me to come to this place and set you free.'

Artemis smiled. Satisfied. 'I imagine there was an incentive offered for our rescue?'

Mulch's beard hair crackled. 'A large incentive. No . . . a *stupendous* incentive.'

'Stupendous, eh? Very well, you shall have it.'

'When?' asked Mulch hungrily.

'Soon. I just need you to do me one more favour.'

'I knew it,' said the dwarf, through grinding teeth. 'Never do the job until you see the cash. Why should I trust you?'

Artemis took a step forward, eyes narrow behind a curtain of dark hair. 'You don't need to trust me, Mulch. You need to be afraid of me. I am a Mud Boy from your future and I could be in your past too, if you choose not to cooperate. I found you once, I could certainly do it again. The next time you break into a car boot, there could be a gun and a badge waiting for you.'

Mulch felt apprehension tingling in his beard hair, and his beard hair was rarely wrong. As his grandmother used to say: *Trust the hair, Mulch. Trust the hair.* This human was dangerous, and he had enough trouble in his life already.

'OK, Mud Boy,' he said grudgingly. 'One more favour. And then you'd better have a stupendous amount of gold for me.'

'I will. Fear not, my pungent friend.'

The dwarf was deeply offended. 'Don't call me *friend*. Just tell me. What. You. Want. Done.'

'Simply follow your nature and dig us a tunnel. I need to steal a lemur.'

U･⊕･◔･�римвⅉ⅊⅋･⊛◻･⊕⅌⅍ⅎ･⅏◉･⅗◉ℬℱ

Mulch nodded as though lemur-napping was the most natural thing in the world.

'And from whom are we stealing it?'

'From me.'

Mulch frowned, then the penny dropped. 'Ah . . . Time travel throws up all sorts of twists, doesn't it?'

Holly slipped the Omnitool into her pocket. 'Tell me about it,' she said.

CHAPTER 7: **TALK TO THE AﬁIMALS**

 THE Fowl Bentley was protected by a fingerprint scanner and a keypad that required an eight-digit code. The code was changed every month, and so it took Artemis a few seconds to mentally rewind almost eight years and remember the right set of numbers.

He slid across the front seat's tan leather upholstery and pressed his thumb to a second scanner tucked behind the steering wheel. A spring-loaded compartment slid smoothly from the dash. It was not a large compartment, but big enough to hold a clip of cash, platinum credit cards and a spare mobile phone in its cradle.

'No gun?' asked Holly when Artemis emerged from the car, though one of Butler's guns would be clunky in her fingers.

'No gun,' confirmed Artemis.

'I wouldn't be able to hit an elephant with one of Butler's pistols even if I had one.'

'Elephants are not the quarry this evening,' said Artemis, speaking in English, now that they were out of the boot. 'Lemurs are. At any rate, as we could hardly shoot at our opponent on this particular adventure, perhaps it's better that we are unarmed.'

'Not really,' said Holly. 'I may not be able to shoot you or the lemur, but I bet that more *opponents* will turn up. You have a knack of making enemies.'

Artemis shrugged. 'Genius inspires resentment. A sad fact of life.'

'Genius *and* robbing stuff,' Mulch chimed from his perch on the lip of the car boot. 'Take it from one who knows: nobody likes a smart thief.'

Artemis drummed his fingers on the fender.

'We have certain advantages. Elfin magic. Digging talents. I have almost eight years' experience in the art of mischief making that the other Artemis does not have.'

'Mischief making?' scoffed Holly. 'I think you're being a little gentle on yourself. Grand larceny is closer to the mark.'

Artemis stopped drumming. 'One of your fairy powers is speaking in tongues, correct?'

'I'm talking to you, aren't I?' responded Holly.

'Just how many tongues can you speak in?'

Holly smiled. She knew Artemis's devious mind well enough to realize exactly where he was going with this.

'As many as you want.'

'Good,' said Artemis. 'We need to split up. You take the overground route into Rathdown Park, Mulch and I travel underground. If we need a distraction, use your gift.'

'It would be a pleasure,' said Holly, and immediately turned translucent as though she were a creature of purest water. The last thing to go was her smile.

Just like the Cheshire Cat.

He remembered a few lines from *Alice's Adventures in Wonderland.*

'*But I don't want to go among mad people,*' said Alice.

'*Oh, you can't help that,*' said the cat. '*We're all mad here.*'

Artemis glanced at the pungent dwarf searching his living beard for stored insects.

We're all mad here too, he thought.

Holly approached the main door of Rathdown Park with care even though she was shielded. The People had thought themselves invisible to Butler once before and had paid with trauma and bruises. She would not underestimate the bodyguard, and the fact that he was once again her enemy set her stomach churning with nervous acid.

The human clothes jumped and scratched along her frame. They were not built for shielding and in a matter of minutes they would shake to pieces.

I miss my Neutrino, she thought, looking at the reinforced-steel door, with the dark unknown beyond it. *And I miss Foaly and his satellite link-ups.*

But at heart Holly was an adventurer, so the idea of quitting never even occurred to her.

It was difficult to operate mechanisms while shielded, so Holly powered down for the few seconds necessary to jimmy the door with her Omnitool. It was an old model, but Holly's mother had paid an extra few ingots for upgrades. The standard Omnitool would open any door operating on a simple mechanical lock-and-key system. This one could short electronic locks too, and even deactivate simple alarms.

But that shouldn't be necessary, she thought. *As far as Artemis remembers, he turned off all the alarms.*

The thought didn't give her much comfort. Artemis had been wrong about this trip already.

In less than five seconds, the Omnitool had done its job and vibrated gently like a cat purring at its own cleverness. The heavy door swung open silently under the lightest touch and Holly buzzed up her shield again.

Stepping into Rathdown Park, Holly felt more mission anxiety than she had in years.

I'm a rookie again. Some kid straight out of the Academy, she realized. *My mind is experienced, but my body is overruling it.*

And then: *I better get this monkey quick before adolescence kicks in.*

Young Artemis had turned off the security on his way into the institute. It had been an easy thing to bypass all the alarms with the director's key card. Earlier in the day, when he had been given the guided tour, he had posed several complicated questions on the validity of the theory of evolution. The director, a committed evolutionist, had allowed his arguments to distract him long enough to have his pocket picked by Butler. Once the key card was in the bodyguard's possession, he simply slotted it into a battery-powered Card Cloner in his breast pocket, and whistled a few bars of Mozart to cover the whirr of the machine.

Two minutes later all the information they needed was stored in the Cloner's memory, the director's card was back in his pocket and Artemis suddenly decided that maybe evolution wasn't a bad theory after all.

'Though there are more holes in it than a Dutch dam made of Swiss cheese,' he'd confided to Butler on the way home from Rathdown Park. Butler had been encouraged by this statement. It was almost a straightforward joke.

Later that evening young Artemis had popped a button camera into the air-con duct at the rear of the Bentley.

All the better to keep an eye on our guests.

The female was interesting. *Fascinating*, actually. The darts would wear off soon and it would be intriguing to watch her reaction, much more so than that of the hirsute teenager, even though his broad forehead suggested intelligence and his general features had a lot in common with the Fowl family's own. In fact, he reminded Artemis of an old photo he had once seen of his father as a boy, working on an archaeological dig in South America. Perhaps the male captive was a distant cousin hoping to claim some kind of birthright now that Father was missing. There was much to be investigated here.

The button camera was broadcasting to his mobile phone and ten-year-old Artemis checked the screen occasionally as Butler guided him through Rathdown Park towards the lemur's cage.

'Focus, Artemis,' chided the bodyguard. 'One dastardly crime at a time.'

Artemis glanced up from his phone. 'Dastardly, Butler? *Dastardly?* Honestly, we are not cartoon characters. I do not have a villainous laugh or an eyepatch.'

'Not yet. Though you'll have an eyepatch soon enough if you don't concentrate on the job at hand.'

They were passing underneath Rathdown Park's aquarium through a perspex tunnel that allowed scientists and the occasional visitor to observe the species housed in the million-gallon tank. The tank mimicked the inhabitants' natural environment as far as possible. Different compartments had different temperatures and different vegetation. Some were saltwater, others were fresh, but all housed endangered or rare creatures.

Tiny bulbs dotted the ceiling above, simulating stars, and the only other light came from the bioluminescence of a lantern shark, which shadowed Artemis and Butler along the tunnel until its snout bumped perspex.

Artemis was more interested in his mobile phone than the shark's eerily glowing photophores.

Events were unfolding on his screen that were close to

incredible. Artemis stopped in his tracks to fully absorb what he was seeing.

The Fowl Manor intruders had escaped the Bentley's boot with the help of an accomplice. Another non-human.

I am entering a new world here. These creatures are potentially more lucrative than a lemur. Should I abandon this venture and concentrate on the non-humans?

Artemis maximized the volume on his handset but the tiny microphone attached to the button camera could only pick up snatches of the conversation.

It was mostly in some alien tongue, but some of the talk was in English and he heard the word *lemur* more than once.

Perhaps this lemur is more valuable than I realized. The animal is the bait that lures these creatures in.

A minute passed with only the small, revolting dwarf-like thing in the screen, perching its disproportionately large backside on the rim of the boot, then the female appeared, only to promptly disappear – Rathdown Park's famous pylons filling the screen where she had been.

Artemis tightened his grip on the phone.

Invisibility? The energy involved in creating a reflective field, or to generate high-speed vibration, must be incredible.

He quickly navigated the phone's menu and activated the digital thermal imager, a decidedly non-standard option, and was relieved to see the female creature's form blossom on screen in warm tones.

Good. Not gone, just hard to see.

Keeping one eye on his phone, Artemis called to his bodyguard.

'Butler, old friend. Slight change of plan.'

The bodyguard knew better than to hope the lemur hunt was off. 'We're still on the trail of a little creature, though, I'll bet.'

'Creatures,' said ten-year-old Artemis. 'Plural.'

Fourteen-year-old Artemis was not enjoying the view. To distract himself he composed a haiku describing the sight before him.

> *Pale, shuddering globes*
> *Churn their poisonous cargo*
> *Bald heads in a bag*

Mulch Diggums was not feeling quite so poetic. He stopped digging and rehinged his jaw.

'Could you please stop shining the torch on my backside? I blister easily. We dwarves are extremely photo-sensitive, even to artificial light.'

Artemis had taken the torch from the Bentley's break-down kit, and was following Mulch through a fresh tunnel to the lemur's cage. The dwarf had assured him that the tunnel was sufficiently short for him to hold in the dirt and air until they reached the other end, making it safe for Artemis to be directly behind him.

Artemis averted the torch for a few seconds, thinking

that a bum blister was the last thing he wanted to see, but after a while the beam strayed back to the pale, wobbling flesh once more.

'Just a quick question. If you can hold in all the diggings, then why does your bum-flap need to be open?'

Mulch was spitting large wads of dwarf phlegm on to the wall to shore up the tunnel.

'In case of emergency,' he explained. 'I could swallow a buried lug of metal, or strip of old tyre. Now, those I would have to evacuate on the spot, annoying Mud Boy to the rear or not. No sense in ruining my trousers too, now is there, dopey?'

'I suppose not,' said Artemis, thinking that with such a wide-bore loaded weapon pointed at him he could bear being called *dopey*.

'Anyway,' continued the dwarf, hawking another wad at the wall, 'you should consider yourself privileged. Not many humans have seen a dwarf working with spit. This is what you might call an ancient art. First you –'

'I know, I know,' interrupted Artemis impatiently. 'First you excavate, then you strengthen the walls with your spittle, which hardens on contact with the air, provided it's out of your mouth, obviously. And it's luminous too – amazing material.'

Mulch's behind wobbled in surprise. 'How do you know these secrets?'

'You told me, or rather you will tell me. Time travel, remember?'

The dwarf peered over his shoulders, eyes red in the glow of his spittle. 'Just how close do we become?'

'Very close. We get an apartment together and after a whirlwind courtship you marry my sister and honeymoon in Vegas.'

'I love Vegas,' said Mulch wistfully. Then: 'Such snide wit. I can see how we might be friends. All the same, keep your comments to yourself or we might have to see how funny you are covered in tunnel waste.'

Artemis swallowed hard and moved the torch beam away from Mulch's behind.

The plan was a simple one. They would tunnel beneath the compound and wait below the lemur's cage for Holly to contact them on the short-range LEP adhesive communicator stuck to Artemis's cheek – part of Mulch's stash. From that point forward, the plan became fluid. Either they would pop up and grab the lemur while Holly caused consternation among the animals, or, if young Artemis had already secured the lemur, Mulch would dig a hole under Butler, making it easier for Holly to relieve the boy of his prize.

All very straightforward, thought Artemis. *Which is unusual for me.*

'OK, Mud Boy,' said Mulch, scooping a bulb-shaped hollow with his flat fingers. 'We are here. X marks the monkey.'

'Lemur,' corrected Artemis automatically. 'Are you certain you can distinguish this particular animal's scent from all the others?'

Mulch held a hand to his heart in mock affront. 'I? *Certain?*

I am a dwarf, human. A dwarf nose can tell the difference between grass and clover. Between black hair and brown. Between dog poo and wolf poo.'

Artemis groaned. 'I shall take that as a yes.'

'And so you should. Keep this up and I may choose not to marry your sister.'

'If I had a sister, I'm sure she would be inconsolable.'

They crouched in the hollow for several minutes, the park's night-time growls and snores drifting down through the clay. By some curious anomaly, once the sounds penetrated the tunnel's coating of dwarf spittle, they were trapped inside and bounced off the walls in conflicting waves. Artemis felt as though he were literally in the lion's den.

As if this wasn't disturbing enough, he noticed that Mulch's cheeks were glowing bright pink. All of them.

'Problems?' he asked, unable to mask a nervous tremor.

'I've been holding in this gas for a long time,' replied the dwarf through clenched teeth. 'It's coming out soon. You got any sinus problems?'

Artemis shook his head.

'Pity,' said Mulch. 'This would have cleared them right up.'

If it wasn't for Artemis's determination to save his mother, he would have bolted right then.

Luckily for Artemis's nasal passages, Holly beeped him on the ad-com. The communicator was a basic vibration model that sent signals directly to Artemis's ear without any external noise. Artemis heard Holly's words but not her voice. The ad-com was only sophisticated enough to produce robotic tones.

'In position. Over.'

Artemis placed a finger on the communicator, completing the circuit that allowed him to speak.

'Received. We are directly below the target's cage. Can you see the opposition?'

'Negative. No visual. But I do see the lemur. He seems to be asleep on a low branch. I can reach him easily.'

'Negative, Holly. Hold your position. We will secure the target. You watch for my younger self.'

'Understood. Don't hang around, Arty. Get up, get down and back to the car.'

Arty?

Artemis was surprised that Holly would call him that. It was his mother's pet name for him.

'Got it. Up, down and back.'

Arty?

Mulch tapped him urgently on the shoulder. 'Whenever you're ready, Mud Boy. Now would be great.'

'Very well. Proceed. Try to be quiet.'

Mulch changed position, pointing the crown of his head at the tunnel roof, squatting low on his haunches.

'Too late for quiet,' he grunted. 'Pull your jacket over your face.'

Artemis barely had time to do what he'd been asked when Mulch released a thundering cylinder of gas and earth, spraying the boy with undigested clods. The shell of dwarf spittle cracked in a thousand places and Mulch was borne aloft by a churning pillar of force, easily punching through to the surface.

Once the dust had settled somewhat, Artemis scrambled after him into the cage. Mulch had pinballed off a low ceiling and was unconscious, blood matting his already tangled hair, his bum-flap fluttering like a windsock while the remainder of the tunnel waste escaped.

Low cage ceiling?

The lemur in the next cage seemed highly amused by all the commotion and hopped up and down on a truncated branch wedged between the bars.

The next cage, realized Artemis. *We are not in the lemur's cage. What cage* are *we in?*

Before he had time to investigate, his cheek beeped and an emotionless robotic voice droned into his ear.

'Get Mulch out of there, Arty. Get back down now.'

What is it? wondered Artemis. *What's in this cage?*

Then a two-hundred-kilo Ugandan mountain gorilla crashed into him, leaving the thought behind like a speech bubble.

Young Artemis and Butler were watching all of this through the slot windows of a camouflaged hide that sat in front of the cages. The hide had been built inside a rockery and water feature and allowed close study of the various animals without disturbing the natural rhythms of their day. The director had been kind enough to let

Artemis sit in the observer's chair earlier that day.

'Some day you could run the hide's thermal-imaging camera and all this equipment from that chair,' he had said.

'Perhaps sooner than that,' Artemis had replied.

'Oh dear,' said Butler, the phrase sounding over-delicate in his gravelly voice. 'That must have really hurt.' He reached into his pocket for the dart gun. 'I better lend a hand or at least a dart.'

Butler had been busy with his darts. Two night workers lay unconscious on cots at the rear of the hide.

Through the slot window they had a clear view of the male intruder being shaken like a rag doll by an enormous gorilla. The cage's third occupant had collapsed and appeared to be wracked by an energetic bout of flatulence.

Incredible, thought Artemis. *This day is full of surprises.*

He tapped a few keys on the computer keyboard before him, redirecting the compound's thermal-imaging camera.

'I don't think a dart will be necessary,' he said. 'Help is already on the way.'

Sure enough, a red-hearted glow bounced across the cobbled walkway, hovering before the gorilla cage.

'Now this should be interesting,' mused ten-year-old Artemis.

Holly was forced into action. She had been discreetly tucked away behind the broad trunk of an imported baobab tree, shield off, conserving magic, keeping an eye out for young Artemis, when Mulch blew a hole in the earth into the wrong cage. He exploded from the ground in a mini-cyclone of debris, bounced off a few surfaces like a cartoon pinball and collapsed on to the cage floor.

The cage's resident, a black-and-grey bull gorilla, shot straight up, woken from deep sleep. Its eyes were wide but blurred, its teeth yellow and bared.

Stay down, Artemis, she thought. *Stay in the hole.*

No such luck. Artemis clambered to the surface, carefully navigating the simple climb. The time stream had not granted him any agility. As Artemis often said, the physical was not his area.

Holly thumbed her ad-com. 'Get Mulch out of there, Arty,' she shouted. 'Get back down now.'

It was too late. The gorilla had decided these newcomers were a threat to be dealt with. It rolled from its nest of leaves and bark, landing on eight knuckles, the impact sending a jarring wave along its arm hair.

Holly buzzed up her shield as she ran, silver strands floating behind her as the wig fell apart, marking her trail.

The gorilla attacked, grabbing a surprised Artemis Fowl by the shoulders, roaring in his face, head back, teeth like a bear trap.

Holly was at the gate, powering down, pulling the Omnitool from her pocket, jabbing the business end into the lock. She surveyed the scene inside the cage while she waited for the tool to work.

Mulch was up and on his elbows now, shaking a groggy head. It would be a moment or two before he was in any shape to help, if he deigned to help a human stranger.

Anyway, it was immaterial: a moment or two would be too late for Artemis.

The Omnitool beeped and the cage door swung open. A narrow walkway extended from the footpath, crossing a moat and slotting into grooves on the habitat floor.

Holly charged across without hesitation, waving her arms, shouting, making herself a target.

The gorilla huffed and snorted, gathering Artemis close to its chest – warning Holly to stay back. Artemis's head flopped on his shoulders and his eyes were half closed.

Holly stopped three metres from the animal, lowering her arms and gaze. A non-threatening stance.

The gorilla made a few fake attacks, thundering to within half a metre of Holly, then contemptuously turning its back, all the while grunting and barking, pressing Artemis to its chest. Artemis's hair was slicked back with blood and a crimson trickle leaked from the corner of his left eye. One arm was broken and blood pouched the sleeve of his tracksuit.

Holly was shocked. Appalled. She felt like crying and running away. Her friend was injured, possibly dead.

Get a grip! she told herself. *You are older than you look.*

One of the fairy magical powers was the gift of tongues and this encompassed a rudimentary grasp of some of the more sophisticated animal tongues. She would never be discussing global warming with a dolphin, but she knew enough for basic communication.

With gorillas it was as much about body language as what was actually said. Holly squatted low, elbows crooked, knuckles on the earth, spine curved forward. The posture of a friend, then funnelled her lips and hooted several times. '*Danger!*' the hoots said. '*Danger is near!*'

The gorilla did a comical double-take, amazed to hear gorilla-speak coming from this creature. It sensed a trick but was not sure what that trick might be. And, when in doubt, beat your chest.

The gorilla dropped Artemis, stood tall on two feet, thrusting forward chin and pectorals, and began beating its chest with open palms.

I am king here. Do not trifle with me, was the clear message.

A wise sentiment indeed, but Holly had no choice.

She darted forward, hooting all the time, throwing in the odd terrified screech, and then, against the advice of every wildlife expert who ever held a steadi-cam, she looked directly into the animal's eyes.

'*Leopard*,' she hooted, layering her voice with the fairy *mesmer*. '*Leopard!*'

The gorilla's fury was replaced by dull confusion, which was in turn pushed aside by terror.

'*Leopard!*' Holly hooted. '*Climb!*'

Moving with less than its customary grace, the gorilla stumbled towards the rear of the cage, moving as though underwater, senses dulled by the *mesmer*. Trees and foliage were batted aside, leaving a wake of sap-crowned trunks and flattened grass. In moments, the animal had disappeared deep into the dark recesses of its artificial habitat.

Fearful gibberings floated from the upper canopy.

Holly would feel bad later for putting the beast under a spell, but now there was not a heartbeat to waste on guilt. Artemis was grievously injured, perhaps mortally so.

The gorilla had dropped Artemis like a carcass that had been picked clean. He lay there, still as the dead.

No. Don't think that.

Holly raced to her friend's side, skidding the final metre on her knees.

Too far gone. He's too far gone.

Artemis's face was pale as bone. His long black hair was matted with blood and the whites of his eyes were twin crescents through hooded lids.

'Mother,' he said, the word riding on a breath.

Holly reached out her hands, magic already dancing on her fingertips, shooting off in arcs like tiny sun flares.

She froze before the magic could make the jump to Artemis's body.

If I heal Artemis, will I also damn him? Is my magic tainted with Spelltropy?

Artemis thrashed weakly and Holly could actually hear bones grating in his sleeve. There was blood on his lips now too.

He will die if I don't help. At least if I heal him there is a chance.

Holly's hands were shaking and her eyes were blurred with tears.

⊖ℬℱ•✦◻•✦◊♌ℬℛℨ•◉◊•ℛℭ◻⟩✦✦¿•◊◊

Pull yourself together. You are a professional.

She didn't feel very professional. She felt like a girl out of her depth.

Your body is playing tricks on your mind. Ignore it.

Holly cupped Artemis's face gently in both hands.

'Heal,' she whispered, almost sobbed.

The magical sparks leaped like dogs unleashed, sinking into Artemis's pores, knitting bones, healing skin, staunching internal bleeding.

The sudden transition from death's door to hale and hearty was rough on Artemis. He shuddered and bucked, teeth chattering, hair frizzing in an electric halo.

'Come on, Artemis,' said Holly, bending over him like a mourner. 'Wake up.'

There was no reaction for several seconds. Artemis looked like a healthy corpse, but then that was how he usually looked. Then his mismatched eyes opened, lids flickering like hummingbird wings as his system rebooted. He coughed and shuddered, flexing fingers and toes.

'Holly,' he said, when his vision cleared. His smile was sincere and grateful. 'You saved me again.'

Holly was laughing and crying at the same time, tears spilling on to Artemis's chest.

'Of course I saved you,' she said. 'I couldn't do without you.' And because she was happy and flushed with magic Holly leaned down and kissed Artemis, magic sparking around the contact like tiny fireworks.

*

Ten-year-old Artemis Fowl was keeping one eye on the drama unfolding in the gorilla cage.

'*Gorilla beringei beringei*,' he commented to Butler. 'Given the name *Troglodytes gorilla* by Doctor Thomas S. Savage, an American missionary to western Africa, who first scientifically described the gorilla in 1847.'

'You don't say,' murmured the bodyguard, who was more interested in the brute's bite radius than its proper name.

They had used the commotion as cover to slip out from the artificial hide and across the small courtyard to the lemur's cage, which was beside the gorilla's cage.

The strange newcomers were far too busy to notice them swipe the cage's key-card lock and open the gate door.

'Look at those two. Wasting time. You wouldn't catch me doing that.'

Butler snorted, as he usually did immediately before delivering a deadpan line.

'Most people never catch you doing anything, Artemis.'

Artemis allowed himself a chuckle. This was an interesting day, and he was enjoying the challenges that it presented.

'And there we are,' said Artemis quietly. 'The last silky sifaka lemur in the world. The hundred-thousand-euro primate.'

The lemur was perched high in a Madagascar palm, clinging to the branches with its long, grasping toes and opposable thumb digits. Its coat was snow white with a brown patch on the chest.

Artemis pointed at the animal. 'That colouring results from chest scent marking with the sternal-gular gland.'

'Uh-huh,' said Butler, who cared slightly less about this than he did about the gorilla's scientific name. 'Let's just get the animal and get out of here before our friends next door regroup.'

'I think we have a moment or two,' said Artemis.

Butler studied the strangers in the adjacent cage. It was surprising that the male was not in pieces by now, but somehow the female had appeared from nowhere and chased the gorilla off. Impressive. That one had a few tricks up her sleeve. There was serious technology behind her. Perhaps some kind of camouflage software in the clothing, which could explain the sparks. The Americans, he knew, were developing an all-terrain camouflage suit. One of his military contacts had sent him a link to a leaked video on the Internet.

There was another creature in the cage, the hairy individual who had released the first two from the Bentley, picking what was supposed to be an unpickable lock in the process. The creature was neither man nor beast, a rough stumpy character who had been propelled through the earth by some force and was now suffering from a debilitating attack of gas. Somehow, this *thing* had managed to dig a thirty-metre tunnel in a matter of minutes. If it hadn't been for the fact that the cages were modular, with overlapping walls, then the creature would have been in the same cage as the lemur. As it was, while it emerged directly below the lemur, it was one cage over.

Butler knew that Artemis would be just itching to study these strange creatures, but now was not the time. They were in a position of total ignorance and people in that position often died without being enlightened.

The bodyguard drew his dart pistol, but Artemis recognized the sound of a gun sliding from a holster and waved his index finger.

'That's our last option. I don't want our little friend breaking his neck on the way down. First we try gentle persuasion.'

From his pocket Artemis tugged a small ziplock bag containing an amber gel flecked with black and green.

'My own concoction,' he explained. 'The sifakas are from the Indriidae family of primates, which, as you know, is a strictly vegetarian family.'

'Who wouldn't know that?' wondered Butler, who had not exactly put away his pistol.

Artemis unzipped the bag, releasing a sweet, thick aroma that wound its way up towards the lemur.

'Sap concentrate, with a potpourri of African vegetation. No lemur could resist this. But if this particular primate's brain is stronger than his stomach, fire away. One shot, if you please, and avoid the head. The needle alone would probably be enough to crack that tiny skull.'

Butler would have snorted, but the lemur was moving. It crawled along the branch, dipping its pointed nose to catch the odour. Touching the smell with a darting pink tongue.

'Hmm,' said the bodyguard. 'That concoction won't work on humans, I suppose.'

'Ask me again in six months,' said Artemis. 'I am doing some pheromone experiments.'

The lemur scampered forward now, hypnotized by the glorious aroma. When the branch ran out, it dropped to the ground and hopped forward on two legs, fingers outstretched towards the bag.

Artemis grinned. 'This game is over.'

'Maybe not,' said Butler. In the cage beside them, the long-haired boy was on his feet and the female was making a very strange noise.

The corona of magic around fourteen-year-old Artemis and Holly faded, and along with it went the dreamlike trance insulating Artemis's mind.

He was instantly alert. Holly had kissed him. Artemis back-pedalled, jumping to his feet, spreading his arms wide to counteract the sudden dizziness.

'Eh, thanks,' he said awkwardly. 'That was unexpected.'

Holly smiled, feeling a little embarrassed. 'Artemis, you're OK. Any more healings and you'll be nothing but scar tissue held together by magic thread.'

Artemis thought that it would be nice to stay here and talk like this, but one cage over his future was escaping with his past.

He understood immediately what had happened. Mulch's nose had led them to the right place, but the cages were built like interlocking blocks and so the lemur had been above them, but also in the next cage. He should have remembered that, if he had been here before. But Artemis had no memory of visiting the central compound. As far as he was aware, the park director had brought the lemur into a special viewing room. This was confusing.

'Very well,' he said. 'I see where we are . . .'

He was thinking aloud, steadying his mind, trying to forget the kiss for now. Think about it later.

Artemis rubbed the red sparks from his eyes, then turned as quickly as the post-healing vertigo would allow. There he was, his younger self, enticing the silky sifaka lemur with a bag of amber paste.

Sap, I bet. Perhaps with a few twigs and leaves. Wasn't I a clever boy?

An immediate solution was needed. A fluid quick-fire plan. Artemis rubbed his eye sockets as if that could sharpen his mind.

'Mulch, can you tunnel?'

The dwarf opened his mouth to answer, but threw up instead.

'I dunno,' he said finally. 'My head's a bit flippy-floppy. Stomach too. That bash really shook me.' His belly made a sound like an outboard motor. ''Scuse me. I think I gotta . . .'

He did indeed *gotta*. Mulch crawled into a fern patch and let fly with the remainder of his stomach contents. Several leaves wilted on the spot.

⊛〇⚶⊛•⊛〇ᗕ•ᘓ〇⟩⊛⊛⸾•ᔔᐱᘓ•⊱⚶⊛

No use, thought Artemis. *I need a miracle or that lemur is gone and dead.*

He grabbed Holly's shoulders. 'Do you have any magic left?'

'A little, Artemis. A few sparks maybe.'

'Can you talk to the animals?'

Holly twisted her chin to the left until her neck bone clicked, checking the tank.

'I could do that, anything except trolls. They don't fall for that trick.'

Artemis nodded, muttering to himself. Thinking.

'OK. OK. I want you to scare that lemur away from me. The younger me. And I need confusion. Can you do that?'

'I can try.'

Holly closed her eyes, breathed deeply through her nose, filling her lungs, then threw her head back and howled. It was a fantastic noise. Lions, apes, wolves and eagles. They were all in there. The howl was punctuated by the staccato chatter of monkeys and the hiss of a thousand snakes.

Artemis the elder stepped back, instinctively terrified. Some primal part of his brain interpreted this message as fear and pain. His skin crawled and he had to fight his every instinct not to run and hide.

Artemis the younger reached down to the lemur, dangling the ziplock bag in front of its twitching nose. The lemur laid the pads of its fingers on Artemis's wrist.

I have him, thought the Irish boy. *The money for the expedition is mine.*

Then a wall of unholy sound blasted him like a force-ten wind. Young Artemis staggered back, dropping the bag of paste, suddenly irrationally terrified.

Something wants to kill me. But what? Every animal in the world, it sounds like.

The park's residents were thoroughly spooked too. They screeched and chattered, rattling their cages, hurling themselves against the bars. Monkeys tried repeatedly to leap across the moats surrounding their islands. An eight-hundred-kilo Sumatran rhino charged the heavy doors to its compound, rattling the hinges with each attack. A red wolf snarled and snapped, an Iberian lynx hissed, slashing the air, and a snow leopard chased its tail, flicking its head and mewling anxiously.

Butler could not help but shift his focus.

'It's the female creature,' he stated. 'Making some kind of sound. It's riling these animals up. I'm a bit disturbed myself.'

Artemis did not take his gaze from the lemur. 'You know what to do,' he said.

Butler knew. If there is an obstacle preventing the completion of a mission, remove the obstacle. He strode quickly to the bars, poked the pistol's muzzle through the mesh and put a dart into the female's shoulder.

She stumbled backwards, her fantastic orchestra of animal sounds squawking to a halt.

Butler felt a shudder of guilt, which almost caused him

to misstep on his way to Artemis's side. Twice now he had tranked this girl, or whatever she was, without having any idea what the chemicals were doing to her non-human system. His only consolation was that he had loaded small-dosage darts as soon as he had secured the night watchman. She shouldn't be out too long. A few minutes tops.

The lemur was spooked now. Tiny hands tickling the space before him. The sap cocktail was tempting, but there was danger here of the worst kind and the urge to live was overriding the desire for a tasty treat.

'No,' said Artemis, seeing fear cloud the creature's eyes. 'It's not real. There is no danger.'

The little simian was not convinced, as if it could read the boy's intention in the sharp angles of his face.

The silky sifaka squeaked once, as though pin-pricked, then scampered along Artemis's arm, over his shoulder and out through the cage door.

Butler lunged for the tail, but missed by a hair. He closed his fingers into a fist.

'Perhaps it's time to admit defeat on this one. We are dangerously unprepared and our adversaries have . . . abilities we know nothing about.'

His charge's reply was to hurry after the lemur.

'Artemis, wait,' sighed Butler. 'If we must proceed, then I will take the lead.'

'They want the lemur,' Artemis panted as he ran. 'And so it becomes more valuable than it was. When we catch the animal, then we are in a position of power.'

Catching the animal was easier said than done. The lemur was incredibly agile and found purchase on the smoothest of surfaces. It darted without a wobble along a metal railing, leaping three metres to the lower branches of a potted palm and from there jumping to the compound wall.

'Shoot!' hissed Artemis.

It occurred to Butler briefly that he did not care for Artemis's expression – almost cruel, his brow creased where a ten-year-old's brow should not have creases – but he would worry about that later; for now he had an animal to sedate.

Butler was quick but the silky sifaka was quicker. In a flash of fur it scaled the wall and dropped outside into the night, leaving a blurred white jet stream in its wake.

'Wow,' said Butler, almost in admiration. 'That was fast.'

Artemis was not impressed by his bodyguard's choice of words. '*Wow*? I think this merits more than a *wow*. Our quarry has escaped and with it the funds for my Arctic expedition.'

At this point Butler was fast losing interest in the lemur. There were other less ignoble ways to raise funds. Butler shuddered to think of the ribbing he would have to endure if an account of this night somehow made it to Farmer's Bar in LA, which was owned by one ex-blue-diamond body-guard and frequented by many more.

But, in spite of his distaste for the mission, Butler's sense of loyalty forced him to share a fact that the park director had mentioned earlier when Artemis was busy studying the alarm system.

'There is something that I know, which you may not know,' he said archly.

Artemis was not in the mood for games. 'Oh, really. And what would that be?'

'Lemurs are tree creatures,' replied Butler. 'That little guy is spooked and he's going to climb the biggest tree he can find, even if it isn't actually a tree. If you see what I mean.'

Artemis saw immediately, which wasn't difficult as the huge structures cast a lattice of moon shadows over the entire compound.

'Of course, old friend,' he said, his frown crease disappearing. 'The pylons.'

Things were going disastrously wrong for Artemis the elder. Mulch was injured, Holly was unconscious *again* – feet sticking out of the dwarf's hole – and he himself was fast running out of ideas. The deafening clamour of a hundred endangered species going berserk was not helping his concentration.

The animals are going ape, he thought. Then: *What a time to develop a sense of humour.*

All he could do was prioritize.

I need to get Holly out of here, he realized. *That is the most important thing.*

Mulch moaned, rolling on to his back, and Artemis saw that there was a bleeding gash on his forehead.

He stumbled to the dwarf's side. 'I imagine you're in great pain,' he said. 'It's to be expected with such a laceration.' Bedside manner was not one of Artemis's strong suits. 'You will have a rather large scar, but then looks are not really important to you.'

Mulch squinted at Artemis through a narrowed eye. 'Are you trying to be funny? Oh, my God, you're not. That was actually the nicest thing you could think of to say.'

He dabbed at his bloody forehead with a finger. 'Ow. That hurts.'

'Of course.'

'I will have to seal it. You know all about *this* dwarf talent, I suppose.'

'Naturally,' said Artemis, keeping a straight face. 'I've seen it a dozen times.'

'I doubt it,' grunted Mulch, plucking a wiggling beard hair from his chin. 'But I don't have much choice, now do I? With the LEP elf in dreamland, I won't be getting any magical help from that quarter.'

Artemis heard a rustling in the undergrowth at the rear of the cage. 'You'd better hurry it up. I think the gorilla is overcoming its fear of fairies.'

Wincing, Mulch introduced the beard hair to his gash. It took off like a tadpole, poking through the skin, stitching the flaps together. Though he groaned and shuddered, Mulch managed to stay conscious.

When the hair had finished its work, and the wound was tied up tighter than a fly in a ball of spider's web, Mulch spat on his hand and rubbed the gooey mess on to the wound.

'All sealed,' he proclaimed, then upon seeing the glint in Artemis's eye: 'Don't get any ideas, Mud Boy. This only works on dwarfs, and, what's more, my beard hair only works on me. You poke one of my lovelies into your skin and all you'll get is an infection.'

The rustling in the undergrowth grew louder, and Artemis Fowl decided to forego further information, which was almost unheard of for him.

'Time we were off. Can you seal the tunnel behind us?'

'I can bring the whole lot down easy as pie. You'd better take the lead though, there are better ways to go than being buried alive in . . . shall we say, recyclings. Need I say more?'

There was no need to say another syllable. Artemis jumped into the hole, grabbed Holly's shoulders and began dragging her down the tunnel, past the blobs of luminous spittle towards the proverbial light at the end. It was like travelling through space towards the Milky Way.

The sounds of his own body were amplified. Gulping breath, drumming heartbeat, the bend and creak of muscle and sinew.

Holly rolled along easily, her suit hissing on the rough surface like a nest of vipers. Or maybe there were snakes down here, the way Artemis's luck was going.

I am trying to do something good for a change, he reminded himself. *And this is how the Fates reward me. A life of crime was infinitely easier.*

Surface noise was amplified by the tunnel's acoustics. The gorilla sounded furious now. Artemis could hear the slap of fists on chest and an enraged huffing.

He realizes he has been tricked.

His theorizing was cut short by Mulch's appearance in the tunnel, the spittle bandage on his forehead casting a zombie glow on his face.

'Gorilla coming,' he said as he gulped down lungfuls of air. 'Gotta go.'

Artemis heard twin thumps as the gorilla landed on the tunnel floor. The huge simian roared a challenge down the hole and the noise grew in ferocity with every metre it travelled.

Holly moaned and Artemis pulled harder on her shoulders.

Mulch sucked down air as fast as he could, bundling Artemis and Holly deeper into the tunnel. Twenty metres to go. They would never make it. The gorilla was advancing, pulverizing each spittle lantern as he passed it, roaring with bloodlust. Artemis swore he saw a flash of teeth.

The tunnel seemed to shudder with each blow. Large sections collapsed. Mud and rock clattered down on Artemis's head and shoulders. Dirt pooled in Holly's eye sockets.

Mulch's cheeks ballooned and he opened his lips the merest fraction to speak. 'OK,' he said in a helium voice. 'The tank is full.'

The dwarf gathered Artemis and Holly in his burly Popeye arms and vented every bubble of air in his body. The resulting jet stream propelled the group down the length of the tunnel. The trip was short, jarring and confusing. The breath was driven from Artemis's lungs and his fingers were stretched to cracking, but he would not let go of Holly.

He could not let her die.

The unfortunate gorilla was blown head-over-rump by the windstorm, yanked back up the tunnel as though tethered to an elastic cable. It whooped as it went, digging its fingers into the tunnel wall.

Artemis, Holly and Mulch popped from the tunnel mouth, bouncing and skittering along the ditch in a tangle of limbs and torsos. The stars above them were speed-streaked and the moon was a smear of yellow light.

An old famine wall halted their progress, crumbling under the impact of three bodies.

'For more than a hundred and fifty years this wall stood,' coughed Artemis. 'Then *we* come along.'

He lay on his back feeling thoroughly defeated. His mother would die and Holly would soon hate him when she worked out the truth.

All is lost. I have no idea what to do.

Then one of the notorious Rathdown pylons sharpened in his vision – more specifically, the figures clambering along its service ladder.

The lemur has escaped, thought Artemis, *and is climbing as high as it can.*

A reprieve. There was still a chance.

What I need to save this situation is a full LEP surveillance and assault kit. Perhaps I will have Number One send one back for me.

Artemis disentangled himself from the others and decided

that underneath the pillar's cornerstone would be a secure spot. He pulled off the remaining stones stacked on top, wiggled his fingers under the final boulder and heaved. It came away easily, revealing nothing but worms and damp earth. No package from the future; for whatever reason, that particular trick would only work once.

So. No help. I must make do with what is available.

Artemis returned to where Holly and Mulch lay. Both were moaning.

'I think I split a gut getting rid of that wind,' said Mulch. 'There was a bit too much fear in the mix.'

Artemis's nose wrinkled. 'Will you be OK?'

'Give me a minute and I'll be plenty strong enough to carry that huge amount of gold you promised me.'

Holly was groggy. Her eyes fluttered as she tried to pull herself out of it and her arms flopped like fish out of water. Artemis did a quick pulse and temperature check. Slight fever but steady heartbeat. Holly was recovering, but it would be several minutes before she could control her mind or body.

I must do this on my own, Artemis realized. *No Holly, no Butler.*

Just Artemis versus Artemis.

And perhaps an Omnitool, he thought, reaching into Holly's pocket.

The Rathdown electricity pylons had been featured in Irish news headlines several times since their erection. Environmentalists protested vehemently that the appearance of the gigantic pylons blighted an otherwise beautiful valley, not to mention the possible detrimental effect the uninsulated power lines could have on the health of anyone or anything living below their arcs. The national electricity board had countered these arguments by pleading that the lines were too high to harm anything and that constructing smaller pylons around the valley would blight ten times more land.

And so a half a dozen of these metal giants bridged Rathdown Valley, reaching a height of one hundred metres at their zenith. The pylon bases were often ringed by protesters, so much so that the power company had taken to servicing the lines by helicopter.

On this night, as Artemis raced across the moonlit meadow, kicking up diamond dewdrops, there were no protesters ringing the pylons, but they had planted their signs like moon flags. Artemis slalomed through this obstacle course while simultaneously craning his neck to track the figures above.

The lemur was on the wire now, silhouetted by the moon, scampering easily along the metal cable, while Artemis the younger and Butler were stranded on the small platform at the pylon's base, unable to venture any further.

Finally, thought Artemis, *a stroke or two of luck.*

Stroke one was that the lemur was suddenly up for grabs. Stroke the second was that while his young nemesis had chosen to follow the silky sifaka directly up the pylon the animal was scaling, he himself could go up the adjacent pole, which just happened to be the service pylon.

Artemis reached the pylon's base, which was secured by a cage. The heavy padlock submitted instantly to a quick jab from the Omnitool, as did the steel equipment locker. Inside were various tools, walkie-talkies and a Faraday suit. Artemis tugged on the heavy overalls, wiggling his fingers into the attached gloves, tucking his long hair inside the hood. The flame-retardant and steel-thread suit had to enclose him completely to act as a protective Faraday cage. Otherwise he could not venture out on the wires without being burned to a criminal-mastermind cinder.

More luck. An elevator platform ran up the side of the pylon. It was locked and key-coded. But locks quailed when faced with an Omnitool, and a key code was of little value when it was a simple matter to unscrew the control panel and activate the pulley manually.

Artemis held tight to the safety rail as the tiny elevator shuddered and whined its way into the night sky. The valley spread out below him as he rose and a westerly wind crept over the hills, tugging a strand of hair from his hood. Artemis gazed north, and for a fanciful moment imagined he could see the lights of Fowl Manor.

Mother is there, he thought. *Unwell now and unwell in the future. Perhaps I can just talk to my younger self. Explain the situation.*

This thought was even more fanciful than the last. Artemis had no illusions about what he had been like at the age of ten. He had trusted no one completely but himself. Not his parents, not even Butler. At the first mention of time travel, his younger self would have his bodyguard shoot a dart first and ask questions later. A *lot* of questions and at great length. There was no time for explanations and debate. This battle would have to be won by wits and guile.

The elevator grated into its brackets at the top of the pylon. A skull and crossbones sign was riveted to the tall safety gate. Even if Artemis had not been a genius the sign would have been difficult to misinterpret, and just in case a total idiot did manage to scale the pylon there was a second sign depicting a cartoon man being zapped by electricity from a cartoon pylon. The man's skeleton was clearly visible, X-ray style.

Apparently electricity is dangerous, Artemis might have commented had Butler been by his side.

There was yet another lock on the safety gate, which delayed Artemis about as long as the first two. Outside the safety gate was a small platform covered with wire mesh, with twin power lines humming directly beneath.

There are half a million volts running through those lines, thought Artemis. *I do hope there are no rips in this suit.*

Artemis squatted low, peering along the line. The lemur had paused halfway between the two pylons and was chattering to itself as if weighing up its options. Luckily for the small creature, it was only touching one line, so no current flowed through its body. If it put so much as a toe on the second line the shock would spin it thirty metres into the air and it would be stone dead before it stopped revolving.

On the far pylon, Artemis the younger scowled at the animal, while simultaneously trying to tempt it back with his bag of paste.

There is nothing to do but go out on the wires and bring the lemur back yourself.

The hot suit was equipped for moving across the wires. There was a safety cord wrapped round his waist and a lightning rod in a long pocket on his thigh. Below the platform was a small sledge on insulated runners that the engineers used to hand-crank themselves between pylons.

Brains count for little now, he realized. *What I need is balance.*

Artemis groaned. Balance was not his forte.

Taking a deep breath, he crouched low, drawing the lightning rod from his pocket. Almost as soon as it cleared the material, jets of white-hot sparks jumped from the power lines connecting with the tip of the rod. The stream buzzed and hissed like a neon snake.

You are equalizing voltage, that's all. The electricity cannot hurt you.

Perhaps not, but Artemis could already feel the hair standing on his neck. Was that anxiety, or were a couple of volts sneaking in somewhere?

Don't be absurd. If there is a hole, all the volts will worm inside, not just a couple.

Artemis was vaguely familiar with the technique for wire-walking, as the national broadcasting service had done a news special on the high-wire daredevils who risked their lives to keep the lights of Dublin burning. It wasn't so much wire-walking as wire-crawling. The cables were extremely taut and the maintenance engineers clipped on their safety lines, lay on the sledge, then turned the winch until they reached the maintenance site.

Simple. In theory. For a professional on a calm morning.

Not so easy for an amateur in the dead of night with only the stars and the ambient light of nearby Dublin to guide him.

Artemis sheathed his lightning rod and gingerly clipped his safety line to one of the cables.

He held his breath, as though that could possibly make a difference, and laid his gloved hands on the metal sledge.

Still alive. A good start.

Artemis inched forward, the metal warm under his clumsy gloved hands, until he was lying flat on the sledge with the double-handled winch in front of his face. It was a delicate manoeuvre and would have been impossible had the cables not been tethered together at regular intervals. He began to twist and almost immediately the strain on his arms was tremendous as he moved his own body weight.

The gym. Butler, you were right. I'll do weights, anything, just get me off these cables with that lemur under my arm.

Artemis slid forward, feeling the runners scrape the rough metal of the cables, their intense hum setting his teeth on edge and sending constant shivers coursing along his arched spine. The wind was low but still threatened to topple him from his lofty perch and the ground seemed like another planet. Distant and uninviting.

꧁•¹⁸⟨Ụ•⟨⟩⟨⟩⟩•⟨⟩⟨•¹⟨⟩•⟨⟩⟨⟩⟨⟩⟨⟩⟨⟩⟨⟩⊕

Ten metres later his arms ached and he was noticed by the opposition.

A voice floated across from the other pylon. 'I advise you to stay where you are, young man. If that suit has the tiniest rip, then one slip and those cables will liquefy your skin and melt your bones.'

Artemis scowled. *Young man?* Had he really been so obnoxious? So patronizing?

'It would take less than a second for you to die,' continued ten-year-old Artemis. 'But that's quite long enough to be in mortal agony, don't you think? And all for nothing, as the lemur will obviously return for this treat.'

Yes, he had been smug as well as obnoxious and patronizing.

Artemis chose not to reply, concentrating his energy on staying alive and enticing the silky sifaka towards him. From his considerable reservoir of knowledge on just about everything, Artemis plucked the fact that smaller simians were comforted by a purring noise. Thank you, Jane Goodall.

So he began to purr, much to the amusement of his younger self.

'Listen, Butler. There's a cat on the wire. A big tom, I would say. Perhaps you should throw him a fish.'

But the mocking tone was undercut with tension. Young Artemis knew exactly what was going on.

More purring and it seemed to be working: the ghostly sifaka took a few cautious steps towards the elder Artemis, his beady black eyes glittering with starlight and perhaps curiosity.

Holly would be proud. I am talking to an animal.

Even as he purred, Artemis winced at how ludicrous the situation had become. It was a typical Fowlesque melodrama. Two parties hunting for a lemur on the highest power lines in Ireland.

Artemis looked along the dip of the lines across to the other pylon, where Butler stood, jacket tail flapping around his thighs. The bodyguard leaned into the wind, and the intensity of his stare seemed to pierce the darkness, honing in on Artemis the elder like a laser.

I miss my bodyguard, thought Artemis.

The lemur scampered closer, encouraged by the purring and perhaps fooled by the steel-grey hot suit.

That's right. I am another lemur.

Artemis's arms were shaking from the strain of turning the handles at such an awkward angle. Every muscle in his body was stretched to its limit, including several he had never used before. His head was dizzy from keeping his balance.

All this and animal impersonations too.

One metre now. That was the distance between Artemis and the lemur. There were no more taunts from the other side. Artemis glanced across and found his nemesis had his eyes closed and was breathing deeply. Trying to come up with a plan.

The lemur jumped on to the sledge and touched Artemis's gloved hand tentatively. Contact. Artemis stayed stock still, apart from his lips, which burbled out a comforting purr.

That's it, little fellow. Climb on to my arm.

Artemis looked into the lemur's eyes and for perhaps the first time realized that it had emotions. There was fear in those eyes, but also a mischievous confidence.

How could I have sold you to those madmen? he wondered.

The lemur suddenly committed itself, scampering on to Artemis's shoulder. It seemed content to sit there while Artemis ferried it back to the service pylon.

As Artemis retreated, he kept his eye fixed on his younger self. He would never simply accept defeat like this. Neither of them would. Young Artemis's eyes suddenly snapped open and met his nemesis's stare.

'Shoot the animal,' he said coldly.

Butler was surprised. 'Shoot the monkey?'

'It's a . . . never mind. Just shoot it. The man is protected by his suit, but the lemur is an easy target.'

'But the fall . . .'

'If it dies, it dies. I will not be thwarted here, Butler. If I cannot have that lemur, then no one will have it.'

Butler frowned. Killing animals was not in his job description, but he knew from experience that there was no point in arguing with the young master. At any rate, it was a bit late to protest now, perched atop a pylon. He should have spoken up more forcefully earlier.

'Whenever you're ready, Butler. The target is not getting any closer.'

Out on the cables, Artemis the elder could scarcely believe what he was hearing. Butler had drawn his pistol and was climbing over the rails to get a better shot.

Artemis had not intended to speak, as interaction with his younger self could have serious repercussions for the future, but the words were out before he could stop them.

'Stay back. You don't know what you're dealing with.'

Oh, the irony.

'Ah, he speaks,' called young Artemis across the abyss. 'How fortunate that we can understand each other. Well, understand this, stranger. I will have that silky sifaka or it will die. Make no mistake.'

'You must not do this. There's too much at stake.'

'I must do it. I have no choice. Now send the animal over, or Butler will shoot.'

Through all of this, the lemur sat perched on fourteen-year-old Artemis's head, scratching the stitching of his hood.

So the two boys who were one boy, locked eyes for a long tense moment.

I would have done it, thought Artemis the elder, shocked by the cruel determination in his own blue eyes.

And so he gingerly reached up one hand and plucked the silky sifaka from his head.

'You have to go back,' he said softly. 'Go back for the nice treat. And, if I were you, I'd stick close to the big human. The little one isn't very nice.'

The lemur reached out and tweaked Artemis's nose, much as Beckett might have done, then turned and trotted along the cable towards Butler, nose sniffing the air, nostrils flaring as they located the sweet scent of Artemis's goodie bag.

In a matter of seconds it sat curled in the crook of young Artemis's elbow, contentedly dipping its long fingers into the sap. The young boy's face glowed with victory.

'Now,' he said, 'I think it best that you stay exactly where you are until we leave. I think fifteen minutes should be fine. After that, I advise you to be on your way and count yourself fortunate that I did not have Butler sedate you. Remember the pain that you are feeling now. The ache of utter defeat and hopelessness. And, if you ever consider crossing swords with me again, review your memory of this pain, and perhaps you will think twice.'

Artemis the elder was forced to watch as Butler stuffed the lemur into a duffel bag, and boy and bodyguard commenced their climb down the service ladder. Several minutes later, the Bentley's headlights scythed the darkness as the car pulled away from Rathdown Park and on to the motorway. Straight to the airport, no doubt.

Artemis reached up and gripped the winch handles. He was not beaten yet, far from it. He intended to cross swords with his ten-year-old self again just as soon as he possibly could. If anything, the boy's mocking speech had fuelled his determination.

Remember the pain? thought Artemis. *I hate myself. I really do.*

𖢧𖣁𖠃𖡣•𖢣𖡣𖡥𖡥•𖣵𖢁𖢫•𖣱𖢻𖢣•𖡧𖢫𖢁𖣐•𖡣𖢣•𖣵𖢧𖡣

CHAPTER 8: A BLOB OF PHLEGM

 BY the time Artemis had made his way down from the pylon, Holly had disappeared. He'd left her by the tunnel mouth, but there was nothing in the spot now except mud and footprints.

Footprints, he thought. *Now, I suppose I need to track Holly. I really must read* The Last of the Mohicans.

'Don't bother following those,' said a voice from the ditch. 'False trail. I laid it in case the big human took our LEP friend along for a snack.'

'That was good thinking,' said Artemis, squinting through the foliage. A shaggy shadow detached itself from a hillock and became Mulch Diggums. 'But why did you bother? I thought the LEP were your enemy.'

Mulch pointed a stubby, mud-crusted finger. 'You are my enemy, human. You are the planet's enemy.'

'And yet you are willing to help me for gold.'

'A *stupendous* amount of gold,' said Mulch. 'And possibly

some fried chicken. With barbecue sauce. And a large Pepsi.
And maybe more chicken.'

'Hungry?'

'Always. A dwarf can only eat so much dirt.'

Artemis didn't know whether to giggle or groan. Mulch
would always have trouble grasping the gravity of situations, or perhaps he liked to give that impression.

'Where's Holly?'

Mulch nodded towards a grave-shaped mound of earth.

'I buried the captain. She was moaning quite loudly. *Arty*
this and *Arty* that, with a few *mothers* thrown in.'

Buried? Holly was claustrophobic.

Artemis dropped to his knees, scooping the earth from
the mound with his bare hands. Mulch let him at it for a
minute, then sighed dramatically.

'Let me do it, Mud Boy. You'll be there all night.'

He strolled over and casually thrust his hand into the
mound, chewing his lip as he searched for a specific spot.

'Here we go,' grunted the dwarf, yanking out a short
branch. The mound vibrated then collapsed into small heaps
of pebbles and clay. Holly was unhurt underneath.

'It's a complex structure called a Na-Na,' said Mulch,
brandishing the twig.

'As in?'

'As in na-na-ne-na-na, you can't see me,' said the dwarf,
then slapped himself on the knee, exploding in a fit of giggles.

Artemis scowled, shaking Holly's shoulders gently.

'Holly, can you hear me?'

Holly Short opened bleary eyes, rolled them around for a while, then focused.

'Artemis, I . . . Oh, gods.'

'It's OK. I don't have the lemur . . . well, actually, I do. The other me, but don't worry, I know where I'm going.'

Holly dragged at her cheeks with delicate fingers. 'I mean *Oh, gods, I think I kissed you.*'

Artemis's head pounded and Holly's mismatched eyes seemed to hypnotize him. She still had a blue eye, even though her body had rejuvenated itself in the tunnel. Another paradox. But, though Artemis felt hypnotized, even slightly dazed, he knew he was not mesmerized. There was no fairy magic here.

Artemis looked into those elfin eyes and he knew that this younger, somehow more vulnerable Holly felt the same way at this particular tangle of time and space as he did.

After all we have been through. Or maybe because of it.

A memory smashed the delicate moment like a rock thrown through a spider's web.

I lied to her.

Artemis rocked backwards with the strength of the thought.

Holly believes that she infected Mother. I blackmailed her.

He knew at that instant there was no recovering from such a brutal fact. If he confessed, she would hate him. If he did not, he would hate himself.

There must be something I can do.

Nothing came to mind.

I need to think.

Artemis took Holly's hand and elbow, helping her to stand and step from the shallow grave-like hole.

'Reborn,' she quipped, then punched Mulch on the shoulder.

'Oww. Whyfore, miss, dost thou torment me?'

'Don't quote Gerd Flambough at me, Mulch Diggums. There was no need to bury me. A simple broadleaf across my mouth would have done.'

Mulch rubbed his shoulder. 'A broadleaf desn't have the same artistry. Anyway, do I look like a fern type of guy? I am a dwarf and we deal in mud.'

Artemis was glad of the banter. It gave him a minute to compose himself.

Forget your adolescent confusion about Holly. Remember Mother wasting away in her bed. There are less than three days left.

'Very well, troops,' he said with forced joviality. 'Let's move it out, as an old friend of mine would say. We have a lemur to catch.'

'What about my gold?' asked Mulch.

'I shall put this as simply as possible. No lemur, no gold.'

Mulch tapped his lips with eight fingers and his beard hairs vibrated like the tendrils of a sea anemone. Thinking.

'How much is *stupendous* exactly, in bucket terms?'

'How many buckets do you have?'

Mulch took this as a serious question. 'I have a lot of buckets. Most of them are full of stuff, though. I could empty them, I suppose.'

Artemis almost gnashed his teeth. 'It was a rhetorical question. A lot of buckets. As many as you like.'

'If you want me to go any further down this monkey road, I need some kind of down payment. A good-faith deposit.'

Artemis slapped his empty pockets. He had nothing.

Holly straightened her silver wig. 'I have something for you, Mulch Diggums. Something better than a stupendous amount of gold. Six numbers, which I will reveal when we get there.'

'Get where?' asked Mulch, who suspected that Holly was being melodramatic.

'The LEP equipment lock-up at Tara.'

Mulch's eyes glowed with dreams of sky skis and dive bubbles, laser cubes and fat vacuums. The mother lode. He'd been trying to crack an LEP lock-up for years.

'I can have anything I want?'

'Whatever you can get on to a hover trolley. One trolley.'

Mulch spat a marbled blob of phlegm into his palm.

'Shake on it,' he said.

Artemis and Holly looked at each other.

'It's your lock-up,' said Artemis, stuffing his hands into his pockets.

'It's your mission,' countered Holly.

'I don't know the combination.'

And then the trump. 'We're here for your mother.'

Artemis smiled ruefully. 'You, Captain Short, are getting as bad as me,' he said, and sealed the deal with a sopping handshake.

CHAPTER 9: THE PRINCE FROG

YOUNG Artemis made a video call from his Powerbook to the the ancient town of Fez in Morocco. Even as he waited for the connection, Artemis silently fumed that it was necessary to make this intercontinental trip at all. Even Casablanca would have been more convenient. Morocco was hot enough without having to drive across country to Fez.

On screen, a window popped open, barely containing the huge head of Doctor Damon Kronski, one of the most hated men in the world, but revered too in certain circles. Damon Kronski was the current president of the Extinctionists' organization. Or, as Kronski said in his most notorious interview: 'The Extinctionists are not just an organization. We are a religion.' Not a statement that endeared him to the peace-loving churches of the world.

The interview had run for months on Internet news sites

and was sampled every time the Extinctionists made the headlines. Artemis had viewed it himself that very morning and was repulsed by the man he was about to do business with.

I am swimming with sharks, he realized. *And I am prepared to become one of them.*

Damon Kronski was an enormous man whose head began its slope into his shoulders just below the ears. His skin was translucent, redhead white with a scattershot of penny freckles, and he wore violet sunglasses clamped in place by the folds of his brow and cheeks. His smile was broad, shining and insincere.

'Little Ah-temis Fowl,' he said with a pronounced New Orleans drawl. 'You find your daddy yet?'

Artemis gripped the armrest of his chair, squeezing dents in the leather, but his smile was as shiny and fake as Kronski's. 'No. Not yet.'

'Well now, that's a pity. Anything I can do to help, you be sure to let your Uncle Damon know.'

Artemis wondered if Kronski's amiable-uncle act would fool a drunken halfwit. Perhaps it was not supposed to.

'Thank you for the offer. In a few hours we may be able to help each other.'

Kronski clapped his hands delightedly. 'You have located my silky sifaka.'

'I have. Quite a specimen. Male. Three years old. More than a metre in length from head to tail. Easily worth a hundred thousand.'

Kronski feigned surprise. 'A hundred? Did we really say a hundred thousand euro?'

There was steel in Artemis's eyes. 'You know we did, Doctor. Plus expenses. Jet fuel is not cheap, as you are aware. I would like to hear you confirm it, or I will turn this plane round.'

Kronski leaned close to the camera, his face ballooning on the screen.

'I'm generally a good judge of character, Ah-temis,' he said. 'I know what people are capable of. But you . . . I have no idea what you might do. I think it's because you haven't reached your limit yet.' Kronski leaned back in his chair, the leather creaking under his weight. 'So, very well. One hundred thousand euro, as we agreed. But a word of warning . . .'

'Ye-es?' said Artemis, stretching the word to two syllables, in the New Orleans fashion, to demonstrate his lack of awe.

'You lose my lemur, my little silky, then you'd better be ready to cover *my* expenses. The trial is all set up, and my people don't like to be disappointed.'

The word *expenses* sounded a lot more sinister when Kronski used it.

'Don't worry,' snapped Artemis. 'You will get your lemur. Just have my money ready.'

Kronski spread his arms wide. 'I've got rivers of gold here, Ah-temis. I've got mountains of diamonds. The only thing I don't have is a silky sifaka lemur. So hurry down here, boy, and make my life complete.'

꙰

And he hung up, a second before Artemis could click the terminate-call button.

Psychologically, that puts Kronski in the power seat, thought Artemis. *I must learn to be quicker on the mouse.*

He closed the Powerbook's lid and reclined his chair. Outside, in the sky, sunlight was burning through the lower layers of mist and jet trails drew tic-tac-toe patterns in the sky.

Still in busy airspace. Not for long. Once we hit Africa, the jet streams will thin out considerably. I need a few hours' sleep. Tomorrow will be a long and distasteful day.

He frowned. *Distasteful, yes, but necessary.*

Artemis hit the recline button and closed his eyes. Most boys his age were swapping football cards or wearing out their thumbs on games consoles. *He* was in a jet six thousand metres over Europe, planning the destruction of a species with a deranged Extinctionist.

Perhaps I am too young for all this.

Age was immaterial. Without his efforts, Artemis Fowl Senior would be lost forever in Russia, and that was simply not going to happen.

Butler's voice came over the jet's intercom. 'All quiet up front, Artemis. Once we get out over the Mediterranean, I'm going to put her on autopilot for an hour and try to wind down . . .'

Artemis stared at the speaker. He could sense that Butler had more to say. Nothing but static and the beep of instruments for a moment, then . . . 'Today, Artemis, when you told me to shoot the lemur, you were bluffing? You were bluffing, weren't you?'

'It was no bluff,' said Artemis, his voice unwavering. 'I will do whatever it takes.'

Tara shuttle port, Ireland

Access to the Tara shuttle port was hindered by several steel doors, various scans and codes, tamper-proof bio-locks and a 360-degree surveillance network at the entrance, which is not as easy to set up as it is to say. Of course, all of this could be bypassed if one knew a secret way in.

'How did you know I have a secret way in?' pouted Mulch.

In response, Artemis and Holly simply looked at him, as though he were an idiot, waiting for the penny to drop.

'Stupid time travel,' muttered the dwarf. 'Told you all about it myself, I suppose.'

'You will,' confirmed Holly. 'And I don't see what you're so upset about. It's not as if I can report you to anyone.'

'True,' admitted Mulch. 'And there is all that lovely loot.'

The three sat in a stolen Mini Cooper outside the boundary fence of the McGraney farm, underneath which was concealed the Tara shuttle port. Ten thousand cubic metres of terminal hidden by a dairy farm. The first light of dawn was diluting the darkness, and the lumpy silhouettes of grazing cows ambled across the meadow. In a year or two, Tara would become a bustling tourist hub for the fairies, but for the moment all tourism had been suspended since the Spelltropy outbreak.

Mulch squinted at the nearest beast through the back window. 'You know something, I'm a tad peckish. I couldn't eat a whole cow, but I'd put a fair dent in one.'

'Mulch Diggums hungry. Stop the presses,' commented Artemis drily. He opened the driver's door, stepping on to the grassy verge. A light mist clung to his face and the clean smell of country air ran through his system like a stimulant.

'We need to get going. I have no doubt that the lemur is already six thousand metres in the air.'

'That's a nimble lemur,' sniggered the dwarf. He climbed over the front seat, and tumbled out on to the verge.

'Nice clay,' he said, giving the ground a lick. 'Tastes like profit.'

Holly stepped from the passenger seat and sideswiped Mulch's behind with her loafer.

'There will be no profit for you if we can't get into the terminal unseen.'

The dwarf picked himself up. 'I thought we were supposed to be friends. Easy with the kicking and the punching. Are you always this aggressive?'

'Can you do it or not?'

'Of course I can. I said so, didn't I? I've been running around this terminal for years. Ever since my cousin –'

Artemis butted in on the conversation. 'Ever since your cousin – Nord, if I'm not mistaken – ever since Nord was arrested on pollution charges and you broke him out. We know. We know everything about you. Now, let's move on with the plan.'

Mulch turned his back to Artemis, casually unbuttoning his bum-flap. This action was among the worst insults in a dwarf's arsenal. Second only to what was known as the Tuba, which involves a cleaning of the pipes in someone's direction. Wars have been fought over the Tuba.

'Moving on, chief. Stay here for fifteen minutes, then make your way to the main entrance. I would take you with me, but this tunnel is too long to hold things in, if you catch my drift.' He paused for a wink. 'And if you stand too close, that's exactly what you'll be catching.'

Artemis smiled through gritted teeth. 'Very well. Most amusing. Fifteen minutes it is, Mister Diggums, the clock is ticking.'

'Ticking?' said Mulch. 'Fairy clocks haven't ticked for centuries.'

Then he unhinged his jaw and leaped, with astonishing grace, diving into the earth like a dolphin slicing through a wave, but without the sunny disposition or cute grin.

Though Artemis had seen this a dozen times, he could not help being impressed.

'What a species,' he commented. 'If they could take their minds off their stomachs for a few minutes, they could rule the world.'

Holly climbed on to the bonnet, resting her back against the windscreen, feeling the sun on her cheeks.

○|•⚒⊛⊘⚯⚒⊛⊕⊘☿•|⚯⚯⊘⊙|)|•☿⋃)

'Maybe they don't want to rule the world. Maybe that's just you, Arty.'

Arty.

Guilt gnawed at Artemis's stomach. He gazed at Holly's familiar fine features and realized that he couldn't keep lying to her any longer.

'It's a pity we had to steal this car,' continued Holly, eyes closed. 'But the note we left was clear enough. The owner should find it without a problem.'

Artemis didn't feel so bad about the car. He had bigger nails in his coffin.

'Yes, the car,' he said absently.

I need to tell her. I have to tell her.

Artemis put a toe on the Mini's front tyre and climbed on to the bonnet beside Holly. He sat there for a few minutes, concentrating on the experience. Storing it away.

Holly glanced at him sitting next to her.

'Sorry about earlier. You know, the thing.'

'The kiss?'

Holly closed her eyes. 'Yes. I don't know what's happening to me. We're not even the same species. And, when we go back, we will be ourselves again.' Holly covered her face with her free hand. 'Listen to me. Babbling. The LEP's first female captain. That time stream has turned me into what you would call a teenager again.'

It was true. Holly was different; the time stream had brought them closer together.

⟨⟩◉⊕⚹⚙•⏚◒◉⊛⊕◒ ⟨⟩⚸⚹•⚸⚑⟊•⊛◒⊕⟊•U

'What if I'm stuck like this? That wouldn't be so bad, would it?'

The question hung in the air between them. A question heavy with insecurity and hope.

If you answer this question, it will be the worst thing you have ever done.

'It wasn't you, Holly,' Artemis blurted, his forehead hot, his calm cracked.

Holly's smile froze, still there but puzzled. 'What wasn't me?'

'You didn't infect my mother. I did it. It was me. I had a few sparks left over from the tunnel and I made my parents forget I'd been missing for three years.'

Holly's smile was gone now.

'I didn't . . . but you told me . . .'

She stopped in mid-sentence, the truth washing across her face like a disease.

Artemis pressed on, determined to explain himself. 'I had to do it, Holly. Mother is dying . . . will be dying. I needed to be certain of your help . . . Please understand . . .'

He trailed off, realizing that there was no explaining away his actions. Artemis allowed Holly several minutes to fume, then spoke again.

'If there had been another way, Holly, believe me . . .'

No reaction. Holly's face was carved in stone.

'Please, Holly. Say something.'

Holly slid from the bonnet, her feet connecting solidly with the earth.

'Fifteen minutes are up,' she said. 'Time to move out.'

She strode across the McGraney boundary without a backward glance, legs cutting twin swathes in the green-black grass. Dawn sunlight shimmered on the tip of each blade and Holly's passage set a surging ripple of light flashing across the meadow.

Extraordinary, thought Artemis. *What have I lost?*

There was nothing to do but trudge after her.

Mulch Diggums was waiting for them inside the holographic bush at the shuttle port's concealed entrance. In spite of a thick coating of mud, his smug expression was easy to read.

'You won't be needing an Omintool, Captain,' he said. 'I got the door open all on my lonesome.'

Holly was more than surprised. The shuttle port's main door needed a twenty-digit code, plus palm-print scan, and she knew that Mulch was about as technologically minded as a stink worm. Not that Holly wasn't relieved, as she had anticipated a thirty-minute slog resetting the log once she'd opened the door herself.

'So . . . tell me.'

Mulch pointed down the corridor towards the subterranean escalator. A small figure was spreadeagled on the ramp, his head covered in a blob of shining goo.

'Commander Root and his heavy mob have cleared out. Only one security guard left.'

Holly nodded. She knew where Julius Root had gone. Back to Haven to wait for her report from Hamburg.

ᛒᚢᚦᛟ → ᚥᚪᚼ → ᚪᚦ → ᛁᛡ → ᚥᚪᚦ → ᛋᚨᛒᚠ ᚢ

'He was on his rounds up here when I tunnelled in, so I swallowed him briefly and gave him a lick of dwarf spit. Everyone reacts differently to the phlegm helmet. This little pixie tried to escape. Slapped the sensor, spouted the code, then staggered around a bit before the sedative got him.'

Artemis pressed past into the access tunnel.

'Perhaps our luck is finally turning,' he said, certain he could feel Holly staring daggers into the back of his head.

'A pity he didn't open the lock-up,' sighed Mulch. 'Then I could have double-crossed you two and made off with the shuttle.'

Artemis froze. 'Shuttle?'

He braved Holly's hostile gaze to ask. 'A shuttle, Holly. Do you think we could still beat my younger self to Morocco?'

Holly's eyes were flat and her tone was neutral. 'It's possible. It depends on how long it takes me to cover our tracks.'

The shuttle was what LEP pilots would call a snowgood, as in *snowgood for anything but the recycling smelter*. Butler, Artemis knew, would have been more straightforward in his assessment of the vehicle.

He could hear the big bodyguard's voice in his head. *I have driven some heaps in my time, Artemis. But this pig is . . .*

'. . . is barely out of the Stone Age,' murmured Artemis, then chuckled ruefully.

'Another joke, Mud Boy?' asked Holly. 'You're really on

fine form today. What is it this time? Did you tell some poor trusting fool that they caused a plague?'

Artemis hung his head wearily. This could go on for years.

Mulch had stumbled across the shuttle when he'd tunnelled to the port wall and wind-blasted a sheet of metal cladding from a service-tunnel wall. He knew the panel would be loose, because he had utilized this point of entry on previous visits. The shuttle had been up on blocks and under a lube-tent and so Mulch could not resist a little peek. Lo and behold, a tunnel scraper, in for refitting. Just the thing for hopping around the People's network of subterranean access tunnels. It had been a simple matter for Holly to reverse the clunky shuttle back down the monorail to the tunnel access hatch.

Meanwhile, Artemis had been covering their tracks, removing all traces of their visit to the shuttle port – wiping video crystals and replacing the lost time with loops. There wasn't much he could do about the unconscious pixie or the loader's worth of LEP hardware they had helped themselves to from the lock-up, but Mulch had had no problem taking credit for those.

'Hey, I'm already public enemy number one,' he had said. 'It's not as if I can go any higher on the list.'

So now they were seated inside the tunnel scraper, which was slotted into a launching bracket, drawing a few minute's charge from the coupling dock before they dropped into the abyss. Holly spent the time falsifying a report for the tunnel authorities.

ᛁᚦᚨ·◉◯◗ᚱ⊕·ᛁ◯ᚼ·ᚨᚱ⊕◯ᚨᛒ·□ᚱ◯◖ᛒ

'I'm telling them that this shuttle's paddle has been upgraded as per the service order and that the ship has been requested by the north African shuttle port to do a supply artery declogging. It's a drone flight, so they won't be looking for any personnel on board.'

Artemis was determined to give the mission every chance of success, in spite of the bridges he had burned. So, if a question had to be asked, he would ask it.

'Will that work?'

Holly shrugged. 'I doubt it. There's probably a smart missile waiting for us on the other side of that door.'

'Really?'

'No. I'm lying. Not nice, is it?'

Artemis shook his head miserably. He would have to think of some way to make it up to Holly. At least partially.

'Of course it will work. For now, at least. By the time Police Plaza puts all of this together, we should have returned to the future.'

'And we can fly without a paddle?'

Holly and Mulch shared a guffaw and a few words in Gnommish that were too fast for Artemis to catch. He did think he heard the word *cowpóg*, which translated as *moron*.

'Yes, Mud Boy. We can fly without a paddle, unless you're planning to scrape some residue from the tunnel walls. Usually we leave that to the robots.'

Artemis had forgotten how cutting Holly could be with people she wasn't fond of.

Mulch sang a few bars of the old human song 'You've

Lost That Lovin' Feelin''. He crooned at Holly, clutching an imaginary microphone in his fist.

Holly was not smiling now. 'You're about to lose all feeling in your legs, Diggums, if you don't shut it.'

Mulch noticed Holly's expression and realized that now was not the best time to be needling her.

Holly decided it was time to terminate the conversation. She remote-opened the access hatch and withdrew the docking clamps.

'Buckle up, boys,' she said, and dropped the small craft into a steep dive down an enormous hole, like dropping a peanut into the mouth of a hungry hippo.

CHAPTER 10: A FOWL MOOD

 TEN-year-old Artemis was about as miserable as Butler could remember seeing him, except for perhaps the time he had lost a science prize to an Australian postgraduate. The bodyguard glanced in the mirror of the rented Land Rover, and saw that his young charge was sitting in a puddle of perspiration, his expensive suit virtually dissolving on his spare frame.

A perforated box sat belted on the seat beside Artemis. Three black fingers poked from one of the holes as the captured lemur explored his prison.

Artemis has barely looked at the creature. He is trying to objectify it. It is no small thing to cause the extinction of a species, even to save one's father.

Artemis, meanwhile, was cataloguing the causes of his misery. A missing father and a mother teetering on the brink of nervous collapse were numbers one and two. Followed by a team of Arctic explorers running up expenses in a Moscow hotel room, doubtless living on room service, caviar with everything. Damon Kronski figured high on the list too. A repulsive man, with repellent ideals.

The local airport, Fez Saïss, had been closed and so Butler had been forced to detour the Learjet to Mohammed V International in Casablanca and rent a Land Rover there. And not a modern Land Rover either. This one belonged in the last millennium and had more holes than a block of Gruyère cheese. The air-conditioning had spluttered its last over a hundred miles ago and the seat padding was worn so thin that Artemis felt like he was sitting on a jackhammer. If the heat didn't bake him, the vibration would shake him to death.

Still, in spite of all these things, a thought struck Artemis, causing the corner of his mouth to twitch in a half smile.

That strange creature and her human companion are utterly fascinating.

They were desperate to have this lemur and they would not give up. He was certain of it.

Artemis turned his attention to the city suburbs bouncing past his window. The desert highway was suddenly thick with traffic as they neared the city centre. Giant trucks thundered past, tyres taller than a grown man, their flat-beds stuffed with sullen human cargo. Harried donkeys' hooves clicked on the broken tarmac, their backs piled high with sticks, laundry or even furniture. Thousands of dusty mopeds slalomed through the lanes, often bearing entire families on their rusting frames. The roadside buildings shimmered in the late afternoon sun like mirages. Ghost houses, with tea-drinking spectres seated out at the front.

Closer to the city centre the buildings were denser with no tracts of desert in between. Dwellings were interspersed with garages and video stores, tea shops and pizza parlours. All were the same sandblasted orange colour, with patches of original paint poking through below the lintels.

Artemis felt, as he always did when visiting developing nations, mild surprise at the coexistence of ancient and modern. Goat herders toted iPods on spangled chains and wore Manchester United shirts. Shacks had satellite dishes bolted to their corrugated roofs.

Until recent times, Fez had been a place of real importance, being the depot for the caravan trade from the south and east. It was known as a centre of Arab wisdom, a holy city, and a place of pilgrimage when the route to Mecca was closed by weather conditions or overrun with bandits.

Now it had become a place where outlawed Extinctionists did deals with desperate Irish criminals.

The world is changing more rapidly now than it ever has before, thought Artemis. *And I am helping to change it, for the worst.*

Not a comforting thought, but comfort was not a luxury he expected to enjoy in the near future.

Artemis's mobile phone buzzed as an incoming text message arrived, having made its way from Fez to Ireland and back to Morocco.

He checked the screen and a mirthless smile exposed his incisors.

The leather souq. Two hours, read the message.

Kronski wished to make the exchange in a public place. *Apparently the doctor trusts me about as much as I trust him.* Smart man.

Holly piloted the shuttle as though she were angry with it, slamming the mining craft round bends until its air brakes screamed and its readout needles shot into the red. She wore a flight helmet hard-wired directly into the shuttle's cameras, so a wraparound view of the shuttle was available to her at all times; she could even choose a remote view beamed to the shuttle from the tunnel's various cameras. This particular stretch of tunnel saw little traffic and so the motion-sensitive lights would pop on barely five miles before the shuttle entered a stretch.

Holly tried hard to enjoy the experience of flying and forget everything else. Being a pilot for the LEP was what she had dreamed of since childhood. As she cut yet another corner with a millimetre to spare, and felt the shuttle strain to its limits in her hands, the tension drained from her body as though absorbed by the craft.

Artemis lied to me and blackmailed me, but he did it for his mother. A good reason. Who's to say that I would not have done the same thing myself? If I could have saved my mother, I would have done whatever I needed to do, including manipulate my friends.

And so she could understand what Artemis had done –
even though she felt it was unnecessary – but that did not
mean she could forgive him just yet.

And how could she forget it? It felt as though she had
completely misjudged their friendship.

That won't happen again.

One thing that Holly was certain of: the most she and
Artemis could ever have now was what they'd always had
– grudging respect.

Holly patched into the passenger-seat bubble-cam on the
shuttle ceiling and was gratified to see Artemis clutching
the armrests on his seat. Perhaps it was the camera feed
or perhaps his face was actually green.

You blew it, Mud Boy, thought Holly, and then, *I hope it's
your face and not the feed.*

There was a natural vent in the Moroccan desert, south of
Agadir, where tunnel gas filtered up through half a mile
of sand. The only evidence of this was a slight discoloration
of the sand above the vent, which was quickly dispersed by
the winds as soon as it reached the surface. Nevertheless, a
thousand years of the process had left the dunes with curious
red streaks, which the local villagers swore was blood from
the victims of Raisuli, a famous twentieth-century bandit.
It was highly unlikely that anyone swallowed these claims,
least of all the villagers themselves, but it made good reading
in the guidebooks and drew visitors to the otherwise un-
remarkable area.

Holly drilled the craft through the vent, sealing the shuttle's own air filters against the tiny sand particles. She was flying virtually blind with only a three-dimensional model of the vent to navigate by. Luckily, it was a short leg of the trip and it took mere seconds for the shuttle to punch through to the African sky. In spite of the craft's insulated skin, its passengers soon began to feel the heat. Especially Mulch Diggums. Unlike the other fairy families, dwarfs were not surface creatures and did not dream of golden sun on their upturned faces. Anything higher than sea level gave them vertigo.

Mulch burped wetly. 'This is too high. I don't like this. Hot, too darned hot. I need to go to the bathroom. For what I'm not sure exactly. Just don't follow me in there. Whatever you hear, don't come in.'

When a dwarf gave this sort of advice, it was wise not to ignore it.

Holly sent a charge through the windscreen to clear it, then pointed the shuttle's nose north-east towards Fez. With a bit of luck, they could still beat little Artemis to the rendezvous point.

She set the autopilot and swivelled her seat to face Artemis, whose face was just returning to its normal pallor.

'You're sure about the rendezvous point?' she asked.

Artemis wasn't sure about anything and this uncertainty fogged his brain.

'Not sure, Holly. But I clearly remember making the exchange at the leather souq in Fez. At the very least it is

181

a place to start. If Kronski and my younger self do not show up, then we proceed to the Extinctionists' compound.'

Holly frowned. 'Hmm. This scheme is not up to your usual standards and our time is running out. We don't have a couple of days to play around with. Time is the enemy.'

'Yes,' agreed Artemis. 'Time is the crux of this entire misadventure.'

Holly took a nutri-block from the tiny refrigerator and returned to her controls.

Artemis studied his friend's back, trying to read her body language. Hunched, rounded shoulders and arms crossed in front of her body. She was cutting herself off, hostile to communication. He needed to produce some masterstroke to get himself back in her good books.

Artemis pressed his nose to the porthole, watching the Moroccan desert flash past in streaks of ochre and gold. There must be something that Holly wanted. Something she regretted not doing that in some way he could facilitate.

After a moment's concentrated thought, it came to him. Hadn't he seen a field holograph pack on one of the storage rails? And wasn't there someone to whom Holly had never said goodbye?

POLICE PLAZA, HAVEN CITY, THE LOWER ELEMENTS

Commander Julius Root was up to the quivering tip of his fungus cigar in paperwork. Not that it was actual paperwork.

There hadn't been any LEP files written on real paper in a centaur's age. It was all saved on a crystal and kept in a central core somewhere in info-space, and apparently now Foaly's people were trying to grow memory plants, which meant that some day information could be stored in plants or dungheaps, or even the cigar sticking out of Root's mouth. The commander did not understand any of this, nor did he want to. Let Foaly have the worlds of nano and cyber technologies. He would take the world of everyday LEP problems. And there were plenty of those.

First, his old enemy Mulch Diggums was running riot above ground. It was almost as if the dwarf were taunting him. His latest crime spree involved breaking into shuttle ports, then selling his booty on to exiled fairies living among the humans. At each site he would leave a nice pyramid of recycled earth in the middle of the floor, like a calling card.

Then there were those blasted swear toads. A couple of college graduate warlocks had granted the power of speech to the common bloated tunnel toad. Naturally, being college graduates, they had only granted the toads the power of bad language. Now, thanks to an unforeseen side effect, namely fertility, there was a virtual epidemic of these toads running around Haven, offending every citizen they hopped into.

The goblin gangs were growing in strength and audacity. Only last week they had fireballed a patrol car on its route through goblin town.

Julius Root leaned back in his swivel chair, allowing the smoke from his cigar to form a cloud around his head. There were days when he felt like hanging up his holster for good. Days when it felt as though there was nothing to keep him in the job.

The hologram ring buzzed on the ceiling like a disco ball. Incoming call. Root checked the caller ID.

Captain Holly Short.

Root allowed himself a rare grin.

Then there were days when he knew exactly what he had to do.

I have to groom the best people to take over when I am gone. People like Captain Kelp, Foaly — gods help me — and Captain Holly Short.

Root had hand-picked Holly from the ranks. Promoted her to captain, the first female to hold the title in the LEP's history. And she had done him proud. Every recon so far had been successful, without a single mind-wipe or time-stop.

She's the one, Julius, said Root's inner voice. *Smart, fearless, compassionate, Holly Short will make a splendid captain. Who knows, maybe a great commander.*

Root wiped the smile from his face. Captain Short did not need to see him smiling proudly, like a doting grandfather. She needed discipline, order and a healthy dollop of respect/fear for her commanding officer.

He tapped the accept pad on his desktop screen, and the hologram ring blasted a Milky Way of stars from its projectors that swirled and solidified into the flickering form of Captain Holly Short wearing a human suit. Undercover obviously. He could see her exactly as she was, but she could not see him until he stepped into the footprint of the holographic ring, which he did.

'Captain Short, all is well in Hamburg, I trust?'

Holly seemed speechless for a moment, her mouth hung open and her hands reached out as if to touch the commander. In her time he was dead, murdered by Opal Koboi, but here and now Julius Root was as vital as she remembered.

Root cleared his throat. 'All *is* well, Captain?'

'Yes. Of course, Commander. All is well, for the moment. Though it might be an idea to have Retrieval on standby.'

Root dismissed this idea with a wave of his cigar. 'Nonsense. Your record so far speaks for itself. You have never needed back-up before.'

Holly smiled. 'Always a first time.'

Root blinked, something on the hologram ring's floating gaseous readout had caught his eye.

'Are you calling me from Africa? What are you doing in Africa?'

Holly slapped her palm against the instrument panel on her end. 'No, I'm in Hamburg, in the observation hide. Stupid machine. The projectors are all wrong too. I look about ten years old on the monitor. I'm going to strangle Foaly when I get back.'

Root couldn't help but smile at that, but he tucked it away quickly.

'Why the hologram, Short? What's wrong with a plain old communicator? Do you know how expensive it is to beam sound and vision through the Earth's crust?'

Holly's image flickered and stared at its feet, then up again.

'I . . . I just wanted to thank you, Jul– Commander.'

Root was surprised. *Thank him*. For months of impossible tasks and double shifts.

'Thank me, Captain? This is most irregular. I'm not sure I'm doing my job right if fairies are thanking me.'

'Yes, yes you are,' blurted Holly's image. 'You do a fine job, more than fine. No one appreciated – appreciates you enough. But I do now. I know what you were – are trying to do for me. So, thank you, and I won't let you down.'

Root was surprised to find that he was actually touched. It wasn't every day he was faced with such genuine emotion.

Look at me, he thought. *Blubbering at a hologram. Wouldn't Foaly love this.*

'I . . . em . . . I accept your thanks and I believe them to be heartfelt. Although I don't expect an expensive hologram call during every mission, just the once will be fine.'

'Understood, Commander.'

'And be careful in Hamburg. Make sure to check your equipment.'

'I will, Commander,' said Holly, and Root could have sworn she rolled her eyes, but it could have been another glitch in the program.

'Anything else, Captain?'

ᚱᚢᚢᛁ᛭·᛭᛭·᛭·᛭᛭᛭·᛭·᛭᛭᛭·᛭·᛭᛭᛭·᛭᛭᛭

Holly reached out her hand; it shimmered and wavered slightly with the motion. Root was not sure what he was supposed to do. Hologram etiquette was very clear: hugging and shaking were not encouraged. After all, who wants to embrace a pixellated image?

But still the hand was there.

'Wish me luck, Commander. One officer to another.'

Root grunted. With any other subordinate he would have suspected toadying, but Captain Short had always impressed him with her candour.

He reached out his hand and felt a slight tingle as it touched Holly's virtual digits.

'Good luck, Captain,' he said gruffly. 'And try to tone down that maverick streak. Some day I won't be around to help you.'

'Will do, Commander. Goodbye,' said Holly, and then she was gone, but in the seconds before her holographic image fizzled out Julius Root could have sworn he saw rough holographic tears glint on her cheeks.

Stupid machine, he thought. *I will demand that Foaly recalibrate the lot of them.*

Holly stepped out of the holo-booth, which resembled an ancient shower unit with rubber curtain. With the touch of a button it collapsed and self-sealed into the portable briefcase.

There were tears in her eyes as she strapped herself into the pilot's chair and flicked off autopilot.

Artemis squirmed slightly in the co-pilot's chair.

'So, are we even?'

Holly nodded. 'Yes. We're even. But your elf-kissing days are over.'

'I see,' said Artemis.

'It's not a challenge, Artemis. Over is over.'

'I know,' said Artemis neutrally.

They sat in silence for a while, watching low mountains speed across the desert towards them, then Holly leaned across and punched Artemis gently on the shoulder.

'Thanks, Arty.'

'You are most welcome. All I did was have an idea.'

Mulch emerged noisily from the bathroom, scratching and grunting.

'Wooo-oh, that's better. Thank the gods for soundproofing, eh?'

Holly winced. 'Close the door and let the extractor fan do its work.'

Mulch slammed the door with a flick of his heel. 'I was thinking in there, you know, rooo-minating.'

'I don't think I want to hear this.'

Mulch ploughed on regardless. 'That little lemur. The silky whatever. You know who he reminds me of with that buzz-cut hairdo?'

They had all been thinking it.

'Commander Root,' said Holly, smiling.

'Yep. A miniature Commander Root.'

'Julius Junior,' said Artemis.

They crested the foothills of the Atlas Mountains and Fez was revealed like the heart of the land, its arteries clogged with vehicles.

'Jayjay,' said Holly. 'That's his name. Now let's go get him.'

She switched on the shuttle's shield and initiated their descent into Fez.

CHAPTER II: PIGEON DROPPINGS

THE LEATHER SOUQ, FEZ MEDINA

 HOLLY inflated a cham pod and suckered it to the shadowy underside of the stone balcony overlooking Fez's leather souq. When the coast was clear, she and Artemis climbed through the tiny access portal, wiggling into the blow-up seats. Artemis's knees knocked against his chin, clicking his teeth.

'Like I said, you're getting tall,' said Holly.

Artemis blew a raven lock from his eye. 'And hairy.'

'Your hair was the only thing that stopped little Arty recognizing himself, so be glad of it.'

Holly had liberated the cham-pod duffel bag from the Tara lock-up along with a single Neutrino handgun and suitable disguises. Artemis wore a knee-length brown shirt and thong sandals, while Holly's fairy characteristics were hidden by a headscarf and an abaya.

The cham pod was an old portable model and was

basically a ball with a transparent outer layer that was inflated by a tank of chromo-variable gas that could change colour to imitate the background. That was about as high-tech as it got. No directional equipment, no on-board weaponry, just a one-way touch screen and two cramped seats.

'No air filters?' wondered Artemis.

'Unfortunately not,' said Holly, pulling her scarf across her nose. 'What is that smell?'

'Diluted pigeon droppings,' replied Artemis. 'Highly acidic and, of course, plentiful. The tannery workers use it to soften the hides before dyeing them.'

The leather souq spread out below them was a spectacular sight. Huge stone vats were arranged across the courtyard in honeycomb patterns, each filled with either acidic softeners or vegetable dyes such as saffron and henna. The leather workers stood in the dye vats, soaking each skin thoroughly, including their own, and, when the hide had attained the desired hue, it was stretched on a nearby rooftop to dry.

'People say that Henry Ford invented the production line,' said Artemis. 'This place has been going for six hundred years.'

The souq was enclosed by high walls painted white but mottled by dye and dust. Ochre stains spread across the ancient brick like the faded map of some exotic archipelago.

'Why did Kronski choose the souq?' wondered Holly. 'The stink is almost unbearable, and I say that as a friend of Mulch Diggums.'

'Since birth Kronski has suffered from anosmia,' Artemis explained. 'He has no sense of smell. It amuses him to conduct his business here, as whoever he happens to be meeting will be virtually assaulted by the smell from the acid vats. Their concentration is shattered and his is unaffected.'

'Clever.'

'Fiendishly so. The area is a tourist attraction, so many people will pass through, but none hang around for too long.'

'Plenty of spectators but not many witnesses.'

'Apart from the locals, and Kronski doubtless has a dozen of those on his payroll, and they will see what he wants them to see.' Artemis leaned forward, his nose brushing the plastic portal. 'And here is our fiendish Extinctionist now. Right on cue.'

The souq below was thronged with leather workers and merchants, long since inured to the sharp odour of the vats. Groups of die-hard tourists flitted through, determined to capture the scene on their cameras but unwilling to suffer the heat and smells for longer than a few shutter clicks. And among them all, serene and smiling, strode Doctor Damon Kronski, dressed in a preposterous tailored camouflage suit, complete with a general's peaked hat.

Holly was sickened by the man and how he obviously relished his surroundings.

'Look at him. He loves this.'

Artemis did not comment. He had sold the lemur and he judged that a crime worse than Kronski's. Instead, he searched the souq for a smaller version of himself.

U•☺•☉ ♫)ʃ♯•⊕□•♡♫⋉•♠☉•⁑⊖ℬ�F

'There I am. West corner.'

Holly switched her gaze to locate young Artemis. He stood almost hidden by a huge tiled urn brimming with mint-green dye. The sinking sun was a chopped silver disc on its surface.

Artemis smiled. *I remember standing in that exact spot, so the glare would distract Kronski. It is the only vat touched by the sun at this time. A little payback for the smell. Childish, perhaps, but then I was a child.*

'It looks like your memory is accurate on this occasion,' said Holly.

Artemis couldn't help but be relieved. His recollection had been hit-and-miss up to now.

He straightened suddenly. *Hit-and-miss. How could he not have seen it? These memory malfunctions could mean only one thing.*

No time to pursue that thought now. The exchange was afoot.

Artemis tapped the touch-screen with his index finger, expanding a section. Closing in on a plinth at the centre of the souq. The low stone tabletop was grooved and curved from centuries of being piled high with hides. Wet henna glistened on its surface and dribbled down its sides, like blood from a head injury.

'There,' said Artemis. 'That's where we agreed to make the exchange. Kronski lays the suitcase on the rock. I hand it over.'

'Him. He's a male, and his name is Jayjay,' said Holly, making it real.

'I hand over Jayjay. Then we go our separate ways, simple as that. There were no complications.'

'Perhaps we should wait until after the handover?'

'No. What happens afterwards is an unknown quantity. At least now we have some foreknowledge.'

Holly studied the scene with a veteran's eye. 'Where's Butler?'

Artemis touched another point on the screen. It rippled slightly, flexed and enlarged his selection.

'In that window. Watching over everything.'

The window was a high rectangle in the flaking white wall, painted black by shade and depth.

'You think you're invisible, don't you, my friend?' Holly whispered, then highlighted the window with a thumb and activated a night-vision filter. In the sudden glow of body heat, a hulking figure appeared in the window, still as stone, except for a beating heart.

'I remember that Butler wanted to make the exchange, but I talked him out of it. He's up there right now, fuming.'

'Butler fuming is not something I want to see up close.'

Artemis laid a hand on her shoulder. 'Then don't get too close. A distraction is all we need. I wish there had been an LEP jumpsuit in that lock-up. If you were invisible to man *and* machine, I would be more comfortable with this.'

Holly twisted her chin, calling her magic, and blobs of her disappeared until there was nothing left in the seat but haze.

'Don't worry, Artemis,' she said, her voice sounding almost robotic because of the vibration. 'I have been on missions before. You are not the only smart one in the souq.'

Artemis was not in the least cheered by this. 'All the more reason to be careful. I wish there'd been a set of wings in the terminal. What sort of lock-up doesn't have wings?'

'Pot luck,' said Holly, her voice floating through the expandable seal of the portal. 'We got what we got.'

'We got what we got,' repeated Artemis, following Holly's progress down the steps and across the courtyard with the infra-red filter. 'Terrible grammar.'

Ten-year-old Artemis felt as though he had been dipped in a jar of honey and left to bake on the surface of the sun. His garments had moulded themselves to his skin and a tornado of flies revolved round his head. Artemis's throat was sandpaper dry, and he could hear his breath and pulse as though he were wearing a helmet.

And the stench. The stench was a hot wind gusting in his nose and eyes.

I must persevere, he thought with a focused determination beyond his years. *Father needs me. Also, I refuse to be cowed by this odious man.*

The souq was a confusing kaleidoscope of pumping limbs, splashing dye and evening shadows. And, from Artemis's point of view, things were even more confusing. Elbows flashed past, urns rang like bells and the air was shattered by sharp bolts of French and Arabic above his head.

Artemis allowed himself a moment to meditate. He closed his eyes, taking shallow breaths through his mouth.

Very well, he thought. *To business, Doctor Kronski.*

Luckily the doctor was enormous, and, as Artemis made his way through the souq, he quickly spotted Kronski on the opposite diagonal.

Look at that poseur. A camouflage suit! Does he honestly believe himself a general in some war against the animal kingdom?

Artemis himself drew surprised stares from the locals. Tourists were not unusual in the souq, but lone ten-year-old boys in formal suits, carrying monkey cages, were rare in any part of the world.

It is a simple matter. Walk to the centre and set down the cage.

But even walking through this souq was not simple. Workers bustled through the lanes between vats, laden with dozens of sopping hides. Strings of dye flew through the air, striping the clothes of tourists and other workers. Artemis was forced to tread carefully and give way several times before he eventually reached the small clearing at the centre.

Kronski was there before him, perched on the tiny stool that folded out from the top of his hunting cane, puffing on a thin cigar.

'Apparently, I'm missing out on half the experience,' he said, as though they were simply continuing a conversation. 'The best part of a cigar is the aroma, and I can't smell a thing.'

Artemis was silently infuriated. The man looked completely

comfortable, with barely a drop of sweat on his brow. He forced himself to smile.

'Do you have the money, Damon?' At least he could annoy the good doctor by neglecting his title.

Kronski did not seem annoyed. 'Got it right here, Ah-temis,' he said, patting his breast pocket. 'A hundred thousand is such a trifling amount, I managed to stuff every last note into my suit pocket.'

Artemis could not resist a jibe. 'And what a lovely suit it is.'

Kronski's violet-coloured glasses flashed in the last rays of the sun. 'Unlike your own, my boy, which appears to be losing its *character* in this heat.'

It was true; Artemis felt that the only thing holding him upright was the dried sweat on his spine. He was hungry, tired and irritable.

Focus. The end justifies the sacrifices.

'Well, obviously I have the lemur, so can we please proceed?'

Kronski's fingers twitched, and Artemis could guess what he was thinking.

Take the lemur from the boy. Just grab it. No need to part with the hundred thousand.

Artemis decided to nip this kind of thinking in the bud.

'In case you're entertaining any rash notions of reneging on our agreement, let me say just one word to you: *Butler*.'

One word was enough. Kronski knew Butler's reputation,

but not his whereabouts. His fingers twitched once more and then were still.

'Very well, Ah-temis. Let's get this business over with. I'm sure you appreciate that I need to inspect the merchandise.'

'Of course. And I'm sure *you* appreciate that I will need to see a sample of your currency.'

'Why, of course.' Kronski wiggled his hand into a pocket and withdrew a fat envelope brimming with purple five-hundred-euro notes. He carelessly selected one and passed it across to Artemis.

'Gonna smell it, are you, Ah-temis?'

'Not exactly.' Artemis flipped open his mobile phone and selected a UV and magnetic currency scanner from its augmented menu. He passed the note in front of the purple light, checking for the watermark and metal strip.

Kronski pressed a hand to his heart. 'I am wounded, boy, injured, that you should think I would cheat you. Why, it would cost more than a hundred thousand to forge a hundred thousand. A good set of plates costs twice that.'

Artemis closed the phone. 'I am not a trusting person, Damon. You'll learn that about me.' He placed the cage on the stone plinth. 'Now, your turn.'

In that moment, Kronski's entire attitude changed. His offhand nature vanished, replaced with a giddiness. He smiled and tittered, tiptoeing to the cage like a child to the Christmas tree.

Perhaps a normal child, thought Artemis sourly. *Christmas morning holds no surprises for me, thanks to the X-ray scanner on my mobile phone.*

Obviously the prospect of extinguishing the life spark of another species excited Kronski hugely. He leaned over the cage daintily, squinting through the airholes.

'Yes, yes. All *appears* to be in order. But I will need to take a closer look.'

'One hundred thousand euro buys you all the closer looks you need.'

Kronski tossed the envelope to Artemis. 'Oh, take it, you tiresome boy. You really distress me, Ah-temis. A boy like you can't have many friends.'

'I've got one friend,' retorted Artemis, pocketing the money. 'And he's bigger than you.'

Kronski opened the box just wide enough to grab the lemur by the scruff of the neck. He hoisted the animal aloft like a trophy, checking him from all angles.

Artemis took a step back, casting suspicious glances around the souq.

Perhaps nothing is going to happen, he thought. *Perhaps those creatures were not as resourceful as I believed. I may have to be content with the hundred thousand for now.*

And then the resourceful creatures arrived.

Holly did not have wings to fly but that did not mean she couldn't cause havoc. There had been no weapons in the LEP lock-up beyond the single Neutrino, but there had been some mining equipment, including a few dozen blaster buttons, which Holly was now sprinkling into the unattended dye vats around the souq, with a double helping underneath Butler's window.

Though she was invisible, Holly took extra care with her movements, as shielding without a suit was wild magic indeed. Any sudden gestures or collisions could cause her body to vent magical fireworks, which would look strange igniting out of thin air.

So, softly, softly was the way to move.

Holly dropped the last of the buttons, feeling totally vulnerable in spite of her invisibility.

I miss Foaly's guidance, she thought. *It's nice to have an all-seeing eye.*

As if he could read her mind, Artemis's voice came from the mike-bud in her ear. Another gift from the lock-up.

'Kronski is opening the cage. Get ready to blow the buttons.'

'All set. I'm at the north-west corner if Jayjay tries to run.'

'I see you on the filter. Detonate at will.'

Holly climbed into an empty vat and fixed her gaze on Kronski. He had the lemur out now, holding it away from his body. Perfect.

She ran a finger along the small strip in her hand, until all the tiny lights turned green. A one-word message scrolled across the strip.

Detonate?

Absolutely, thought Holly, and pressed the *yes* box.

⬡ • ⬡⬡⬡ • ⬡⬡⬡⬡⬡⬡⬡⬡⬡⬡ • ⬡ ⬡⬡⬡⬡ •

A vat blew, sending a column of red dye shooting six metres into the air. Several more vats quickly followed suit, thumping like mortars, hurling their contents into the Morocco sky.

A symphony of colour, thought Artemis from his perch. *Butler's view is totally obscured.*

Below in the souq, pandemonium was instantaneous. The leather workers roared and shouted, oohing like spectators at a fireworks show as each new coloured fountain erupted. Some realized that their precious leathers were being coated with the wrong hues and began to feverishly gather their wares and tools. Within seconds it was raining gouts of dye, and the spaces between the vats were thronged with frantic workers and spooked tourists.

Young Artemis stood stock still, ignoring the flying dye, his gaze fixed on Damon Kronski and the lemur in his fist.

Watch the animal. They want the animal.

Kronski squealed with each explosion, balancing on a single leg like a scared ballet dancer.

Priceless, thought Artemis, and shot a few seconds of video on his phone. Something else was about to happen; he felt sure of it.

And he was right. Artemis had a vague impression that the earth exploded in front of Kronski's feet. Mud mushroomed upwards, something moved in the curtain of earth and then the lemur was gone.

Doctor Kronski was left holding a blob of slime, which glowed slightly in the evening shadows.

The last drops of dye fell, and slowly the chaos retreated. The leather workers shook their heads in wonder, then began to curse their luck. A day's profit gone.

Kronski squealed for several seconds after the dust had cleared, holding the note like an opera singer.

Artemis grinned nastily. 'It isn't over until the fat lady sings, so I suppose it's over.'

The doctor was snapped out of it by Artemis's tones. He composed himself, standing on two feet and breathing deeply as the red spots retreated from his cheeks. It was not until he tried to wipe the gunk from his hand that he realized the lemur was no longer in his grasp.

As he stared in disbelief at his fingers, Kronski felt the stuff coating his fingers harden into a glowing gauntlet.

'What have you done, Artemis?'

Ah, thought Artemis. *Suddenly you can pronounce my name.*

'I have done nothing, Damon. I delivered the lemur; you lost him. The problems here are all yours.'

Kronski was livid. He tore off his glasses to reveal red-rimmed eyes. 'You have tricked me, Fowl. Somehow, you are a participant in this. I cannot host an Extinctionist conference without a strong opening. The execution of that lemur was my big *hello, everyone.*'

Artemis's phone beeped and he glanced at the screen. A brief text from Butler.

Mission accomplished.

He pocketed the mobile phone and smiled broadly at Kronski.

'A strong opening. I may be able to help you with that. For a price, naturally.'

Artemis the elder sat in the cham pod, watching events unfurling below. Everything went exactly to plan, with the exception of the dye vats, which actually exceeded Artemis's expectations.

Butler's view is completely blocked, he thought. And then he froze suddenly. *Of course! I wouldn't have placed Butler in that window at all. I would have put a decoy there, as it is one of the five logical places for a sniper to set up. In fact, I would have put a decoy in all five spots and then have Butler hide himself somewhere on the souq floor, ready to step in if those pesky lemur-nappers showed up again, which they very well could, as they seem to know my every move. I, Artemis Fowl, have been bamboozled by myself.*

Suddenly, a horrifying thought struck him.

'Holly!' he shouted into the microphone pad adhered to his thumb. 'Abort! Abort!'

'What . . .' came the crackly response. 'The noise . . . I think . . . damaged.'

Then a few seconds of white noise, sharp snaps and silence.

It was too late. Artemis could only press his face against the screen and watch helplessly as one of the leather workers shrugged off his shoulder blanket and straightened, revealing himself to be far taller than he had previously appeared. It was, of course, Butler, with a hand-held infra-red scanner extended before him.

Butler. Don't do it, old friend. I know you were never comfortable with my schemes.

In three quick strides, the bodyguard moved to Holly's vat and netted the elf in his blanket. She struggled and fought, but never had a chance against Butler's formidable strength. In ten seconds, Holly was hog-tied and hoisted over the bodyguard's shoulder. In five more seconds Butler was out of the gate and lost in the gathering crowds of the medina.

It all happened so quickly that Artemis's jaw did not have time to drop. One moment he was in control, enjoying the smugness that comes with being the smartest person in the metaphorical room. The next, he was crashing back to earth, having sacrificed his queen for a rook, realizing he was up against somebody just as smart as he was, only twice as ruthless.

He felt the pallor of desperation creep across his forehead, leaving pins and needles in its wake.

They have Holly. The Extinctionists will put her on trial on charges of breathing human air.

A thought occurred to him. *Every defendant is entitled to a good lawyer.*

CHAPTER 12: GONE FOREVER

LE DOMAINE DES HOMMES, EXTINCTIONISTS' COMPOUND, FEZ

 ARTEMIS the younger agreed to accompany Doctor Kronski to his gated compound near the medina. Kronski's Land Rover was considerably more luxurious than Artemis's rented model, complete with powerful air-conditioning, water cooler and white-tiger upholstery.

Artemis ran a finger through the fur and was not surprised to find that it was real.

'Nice seats,' he commented drily.

Kronski did not answer. He hadn't spoken much since losing the lemur, except to mutter to himself, cursing the unfairness of it all. It didn't seem to bother him that his suit was covered in dye, which was transferring itself to his expensive upholstery.

Though it took barely five minutes to reach the compound,

Artemis was glad of the thinking space. By the time the Land Rover was cleared through the reinforced gates, he had any wrinkles in his strategy straightened out and he'd used the spare two minutes to plot one of the romance novels he occasionally wrote under the pseudonym Violet Tsirblou.

A guard with bulk to match Butler's waved them through underneath a walkway arch in the four-metre-high wall. Artemis kept his eyes open on the way in, noting the armed guards patrolling the ten-acre compound, and the position of the generator hut and the staff quarters.

Information is power.

The residential chalets were built in the style of Californian beach houses, flat roofs and plenty of glass, clustered around a man-made beach, complete with wave machine and lifeguard. There was a large conference centre in the middle of the compound, with a scaffold-clad spire jutting from its roof. Two men were perched on the scaffolding, putting the finishing touches to a brass icon on the spire's tip. And even though most of the icon was wrapped in canvas, Artemis could see enough to know what it was. A human arm with the world in its fist. The symbol of the Extinctionists.

Kronski's driver parked in front of the compound's grandest chalet and the doctor led the way inside wordlessly. He flapped a hand towards a hide-covered sofa, and disappeared into his bedroom.

Artemis was hoping for a shower and a change of clothes,

but apparently Kronski was too upset for courtesy, so Artemis was forced to tug at the collar of his itchy shirt and wait for his host's return.

Kronski's reception lounge was a macabre space. One wall was covered with certificates of extinction, complete with photographs of the unfortunate animals and the dates on which the Extinctionists managed to murder the last one of the particular species.

Artemis browsed the photo wall. Here was a Japanese sea lion, and a Yangtze river dolphin. A Guam flying fox and a Bali tiger.

All gone forever.

The only way to see these creatures was to somehow build up enough momentum to travel faster than the speed of light and go back in time.

There were further horrors in the room, all labelled for educational purposes. The sofa was upholstered with the pelts of Falkland Island wolves. The base of a standing lamp was fashioned from the skull of a western black rhinoceros.

Artemis struggled to maintain his composure.

I need to get out of here as quickly as possible.

But the faint voice of his conscience reminded him that leaving would not mean that this place no longer existed, and selling the strange creature to Kronski would only draw more people to it.

Artemis conjured a picture of his father in his mind.

Whatever it takes. Whatever I have to do.

Kronski entered the room showered and wearing a flowing kaftan. His eyes were red-rimmed, as though he'd been crying.

'Sit down, Ah-temis,' he said, gesturing towards the sofa with a hide-bound fly swatter.

Artemis eyed the seat. 'No. I think I'll stand.'

Kronski sank into an office chair. 'Oh, I get it. Grown-up sofa. It's difficult to be taken seriously when your feet don't touch the ground.'

The doctor rubbed his eyes with stubby thumbs, then donned his trademark glasses.

'You have no idea what it's been like for me, Ah-temis. Hounded from country to country because of my beliefs, like some common criminal. And now that I have *finally* found somewhere to call home, now that I have persuaded the committee to meet here, I lose my trial animal. That lemur was the centrepiece of the entire conference.'

Kronski's voice was steady and he seemed to have recovered himself since his breakdown at the leather souq.

'The Extinctionists' committee members are very powerful men, Ah-temis. They are accustomed to comfort and convenience. Morocco is hardly convenient. I had to build this compound to entice them down here, and promise a big opening to the conference. And now all I have to show is a shining hand.'

Kronski brandished his hand, which was largely slime free, but did seem to glow faintly.

'All is not lost, Doctor,' said Artemis soothingly. 'I can

provide you with something that will rejuvenate your society and make it globally relevant.'

Kronski's frown was sceptical, but he leaned forward, arms slightly outstretched.

His face says no, thought Artemis. *But his body language says yes.*

'What are you selling, Ah-temis?'

Artemis opened the gallery on his phone, selecting a photograph.

'This,' he said, passing the phone to Kronski.

The doctor studied the photograph and the scepticism in his eyes grew more pronounced.

'What is this? Photo manipulation?'

'No. Genuine. This creature is real.'

'Come on, Ah-temis. What we've got here are latex and bone implants. Nothing more.'

Artemis nodded. 'That's a fair reaction. So you don't pay until you're satisfied.'

'I already paid.'

'You paid for a lemur,' Artemis countered. 'This is an undiscovered species. Possibly a threat to mankind. This is what the Extinctionists are all about. Imagine how many members will clamour to donate to your church when you uncover this threat.'

Kronski nodded. 'You put together a good argument for a ten-year-old. How much do I pay?'

'You pay five million euro. Non-negotiable.'

'Cash?'

⊖β૬•ᘮᗏ⏋⏋⅄ᚨᑉ⦰◑•⊛◻⅄⊛•ᘚᐁᗃ◑•βᏇᗃᑉ•

'Diamonds.'

Kronski pouted. 'I won't pay a single stone until I verify the authenticity of your product.'

'That's fair.'

'That's mighty accommodating of you, Fowl. How do you know I won't double-cross you? After all, I'm pretty sure that you had a hand in whatever happened back at the souq. Payback is fair play where I come from.'

'You might double-cross me, Damon. But you won't double-cross Butler. You are not a stupid man.'

Kronski grunted, impressed. 'I got to hand it to you, boy. You have all the angles figured. You present 'em well too.' He stared absently at his glowing hand. 'You ever think it strange, Ah-temis, how a kid like you winds up going eyeball to eyeball with an old crook like me?'

'I don't understand the question,' said Artemis truthfully.

Kronski clapped his hands and laughed. 'It delights me, Ah-temis,' he said, 'that a boy such as you exists. It makes my day.' The laughter stopped suddenly, as though cut off by a guillotine. 'Now, how soon can I inspect the creature?'

'Immediately,' replied Artemis.

'Good. Well, text your man to come hither. Let's say it takes him thirty minutes to get here, another ten to clear security. We can meet him in the grand lodge in one hour.'

'I said immediately,' said Artemis, clicking his fingers. Butler stepped out from behind a curtain, a Kevlar duffel bag under one arm.

Kronski squealed briefly, then rolled his eyes in frustration.

'I can't control that . . . Ever since the koala in Cleveland. It's so embarassing . . .'

File and save, thought Artemis. *Koala in Cleveland.*

'Anyway,' continued the doctor, 'how did he get in here?'

Butler shrugged. 'I came in the same way you did, Doctor.'

'You were in the Land Rover,' breathed Kronski. 'Very clever.'

'Not really. More lax on your part than clever on ours.'

'I will remember that. Do you have the merchandise with you?'

Butler's mouth tightened and Artemis knew that he was pushed to the limits of his loyalty by this transaction. The lemur had been bad enough, but this female in the bag was some kind of person.

Wordlessly, the bodyguard placed the duffel on the desk. Artemis tugged on the zipper, but Butler stopped him.

'She has some kind of hypnotizing skills. I once met a guy in Laos who could put the whammy on you, but nothing like this. She tried it on outside the souq and I nearly ran into a camel, so I taped her mouth. Also, as we know, she can turn invisible. When I opened the bag first, she wasn't there. I think her juice is running out, though. There could be more stunts – who knows what tricks she has hidden in those pointed ears? Are you prepared to take that risk?'

'Yes,' said Kronski, almost foaming at the mouth. 'Absolutely, yes. Open the bag.'

Butler removed his hand and Artemis unzipped the duffel, exposing the figure inside.

Kronski stared into the mismatched eyes. Ran a hand across the inhumanly wide brow, tugged one of the ears, then staggered to the office bar, pouring himself a glass of water with shaky hands.

'Five million at today's market price,' he said. 'You said five and we agreed. No upping the price now.'

Artemis smiled. The doctor was hooked.

'Five million,' he said. 'Plus expenses.'

Artemis the elder rode back to the landing site on a collapsible LEP scooter designed to resemble a 1950s human Lambretta. The resemblance was only bumper deep, as there were not many Lambrettas that came equipped with clean nuclear batteries, Gnommish satellite navigation and self-destruct buttons.

The Ifrane road outside the imperial city was part of the fertile Fez river basin and was lined with olive groves and golf courses.

Ancient and modern. Coexisting.

Overhead the stars seemed closer and fiercer than at home in Ireland, shining down like stadium lights, as though Africa were somehow closer to the rest of the universe.

I lost her. I lost Holly.

But he did have a plan. A half-decent plan. All it needed

was a bit of fairy technology to open a few doors and then there was still a chance. Because, without Holly, all was lost. There would be no future for any of them.

It took almost an hour to find the particular golf course where Holly had parked the LEP shuttle. Not that there was much evidence of a craft on the spot besides a slightly flat plane of sand in the bunker. Holly had nosed the shuttle deep into the dry sand and left the shield powered on. Artemis only found it himself with the help of the bike's navigation systems.

He collapsed the scooter into a Frisbee-sized disc and climbed down through the roof hatch.

Mulch Diggums was idly swivelling himself in the pilot's chair.

'That's my scooter, Mud Boy,' he said. 'That came off the trolley, so I take it with me.'

Artemis shut the hatch behind him. 'Where's the lemur? Where's Jayjay?'

Mulch answered these questions with some of his own. 'Where's Holly? Have you lost her?'

'Yes,' Artemis admitted miserably. 'The boy outwitted me. He knew we would come for the lemur. He sacrificed it for Holly.'

'Smart,' said Mulch. 'Anyway, I'm off. See you . . .'

'See you? *See you?* One of your fairy comrades is in danger and you're just going to desert her?'

Mulch raised his palms. 'Hey, calm down, Mud Boy. The

LEP are not my comrades. We had a deal; I get you the little furry fellow and you get me a trolley of LEP tech goodies. Job done, both parties happy.'

At that moment, Jayjay poked his head round the bathroom door.

'What's he doing in there?'

Mulch grinned. 'Take two guesses.'

'Lemurs cannot use advanced plumbing.'

'See for yourself. Whatever's in there, I'm blaming Jayjay.'

He clicked his furry fingers and the lemur ran along his arm, on to his head.

'See. He accepts responsibility.' Mulch frowned. 'You're not going to trade this fellow for Captain Short, are you?'

'No point,' said Artemis, accessing the LEP central database. 'It would be like trying to trade a hairpin for Excalibur.'

Mulch chewed his lip. 'I'm familiar with the Excalibur story, so I know what you're trying to say there. A hairpin is useless, Excalibur is wonderful, and so on. But in some instances a hairpin is extremely useful. Now, if you had said a *rubber* hairpin. Do you see what I'm getting at?'

Artemis ignored him, tapping furiously at the v-board that had appeared in front of him. He needed to know everything he could about the Extinctionists and Foaly had an extensive file on them.

Mulch tickled Jayjay under the chin. 'I was getting pretty fond of Captain Short, against my better judgement. I suppose I could dig in and rescue her.'

⟨ᘒᕼᒷ•⊗ᗢ•ᔑᖇ ᘒ⊗ᒷᕊ•ᗢ•ᕼᕼᘖᘿᑌ•⟩

This was a genuine offer and a fair point, so Artemis spared a moment to address it.

'Not possible. Kronski has seen the tunnel rescue before and he won't fall for it again. At any rate, you wouldn't survive the temperature during the day. Even underground you wouldn't be safe. The earth is so dry that cracks can penetrate up to fifteen metres in open ground. One pinprick of midday sun and you would crisp like an old book in a furnace.'

Mulch winced. 'Now, you see, *that* image works really well. So what are you going to do?'

Artemis used the advanced fairy technology to print off a leopard-print card with an Extinctionists' hologram flashing silver and purple in the centre.

'I'm going to the Extinctionists' banquet tonight,' he said, flicking the card with his forefinger. 'After all, I have been invited. All I need is a disguise and some medical supplies.'

Mulch was impressed. 'That's very good. You're almost as devious as I am.'

Artemis turned back to the v-board. It would take time to firm up his cover.

'You have no idea,' he said.

The night of the Extinctionists' banquet was upon him and Kronski's nerves were frazzled. He danced around his chalet wearing nothing but a bath towel, anxiously humming his way through the tunes from *Joseph and the Amazing Technicolor Dreamcoat*. Kronski often dreamed that *he* was wearing the Technicolor coat and it was fashioned from the pelts of all the animals he had hunted to extinction. He always awoke smiling.

Everything has to be perfect. This is the biggest night of my life. Thank you, little Ah-temis.

There was a lot riding on this conference, and the banquet generally set the tone for the entire weekend. Pull off something big at the banquet trial and the members would be buzzing about it for days. The Internet would be alive with chatter.

And it doesn't get any bigger than a brand-new sentient species. The Extinctionists are about to go global.

And just in time. Truth be told, the Extinctionists were old news. Subscriptions were dropping off and, for the first time since its inception, the conference was not a total sell-out. In the beginning it had been wonderful – so many exciting species to hunt and nail to the wall. But now countries were protecting their rare animals, especially the big ones. There was no flying into India for a tiger shoot any more. And the sub-Saharan nations took it extremely badly if a group of well-armed Extinctionists showed up at one of their reserves and began taking pot shots at elephants. It was getting to the point where government officials were refusing bribes. *Refusing bribes.*

There was another problem with the Extinctionists, though Kronski would never admit it aloud. The group had become a touchstone for the lunatic fringe. His heart-felt hatred for the animal kingdom was attracting blood-thirsty crazies who could not see past putting a bullet in a dumb beast. They could not grasp the philosophy of the organization. Man is king, and animals survive only so long as they contribute to the comfort of their masters. An animal without uses is wasting precious air and should be wiped out.

But this new creature changed everything. Everyone would want to see her. They would film the entire trial and execution, leak the tape and then the world would come to Damon Kronski.

One year of donations, thought Kronski. *Then I retire to enjoy my wealth.*

Five million. This fairy, or whatever it is, is worth ten times that. A hundred times.

Kronski jiggled in front of the air-conditioner blast for a minute then selected a suit from his wardrobe.

Purple, he thought. *Tonight I shall be emperor.*

As an afterthought he plucked a matching tasselled Caspian tiger-skin hat from an upper shelf.

When in Fez, he thought brightly.

THE FOWL LEARJET, 10,000 METRES OVER GIBRALTAR

Ten-year-old Artemis Fowl tried his best to relax in one of the Learjet's plush leather chairs, but there was a tension knot at the base of his skull.

I need a massage, he thought. *Or some herbal tea.*

Artemis was perfectly aware what was causing the tension.

I have sold a creature . . . a person to the Extinctionists.

Being as smart as he was, Artemis was perfectly capable of constructing an argument to justify his actions.

Her friends will free her. They almost outsmarted me; they can certainly outsmart Kronski. That fairy creature is probably on her way back to wherever she came from right now, with the lemur under her arm.

Artemis distracted himself from this shaky reasoning by concentrating on Kronski.

Something really should be done about that man.

A titanium Powerbook hummed gently on Artemis's fold-out tray. He woke the screen and opened his personal Internet browser program that he had written as a school project. Thanks to a powerful and illegal antenna in the jet's cargo bay he was able to pick up radio, television and Internet signals almost anywhere in the world.

Organizations like the Extinctionists live and die on their reputations, he thought. *It would be an amusing exercise to destroy Kronski's reputation using the power of the web.*

All it would take was some research and the placement of a little video on a few of the Net's more popular networking sites.

Twenty minutes later, Artemis Junior was putting the finishing touches to his project when Butler ducked through the cockpit door.

'Hungry?' asked the bodyguard. 'There's some hummus in the fridge and I made yoghurt and honey smoothies.'

Artemis embedded his video project on to the final website.

'No, thank you,' mumbled Artemis. 'I'm not hungry.'

'That will be the guilt gnawing at your soul,' said Butler candidly, helping himself from the fridge. 'Like a rat on an old bone.'

'Thank you for the simile, Butler, but what's done is done.'

'Did we have to leave Kronski the weapon?'

'Please, I put remote destruct charges in my hardware. Do you really think such an advanced race will leave their technology unprotected? I wouldn't be surprised if that gun is melting in Kronski's hands. I had to leave it as a sweetener.'

'I doubt the creature is melting.'

'Stop this, Butler. I made a deal and that's the end of it.'

Butler sat opposite him. 'Hmm. So you are governed by some sort of code now. Honour among criminals. Interesting. So, what's that you're cooking up on your computer?'

Artemis rubbed the tense spot on his neck. 'Please, Butler. All of this is for my father. You know it must be done.'

'One question,' said Butler, ripping the plastic from a cutlery set. 'Would your father want it to be done this way?'

Artemis did not answer, just sat and rubbed his neck.

Five minutes later, Butler took pity on the ten-year-old. 'I thought we might turn the plane around and give those strange creatures a little help. Fez Saïss airport has re-opened so we could be back there in a couple of hours.'

Artemis frowned. It was the right thing to do, but it was not on his agenda. Returning to Fez would not save his father.

Butler folded his paper plate in half, trapping the debris from his meal inside.

'Artemis, I would like to swing the jet around, and I intend to do that unless you instruct me not to. All you need to do is say the word.'

Artemis watched his bodyguard return to the cockpit, but said nothing.

MOROCCO

Le Domaine des Hommes was buzzing with limo-loads of Extinctionists coming in from the airport, each one wearing their hatred for animals on their sleeve, or on their heads or feet. Kronski spotted a lady sporting thigh-length ibex boots. Pyrenean, if he wasn't mistaken. And there was old Jeffrey Coontz-Meyers with his quagga-backed tweed jacket. And Contessa Irina Kostovich, her pale neck protected from the evening chill by a Honshu-wolf stole.

Kronski smiled and greeted each one warmly and most by name. Every year there were fewer newcomers to the ranks, but that would all change after the trial tonight. He skipped along towards the banquet hall.

The hall itself had been designed by Schiller-Haus in Munich, and was essentially a huge prefabricated kit which had arrived in containers and been erected by German specialists in less than four weeks. Incredible really. It was an impressive structure, more formal in appearance than the chalets, which was only proper, as serious business was conducted inside. Fair trials and then executions.

Fair trials, thought Kronski, and giggled.

The main doors were guarded by two burly Moroccan gentlemen in evening wear. Kronski had considered crested jumpsuits for the guards, but dismissed the idea as too Bond.

I am not Doctor No. I am Doctor No-Animals.

Kronski breezed past the guards, down a corridor carpeted with sumptuous local rugs and into a double-height banquet hall with a triple-glazed glass roof. The stars seemed close enough to reach out and capture.

The decor was a tasteful blend of classic and modern. Tasteful except for the gorilla-paw ashtrays dotted on each table and the row of elephant-foot champagne coolers on stands outside the kitchen doors. Kronski squeezed through the double doors, past a brushed-steel kitchen, to the walk-in freezer at the rear.

The creature sat flanked by three more guards. She was cuffed to a plastic baby chair borrowed from the compound's crèche. Her features were alert and sullen. Her weapon lay out of reach on a steel trolley.

If looks were bullets, thought Kronski, picking up the tiny weapon and weighing it on his palm, *I would be riddled.*

He pointed the weapon at a frozen ham hock hanging on a chain and pulled the tiny trigger. There was no kickback and no obvious flash of light, but the ham was now steaming and ready to serve.

Kronski raised the violet-coloured sunglasses that he wore day and night, to make sure his vision was accurate.

'My goodness,' he said in wonderment. 'This is quite a toy.'

He stamped on the steel floor, sending a bong reverberating through the chamber.

'No tunnelling out this time,' he announced. 'Not like the souq. Do you speak English, creature? Do you know what I am saying to you?'

The creature rolled her eyes.

I would answer you, her expression said, *but there is tape across my mouth.*

'And for good reason,' said Kronski, as though the sentence had been spoken aloud. 'We know all about your hypnotism tricks. And the invisibility.' He pinched her cheek, as one would a cute infant. 'Your skin feels almost human. What are you? A fairy, is that it?'

Another eye roll.

If eye-rolling were a sport, this creature would be a gold-medal winner, thought the doctor. *Well, perhaps silver medal. Gold would surely go to my ex-wife, who's no slacker in the eye-rolling department herself.*

Kronski addressed the guards.

'Has she moved?' he asked.

The men shook their heads. It was a stupid question. How could she move?

'Very well. Good. All proceeds according to my plan.'

ℛ•ⵚⵔⵔⵕⵓⵔ•⊖•◌•ℛⵔⵔⵔⵔ◬ℬⵗ•◌ⵕⵉ

Now Kronski rolled his own eyes. 'Listen to me. *All proceeds according to my plan.* That is *so* Doctor No. I should go and get myself some metal hands. What do you think, gentlemen?'

'Metal hands?' said the newest guard, unaccustomed to Kronski's rants. The other two were well aware that many of the doctor's questions were rhetorical, especially the ones about Andrew Lloyd Webber or James Bond.

Kronski ignored the new guy. He placed a finger on pursed lips for a moment, to communicate the importance of what he was about to say, then took a deep whistling breath through his nose.

'OK, gentlemen. Everyone listening? This evening couldn't be more important. The future of the entire organization depends on it. Everything must be totally perfect. Do not take your eyes off the prisoner and do not remove her restraints or gag. No one is to see her until the trial begins. I paid five million in diamonds for the privilege of a grand reveal, so no one gets in here but me. Understood?'

This was not a rhetorical question, though it took the new guy a moment to realize it.

'Yes, sir. Understood,' he blurted a fraction after the other two.

'If something does go wrong, then your final job of the evening will be burial duty.' Kronski winked at the new guard. 'And you know what they say, last in first out.'

The atmosphere at the banquet was a little jaded – until the food arrived. The thing about Extinctionists was that they were picky eaters. Some hated animals so much that they were vegetarians, which limited the menu somewhat. But this year Kronski had managed to poach a chef from a vegetarian restaurant in Edinburgh who could do things with a courgette that would make the most hardened carnivore weep.

They started with a subtle tomato-and-pepper soup in baby turtle shells. Then a light parcel of roast vegetables in pastry with a dollop of Greek yoghurt, served in a monkey-skull saucer. All very tasty, and by now the wine was relaxing the guests.

Kronski's stomach was so churned with nerves that he could not eat a single bite, which was most unusual for him. He hadn't felt this giddy since his very first banquet in Austin all those years ago.

I am on the verge of greatness. Soon my name will be mentioned in the same sentence as Bobby Jo Haggard or Jo Bobby Saggart. The great evangelist Extinctionists. Damon Kronski, the man who saved the world.

Two things would make this banquet the greatest ever held.

The entrée and the trial.

The entrée would delight everyone, meat eaters and vegetarians alike. The vegetarians could not eat it, but at least they could marvel at the artistry it took to prepare the dish.

Kronski tapped a small gong beside his place setting and stood to introduce the dish, as was the custom.

🐦︎⟩◐⊕•🐍︎𝑘•▢🐊⟩🐍🐍•⊕𝓢◐𝓑☎︎🦀𝑘•𝑘

'Ladies and gentlemen,' he began, 'let me tell you a story of extinction. In July 1889, Professor D. S. Jordan visited Twin Lakes in Colorado and published his discoveries in the 1891 *Bulletin of the United States Fish Commission*. He found what he declared to be a new species, the "yellowfin cutthroat". In his report Jordan described the fish as silvery olive with a broad lemon-yellow shade along the sides, lower fins bright golden yellow in life and a deep red dash on each side of the throat, hence the "cutthroat". Until about 1903, yellowfin cutthroats survived in Twin Lakes. The yellowfin died out soon after rainbow trout were introduced to Twin Lakes. Other trout interbred with the rainbows, but the yellowfins quickly disappeared and are now completely extinct.'

Nobody shed a tear. In fact there was a smattering of applause for the *E* word.

Kronski raised a hand. 'No, no. This is not a cause for joy. It is said that the yellowfin was a very tasty fish, with a particulary sweet flavour. What a pity we shall never taste it.' He paused dramatically. 'Or shall we . . .'

At the rear of the room, a large false wall slid aside to reveal a red velvet curtain. With great ceremony, Kronski pulled a remote control from his jacket and zapped the curtain, which drew back with a smooth swish. Behind it was an enormous trolley bearing what appeared to be a miniature glacier. Silver and steaming.

The guests sat forward, intrigued.

'What if there was a flash freeze over a hundred years ago in Twin Lakes.'

A twittering began among the diners.

No.

Surely not.

Impossible.

'What if a frozen chunk of lake was trapped by a landslide deep in an uncharted crevasse and kept solid by near-zero currents.'

Then that would mean . . .

Inside that chunk . . .

'What if that chunk surfaced a mere six weeks ago on the land of my good friend Tommy Kirkenhazard. One of our own faithful members.'

Tommy stood to take a bow, waving his Texas-grey-wolf stetson. Though his teeth were smiling, his eyes were shooting daggers at Kronski. It was obvious to the entire room that there was bad blood between the two.

'Then it would be possible, outrageously expensive and difficult but possible, to transport that chunk of ice here. A chunk that contains a sizeable shoal of yellowfin cutthroat trout.' Kronski drew breath to allow this information to sink in. 'Then we, dear friends, could be the first people to eat yellowfin in a hundred years.'

This prospect even had a few of the vegetarians salivating.

'Watch, Extinctionists. Watch and be amazed.'

Kronski clicked his fingers and a dozen kitchen staff wheeled the ponderous trolley into the centre of the banqueting area, where it rested on a steel grille. The workers then stripped off their uniforms to reveal monkey costumes underneath.

Have I gone over the top with the monkey rigs? Kronski wondered. *Is it just too Broadway?*

But a quick survey of his guests assured him that they remained enthralled.

The kitchen staff were actually trained circus acrobats from one of the Cirque du Soleil knock-offs touring north Africa. They were only too glad to take a few days out from their schedule to put on this private show for the Extinctionists.

They swarmed up the huge ice-block, anchoring themselves on with ropes, crampons or grappling hooks, and began demolishing it with chainsaws, flaming swords and flamethrowers, all produced seemingly from nowhere.

It was a spectacular indulgence. Ice flew, showering the guests, and the buzz of machinery was deafening.

Quickly the shoal of yellowfin poked through the blue murk of ice. They hung wide-eyed and frozen in mid-turn, their bodies caught by the flash freeze.

What a way to go, thought Kronski. *With absolutely no inkling. Wonderful.*

The performers began carving the fish in blocks from the ice, and each one was passed down to one of a dozen line cooks who had appeared from the side doors, wheeling gas burners. Each individual block was slid into a heated colander to steam off excess ice, then the fish were expertly filleted and fried in olive oil with a selection of chunky-cut vegetables and a crushed clove of garlic.

227

For the vegetarians there was a Champagne mushroom risotto, though Kronski did not anticipate many takers. The non-meat eaters would accept the fish just to stab it.

The meal was a huge success and the level of delighted chatter rose to fill the hall.

Kronski managed to eat half a fillet, in spite of his nerves. *Delicious. Exquisite.*

They think that was the highlight, he thought. *They ain't seen nothing yet.*

After coffee, when the Extinctionists were loosening their cummerbunds or turning fat cigars for an even burn, Kronski instructed his staff to set up the courtroom.

They responded with the speed and expertise of a Formula One pit-team, as well they should after three months of being whipped into shape. Literally. The workers swarmed across the grid where the melted ice sloshed below like a disturbed swimming pool, a few stray yellowfins floating on the surface. They covered this section of floor and exposed a second pit, this one lined with steel and covered with scorch marks.

Two podiums and a dock were wheeled into the centre of the hall, taking the place of the ice-trolley. The podiums had computers on their swivel tops, and the wooden dock was occupied by a cage. The cage's resident was masked by a curtain of leopard skin.

The diners' chatter ceased as they held their breath for the big reveal. This was the moment everyone was waiting for, these millionaires and billionaires paying through the nose for a few moments of ultimate power: holding the fate of an entire species in their hands. Showing the rest of the planet who was boss. The guests did not notice the dozen or so sharpshooters placed discreetly on the upper terrace in case the creature on trial displayed any new magical powers. There was little chance of a subterranean rescue as the entire hall was built on a foundation of steel rods and concrete.

Kronski milked the moment, rising slowly from his seat, sauntering across to the prosecutor's podium.

He steepled his fingers, allowing the tension to build, then began his presentation.

'Every year we put a rare animal on trial.'

There were a few hoots from the audience, which Kronski waved away good-naturedly.

'A *real* trial where the host prosecutes and one of you lucky people gets to defend. The idea is simple. If you can convince a jury of your unprejudiced peers . . .'

More hooting.

'. . . that the creature in this cage contributes positively to human existence on this planet, then we will free the creature. This, believe it or not, did happen once in 1983. A little before my time, but I am assured it actually happened. If the defence counsel's peers are not convinced of the animal's usefulness, then I press this button.' And here Kronski's bulbous fingers twiddled playfully with an oversized red button on his remote control. 'And the animal drops from its cage into the pit, passing the laser beam that activates the gas-powered flame jets. *Voilà*: instant cremation.

'Allow me to demonstrate. Indulge me, it's a new pit. I've been testing it all week.'

He nodded at one of the staff, who yanked up a section of the grid with a steel hook. Kronski then picked a melon from a fruit platter and tossed it into the pit. There was a beep, followed by an eruption of blue-white flame gouts from nozzles ranged around the pit walls. The melon was burned to black floating crisps.

The display drew an impressed round of applause, but not everyone appreciated Kronski's grandstanding.

Jeffrey Coontz-Meyers cupped both hands round his mouth. 'Come on, Damon. What have we got tonight? Not another monkey. Every year it's monkeys.'

Generally interruptions would irritate Kronski, but not tonight. On this night all hectoring, however witty, would be swept from people's memories the second that curtain was drawn aside.

'No, Jeffrey, not another monkey. What if . . .'

Jeffrey Coontz-Meyers groaned vocally. 'Please, no more *what ifs*. We had half a dozen with the fish. Show us the blasted creature.'

Kronski bowed. 'As you wish.'

He thumbed a button on his remote control and a large-view screen descended from the rafters, covering the back wall. Another button pushed and the curtain concealing the caged creature swished smoothly to one side.

Holly was revealed, cuffed to the baby chair, her eyes darting and furious.

At first the main reaction was puzzlement.

Was it a little girl?

It's just a child.

Has Kronski gone mad? I knew he sang to himself, but this?

Then the Extinctionists' eyes were drawn to the screen, which was displaying a feed from a camera clamped to the cage.

Oh, my Lord. Her ears. Look at her ears.

She's not human.

What is that? What is it?

Tommy Kirkenhazard stood. 'This better not be a hoax, Damon. Or we'll string you up.'

'Two points,' said Kronski softly. 'First, this is no hoax. I have unearthed an undiscovered species – as a matter of fact, I believe it to be a fairy. Second, if this were a hoax, you would not be stringing anyone up, Kirkenhazard. My men would cut you down before you could wave that ridiculous hat of yours and shout *yee-haw*.'

Sometimes it was good to send a shiver down people's spines. Remind them where the power was.

'Of course, your scepticism is to be expected, welcomed in fact. To put your minds at rest, I will need a volunteer from the audience. How about you, Tommy? How's that backbone of yours?'

Tommy Kirkenhazard gulped down half a glass of whiskey to bolster his nerves, then made his way to the cage.

Good performance, Tommy, thought Kronski. *It's almost as if we hadn't arranged this little confrontation to give me a bit more credibility.*

Kirkenhazard stood as close to Holly as he dared, then reached in slowly to tweak her ear.

'My saints, it's no fake. This is the real deal.' He stood back and the truth of what was happening filled his face with joy. 'We got ourselves a fairy.'

Kirkenhazard rushed across to Kronski's podium, pumping his hand, clapping his back.

And so my biggest critic is converted. The rest will follow like sheep. Useful animals, sheep.

Kronski silently congratulated himself.

'I will prosecute the fairy, as is the tradition,' Kronski told the crowd. 'But who will defend? Which unlucky member will draw the black ball? Who will it be?'

Kronski nodded at the maître d'.

'Bring the bag.'

Like many ancient organizations, the Extinctionists were bound by tradition, and one of these traditions was that the creature on trial could be defended by any member of the assembly and, if no member were willing, one would be chosen by lottery. A bag of white balls, with one black. The spherical equivalent of the short straw.

'No need for the bag,' said a voice. 'I will defend the creature.'

Heads turned to locate the speaker. It was a slender young man with a goatee and piercing blue eyes. He was wearing tinted glasses and a lightweight linen suit.

Kronski had noticed him earlier, but could not put a name to the face, which disturbed him.

'And you are?' he asked, while swivelling his laptop so that the built-in camera was aimed at this stranger.

The young man smiled. 'Why don't we give your identification software a moment to whisper the answer to you.'

Kronski thumbed *enter*, the computer captured an image and five seconds later plucked membership details from the Extinctionists' file.

Malachy Pasteur. Young French-Irish heir to an abattoir empire. Made a sizeable donation to the Extinctionists' coffers. His first conference. Like all the attendees, Pasteur was thoroughly vetted before his invitation was issued. A valuable addition to the ranks.

Kronski was all charm.

'Master Pasteur, we are delighted to welcome you to Morocco. But, tell me, why would you wish to defend this creature? Her fate is almost certainly sealed.'

The young man walked briskly to the podium. 'I enjoy a challenge. It is a mental exercise.'

'Defending *vermin* is an exercise?'

'*Especially* vermin,' retorted Pasteur, lifting the lid on his laptop. 'It is easy to defend a servile, useful animal like the common cow. But this? This will be a hard-fought battle.'

'A pity to be crushed in battle so young,' said Kronski, his lower lip hanging with mock sympathy.

Pasteur drummed his fingers on the podium. 'I have always liked your style, Doctor Kronski. Your commitment to the ideals of Extinctionism. For years I have followed your career, since I was a boy in Dublin, in fact. Lately, however, I feel that the organization has lost its way, and I am not the only one with this notion.'

Kronski ground his teeth. So that was it. A naked challenge to his leadership.

'Be careful what you say, Pasteur. You tread on dangerous ground.'

Pasteur glanced at the floor below him, where ice water still sloshed in the pit beneath. 'You mean I could sleep with the fishes. You would kill me, Doctor? A mere boy. I don't think that would bolster your credibility much.'

He's right, fumed Kronski. *I can't kill him; I must win this trial.*

The doctor forced his mouth to smile. 'I don't kill *humans*,' he said. 'Just animals. Like the animal in this cage.'

Kronski's many supporters applauded, but that still left many silent.

I was wrong to come here, Kronski realized. *It is too remote. Nowhere for private jets to land. Next year I will find somewhere in Europe. I will announce the move as soon as I crush this whelp.*

'Allow me to explain the rules,' continued Kronski, thinking, *Explaining the rules puts me in charge, giving me the upper hand, psychologically speaking.*

'No need,' said Pasteur brusquely. 'I have read several transcripts. The prosecutor puts his case, the defender puts his case. A few minutes of lively debate, then each table votes. Simple. Can we please proceed, Doctor? No one here appreciates their time being wasted.'

Clever, young man. Putting yourself on the same side as the jury. No matter. I know these people and they will never acquit a beast, no matter how pretty she is.

'Very well. We shall proceed.' He selected a document on his desktop. His opening statement. Kronski knew it by heart, but it was comforting to have the words easily accessible.

'People say that we Extinctionists hate animals,' began Kronski. 'But this is not the case. We do not hate poor dumb animals, rather we love humans. We love humans and will do whatever it takes to ensure that we, as a race, survive for as long as possible. This planet has limited resources and I, for one, say we should hoard them for ourselves. Why should humans starve when dumb animals grow fat? Why should humans freeze when beasts lie toasty warm in their coats of fur?'

Malachy Pasteur made a noise somewhere between a cough and a chuckle. 'Really, Doctor Kronski, I have read several variations on this speech. Every year, it seems, you trot out the same simplistic arguments. Can we please focus on the creature before us tonight?'

A tittering ripple spread among the banquet guests, and Kronski had to struggle to contain his temper. It seemed he had a battle on his hands. Very well, then.

'Most amusing, boy. I was going to take it easy on you, but now the gloves are off.'

'We are delighted to hear it.'

⊛ ☝ •⊛ ♫ •¡♫ •◊ ℱ □ ⊛ ☉ ♢ δ •¡♫ ℛ ♢

We? We? Pasteur was swinging the Extinctionists his way without them even knowing it.

Kronski summoned every last drop of charisma from inside himself, flashing back to his youth, to those long summer days spent watching his evangelist daddy whip up the crowds inside a canvas tent.

He raised his arms high, each finger bent back until the tendons strained.

'This is not what we are about, people,' he thundered. 'We did not travel all this way for some petty verbal sparring. *This* is what the Extinctionists are about.' Kronski pointed a rigid finger at Holly. 'Ridding our planet of creatures like this.'

Kronski shot a sideways glance at Pasteur, who was leaning, chin on hands, a bemused look on his face. Standard opposition behaviour.

'We have a new species here, friends. A *dangerous* species. It can make itself invisible, it can hypnotize through speech. It was *armed*.'

And, to much oohing from the crowd, Kronski drew forth Holly's Neutrino handgun from his pocket.

'Do any of us wish to face a future where this could be pointed in our faces? Do we? The answer, I think, is clearly no. Now, I'm not going to pretend that this is the last one of its kind. I feel certain that there are thousands of these fairies, or aliens, or whatever, all around us. But does that mean we should grovel and release this little creature? I say no. I say we send a message. Execute one and the rest will know we mean business. The governments of the world despise us now, but tomorrow they will come banging down our door for guidance.' Time for the big finish. 'We are Extinctionists, and our time is now!'

It was a good speech and drew wave after wave of applause, which Pasteur rode out with the same bemused expression.

Kronski accepted the applause with a boxer's rolling of the shoulders, then nodded towards the opposite podium.

'The floor is yours, boy.'

Pasteur straightened and cleared his throat . . .

. . . Artemis straightened and cleared his throat. The fake beard glued to his chin itched like crazy, but he resisted the impulse to scratch it. In a fair arena, he would destroy Kronski's arguments in about five seconds, but this was not a fair arena, or even a sane one. These people were bloodthirsty, jaded billionaires, using their money to buy illicit excitement. Murder was just another service that could be purchased. He needed to handle this crowd carefully. Push the right buttons. First of all he had to establish himself as one of them.

'When I was young, and the family wintered in South Africa, my grandfather would tell me stories of a time when people had the right attitude towards animals. *We kill 'em when it suits us*, he said to me. *When it serves our purposes.* This is what the Extinctionists used to be about. A species was not *protected* unless we humans benefited from its survival.

We kill when it *benefits* us. If an animal is using the planet's resources and not directly contributing to our health, safety and comfort, we wipe it out. Simple as that. This was an ideal worth fighting for. Worth killing for. But this . . .' Artemis pointed at the pit below him and Holly in her cage. 'This is a circus. This is an insult to the memory of our ancestors, who gave their time and gold to the Extinctionists' cause.'

Artemis worked hard on his eye contact, connecting with as many people as possible in the audience. Lingering for a moment with everyone.

'We have an opportunity to learn from this creature. We owe it to our predecessors to find out if she can contribute to our coffers. If this is in reality a fairy, then who knows what magic it possesses. Magic that could be yours. If we kill this *fairy*, we will never know what unimaginable wealth dies with it.'

Artemis bowed. He had made his point. It would not be enough to sway the bloodthirsty Extinctionists, he knew, but it might be enough to make Kronski feel a little less cocky.

The doctor was waving his hands before the echo of Artemis's voice faded.

'How many times must we listen to this argument?' he wondered. 'Master Pasteur accuses me of repeating myself while he repeats the tired argument of every defence counsel we have ever listened to.' Kronski tapped his lips in horror. 'Ooh, let us not kill the creature for it is potentially the source of all our power and wealth. I remember spending a fortune on a sea slug that was supposed to cure arthritis. All we got was very expensive goo. This is all supposition.'

'But this creature is magical,' objected Artemis, banging the podium with a fist. 'We have all heard how she can turn invisible. Even now her mouth is taped so she cannot hypnotize us. Imagine the power we could wield if we were to unlock the secrets of these gifts. If nothing else, they would better prepare us to deal with the rest of her kind.'

Kronski's main problem was that he agreed with much of his opposition's argument. It made perfect sense to save the creature and tease her secrets from her, but he could not afford to lose this argument. If he did, he might as well hand over the leadership.

'We have tried to interrogate her. Our best men tried and she told us nothing.'

'It is difficult to talk with a taped mouth,' Artemis noted drily.

Kronski drew himself to his full height, lowering the timbre of his voice for effect. 'The human race faces its most deadly enemy and you want to cosy up to it. That is not how we Extinctionists do things. If there is a threat, we wipe it out. That is how it has always been.'

This brought a roar of approval from the crowd, bloodlust trumping logic every time. Several members were on their feet, hollering. They had had enough of argument and wanted some action.

Kronski's face was flushed with victory.

᚛᚛ • ᚐᚑᚁᚑᚐᚁ᚛ • ᚛ᚐᚑ • ᚑ᚛᚛᚜ • ᚐᚐᚑᚁᚐᚐ

He thinks it's over, thought Artemis. *Poor man*, and then, *This beard really itches.*

He waited calmly until the furore had trailed away, then came out from behind the podium.

'I was hoping to spare you this, Doctor,' he said. 'Because I respect you so much.'

Kronski flapped his lips. 'Spare me what, Master Pasteur?'

'You know what. I think you have pulled the wool over everyone's eyes long enough.'

Kronski was not in the least worried. The boy was beaten and everything else was was just irritating chatter. Still, why not let Pasteur dig a hole for himself?

'And what wool would that be?'

'Are you certain you want me to continue?'

Kronski's teeth glittered when he smiled. 'Oh, absolutely certain.'

'As you wish,' said Artemis, approaching the dock. 'This creature was not our original defendant. Up until yesterday we had a lemur. Not quite a monkey, Mister Kirkenhazard, but close enough. I *say* we had a lemur, but in truth we almost had a lemur. It went missing at the pick-up. Then, and this is important, then we were sold this creature by the *same* boy who almost sold us the lemur, undoubtedly paid for from Extinctionists' funds. Does anyone else think this is a little off? I do. This boy keeps his lemur and sells us a supposed fairy.'

Kronski was not so cocky now. This Pasteur fellow had a lot of information.

240

'*Supposed* fairy?'

'That's right. Supposed. We have only your word for it, and of course that of Mister Kirkenhazard, who apparently is your worst enemy. Nobody is falling for that ruse, I assure you.'

'Examine the thing yourself,' blurted Kronski, glossing over the Kirkenhazard accusation. 'This is an easy argument to win.'

'Thank you, Doctor,' said Artemis. 'I believe I shall.'

Artemis approached the cage. This was the tricky part as it required sleight of hand and coordination, which were the elements in every plan that he usually left to Butler.

His pocket bulged slightly with a couple of adhesive Nu-skin bandages taken from Mulch's medi-kit. He had told the security guard they were nicotine patches and so he had been allowed bring them through to the banquet. The bandages' adhesive was activated by skin contact and they moulded themselves to the contours they were applied to, assuming the colour and texture of the surrounding skin.

Artemis's fingers hovered over his pocket, but it was not yet time to touch a bandage. It would simply stick to his own hand. Instead, he reached into his other pocket for the phone he had stolen from the Bentley back at Rathdown Park.

'This phone is invaluable to me,' he told the Extinctionists. 'It's a little bulkier than other phones, but that is because I have been installing add-ons for years. It is an amazing thing, really. I can stream television, watch movies, check my stocks, all the standard stuff. But I also have an X-ray camera and display. Just give me a second.' Artemis pressed a few buttons, linking the phone by Bluetooth to the laptops and from there to the large-view screen.

'Ah, here we are,' Artemis said, passing the phone in front of his hand. On screen an arrangement of phalanges, metacarpals and carpals stood out darkly inside a pale foam of flesh. 'You see the bones of my hand quite clearly. This is a very good projection system you have, Doctor Kronski. I congratulate you.'

Kronski's smile was as fake as the congratulations had been.

'Do you have a point, Pasteur, or are you just showing us how clever you are?'

'Oh, I have a point, Doctor. And the point is that were it not for the wideness of the brow and the pointed ears, this creature would seem remarkably like a little girl.'

Kronski snorted. 'A pity about the ears and brow. But for them you would have an argument.'

'Precisely,' said Artemis, and passed the phone before Holly's face. On screen, he played a short movie file he had constructed back in the shuttle. It showed Holly's skull with dark dense shapes on temples and ears.

'Implants,' crowed Artemis. 'Clearly the result of surgery. This *fairy* is a clever fake. You have tried to dupe us, Kronski.'

Kronski's denials were lost in the roar of the crowd. The Extinctionists surged to their feet, decrying this despicable con-job.

'You lied to me, Damon!' shouted Tommy Kirkenhazard, with something like anguish. 'To *me*.'

'Put *him* in the pit,' called Contessa Irina Kostovich, her face as feral as that of the Honshu wolf on her shoulder. 'Make *Kronski* extinct. He deserves it for dragging us here.'

Kronski upped the volume on his podium mike. 'This is ridiculous. If you have been tricked, then so have I. No! I will not believe it. This boy, this Pasteur, is lying. My fairy is real. Just give me a chance to prove it.'

'I have not finished, Doctor,' cried Artemis, stepping boldly to the dock. In both hands he held a Nu-skin patch, slipped into his palms during the confusion. He could feel pinpricks of heat on his flesh as the adhesive was activated. He had to act quickly or his plans would be reduced to two flesh-coloured pads on his own hands.

'These ears do not seem right to me. And your friend Mister Kirkenhazard was most gentle with them.'

Artemis scrunched one Nu-skin patch into a rough cone, sealing the adhesive on itself. He thrust the other hand through the bars and made a great show of tugging on the tip, while in reality spreading the second bandage over Holly's ear. Covering the entire tip and most of the auricle.

'It's coming away,' he grunted, making sure to mask the cage's camera with his forearm. 'I have it.'

Seconds later the bandage was dry and one of Holly's ears was totally obscured. Artemis looked her in the eye and winked.

Ө•ᏒᎩ•ꝰ)◊•ᏻᏜᎠ)•ᏒᏖᎾ➤•ᏄᎾᏇᏸᏜᏒᏇᏜᏒ

Play along, the wink said. *I will get you out of this.*

At least Artemis hoped this was what his wink communicated and not something like *any chance of another kiss later?*

Back to business.

'It's a fake,' called Artemis, holding high the crumpled flesh-coloured bandage. 'It came off in my hand.'

Holly obligingly presented her profile to the web cam. No more pointed ear.

Outrage was the dominant reaction from the Extinctionists.

Kronski had tricked them all or, even worse, he had been bamboozled by a boy.

Artemis held the supposed fake ear aloft, squeezing it as though he were strangling a poisonous snake.

'Is this the man we want to lead us? Has Doctor Kronski displayed sound judgement in this case?'

Artemis threw the 'ear' to the ground. 'And *supposedly* this creature can hypnotize us all. I rather think her mouth is covered so she cannot speak.'

With one sharp movement, he ripped the tape from Holly's mouth. She winced and shot Artemis a dour glare, but then quickly dissolved into tears, playing the part of human victim to perfection.

'I didn't want to do it,' she sobbed.

'Do what?' Artemis prompted.

'Doctor Kronski took me from the orphanage.'

Artemis raised an eyebrow. *The orphanage?* Holly was ad-libbing.

'He told me if I had the implants, then I could live in America. After the operation I changed my mind, but the doctor wouldn't let me go.'

'An orphanage,' said Artemis. 'Why, that's bordering on the unbelievable.'

Holly's chin dropped. 'He said he'd kill me if I told.'

Artemis was outraged. 'He said he'd kill you. And this is the man steering our organization. A man who hunts humans as well as animals.' He pointed an accusing finger at a bewildered Kronski. 'You, sir, are worse than the creatures we all despise, and I demand you release this poor girl.'

Kronski was finished and he knew it. But something could still be salvaged from this mess. He still had the group's account numbers and he was the only one with the combination to the compound safe. He could be out of this place in two hours with enough riches to last a few years. All he had to do was somehow stop this Pasteur boy hamming it up.

And then he remembered. Ham!

'And what about this?' he shouted, brandishing Holly's gun. 'I suppose this is fake too.'

The Extinctionists drew back. Cowering behind their seats.

'Absolutely,' sneered Artemis. 'A child's toy. Nothing more.'

'Would you stake your life on it?'

Artemis appeared to hesitate. 'N-no need for dramatics, Doctor. Your cause is lost. Accept it.'

'No,' snapped Kronski. 'If the gun is real, then the creature is real. And if she is not real, as you insist, then you have nothing to fear.'

Artemis summoned his courage. 'Very well, do your worst.' He stood squarely before the tiny needle barrel, offering his chest.

'You are about to die, Pasteur,' said Kronski, without much sympathy.

'Perhaps I would be, if you could squeeze your chubby finger into the trigger guard,' said Artemis, almost as if he were goading the doctor into action.

'To hell with you, then!' barked Kronski, and pulled the trigger.

Nothing much happened. A spark and a slight hum from the inner workings.

'It's broken,' gasped the doctor.

'You don't say,' said Artemis, who had remote-destructed the Neutrino's charge pack from the shuttle.

Kronski raised his palms. 'OK, boy. OK. Give me a moment to think.'

'Just let the girl go, Doctor. Save a shred of dignity. We don't execute humans.'

'I am in charge here. I just need a second to gather myself. This wasn't supposed to happen. This is not how she said it would go . . .'

The doctor rested his elbows on the lectern, rubbing his eyes beneath the round tinted spectacles.

How she said it would go? thought Artemis. Were there unseen forces at work here?

While Artemis was puzzling and Kronski's world collapsed around his ample shoulders, mobile phones began to ring in the banqueting hall. A lot of people were receiving messages all of a sudden. In moments the room rang with a discordant symphony of beeps, brrrs and polyphonic tunes.

Kronski ignored this strange development, but Artemis was anxious. He had things under control now and did not need anything to redress the scales, or for that matter tip Kronski over the edge.

The reactions to the incoming messages were a mixture of shock and glee.

Oh, my God. Is this true? Is it real?

Play it again. Turn up the volume.

I don't believe this. Kronski, you fool.

That's the last straw. We are a joke. The Extinctionists are finished.

Artemis realized that all these messages were in fact the same message. Someone had an Extinctionists' database and was sending them all a video.

Artemis's own phone trilled gently. Of course it would, he had put his fake identity on every Extinctionist database he could find. And as his phone was still linked to the giant screen, the video mail began to play automatically.

Artemis recognized the scene immediately. The leather souq. And the main player was Kronski, standing on one leg, squealing with a high-pitched ruptured-balloon intensity. Comical was not the word for it. Ridiculous, farcical and pathetic were words that came close. One thing was certain, having seen the video, no one in their right mind could respect this man ever again, much less follow his lead.

While the video played, a short message scrolled below the picture.

Here we see Doctor Damon Kronski, the president of the Extinctionists, displaying surprising balance for a man his size. This reporter has learned that Kronski turned against animals when he was mauled by an escaped koala at one of his politician father's rallies in Cleveland. Witnesses to the mauling say that young Damon 'squealed so sharp he coulda cut glass'. A talent the good doctor does not seem to have lost. Squeal, baby, squeal.

Artemis sighed. *I did this*, he realized. *It's just the kind of thing I would do.*

At another time, he would have appreciated this touch, but not now. Not when he was so close to freeing Holly.

Speaking of Holly.

'Artemis, get me out of here,' she hissed.

'Yes, of course. Time to go.'

Artemis rifled his pockets for a handy wipe. Inside the wipe were three long, coarse hairs donated by Mulch Diggums. Dwarf hairs are actually antennae that dwarfs use to navigate in dark tunnels, and have been adapted by the resourceful race to serve as skeleton keys. No doubt, Holly's Omnitool would have been handier, but Artemis could not risk losing that to security. The wipe had kept the hairs moist and pliable until they were needed.

Artemis removed the first hair, blew a speck of moisture

from its tip and inserted it into the cage lock, working it through the cogs. As soon as he felt the hair harden in his fingers, he turned the makeshift key and the door sprang open.

'Thank you, Mulch,' he whispered, then went to work on Holly's centrally locked cuffs. The third hair would not even be needed. In seconds Holly was free and rubbing her wrists.

'Orphanage?' said Artemis. 'You don't think that was overdoing it?'

'Boo hoo,' said Holly briskly. 'Let's just get back to the shuttle.'

It was not to be that straightforward.

Kronski was being herded into a corner by a group of Extinctionists. They harangued and even prodded and poked the doctor, ignoring his arguments, while overhead the video message played again and again.

Oops, thought Artemis, closing his phone.

Inevitably perhaps, Kronski cracked. He batted his tormentors aside like bowling pins, clearing a circle of breathing space for himself, then, panting, he pulled a walkie-talkie from its clip on his belt.

'Secure the area,' he wheezed into the device. 'Use all necessary force.'

Even though Le Domaine des Hommes security guards were technically working for the Extinctionists, their loyalties lay with the man who paid their salaries. That man was Damon Kronski. He might dress like a demented peacock and have the manners of a desert dog, but he knew the combination to the safe and paid the wages on time.

The sharpshooters on the upper terrace sent a few warning shots over the crowd's head, which caused utter pandemonium.

'Lock the building down,' said Kronski into the walkie-talkie. 'I need time to gather my funds. Ten thousand dollars in cash for every man who stands by me.'

There was no need for further incentive. Ten thousand dollars was two years' wages to these men.

Doors and shutters were slammed down and manned by burly guards, each one brandishing a rifle or a custom-made Moroccan nimcha sword with rhino grip that Kronski had had made for the security team.

The spooked Extinctionists bolted towards bathrooms or alcoves, anywhere that might have a window. They frantically punched numbers into their phones, screaming for help from anyone, anywhere.

A few were more resourceful. Tommy Kirkenhazard pulled out a ceramic handgun he had smuggled in under his hat and took a few potshots at the upper terrace from behind a heavy teak bar. He was answered by a volley from above, with shattered bottles, mirrors and glasses sending slivers flying like arrowheads.

With a straight-fingered jab to the solar plexus, a tall Asian man quickly disarmed a door guard.

'This way!' he called, flinging the fire door wide. The portal was quickly jammed with Extinctionist torsos.

◊◌✸☠•❗️🅱️◌✸🅱️◌ ☾◊☠ • ☾🅱️✦ •◌🅱️🆓•◡

Artemis and Holly sheltered behind the cage, watching for a way out.

'Can you shield?'

Holly twisted her chin and one arm rippled out of sight. 'I'm low on juice. I have just about enough for a minute or two. I've been saving it.'

Artemis scowled. 'You are always low on juice. Didn't Number One fill you up with his signature magic?'

'Maybe if your bodyguard hadn't plugged me with a dart – twice. Maybe if I hadn't had to heal you at Rathdown Park. And maybe if I hadn't been shielding in the souq, trying to find your monkey.'

'Lemur,' said Artemis. 'At least we saved Jayjay.'

Holly ducked as a hail of glass shot over her head. 'My goodness, Artemis. You sound like you actually care about an animal. Nice beard by the way.'

'Thank you. Now, do you think you could shield for long enough to disarm those two guards on the kitchen door behind us?'

Holly sized the two men up. Both had shotguns and were radiating enough malevolence to ripple the air. 'Shouldn't be a problem.'

'Good. Do it quietly. We don't want another bottleneck. If we do get separated, let's meet somewhere close. At the souq.'

'OK,' said Holly, vibrating into invisibility.

A second later Artemis felt a hand on his shoulder, and heard a disembodied voice in his ear.

'You came for me,' whispered Holly. 'Thank you.'

Then the hand was gone.

All magic has a price. When fairies shield, they sacrifice fine motor skills and clear thought. It is infinitely more difficult to do a jigsaw when your body is vibrating faster than a hummingbird's wings, even if your brain could stop rattling for long enough to focus on the puzzle.

In the LEP Academy, Holly had picked up a tip from an Atlantean gym coach. It really helped to beat the shield-shakes if you sucked your lower abdominals in and up, strengthening your core. It gave you something to focus on and held your torso a little tighter.

Holly practised the exercise as she crossed the banquet floor towards the kitchen. When a frantic, butter-knife-wielding Extinctionist missed her by a shade, she thought that sometimes being invisible was more dangerous than being in plain sight.

The two guards on the door were actually growling at anyone who ventured too close. They were big, even for humans, and Holly was glad that no fine motor skill would be called for. Two quick jabs into the nerve cluster above the knee should be plenty to bring these guys down.

Simple, thought Holly, then, *I shouldn't have thought that. Whenever you think that, something goes wrong.*

Of course she was dead right.

Someone started firing on Kronski's guards. Silver darts

streaked through the air, then punctured skin with a sickening thunk.

Holly knew instinctively who the shooter was, then her suspicions were confirmed when she spotted a familiar silhouette anchored in the roof beams.

Butler!

The bodyguard was draped in a desert blanket, but Holly identified him from the shape of his head and also from his unmistakable shooting position: left elbow cocked out a little more than most marksmen preferred.

Young Artemis sent him back to clear a path for us, she realized. *Or maybe Butler made the decision himself.*

Whichever it was, Butler was not helping as much as he hoped. With the guards dropping at the fire exit, the Extinctionists were piling over their fallen captors, desperate to be free of this building.

Caged Extinctionists, thought Holly. *I'm sure Artemis appreciates that irony.*

Just as Holly drew back her fists, the two guards at the kitchen door clutched their necks and pitched forward, unconscious before they hit the floor.

Nice shooting. Two shots in under a second from eighty metres out. With darts too, which are about as accurate as wet sponges.

She was not the only one to notice the unguarded door. A dozen hysterical Extinctionists rushed the portal, screaming like rock-band fans.

We need to exit this building. Now.

⬠⏚⌇⏛⎔⟊⟆⫯•⎔⎔⎔⬡•⊙•⌇⟆⏚⊙⊘•⬢⊙⟆⬢•

Holly turned towards Artemis, but he was lost in a clump of advancing Extinctionists.

He must be somewhere in there, she thought, then she was pinned by the mob, borne aloft and into the kitchen.

'Artemis,' she called, completely forgetting that she was still invisible. 'Artemis!'

But he was nowhere to be seen. The world was a melee of elbows and torsos. Sweat and screams. Voices were in her ears and ragged breath on her face, and by the time she had disentangled herself from the pack, the banquet hall was virtually deserted. A few stragglers, but no Artemis.

The souq, she thought. *I will find him in the souq.*

Artemis tensed himself to run. As soon as Holly took the guards out of commission, he would sprint as fast as he could and pray that he didn't trip and fall. Imagine, to endure all of this only to be defeated by a lack of coordination. Butler would be sure to say *I told you so* when they met in the afterlife.

Suddenly the pandemonium level jumped a few notches, and the screaming of the Extinctionists reminded Artemis of Rathdown Park's panicked animals.

Caged Extinctionists, he thought. *Oh, the irony.*

The kitchen-door guards fell, clutching their throats.

Nice work, Captain.

Artemis bent low, like a sprinter waiting for the gun, then catapulted himself from his hiding place behind the dock.

Kronski hit him broadside with his full weight, tumbling them both through the railings into the dock. Artemis landed heavily on the baby chair and it collapsed underneath him, one of its arms raking along his side.

'This is all your fault,' squealed Kronski. 'This was supposed to be the best night of my life.'

Artemis felt himself being smothered. His mouth and nose were jammed by sweat-soaked purple material.

He intends to kill me, thought Artemis. *I have pushed him too far.*

There was no time for planning and, even if there were time, this was not one of those situations where a handy mathematical theorem could be found to get Artemis out of his predicament. There was only only one thing to do: lash out.

So Artemis kicked, punched and gouged. He buried his knee in Kronski's ample stomach and blinded him with his fists.

All very superficial blows which had little lasting effect, except one. Artemis's right heel brushed against Kronski's chest. Kronski didn't even feel it. But the heel connected briefly with the oversized button on the remote control in the doctor's pocket, releasing the dock trapdoor.

The second his brain registered the loss of back support, Artemis knew what had happened.

I am dead, he realized. *Sorry, Mother.*

Artemis fell bodily into the pit, breaking the laser beam with his elbow. There was a beep and half a second later the pit was filled with blue-white flame that blasted black scorch marks in the walls.

Nothing could have survived.

Kronski braced himself against the dock rails, perspiration dripping from the tip of his nose into the pit, evaporating on the way down.

Do I feel bad about what just happened? he asked himself, aware that psychologists recommended facing trauma head-on in order to avoid stress in later life.

No, he found. *I don't. In fact, I feel as though a weight has been lifted from my shoulders.*

Kronski raised himself up with a great creaking and cracking of knees.

Now, where's the other one? he wondered. *I still have some weight to lose.*

Artemis saw the flames blossom around him. He saw his skin glow blue with their light and heard their raw roar, then he was through, unscathed.

Impossible.

Obviously not. *Obviously*, these flames had more bark about them than bite.

Holograms?

The pit floor yielded beneath his weight with a hiss of pneumatics, and Artemis found himself in a sub-chamber looking up at heavy steel doors swinging closed above him.

The view from inside a swing-top bin.

A very high-tech swing-top bin, with expanding gel hinges. Fairy design, without a doubt.

Artemis remembered something Kronski had said earlier.

This is not how she said it would go . . .

She . . . she.

Fairy design. Endangered species. What fairy had been harvesting lemur brain fluid even before the Spelltropy epidemic?

Artemis paled. Not her. Please not her.

What do I have to do? he thought. *How many times must I save the world from this lunatic?*

He scrambled to his knees and saw he had been funnelled on to a padded pallet. Before he could roll off, Octobonds sprang from recessed apertures along the pallet's steel rim, trussing him tighter than a tumbled rodeo cow. Purple gas hissed from a dozen overhead nozzles, shrouding the pallet.

Hold your breath, Artemis told himself. *Animals don't know to hold their breaths.*

He held on until it felt as though his sternum would split, and then just as he was about to exhale and suck in a huge breath, a second gas was pumped into the chamber, crystallizing the first. It fell on to Artemis's face like purple snowflakes.

You are asleep now. Play possum.

A small door sank smoothly into the floor with a sound like air being blown through a straw.

Artemis peeked through one half-closed eye.

Magnetic field, he thought dully, a band of steel creasing his forehead.

I know what I will see, but I have no wish to see it.

A pixie stood framed in the doorway, her tiny, beautiful features twisted with their customary pouting cruelty.

'This,' squealed Opal Koboi, pointing a vibrating finger, 'is not a lemur.'

CHAPTER 13: THE HAİRY ONE İS DEAD

THE LEATHER SOUQ

 BUTLER jogged from the Extinctionists' compound to the leather souq. Artemis was waiting in the building in which they had planned the previous day's exchange. Police presence in Fez amounted to no more than a couple of two-man patrols and so it was easy for someone of Butler's experience to sneak around without being detected. Though it was hardly illegal to visit a medina, it was certainly frowned on to stroll around a tourist area with a large rifle strapped to one's back.

Butler ducked into a dark corner and quickly broke down his dart rifle into almost a dozen parts, slotting them into various rubbish tips. It was possible that he could slip the Fez Saïss airport customs men some baksheesh and simply stow the weapon under his seat, but these days it was better to be safe than sorry.

Ten-year-old Artemis was sitting at a pre-arranged spot in one of the sniper windows, picking non-existent lint from his jacket sleeve, which was his version of nervous pacing.

'Well?' he asked, steeling himself for the answer.

'The female got out,' said Butler. He thought it better not to mention that the long-haired male had had everything under control until Artemis's video arrived.

Artemis caught the implication. 'The female? The other one was there too?'

Butler nodded. 'The hairy one is dead. He attempted a rescue and it didn't work out.'

Artemis gasped. 'Dead?' he said. 'Dead?'

'Repeating the word won't change its meaning,' said Butler sharply. 'He tried to rescue his friend and Kronski killed him for it. But what's done is done, eh? And at least we have our diamonds.' Butler checked his temper. 'We should move out for the airport. I need to run the preflight checks.'

Artemis was left stunned and silent, unable to take his eyes from the bag of diamonds that winked accusingly from their slouched perch on his lap.

Holly was not having any luck. Her shield was so weak that she switched it off to save her last spark for a small healing if it was needed, and no sooner had her image solidified than one of Kronski's goons spotted her and walkie-talkied his entire squad. Now she was running for her life through the medina, praying that Artemis was at the meeting point *and* that he had thought to bring the scooter.

No one was taking potshots at her, which was encouraging, unless Kronski wanted to do the potshotting himself.

No time to think about that now. Survival was the priority.

The medina was quiet this late in the evening, with only a few straggling tourists and die-hard merchants still walking the streets. Holly dodged between them, pulling down whatever she could reach to get in the way of the stampede of security men behind her. She tugged over towers of baskets, upended a kebab stand and shouldered a table of spices, dashing a white wall with multicoloured arcs.

The thunder of footsteps behind her did not recede in the least. Her tactics were not working. The security guards were simply too large and were bustling past the obstacles.

Dodge and weave, then. Lose them in the alleyways.

This tactic was no more successful than the last. Her pursuers were familiar with the medina's layout and co-ordinated their pursuit on hand-held radios, herding Holly towards the leather souq.

Where I'll be in the open. An easy target.

Holly raced on, Artemis's loafers cutting into her heels. A series of cries and curses arose behind her as she barged without apology through bands of tourists, and shoulder-slammed tea boys, sending trays flying.

I am corralled, she thought desperately. *You'd better be waiting, Artemis.*

It occurred to Holly then that she was leading the posse directly to Artemis, but there was no other option. If he were waiting, then he could help; if not, then she was on her own anyway.

She jinked left but four huffing guards blocked the alleyway, all hefting vicious long-bladed knives.

The other way, I think.

Right, then. Holly skidded into the leather souq, heels throwing up dust fans.

Where are you, Artemis?

She cast her gaze upwards towards their observation point, but there was nothing there. Not even the telltale shimmer of a hide.

He's not here.

She felt panic scratch at her heart. Holly Short was an excellent field officer, but she was way out of her jurisdiction, her league and her time.

The leather souq was quiet now, with only a few workers scraping skins on the surrounding rooftops. Lanterns crackled below the roofline and the giant urns lurked like alien pods. The smell was just as bad as it had been the previous day, possibly worse, as the vats had had longer to cook. The stench of droppings hit Holly like a soft, feverish glove, further addling her mind.

Keep running. Find a nook.

Holly spent half a moment considering which body part

she would trade for a weapon, then sprinted for a doorway in the adjacent wall.

A guard appeared, dragging his knife from his sheath. The blade was red. Maybe blood, maybe rust. Holly switched direction, losing a shoe in the turn. There was a window one floor up, but the wall was cracked – she could make the climb.

Two more guards. Grinning. One held a net, like a gladiator.

Holly slid to a halt.

We're in the desert! Why does he have a fishing net?

She tried again. An alleyway barely broad enough for an adult human. She was almost there when a fat guard with a ponytail to his waist and a mouthful of yellowed teeth wedged himself into the avenue, blocking it.

Trapped. Trapped. No escape and not enough magic to shield. Not even enough to mesmerize.

It was difficult to stay calm, in spite of all her training and experience. Holly could feel her animal instincts bubble in the pit of her stomach.

Survive. Do what you have to do.

But what could she do? One unarmed, child-sized fairy against a squadron of armed muscle.

They formed a ragged circle around her, weaving between the urns in a slow-motion slalom. Every set of greedy glittering eyes focused on her face. Closer and closer they came, spreading their arms wide in case their prey made a dart for freedom.

Holly could see their scars and pockmarks, see the desert in their nails and on their cuffs. Smell their breath and count their fillings.

She cast her eyes towards the heavens.

'Help,' she cried.

And it began to rain diamonds.

Below the Extinctionists' compound

'That is not a lemur,' repeated Opal Koboi, drumming a tiny toe on the floor. 'I know it is not a lemur because it has no tail and it seems to be wearing clothes. This is a human, Mervall. A Mud Boy.'

A second pixie appeared in the doorway. Mervall Brill. One of the infamous Brill brothers who would break Opal out of her padded psych cell some years later. His expression was a mixture of puzzlement and terror. Not pretty on any face.

'I don't understand it, Miss Koboi,' he said, twiddling the top button on his crimson lab coat. 'It was all set up for the lemur. You mesmerized Kronski yourself.'

Opal's nostrils flared. 'Are you suggesting this is somehow my fault?' She clutched her throat, as if the very idea caused her breath to fail.

'No, no, no,' said Mervall hurriedly. 'It could not be Miss Koboi's fault. Miss Koboi is, after all, perfection itself. Perfection does not make mistakes.'

�ᚉᚋᚃ•ᚉᚁᚏᚑᚇᚕ•ᚅᚇᚖᚑᚋᚁ•ᚐᚖᚐ•▢

This outrageous statement would be recognized as blatant toadying by right-minded people, but Opal Koboi found it fair and rational.

'Exactly. Well said, Mervall. A pity your brother does not have a tenth of your wisdom.'

Mervall smiled and shuddered. The smile was in acceptance of the compliment, the wince was because the mention of his twin had reminded him that his brother was at this moment locked in a cage with a red river hog, as punishment for not complimenting Opal on her new boots.

Miss Koboi was having a bad day. Currently, two out of seven were bad. If things got any worse, even though the wages were astronomical, the Brill brothers might be forced to seek alternative employment.

Mervall decided to distract his boss. 'They're going crazy up there. Firing weapons. Duelling with cutlery. Those Extinctionists are an unstable lot.'

Opal leaned over Artemis, sniffing gently, wiggling her fingers to see if the human was awake.

'The lemur was the last one. I was *this* close to being all-powerful.'

'How close?' asked Mervall.

Opal squinted at him. 'Are you being funny?'

'No. I sincerely wondered —'

'It's an expression,' snapped the pixie, striding back towards the main chamber.

Mervall nodded slowly. 'An expression. I see. What should I do with the human?'

Opal did not break her stride. 'Oh, you might as well harvest him. Human brain fluid is a good moisturizer. Then we pack up and find that lemur ourselves.'

'Should I dump his drained corpse in the animal pit?'

Opal threw up her arms. 'Oh, for heaven's sake. Must I tell you how to do everything? Can't you show a little initiative?'

Mervall wheeled the pallet after his boss.

The animal pit it is, then, he thought.

THE LEATHER SOUQ

Diamonds rained down in glittering showers. Falling stars twinkling in the lamp light.

Young Artemis's fee, Holly realized. *He is throwing me a life-line.*

For a moment the guards were transfixed. Their faces wore the dazed expression of children who have woken and are surprised to find themselves in a good mood. They stretched out their fingers, watching the diamonds bounce and tumble.

Then one broke the spell. '*Des diamants!*' he cried.

Hearing the word spoken aloud galvanized his companions. They dropped to their knees, patting the dusky ground for the precious stones. More dived into the pungent vats as they registered tiny plops made by stones impacting on liquid.

Mayhem, thought Holly. *Perfect*.

She glanced upwards just in time to see a small hand withdraw into the black rectangle of a window.

What made him do it? she wondered. *That was a most un-Artemis-like gesture.*

A guard diving past her leg reminded her that things were still pretty dire.

In their greed they have forgotten me, but perhaps they will remember their duty when the stones are pocketed.

Holly spared a moment to salute up at young Artemis's window, then raced out of his view towards the nearest alley, only to be flattened by a puffing Damon Kronski.

'Two for two,' he huffed. 'I got both of you. This must be my lucky day.'

When will this end? thought Holly incredulously. *How can these things continue to happen?*

Kronski pressed down on her like an enraged elephant, frown lines framing his tinted glasses, sweat flowing in sheets down his face, dripping from his pouting lip.

'Except, this is *not* my lucky day, is it?' he shouted, a keen note of hysteria on the edge of his tones. 'You saw to that. You and your accomplice. Well, my gas chamber took care of him. Now I will take care of you!'

Holly was stunned.

Artemis dead?

She would not believe it. Never. How many people had written Artemis Fowl off and lived to regret it? Plenty. She was one of them.

Holly, on the other hand, was proving easier to kill. Her vision was blurring, her limbs were treading water and the weight of the world was on her chest. The only sense firing on all cylinders was her sense of smell.

What a way to go. Inhaling motes of pigeon dropping with your last breath.

She heard her ribs groan.

I wish Kronski could smell this.

An idea sparked in her brain, the last ember in a dying grate.

Why shouldn't he smell it? It's the least I can do.

Holly reached deep into her core of magic, searching for that last spell. There was a flicker deep inside. Not enough to shield, or even mesmerize, but perhaps a minor healing.

Usually healing spells were used on recent wounds, but Kronski's anosmia was a lifelong ailment. Fixing it now could be dangerous and would almost certainly be painful.

Oh well, thought Holly. *If it hurts him, it hurts him.*

She reached up a hand past the forearm on her throat, inching it along Kronski's face, willing the magic into her fingertips.

Kronski did not feel threatened. 'What's this? Are you playing *got your nose?*'

Holly did not answer. Instead she closed her eyes, jammed two fingers up Kronski's nostrils and sent her last sparks of magic down those channels.

'Heal,' she said. A wish and a prayer.

Kronski was surprised but not initially upset.

'Hey, what the –' he said, then sneezed. The sneeze was powerful enough to pop his ears and roll him off his captive. 'What are you, five years old? Sticking fingers up my nose.' Another sneeze. Bigger this time. Blowing a trumpet of steam from each nostril.

'This is pathetic. You people are really –'

A third sneeze, this one traumatizing the entire body. Tears streamed down Kronski's face. His legs jittered and his glasses shattered in their frames.

'Oh my,' said Kronski, when he had his limbs under control. 'Something's different. Something has changed.'

Then the smell hit him.

'Aarrgh,' said Kronski, and began to squeal. His tendons tightened, his toes pointed and his fingers ripped holes in the air.

'Wow,' said Holly, massaging her throat. This was a stronger reaction than expected.

The smell was bad, but Kronski acted like he was dying. What Holly had not fully grasped was the power of the doctor's awakened sense of smell. Imagine the joy of seeing for the first time, or the euphoria of a first step. Then square that feeling and make it negative. Take a ball of poison, dip it in thorns and manure, wrap it in a poultice of festering bandages, boil the whole lot in a cauldron of unspeakably vile excretions and shove it up your nose.

⊕◉◮ᐖℛ•◉◖ᐃᛯ•⨳ᐁ◗•◉◉ᐔℱ•◊ᐃᛁᛁℛᛒ

This is what Kronski could smell, and it was driving him out of his mind.

He lay flat on his back, flinching and pawing the sky.

'Foul,' he said, repeating the word over and over. 'Foul, foul. Fowl, Fowl.'

Holly crawled to her knees, coughing and spitting on to the dry sand. Her entire being felt battered and bruised from back to spirit. She looked at Kronski's expression and realized that there was no point in asking him questions. The president of the Extinctionists was beyond logical conversation for the time being.

Possibly for good, she thought. *I don't see him leading any international organizations for a while.*

Holly noticed something. One of Kronski's lenses had completely shattered, revealing the eyeball underneath. The iris was a strange violet, almost the same shade as the spectacles had been, but this was not what caught Holly's attention. The edge of the retina was ragged, as though it had been nibbled on by tiny sclera fish.

This man has been mesmerized, Holly realized. *A fairy is controlling him.*

She climbed to her feet and hobbled one-shoed down the nearest alley, the voices of squabbling greed fading behind her.

If a fairy is involved, then nothing is as it seems. And, if nothing is as it seems, then perhaps Artemis Fowl still lives.

BELOW THE EXTINCTIONISTS' COMPOUND

Mervall Brill winked at himself in the chrome door of a body freezer.

I am a handsome chap, he thought, *and this lab coat covers the paunch rather well.*

'Brill!' called Opal from her office. 'How is that brain fluid coming?'

Merv jumped. 'Just sucking him dry now, Miss Koboi.'

The pixie put his weight behind the trolley with its human cargo, trundling it down a short corridor to the lab itself. Being stuck in this tiny facility with Opal Koboi was no picnic. Just the three of them for weeks on end, draining the fluids from endangered species. Opal could afford to hire a thousand lab assistants to work for her, but she was über-paranoid about secrecy. Opal's level of paranoia was such that she had begun to suspect plants and inanimate objects of spying on her.

'I can grow cameras!' she had shrieked at the Brill brothers during one briefing. 'Who's to say that despicable centaur Foaly hasn't succeeded in splicing surveillance equipment to plants. So get rid of all the flowers. Rocks too. I don't trust them. Sullen little blëbers.'

So the Brill twins had spent an afternoon scouring the facility for anything that might contain a bug. Even the re-cycling toilet-scent blocks had to go, as Opal was convinced they were photographing her when she used the facilities.

Still, though, Miss Koboi is right to be paranoid, Merv

𐑐•𐑁𐑉𐑼•𐑣𐑦𐑥𐑕𐑧𐑤𐑓•𐑢𐑦𐑯𐑒𐑛•𐑨𐑑•𐑣𐑦𐑥𐑕𐑧𐑤𐑓

admitted, as he barged through the lab double doors. *If the LEP ever found out what she was doing here, they would lock her up forever and a day.*

The double doors led to a long, triple-height laboratory. It was a place of misery. Cages were stacked to the ceiling, each one filled with a trapped animal. They moaned and keened, rattling their bars, butting the doors. A robot food-pellet dispensing machine whirred along the network, spitting grey pellets into the appropriate cages.

The centre island was a series of operating pallets. Scores of animals lay sedated on the tables, secured, like Artemis, with rigid Octobonds. Artemis caught sight of a Siberian tiger, paws in the air and bald patches shaved into its skull. On each patch, there sat what looked like a tiny slice of liver. As they passed, one of the slices made a squelching sound and a tiny light-emitting diode on its ridge flashed red.

Merv stopped to peel it off and Artemis saw to his horror that the thing's underside was spiked with a dozen dripping spines.

'Full to the brim, Mister Super Genetically Modified Leech Mosquito thing. You are a disgusting abomination, yes you are. But you sure know how to siphon brain fluid. I'd say you're due a squeezing.'

Merv pumped a foot pedal to open a nearby fridge and finger-tinkled the beakers inside until he found the right one.

'Here we go. SibTig BF.'

He placed the beaker on a chrome work surface, then squeezed the leech like a sponge until it surrendered its bounty of brain fluid. Afterwards the leech was casually tossed into the trash.

'Love you lots,' said Mervall, returning to Artemis's pallet. 'Miss you loads.'

Artemis saw everything through the slit of a closed eye. This was a depraved, horrible place and he had to get out of here.

Holly will come for me, he thought, and then, *No, she won't. She'll think I'm dead.*

This realization chilled his blood.

I went into the flames.

He would have to save himself, then. It would not be the first time. Stay alert, a chance will come and you must be ready to take it.

Mervall found room on the operating section and parked Artemis neatly in it.

'And he squeezes it into an impossible space. They said it couldn't be done. They were wrong. Mervall Brill is the king of trolley parking.' The pixie belched. 'Which is not the future I had in mind for myself as a younger pixie.'

Then, somewhat moodily, he trawled a low-level aquarium with a perforated jug until it was full of convulsing super leeches.

Oh no, thought Artemis. *Oh, please.*

And then he was forced to close his eyes as Mervall turned to face him.

⊗ • ⊗ ▢ ⚷⊗ • ♒⧓Ⴑ • ⊖ • ◉ ⚹⟩⎎⚸ • ⊗ ▢ • ⊖

Surely he will see my chest heaving. He will sedate me, and it will all be over.

But Mervall apparently did not notice.

'Ooh, I hate you guys. Disgusting. I tell you something, human, if your subconscious can hear me, be glad you're asleep, because you do *not* want to go through this awake.'

Artemis almost cracked then. But he thought of his mother, with less than a day left to her, and he kept silent.

He felt his left hand being tugged, and heard Mervall grunt.

'Stuck tight. Just a tick.'

The grip loosened and Artemis tracked Mervall's movement with his ears and nose. A brush of soft belly on his elbow. Breath blowing past his ear. Mervall was at his left shoulder, reaching across.

Artemis opened his right eye just enough, and rolled his pupil into the slit. There was a theatre light directly overhead, craned in above the operating table on a thick, flat chrome arm.

Chrome. Reflective.

Artemis watched Mervall's actions in the surface. The pixie tapped the Octobond's touch-sensitive control pad, revealing a Gnommish keyboard. Then, singing a popular pixie pop song, he tapped in his password. One number with each beat of the chorus.

'Pixies rock hard!' he sang. 'Extreme pixie hard rock, baby.'

Which seemed unlikely to Artemis, but he was glad of
the song as it gave him time to file Mervall's passcode.

Mervall released one of the bonds, allowing him to
extend Artemis's forearm. Even if the human did happen
to wake up, all he could do was flail.

'Now, my little leech, do your nasty work for Aunt
Opal, and I will reward you by squeezing your innards
into a bucket.' He sighed. 'Why are all my best lines wasted
on annelids.'

Then he plucked a leech from the jug, pinched it to
make the spines stick out and slapped it on to Artemis's
exposed wrist.

Artemis felt nothing but an immediate sense of well-being.

I'm being sedated, he realized. *An old troll trick. Cheer you
up before you die. It's a good ploy and anyway, how bad can dying
be? My life has been one trial after another.*

Mervall was checking his chronometer. His brother had
been in that recycling cage behind the galley for an awfully
long time. That red river hog might decide to have himself
a bite of pixie meat.

'I'll just check,' he decided. 'Be back before the leech
is full. First blood, then brain. You should have compli-
mented Miss Opal's boots, brother.'

And off he toddled down the centre aisle, plucking
the mesh of each cage as he passed, driving the animals
wild.

'Pixies rock hard!' he sang. 'Extreme pixie hard rock, baby.'

*

Artemis was finding it hard to motivate himself. It felt so easy lying on the pallet, just letting all his troubles run out of his arm.

When you decide to die, Artemis thought sluggishly, *it doesn't matter how many people want to kill you.*

He did wish the animals would calm down. Their chattering and chirping were interfering with his mood.

There was even a parrot somewhere squawking a phrase.

'Who's your momma?' it asked over and over again. 'Who's your momma?'

My momma is Angeline. She's dying.

Artemis's eyes opened.

Momma. Mother.

He lifted his free arm and bashed the unwelcome leech against one of the Octobonds. It exploded in a spatter of mucus and blood, leaving half a dozen spines jutting from Artemis's arms like the spears of tiny soldiers.

That's going to hurt eventually.

Artemis's throat was dry, his neck was twisted and his vision was impaired, but, even so, it took him barely a minute to activate the keypad with Mervall's code and retract the bonds.

If these are alarmed, I'm in trouble.

But there was no klaxon. No pixies came running.

I have time. But not much.

He picked the spines from his skin, wincing not from pain, but from the sight of the red-rimmed holes in his wrist. A rivulet of blood ran from each wound, but it was slow and watery. He would not bleed to death.

Coagulent in the spines. Of course.

Artemis zombie-walked across the lab, gradually straightening out the kinks. There were hundreds of eyes on him. The animals were silent now, noses, beaks or snouts pressed against the wire mesh, waiting to see what would develop. The only sound came from the food-pellet robot zipping through its routine.

All I need to do is escape. No need for confrontation or saving the world. Leave Opal be, and run away.

But, of course, in the world of Artemis Fowl things are rarely straightforward. Artemis donned network goggles he found hanging from a low peg, activated the v-board and used Mervall's password to log on to the network. He needed to know where he was and how to get out.

There were design plans to the entire facility stored on a desktop file. No security, no encryption. Why would there be? It wasn't as if any of the humans above would wander down and, even if they did, humans could not read Gnommish.

Artemis studied the plans with care and growing anxiety. The facility consisted of a series of interconnected modules, housed in ancient tunnels beneath the Extinctionists' compound, but there were only two ways out. He could go out the way he had come in, which was not ideal as it led straight back up to Kronski. Or he could choose the shuttle port on the lower level, which would mean stealing and piloting a shuttle. His chances of overriding complicated theft-prevention safeties before Opal had him vaporized were minimal. He would have to go up.

'Do you like my little laboratory?' said a voice.

Artemis stared past the goggle display. Opal stood before him, hands on hips.

'Quite a place, isn't it?' she continued, in English. 'All these tunnels were just here, waiting for us. Perfect. As soon as I found them, I knew I had to have them, which is why I persuaded Doctor Kronski to move here.'

Information is power, thought Artemis. *Don't give her any.*

'Who are you?' he asked.

'I am the future queen of this world, at the very least. You may refer to me as Miss Koboi, for the next five minutes. After that you may refer to me as *aaaaarrrrgh*, hold your throat, die screaming, and so on.'

As pompous as I remember.

'I seem to be bigger than you, Miss Koboi. And, as far as I can see, you have no weapons.'

Opal laughed. 'No weapons?' she cried, spreading her arms. 'These creatures have given me all the weapons I need.' She stroked the sleeping tiger. 'This big kitty augments my mind control. Those sea slugs focus my energy beams. A shot of liquidized dolphin fin mixed with just the right amount of cobra venom turns the clock back a hundred years.'

'This is a weapons factory,' breathed Artemis.

'Exactly,' said Opal, gratified that *someone* finally understood. 'Thanks to these animals and their fluids, I have become the most powerful magician since the demon warlocks. The

Extinctionists have been rounding up the creatures I need. Fools. Tricked by a cheap blast of holographic flames. As if I would kill these wonderful creatures before I drain their juices. You humans are such idiots. Your governments spend their fortunes looking for power when all the time it is cavorting around your jungles.'

'That's quite a speech,' said Artemis, wiggling his fingers, tapping the v-board that only he could see.

'Soon I will be –'

'Don't tell me – soon you will be invincible.'

'No, actually,' said Opal, with admirable patience. 'Soon I will be able to manipulate time itself. All I need is the –'

And suddenly everything fell into place for Artemis. Everything about this whole affair. And he knew he would be able to escape.

'The lemur. All you need is the lemur.'

Opal clapped. 'Exactly, you bright Mud Boy. That wonderful lemur brain fluid is the last ingredient I need for my magic boosting formula.'

Artemis sighed. 'Magic boosting formula? Listen to yourself.'

Opal missed the mocking tone, possibly because she didn't hear it a lot. 'I had a whole bunch of lemurs before, but the LEP appropriated them to cure some plague and I lost the rest in a fire. All my test subjects gone, and their fluids are quite impossible to replicate. There is *one* left and I need him. He is my cloning model. With that lemur I will control time itself.' Opal stopped speaking for a moment,

ᛒᚱᚼ�oᛒᚠ•ᚨᛒᚱᚢ•ᚨᛋᛒ•ᛁᚤ•ᚤ•ᚼ•ᚢ•ᛒᚨᛋ

tapping her bow lips with a finger. 'Wait a moment, human. What do you know of my lemur?' She took the finger away from her mouth and ignited a pulsing sphere of flame at its tip, melting her nail varnish. 'I asked you, what do you know of my lemur?'

'Nice boots,' said Artemis, then selected an option on the goggle screen with a flick of his finger.

Are you sure you wish to open all the cages? asked the computer.

The Extinctionists were sneaking back into the compound led by the intrepid Tommy Kirkenhazard, who brandished his empty pistol with decidedly more bravado than he felt.

'I got stuff in that compound,' he repeatedly told the mass huddled behind him. 'Expensive stuff. And I ain't leaving it behind.'

Most of the rest had *expensive stuff* too, and now that Kronski was catatonic in the souq and his guards seemed to have fled with their sparkling booty, this would appear to be the best time to reclaim their belongings and head for the airport.

Much to Kirkenhazard's relief, the compound seemed utterly deserted, though the gelatinous group was spooked several times by night shadows jumping in the Moroccan wind.

I ain't never shot nothing with an empty gun, he thought. *But I don't imagine it's too effective.*

They reached the door to the main hall, which hung from the frame on a single hinge.

⬖⬚ ⚶⬡ ⬖⬡⬚◗↺ ⬩⚗◊⚰◻⬩ⓞ⬠⟠⬡ ⬩⬥⬩

'OK, folks,' said Kirkenhazard. 'There ain't no porters around to carry our stuff, so you got to hump it yourselves.'

'Oh, my Lord,' said Contessa Irina Kostovich, and swooned into the arms of a Scottish oil baron.

'Gather whatever you can and we meet back here in fifteen minutes.'

The contessa was muttering something.

'What was that?' asked Kirkenhazard.

'She said she has a pedicure booked for the morning.'

Kirkenhazard held up a hand, listening. 'No. Not that. Does anyone else hear rumbling?'

The animals charged through the open cage doors with savage glee, hopping, jumping, flying and sliming. Lions, leopards, various monkeys, parrots, gazelles, hundreds of creatures all with one idea in mind: *escape*.

Opal was not amused.

'I cannot believe you did that, Mud Person. I will wring your brain out like a sponge.'

Artemis ducked his head low, not caring at all for the brain/sponge imagery. If he avoided Opal's regal stare, then she could not mesmerize him. Unless her augmented powers allowed her access to the brain without the conduit of the optic nerve.

Even if he had not ducked, he would have been shielded by the tide of creatures that engulfed him, snapping, buffeting and kicking.

This is ridiculous, he thought, as a monkey's elbow drove

the air from his lungs. *If Opal does not get me, the animals will. I need to direct this stampede.*

Artemis ducked behind one of the operating tables, pulling out the tiger's anaesthetic drip as he passed, and squinted through the spokes of passing legs for an appropriate animal.

Opal roared at the creatures in an amalgamation of their tongues. It was a piercing sound and split the animal phalanx down the centre so that it flowed around her. As the herd passed, Opal took potshots with pulsing blasts of energy that erupted from her fingers and scythed through entire rows of creatures, knocking them senseless to the ground. Cages tumbled like building blocks, refrigerators spewed their contents across the tiles.

My distraction is being chopped down, thought Artemis. *Time for an exit.*

He spied a set of hooves stomping towards him and steadied himself for a jump.

It's a quagga, he realized. *Half horse, half zebra and there hasn't been one in captivity for a hundred years. Not exactly a thoroughbred stallion but it will have to do.*

The ride was a little rougher than Artemis was accustomed to on the Fowl Arabians. No steadying stirrups, no creaking saddle, no snapping reins. Not to mention the facts that the quagga was unbroken and scared out of its wits.

Artemis patted its neck.

Ludicrous, he thought. *This entire affair. A dead boy escaping on an extinct animal.*

Artemis grabbed tufts of the quagga's mane and tried

to direct it towards the open doorway. It bucked and kicked, whipping its striped head round to nip at Artemis with strong, square teeth. He dug in his heels and held on.

Opal was busy protecting herself from a wave of animal vengeance. Some of the larger predators were not as cowed as their cousins and decided that the best way to remove the threat posed by Opal Koboi was to eat her.

The tiny pixie twirled like a demonic ballerina, shooting blasts of magical energy that ballooned at her shoulders, gathered force in roiling spheres at her elbows and shot forth with liquid pulsations.

Artemis had never seen anything like it. Stricken animals simply froze in mid-air, momentum utterly drained, dropping to the ground like statues. Immobile but for their terrified rolling eyes.

She is powerful indeed. I have never seen a force like this. Opal must never be allowed to capture Jayjay.

Opal was running out of magic. Her bolts fizzled out or spiralled off target like errant squibs. She abandoned them and drew two pistols from her belt. One was immediately batted from her hand by the tiger that had lumbered to join the fray, but Opal did not submit to hysteria. She quickly thumbed the other gun to a broad-spread setting and slashed the barrel from side to side as she fired, releasing a fan of silver energy.

The tiger was the first to drop, with a look on his face that said *not again*. Several more followed, cut off in mid-screech, howl or hiss.

Artemis hauled back on the quagga's spiked mane, jumping it on to an operating table. The beast snorted and complained, but did as it was bid, skittering the length of one table and leaping across to the next one.

Opal loosed a shot in their direction, but it was absorbed by a brace of condors.

The door was directly before them, and Artemis feared the quagga would falter, but no – it butted through to the corridor connecting the lab to the holographic-flame chamber.

Artemis quickly opened the control panel in his stolen network goggles and chose the ramp setting.

It took maddening moments for the platform to extend itself, and for those seconds Artemis rode the quagga round in circles to take its mind off dislodging the unwelcome rider on its back, and to make them both a more difficult target if Opal followed them through the corridor.

An eagle swooped by, its feathers raking Artemis's cheek. A muskrat clambered along his torso, hopping to the rising platform.

There was light above, the sickly wavering beams of a faulty strip light. But light nevertheless.

'Come on, girl,' said Artemis, feeling very much the cowboy. 'Yee-haw.'

The Extinctionists gathered around Tommy Kirkenhazard's raised finger, listening intently as if the noise emanated from inside the finger.

'Ah, I don't hear nothing,' admitted Tommy. 'I must have

been dreaming. After all, it's been a stressful night for human-lovers.'

Then the lodge burst open and the Extinctionists were utterly engulfed in a sea of beasts.

Kirkenhazard went down under a couple of chacma baboons, vainly pulling the trigger on his empty gun and shouting over and over, 'But we killed you, darn it. We killed you.'

Though there would be no fatalities in the compound that night, eighteen people were hospitalized with bites, skin burns, broken bones and various infestations. Kirkenhazard fared the worst. The baboons ate his gun and the hand holding it and then turned the unfortunate man over to a groggy tiger, who found himself waking in a very bad mood.

Not one of the Extinctionists noticed a small dark craft rising silently from behind one of the chalets. It flew across the central park and scooped up a long-haired youth from the back of what looked like a small stripy donkey. The craft spun in a tight arc, like a stone in a sling, then hurtled into the night sky, as though it had to be somewhere in a real hurry.

Pedicures, and indeed all spa treatments, were cancelled for the next day.

Opal was desolate to find that, on top of everything else, her boots were ruined.

'What is that stain?' she demanded of Mervall and his recently liberated twin, Descant.

'Dunno,' muttered Descant, who was still a bit moody from his time in the cage.

285

'It's a dropping of some kind,' volunteered Mervall quickly. 'Judging from the size and texture, I would say one of the big cats got a little nervous.'

Opal sat on a bench, extending the boot. 'Pull it off, Mervall.'

She placed her sole on Mervall's forehead and pushed until he tumbled backwards, clutching the dropping-laden footwear.

'That Mud Boy. He knows about my lemur. We must follow him. He is tagged, I take it.'

'Oh yes,' confirmed Mervall. 'All the newcomers are sprayed on landing. There's a radioactive tracer in his every pore right now. Harmless, but there's nowhere on this planet that he can hide from us.'

'Good. Excellent, in fact. I think of everything, do I not?'

'You do, Miss Koboi,' droned Descant. 'Brilliant you are. Astounding is your fabulosity.'

'Why thank you, Descant,' said Opal, as ever oblivious to sarcasm. 'And I thought you'd be upset after the pig pen. Fabulosity isn't a word, by the way. In case you're thinking of writing how wonderful I am in your diary.'

'Point taken,' said Descant seriously.

Opal offered her other foot to Mervall. 'Good. Now set the self-destructs on this place and let's get the shuttle prepped. I want to find this human and kill him immediately. We were too nice last time, with the leeches. This time immediate death.'

Mervall winced. He was holding two boots covered in

tiger droppings, and he'd prefer to wear those than be in that human's shoes.

Artemis lay flat on his back in the cargo hold, wondering if he could possibly have dreamed the past few minutes. Super-leeches, sleeping tigers and a grumpy quagga.

He felt the floor vibrate beneath him and knew that they were moving at several times the speed of sound. Suddenly the vibration disappeared, to be replaced by a far more sedate hum. They were slowing down!

Artemis hurried to the cockpit, where Holly was glaring at a readout as if she could change the information displayed there. Jayjay was in the co-pilot's seat and seemed to be in charge of steering.

Artemis pointed at the lemur. 'This may seem like a silly question, but is Jayjay . . .'

'No. Autopilot. And nice to see you alive, by the way. You're welcome for the rescue.'

Artemis touched her shoulder. 'Once again, I owe you my life. Now, I hate to move directly from gratitude to petulance, but why have we slowed down? Time is running out. We had three days, remember? There are only hours left.'

Holly tapped the readout. 'We were pinged by something at the compound. Someone's computers have downloaded our schematics. Can you tell me any more about that?'

'Opal Koboi,' said Artemis. 'Opal is behind everything.

She's harvesting animal fluids to increase her own magic. If she gets her hands on Jayjay, she'll be invincible.'

Holly did not have time to be incredulous. 'That's wonderful. Opal Koboi. I knew this little trip was missing a psychotic element. If Opal pinged us, then she'll be on our tail in something a little more war-worthy than this clunker.'

'Shields?'

'Nothing much. We might fool human radar but not fairy scanners.'

'What can we do?'

'I need to keep us up here in the air-lanes with all the human traffic. We stay sub-sonic and don't draw attention to ourselves. Then at the last moment we make a break for Fowl Manor. It won't matter if Opal sees us then, because by the time she catches us we'll be back in the time stream.'

Mulch Diggums poked his head through from the mail box. 'Nothing much in here. A few gold coins. What say I keep them? And did I hear someone mention Opal Koboi?'

'Don't worry about it. Everything is under control.'

Mulch guffawed. 'Under control? Like Rathdown Park was under control. Like the leather souq was under control.'

'You're not seeing us at our best,' Artemis admitted. 'But in time you will come to respect Captain Short and me.'

Mulch's expression doubted it. 'I'd better go and look up *respect* in the dictionary, because it mustn't mean what I think it means, eh, Jayjay?'

The lemur clapped his delicate hands and chattered with what sounded like laughter.

〰️ ⬧ •⬡⬧⬡⬧ ⬧ •⬡⬡⬡• ⬡⬡⬡ •⬡⬡⬡⬡ ⬧⬡⬡ •⬡⬡⬡⬡ 〰️

'It looks like you've found an intellectual equal, Mulch,' said Holly, returning to her instruments. 'It's a pity he isn't a girl; then you could marry him.'

Mulch imitated shock. 'Romance outside your species. Now *that's* disgusting. What kind of weirdo would kiss someone when they weren't even part of the same species?'

Artemis massaged his suddenly pounding temples.

It's a long way to Tipperary, he thought, *and then a few more miles to Dublin.*

'A shuttle?' said Opal. 'A fairy shuttle?'

The Koboi craft was hovering at an altitude of thirty miles, tipping the border of space. Starlight winked on the hull of their matt-black shuttle and the Earth hung below them, wearing a stole of clouds.

'That's what the sensors show,' said Mervall. 'An old mining model. Not much under the hood and zero firepower. We should be able to catch it.'

'Should?' said Opal, stretching an ankle to admire her new red boots. 'Why *should*?'

'Well, we had her for a while. Then she went sub-sonic. I would guess their pilot is riding the human flight lanes until they feel safe.'

Opal smiled devilishly. She liked a challenge.

'OK, let's give ourselves every advantage. We have the speed and we have the weapons. All we need is to point ourselves in the right direction.'

'What an incrediferous idea,' smirked Descant.

◊•🙢⊙⊃⊠⊕⊟ꜛ•◊⊖ᒋ⊡⊗•⚘⊙◊➤•🙜⚘❖

Opal was pained. 'Please, Descant. Use short words. Don't force me to vaporize you.'

This was a hollow threat, as Opal had not been able to produce so much as a spark since the compound. She still had the basics – mind control, levitation, that kind of thing – but she would need some serious bed rest before she could muster a lightning bolt. The Brills did not need to know that, though.

'Here's my idea. I ran the lab tapes through voice recognition and got a regional match. Whoever that Mud Boy is, he lives in central Ireland. Probably Dublin. I want you to get us down there as fast as you can, Descant, and when that mining shuttle drops out of the air lanes . . .' Opal closed her tiny fingers round an imaginary ant, squeezing the blood from its body. 'We will be waiting.'

'Fabulicious,' said Descant.

FOWL MANOR

The sun had risen and was sinking again by the time Holly dragged the spluttering shuttle over the Fowl estate wall.

'We're close to the deadline and this piece of junk is close to dead,' she said to Artemis. Holly placed a hand on her heart. 'I can feel Number One's spark dying inside, but there's still time.'

Artemis nodded. The sight of the manor somehow made his mother's plight seem even more urgent.

I have to go home.

꙰ꙮ — ꙩ — ꙭ — ꙮꙭꙭ — ꙩꙩ꙯ — ꙮꙭꙮꙮꙭꙭꙮꙩ — ꙮ

'Well done, Holly. You did it. Set us down in the rear courtyard. We can access the house by the kitchen door.'

Holly pressed a few buttons. 'Around the back it is. Scanning for alarms. Found two and a sneaky third. Motion sensors, if I'm not mistaken. Only one alarm is being remotely monitored and the other two are self-contained. Should I disable the remote alarm?'

'Yes, Holly, please disable the alarm. Anybody home?'

Holly checked the thermal imaging. 'One warm body. Top floor.'

Artemis sighed. Relieved. 'Good. Just Mother. She will have taken her sleeping tablets by now. Little me can't be back yet.'

Holly set the shuttle down as gently as she could, but the gears were stripped and the suspension bags were drained. There were dents in the stabilizers and the gyro-scope was spinning like a weathervane. The landing gear stripped a channel of cobblestones from the courtyard surface, tumbling them like bricks of turf before the plough.

Artemis gathered Jayjay in his arms.

'Are you ready for more adventures, little man?'

The lemur's round eyes were filled with anxiety and he looked to Mulch for reassurance.

'Always remember,' said Mulch, tickling the creature's chin, 'that *you* are the smart one.'

The dwarf found an old duffel bag and began stuffing the remaining contents of the fridge inside.

'No need for that,' said Holly. 'The ship is yours. Take it, dig up your booty and fly far away. Dump this heap in the sea and live off your earnings for a few years. Just promise me that you won't sell to humans.'

'Only the junk,' said Mulch. 'And did you say that I could keep the shuttle?'

'Actually, I'm asking you to scrap it. You'll be doing me a favour.'

Mulch grinned. 'I'm a generous person. I could do you a favour.'

Holly smiled back. 'Good. And remember, when we meet again, none of this ever happened, or it probably won't.'

'My lips are sealed.'

Artemis squeezed past him. 'Now there's something I would pay to see. Mulch Diggums with his mouth closed.'

'Yes, nice meeting you too, Mud Boy. I look forward to robbing you in the future.'

Artemis shook his hand. 'I look forward to it myself, believe it or not. We will have some fine times.'

Jayjay reached out for a handshake.

'You look after the human, Jayjay,' said Mulch seriously. 'He's a bit dim, but he means well.'

'Goodbye, Mister Diggums.'

'Later, Master Fowl.'

Opal was on her third round of the Gola Schweem meditative circle chant when Mervall burst into her private chamber.

'We found the shuttle, Miss Koboi,' he panted, clutching

a flexi-screen to his chest. 'They went supersonic for barely a minute over the Mediterannean. But it was enough.'

'Humm humm haaa. Rahmumm humm haaaa,' intoned Opal, finishing her chant. 'Peace be inside me, tolerance all around me, forgiveness in my path. Now, Mervall, show me where the filthy human is, so that I may feed him his organs.'

Mervall proffered the flexi-screen. 'Red dot. East coast.'

'Military?'

'No, surprisingly. It's a residence. No defences whatsoever.'

Opal climbed out of her snuggle-me chair. 'Good. Run a few scans. Warm up the cannons and get me down there.'

'Yes, Miss Koboi.'

'And Mervall?'

'Miss Koboi?'

'I think little Descant has a crush on me. He told me earlier that I was very phototractive. Poor little simpleton. Could you tell him that I am unavailable? If you don't, I shall have to have him killed.'

Merv sighed. 'I shall tell him, Miss Koboi. I feel sure he will be disconnipted.'

Artemis found himself scratching Jayjay's head as they moved through the manor.

'Be calm, little chap. No one can hurt you now. We're safe.'

Holly was behind him on the stairs, guarding the rear,

⊙◊·♆○◗⊕⊗§·◊◌⌂⊗·⚚◉◊→·⊙♭·

two fingers rigidly extended. The fingers were not a loaded weapon but they could break bones with enough momentum behind them.

'Come on, Artemis. Number One is weaker now, so we have to jump soon.'

Artemis stepped round a weight-sensitive pad on the twelfth step. 'Nearly there. Seconds away.'

His study was exactly as he had left it, the wardrobe still open, a scarf drooping from the top shelf like an escaping snake.

'Good,' said Artemis, his confidence growing. 'This is the spot. The exact spot.'

Holly was panting. 'About time. I'm having trouble holding on to the signal. It's like running after a smell.'

Artemis put an arm round her shoulder. A group of three – tired, hungry but excited.

Holly's shoulders shook with an exhaustion and tension she had kept hidden until now.

'I thought you were dead,' she said.

'Me too,' admitted Artemis. 'Then I realized that I couldn't die, not in this time.'

'I presume you're going to explain that to me.'

'Later. Over supper. Now can we open the time stream, friend?'

There was a sudden swish as the bay-window curtain slid back. Young Artemis and Butler were there, both wearing foil suits. Butler unzipped his suit to reveal a large gun strapped across his chest.

⊙ ⅃Ʊ⊕ ∙Ⅎⅉↄ⅃ ∙ꙅↄ ∙⅌⊙Ƀⅎ ∙ ℛⅉↄ∪ⅉℛ

'What was that about a time stream?' asked ten-year-old Artemis.

Mulch Diggums was burying a gold coin as a sacrifice to Shammy, the dwarf god of good fortune, when the earth exploded underneath him and he found himself straddling the blade of a shuttle ice-breaker prow.

I never even heard that coming, he thought, and then, *So much for Shammy.*

Before he could gather himself sufficiently to figure up from down, Mulch found himself tumbled to the base of a silver ash tree with the barrel of a Neutrino restricting the movement of his Adam's apple. His beard hairs instinctively realized that the gun was not friendly and twined themselves round the barrel.

'Nice shuttle,' said Mulch, playing for time until the stars in his vision flickered out. 'Whisper engine, I'm guessing.'

Three pixies stood before him. Two males and a female. Generally pixies were not very threatening creatures, but the males were armed and the female had a look in her eyes.

'I bet,' said Mulch. 'That you would set the world on fire, just to watch it burn.'

Opal tapped the suggestion into a small electronic notepad on her pocket computer.

'Thanks for that. Now tell me everything.'

I'll resist for a minute, then feed her some misinformation, thought Mulch.

⊗◉∪➝•⚡⚙∪☏◉⌑Ϝ•⚡•◉•◑⚡☖•⊗⬜•◖↺�

'I'll tell you nothing, pixie she-devil,' he said, Adam's apple knocking nervously against the gun barrel.

'Oooh,' said Opal, stamping with frustration. 'Isn't anyone afraid of me?'

She stripped off a glove, placing a thumb on Mulch's temple.

'Now, show me everything.'

And with a few remaining sparks of ill-gotten magic, she sucked every memory of the past few days from Mulch's brain. It was an extremely unpleasant sensation, even for someone used to expelling large amounts of material from his person. Mulch gibbered and bucked as the last few days were vacuumed from his head. When Opal had what she wanted, the dwarf was left unconscious in the mud.

He would wake up an hour later with the starter chip for an LEP shuttle in his pocket and no idea how he'd got there.

Opal closed her eyes and flicked through her new memories.

'Ah,' she said, smiling. 'A time stream.'

'There isn't time for this,' insisted Artemis.

'I think there is,' argued ten-year-old Artemis. 'You have broken into my house again, the least you can do is explain that *time stream* comment. Not to mention the fact that you are alive.'

Artemis the elder flicked his hair away from his face.

'You must recognize me now. Surely.'

'This is not a shampoo commercial. Please stop flicking your hair.'

Holly was bent almost double, her hand on her heart.

'Hurry,' she groaned. 'Or I'll have to go without you.'

'Please,' Artemis pleaded. 'We need to go. It's a matter of life and death.'

Young Artemis was unmoved. 'I had a feeling you would be back. This is where it all began, right on this spot. I reviewed the security tapes and you simply appeared in this room. Then you followed me to Africa, so I thought if I saved the creature's life you might end up back here with my lemur. We simply blocked our heat signatures and waited. And here you are.'

'That's pretty flimsy reasoning,' said Artemis the elder. 'We were obviously after the lemur. Once we had the lemur, why would we return here?'

'I realize the logic was flawed, but I had nothing to lose. And, as we can see, a lot to gain.'

Holly did not have the patience for a Fowl gloating session.

'Artemis, I know you have a heart. You're a good person even if you don't know it yet. You sacrificed your diamonds to save my life. What will it take for you to let us go?'

Young Artemis considered this for an infuriating minute and a half.

'The truth,' he said eventually. 'I need to know the absolute truth about all of this. What kind of creature are *you*? Why does *he* look so familiar? What makes the lemur so special? Everything.'

⏀ᛒ⟶•◌•ᔑ�⬡⊛ᚪ•◉•ᗺ◊•⊛▢◊•ᔑᗗᔔ•

Artemis the elder clutched Jayjay to his chest. 'Get me a pair of scissors,' he said.

Opal ran into the manor, casually squashing the magical nausea that flared upon entering a human dwelling without permission.

A time stream, she thought, almost giggling with excitement. *Finally I can test my theories.*

The manipulation of time had long been Opal's ultimate goal. To be able to control one's passage through time was the greatest power. But her magic was not strong enough without the lemur. It took teams of LEP warlocks to slow time down for a few hours; the magic required to open a door to the tunnel was stupendous. It would be easier to shoot down the moon.

Opal tapped this into her notepad.

Reminder. Shoot down the moon? Viable?

But, if she could gain entrance to the tunnel, Opal felt sure that she would quickly master the science involved.

It's more than likely an intuitive organism and, after all, I am a genius.

She scaled the stairs, mindless of the scuff marks the high human steps inflicted on her new boots. Mervall and Descant trailed behind, surprised at this lack of footwear prudence.

'I got thrown in the pig pen for boots,' muttered Descant. 'Now, she's scratching those ones on the stairs. Typical Koboi inconsistency. I think I'm getting an ulcer.'

Opal reached the upper landing and raced immediately through an open doorway.

'How does she know that's the right room?' wondered Descant.

'Oh, I don't know,' said Mervall, resting his hands on his knees. Scaling human steps is not easy for pixies. Big heads, short legs, tiny lungs. 'Maybe it's the magical red glow coming from the doorway, or perhaps it's the deafening howl of the temporal winds.'

Descant nodded. 'You could be right, brother. And don't think I don't know sarcasm when I hear it.'

Opal traipsed from the room, her expression sour.

'They have gone,' she announced. 'And the tunnel is about to close. Also my boots are ruined. So, boys, I am looking for someone to blame.'

The Brill brothers took one look at each other, then turned and ran as fast as their tiny legs would carry them.

Not fast enough.

CHAPTER 14: **THE HOLE İN THE ACE**

HOLLY felt herself relax as soon as they entered the stream.

Safe for the moment.

Jayjay was safe. Soon Artemis's mother would be well, and when that was accomplished Holly decided that she would punch her erstwhile friend in his smug face.

I did what I had to do, Artemis had said. *And I would do it again.*

And she had kissed him. Kissed him!

Holly understood Artemis's motives, but it wounded her deeply that he had felt the need to blackmail her.

I would have helped anyway. Definitely.

Would you? Would you have disobeyed orders? Was Artemis right to do it his way?

These were questions that Holly knew would haunt her for years. If she had years left to her.

The journey was more arduous than before. The time

stream was eroding her sense of self and there was a syrupy temptation to relax her concentration. Her world seemed less important wrapped in its sparkling waves. Being part of an eternal river would be a pleasant way to exist. And if the fairy races were wiped out by plague, what of it?

N°1's presence pricked her consciousness, bolstering her resolve. The little demon's power was evident in the stream, a shimmering thread of crimson pulling them on through the miasma. Things moved in the shadows. Darting, sharp things. Holly sensed teeth and hooked fingers.

Had Number One mentioned something about quantum zombies? That was probably a joke. Please let that be a joke.

Concentrate! Holly told herself. *Or you will be absorbed.*

She could feel other presences travelling with her. Jayjay was surprisingly calm, considering his surroundings. Somewhere in the periphery was Artemis, his sense of purpose keen as a blade.

Number One is going to get a shock, thought Holly, *when he sees us pop through.*

N°1 didn't seem very shocked when the group tumbled from the stream, solidifying on the floor of Artemis's study.

'See any zombies?' he asked with a spooky wiggling of his fingers.

'Thank the gods,' proclaimed Foaly from the television screens, then exhaled loudly through his broad nostrils. 'That was the longest ten seconds of my life. Did you get the lemur?'

🜁•⊕🔲🜚⊕•🜔•🝮🜋🌙🜊🝞•🝐•🜔🜋🝥🜚➙•🜔

There was no need for an answer as Jayjay decided he liked the sound of Foaly's voice and gave the nearest screen a lick. The little primate's tongue crackled and he scampered back, shooting Foaly a glare.

'One lemur,' said the centaur. 'No female?'

Holly shook the stars from her eyes, the fog from her head. The stream lingered in her head like the last moments of sleep.

'No. No female. You'll have to clone him.'

Foaly peered past Holly to the shuddering form on the ground behind her.

The centaur raised an eyebrow.

'I see we have an –'

'Let's talk about that later,' said Holly sharply, interrupting the centaur, 'for now we have work to do.'

Foaly nodded thoughtfully. 'I'm guessing, from the look of things, that Artemis has a plan of some sort. Is that going to be a problem for us?'

'Only if we try to stop it,' said Holly.

Artemis took Jayjay into his arms, stroking the little lemur's mohican, calming him with a rhythmic clicking of his tongue.

Holly felt that she too would be calmed, not by Artemis's clicking but by the sight of her own face in the mirror. She was herself again; her one-piece fitted snugly. A grown woman. No more teenage confusion. She would feel even better once she retrieved her gear. There was nothing like a Neutrino on the hip for a self-confidence boost.

'Time to see Mother,' said Artemis grimly, selecting a suit from the wardrobe. 'How much fluid should I administer?'

'It's powerful stuff,' said Foaly, entering some calculations on his keyboard. 'Two cc's. No more. There is a syringe gun in Holly's medi-kit bedside table. Be very careful with the brain drain. There's an anaesthetic tab in there too. Give Jayjay a swab and he won't feel a thing.'

'Very well,' Artemis said, pocketing the kit. 'I shall go in alone. I do hope Mother recognizes me.'

'So do I,' agreed Holly. 'Or she may object to lemur brain juice being injected into her by a total stranger.'

Artemis's hand hovered over the crystal doorknob on his parents' bedroom door. In its facets he could see a dozen reflections of his own face. Each one was drawn and worried.

Last chance. My last chance to save her.

I am forever trying to save people, he thought. *I'm supposed to be a criminal. Where did it all go wrong?*

No time for drifting. There was more at stake here than gold or notoriety. His mother was dying, and her salvation was perched on Artemis's shoulder, searching his scalp for ticks.

Artemis closed his fingers over the knob. Not another moment to waste on thoughts, time now for action.

The room seemed colder than he remembered, but this was doubtless his imagination.

All minds play tricks. Even mine. The perceived cold is a projection of my mood, nothing more.

His parents' bedroom was rectangular in shape, stretching along the west wing from front to rear. It was actually more of an apartment than a room, with a lounge area and office corner. The large four-poster bed was angled so that tinted light from a medieval stained-glass porthole would fall across the studded headboard in summer.

Artemis placed his feet carefully on the rug like a ballet dancer, avoiding the vine pattern in the weave.

Step on a vine, count to nine.

Bad luck was the last thing he needed.

Angeline Fowl was splayed on the bed, as though thrown there. Her head was angled back so sharply that the line from her neck to chin was almost straight, and her skin was pale enough to seem translucent.

She's not breathing, thought Artemis, panic fluttering in his chest like a caged bird. *I was wrong. I am too late.*

Then his mother's entire frame convulsed as she dragged down a painful breath.

Artemis's resolve almost left him then. His legs were boneless rubber and his forehead burned.

This is my mother. How can I do what needs to be done?

But he would do it. There wasn't anyone else who could.

Artemis reached his mother's side and gently pushed strands of hair back from her face.

'I am here, Mother. Everything will be fine. I found a cure.'

Somehow, Angeline Fowl heard her son's words and her eyes flickered open. Even her irises had lost their colour, fading to the ice blue of a winter lake.

'Cure,' she sighed. 'My little Arty found the cure.'

'That's right,' said Artemis. 'Little Arty found the cure. It was the lemur. Remember, the Madagascan lemur from Rathdown Park?'

Angeline raised a bone-thin finger, tickling the air before Jayjay's nose. 'Little lemur. Cure.'

Jayjay, unsettled by the bedridden woman's skeletal appearance, ducked behind Artemis's head.

'Nice lemur,' said Angeline, a weak smile twitching her lips.

I am the parent now, thought Artemis. *She is the child.*

'Can I hold him?'

Artemis took a half-step back. 'No, Mother. Not yet. Jayjay is a very important creature. This little fellow could save the world.'

Angeline spoke through her teeth. 'Let me hold him. Just for a moment.'

Jayjay crawled down the back of Artemis's jacket, as though he understood the request and did not want to be held.

'Please, Arty. It would comfort me to hold him.'

Artemis nearly handed the lemur over. Nearly.

'Holding him will not cure you, Mother. I need to inject some fluid into one of your veins.'

Angeline seemed to be regaining her strength. She inched

backwards, sliding her head up the headboard. 'Don't you want to make me happy, Arty?'

'I prefer *healthy* to happy for the moment,' said Artemis, making no move to hand over the lemur.

'Don't you love me, son?' crooned Angeline. 'Don't you love your mummy?'

Artemis moved briskly, tearing open the medi-kit, closing his fingers round the transfusion gun. A single tear rolled down his pale cheek.

'I love you, Mother. I love you more than life. If you could only know what I have been through to find little Jayjay. Just be still for five seconds, then this nightmare will be over.'

Angeline's eyes were crafty slits. 'I don't want you to inject me, Artemis. You're not a trained nurse. Wasn't there a doctor here, or was I dreaming that?'

Artemis primed the gun, waiting for the charge light to flash green. 'I *have* administered shots before, Mother. I gave you your medicine more than once the last time you were . . . *ill*.'

'Artemis!' snapped Angeline, the flat of her hand slapping the sheet. 'I *demand* that you give the lemur to me now! This instant! And summon the doctor.'

Artemis plucked a vial from the medi-kit. 'You are hysterical, Mother. Not yourself. I think I should give you a sedative before I administer the antidote.' He slid the vial into the gun, reaching for his mother's arm.

'No,' Angeline virtually screeched, slapping him away

with surprising strength. 'Don't touch me with your LEP sedatives, you stupid boy.'

Artemis froze. 'LEP, Mother? What do you know of the LEP?'

Angeline tugged her lip, a guilty child. 'What? Did I say LEP? Three letters, no more. They mean nothing to me.'

Artemis took another step away from the bed, gathering Jayjay protectively in his arms.

'Tell me the truth, Mother. What is happening here?'

Angeline abandoned her innocent act, pounding the mattress with delicate fists, squealing in frustration.

'I despise you, Artemis Fowl. You bothersome human. How I loathe you.'

Not words one expects to hear from one's mother.

Angeline lay flat on the bed, steaming with rage. Literally steaming. Her eyeballs rolled in their sockets and tendons stood out like steel cables on her arms and neck. All the time she ranted.

'When I have the lemur, I will crush you all. The LEP, Foaly, Julius Root. All of you. I will send laser dogs down every tunnel in the Earth's crust until I flush out that odious dwarf. And as for that female captain, I will brainwash her and make her my slave.' She cast a hateful look at Artemis. 'Fitting revenge. Don't you agree, *my son*.' The last two words dripped from her lips like poison from a viper's fangs.

Artemis held Jayjay close. He could feel the small creature shiver against his chest. Or perhaps the shivering was his own.

'Opal,' he said. 'You followed us home.'

'Finally!' shouted Artemis's mother, in Opal's voice. 'The great boy genius sees the truth.' Angeline's limbs stiffened and she levitated from the bed, surrounded by a roiling mist of steam. Her pale blue eyes cut through the fog, spearing Artemis with their mad glare.

'Did you think you could win? Did you believe that the battle *was* won? How charmingly deluded. You do not even possess any magic. I on the other hand have more magic than any other fairy since the demon warlocks. And, once I have the lemur, I will be immortal.'

Artemis rolled his eyes. 'Don't forget invincible.'

'I *haaate* you,' squealed Opal/Angeline. 'When I have the lemur, I will . . . I will . . .'

'Kill me in some horrible fashion,' suggested Artemis.

'Precisely. Thank you.'

Angeline's body pivoted stiffly until she hovered upright, her halo of charged hair brushing the ceiling.

'Now,' she said, pointing a skeletal finger at the cowering Jayjay. 'Give me that creature.'

Artemis wrapped the lemur in his jacket.

'Come and get him,' he said.

In the study, Holly was running through Artemis's theory.

'That's it?' said N°1 when Holly had finished explaining. 'You're not forgetting some crucial detail? Like the part that makes sense?'

'The whole thing is ridiculous!' interjected Foaly from

the monitors. 'Come on, fairies. We've done our bit. Time
to head below ground.'

'Soon,' said Holly. 'Let's just give Artemis five minutes
to check it out. All we need to do is be alert.'

Foaly's sigh crackled through the speakers. 'Well, at least
let me raise the shuttle. The troops are holding at Tara,
waiting for a call-back.'

Holly thought about this. 'That's good. You do that.
Whatever happens, we need to be ready to move out. And
when you're finished do a sweep of the estate – see where
that nurse is.'

Foaly's focus shifted left while he put a call in to Tara.

Holly pointed at N°1. 'You just have a little of that signature magic dancing on your fingertips in case we need it.
I won't feel completely safe until Angeline is well, and
we're drinking sim-coffee in a Haven bar.'

N°1 raised his hands, and soon they were enveloped in
ripples of red power. 'No problem, Holly. I'm ready for
anything.'

It was a statement that was missing an *almost*.

In the same split second, the monitors blacked out and
the door burst open with a force that actually drove the
doorknob into the wall. Butler's huge frame filled the gap.

Holly's smile slipped when she noticed the pistol in the
bodyguard's fist and the mirrored sunglasses covering his eyes.

He's armed and doesn't want to be mesmerized.

Holly was quick, but Butler was quicker and he had the
element of surprise – after all, he was supposed to be on

his way to China. Holly went for her gun, but realized that she had not yet reclaimed it from the safe.

We have other tricks, thought Holly. *We have magic. Number One will knock your socks off.*

Butler dragged something into the room on a trolley. A steel barrel with runes etched on the metal.

What's this? What's he doing?

N°1 managed to get off a single bolt. Indoor lightning that scorched Butler's shirt, knocking him back a pace, but even as he stumbled backwards the bodyguard swung the trolley past him, slingshotting it into the room. A thick slime slopped from the barrel's open mouth, splashing on N°1's legs. It trundled forward, knocking Holly and N°1 aside like skittles.

N°1 stared at his fingers as the magic on each tip winked out like candles in a breeze.

'I don't feel so great,' he groaned, then keeled over, eyes flickering, lips muttering ancient spells which did not one iota of good.

What is in that barrel? wondered Holly.

Butler bent low and grabbed Holly's ankle, flipping her ignominiously into the barrel. She felt the thick gunk close over her like a wet fist, blocking her nose, filling her throat.

The smell was repulsive.

Animal fat, she realized, with a spasmodic shudder of horror. *Pure rendered fat, with a few hexes stirred into it.*

Animal fat had been used as a magic suppressor for

millennia. Even the most powerful warlock was helpless when dipped in rendered fat. You throw a warlock in a barrel of fat, seal it with woven willow bark and bury it in a consecrated human graveyard, and that warlock was as helpless as a kitten in a sack. The experience would be made even more terrible by the fact that most fairies are devout vegetarians and would be perfectly aware how many animals had to die to produce an entire barrel of fat.

Who told Butler about this? Holly wondered. *Who is controlling him?*

Then N°1 was jammed in beside her and the fat level rose to cover their heads. Holly surged upwards, clearing her eyes just in time to see a lid bearing down on the barrel mouth, eclipsing the ceiling light.

No helmet, she lamented. *I wish I had my helmet.*

Then the lid was on and sealed. The fat found the neck-hole in her one-piece and wormed inside, probing her face and invading her ears. Hexes swirled like malevolent snakes, keeping her magic at bay.

Lost, thought Holly. *The worst death I can imagine. Sealed in a small space. Like my mother.*

N°1 convulsed beside her. The little warlock must feel like the soul was being sucked right out of him.

Holly panicked. She kicked and fought, bruising her elbows, tearing the skin from her knees. Where magic tried to heal her wounds, the hex snakes zoomed in, swallowing the sparks.

She almost opened her mouth to scream. The merest thread of reason stopped her. Then something brushed against her face. A corrugated tube. There were two.

Breathing tubes . . .

With frantic fingers, Holly felt her way to the end of the tube. She fought her natural instinct to jam the tube into Nº1's mouth.

In the event of an emergency, always take care of yourself first before you attend to civilians.

So Holly used her absolute last puff of air to clear the pipe as a diver would clear his snorkel. She imagined blobs of fat spraying the room outside.

I hope Butler's suit is ruined, she thought.

No choice now but to inhale. Air whistled down to her, mixed with wormy slivers of fat. Holly blew again, clearing the last traces of gunk.

Now for Nº1. His wriggling grew weaker as his power waned. For someone with such power, this dunking must be almost intolerable. Holly blocked her own tube with a thumb, then cleared the second one before twisting it into Nº1's slack mouth. For a moment there was no reaction, and she thought it was too late, then Nº1 jerked, spluttered and started, like an old engine on a frosty morning.

Alive, thought Holly. *We are both alive. If Butler wanted us dead, then we already would be.*

She braced her feet on the base of the barrel and hugged Nº1 tightly. Calm was needed here.

Calm, she broadcast, though she knew N°1's empathy would be muted. *Calm, little friend. Artemis will save us.*

If he is alive, she thought, but did not broadcast.

Artemis backed away from the nightmare version of his mother that hovered before him. Jayjay screeched and bucked in his arms, but Artemis held him tightly, automatically scratching the tiny brush of hair on his crown.

'Hand over that creature,' demanded Opal. 'You have no choice.'

Artemis circled Jayjay's neck with his thumb and forefinger.

'Oh, I think I have a choice.'

Opal was horrified. 'You wouldn't kill an innocent creature.'

'I did it before.'

Opal studied his eyes. 'I don't think you would do it again, Artemis Fowl. My fairy intuition tells me that you are not as cold-hearted as you pretend to be.'

It was true. Artemis knew he couldn't harm Jayjay, even to derail Opal's plans. Still, no reason to tell Opal that.

'My heart is cold, pixie. Believe it. Use some of that magical empathy to search my soul.'

His tone gave Opal pause. There was steel there, and he was hard to read. Perhaps she should not gamble so recklessly with him.

'Very well, human. Hand over the creature and I will spare your friends.'

•⚹⊕◊⌇⚹⊕⊖⊚•⚹•⟩⊕•⊕⚺•⎊⚹⋃•⚹⚹

'I have no friends,' Artemis shot back, though he knew it was a transparent bluff. Opal had been here for a few days at least. She had doubtless hijacked the manor's surveillance and security.

The Angeline Opal scratched her chin. 'Hmm, no friends. Apart from the LEP elf who accompanied you to the past, and of course the demon warlock who sent you back. Not to mention your big burly bodyguard.'

Alliteration, thought Artemis. *She's toying with me.*

'Then again,' mused Opal/Angeline, 'Butler is not really your friend any more. He's mine.'

This was a worrying statement, and perhaps true. Artemis, usually an expert interpreter of body language and telltale tics, was flummoxed by this crazed version of his mother.

'Butler would never willingly befriend you!'

Opal shrugged. It was a fair point. 'Who said anything about willingly?'

Artemis paled.

Uh-oh.

'Let me explain what happened,' said Opal sweetly. 'I scrambled the brains of my little helpers somewhat, so they could not report on me, then had them fly the shuttle back to Haven. Then I hitched a ride on your time stream before it closed. Oh so simple for someone with my skill set. You didn't even leave a hex at the hole.'

Artemis snapped his fingers. 'I knew I had forgotten something.'

314

Opal smiled thinly. 'Amusing. Anyway, it became obvious to me that I was or would be responsible for this entire affair, so I dropped out of the stream a few days early and took my time getting to know your group. Mother, father, Butler.'

'Where is my mother?' shouted Artemis, anger punching through his calm exterior, like a hammer through ice.

'Why I'm right here, darling,' said Opal in Angeline's voice. 'I am really sick and I need you to go into the past and fetch a magic monkey for me.' She laughed mockingly. 'Humans are such fools.'

'So this is not some kind of shape-shifting spell?'

'No, idiot. I was perfectly aware that Angeline would be examined. Shape-shifting spells are only skin deep, and even an adept such as myself can only hold one for short periods.'

'This means that my mother is not dying?' Artemis knew the answer, but he had to be certain.

Opal ground her teeth, torn between impatience and the desire to explain the brilliance of her plan.

'Not yet. Though soon the damage to her systems will be irreversible. I have possessed her from a distance. An extreme form of the *mesmer*. With power like mine, I can manipulate her very organs. Imitating Spelltropy was child's play. And once I have little Jayjay I can open my own hole in time.'

'So you are nearby? Your real self?'

Opal had had enough of questions. 'Yes, no. What does it matter? I win, you lose. Accept it, or everyone dies.'

Artemis edged towards the door. 'This game is not over yet.'

Footsteps outside and a strange rhythmic squeaking. A wheelbarrow, Artemis guessed, though he did not have much experience with gardening aids.

'Oh, I think this game is over now,' said Opal slyly.

The heavy door bounced in fits as it was butted from the outside. Butler pushed the trolley into the room, stumbling after it, hunched and shivering.

'He is strong, this one,' said Opal, almost in admiration. 'I mesmerized him, but still he refused to kill your friends. The stupid man's heart almost burst. It was all I could do to force him to construct the barrel and fill it with fat.'

'To smother fairy magic,' Artemis guessed.

'Obviously, idiot. Now, the game is absolutely over. Finished. Butler is my ace in the hole, as you humans might say. I hold all the aces. You are alone. Give me the lemur and I will go back to my own time. Nobody has to suffer.'

If Opal gets the lemur, then the entire planet will suffer, thought Artemis.

Opal snapped her fingers. 'Butler, seize the animal.'

Butler took a single step towards Artemis, then stopped. Shudders racked his broad back, and his fingers were claws wringing an invisible neck.

'I said get the animal, you stupid human.'

The bodyguard dropped to his knees, pounding the floor, trying to drive the voice from his head.

'Get the lemur now!' shrieked Opal.

Butler had enough strength for three words. 'Go . . . to . . . hell.'

Then he clutched at his arm and collapsed.

'Oops,' said Opal. 'Heart attack. I broke him.'

Stay focused, Artemis ordered himself. *Opal may hold all the aces, but perhaps there is a hole in one of those aces.*

Artemis tickled Jayjay under the chin.

'Hide, little friend. Hide.'

And with that he tossed the lemur towards a chandelier suspended from the ceiling. Jayjay flailed in the air, then latched on to a glass strut. He pulled himself nimbly into the light, hiding behind sheets of dangling crystal.

Opal immediately lost interest in Artemis, concentrating on levitating Angeline's body to the level of the chandalier. With a squeal of frustration she realized that such remote elevation was beyond even a being of her power.

'Doctor Schalke!' she called, and somewhere her real mouth was calling it too. 'Into the bedroom, Schalke!'

Artemis filed this information, then ducked below Opal to his mother's bedside. A mobile defibrillator cart was parked among the row of medical equipment ranged around the four-poster, and Artemis quickly switched it on, dragging the entire contraption to the limit of its lead to where Butler had collapsed.

The bodyguard lay face up, hands thrown back as though there were an invisible boulder on his chest. His face was stretched with the effort of moving the great stone. Eyes closed, sweat sheened, teeth clenched.

•◊⊖ᚷ�□⊕ ⊙ ⟩�8 •1⚶ ⨂⬡⬠⊖⚼ß •⅍↺ •⊛⁑⟩

He unbuttoned Butler's shirt, exposing a barrel chest, hard with muscle, scars and tension. A cursory examination told him that there was no heartbeat. Butler's body was dead; only his brain was left alive.

'Hold on, old friend,' murmured Artemis, trying to keep his mind focused.

He pulled the defibrillator paddles from their holsters, peeling back their disposable safety covers, leaving a thin coating of conductive gel on the contact surfaces. The paddles seemed to grow heavier as he waited for the unit to charge, and by the time the *go* light flashed green, they felt like rocks in his hands.

'Clear!' he called to no one in particular, then positioned the paddles firmly on Butler's chest and hit the shock button under his thumb, sending 360 joules of electricity into his bodyguard's heart. Butler's body arched, and the sharp smell of burning hair and skin assailed Artemis's nostrils. Gel crisped and sparked, burning twin rings where the pads had made contact. Butler's eyes flew open and his massive hands gripped Artemis's shoulders.

Is he still Opal's slave?

'Artemis,' breathed Butler, but then frowned in confusion. 'Artemis? How?'

'Later, old friend,' said the Irish boy brusquely, mentally progressing to the next problem. 'Just rest for now.'

This was not an order he would have to repeat. Butler sank immediately into exhausted unconsciousness, but his heart beat strongly inside his chest. He had not been dead long enough to have suffered brain damage.

Artemis's next problem was Opal, or more specifically how to get her out of his mother's body. If she did not vacate soon, Artemis had no doubt that his mother would not recover from the ordeal.

Gathering his nerve with several deep breaths, Artemis switched his full attention to his mother's hovering body. She was twirling below the chandelier as though suspended from it, clawing at Jayjay, who appeared to be taunting her by waving his hind quarters in her direction.

Can this situation get any more surreal?

Just then Doctor Schalke entered the room, brandishing a pistol that seemed too large for his delicate hands.

'I am here, you creature. Though I must say I don't like your tone. I may be spellbound, but I am not an animal.'

'Do shut up, Schalke. I can see I will have to fry a few more of your brain cells. Now, please. Fetch that lemur!'

Schalke pointed four fingers of his free hand towards the chandelier. 'The lemur is at a considerable height, yes? How do you suggest I fetch him? Perhaps I could shoot him dead?'

Opal swooshed low, arms and legs twirling like a harpy. 'No!' she shrieked, striking him around the head and shoulders. 'I would shoot a hundred of you, a thousand, before I let you harm one hair of that creature's fur. He is the future. My future! The world's future!'

'Indeed,' said the doctor. 'Were I not mesmerized, I suspect I should be yawning.'

☎ •✦⚹• ⬡✦⚜ •⬦✦• ✳◻◯↻• ⨃✦✦ •✦✦⬟✦ •◯

'Shoot the humans,' commanded Opal. 'The boy first, he is the most dangerous.'

'Are you certain? The man mountain looks more dangerous to me.'

'Shoot the boy!' howled Opal, frustration sending tears streaming down her cheeks. 'Then Butler and then yourself.'

Artemis swallowed. This was cutting things a bit fine; his accomplice had better get a move on.

'Very well,' said Schalke, fiddling with the safety on Butler's Sig Sauer. 'Anything to escape these theatrics.'

I have seconds before he figures out that catch, thought Artemis. *Seconds to distract Opal. Nothing to do but reveal the hole in her ace.*

'Come now, Opal,' Artemis said, with a calmness he did not feel. 'You wouldn't shoot a ten-year-old boy, would you?'

'I absolutely would,' said Opal without a heartbeat's hesitation. 'I am considering cloning you so that I can kill you over and over again. Heaven.'

Then *all* of what Artemis had said registered.

'Ten? Did you say you were ten years old?'

Artemis forgot all about the danger surrounding him, lost in the sweet moment of triumph. It was intoxicating.

'Yes, that is what I said. I am ten. My *real* mother would have noticed immediately.'

Opal chewed the knuckles of Angeline's left hand. Thinking.

'You are the Artemis Fowl from *my* time? They brought you back!'

'Obviously.'

Opal reared back through the air, as though taken by the wind.

'There is another one. Here somewhere, another Artemis Fowl.'

'Finally!' said Artemis smirking. 'The great pixie genius sees the truth.'

'Find him,' shrieked Opal. 'Find him immediately. At once.'

Schalke straightened his glasses. 'At once *and* immediately. This must be important.'

Opal watched him go with real hatred in her eyes. 'When this is over, I am going to destroy this entire estate just for spite. And then, when I return to the past, I shall –'

'Don't tell me,' interrupted ten-year-old Artemis Fowl. 'You will destroy it again.'

ALMOST EIGHT YEARS AGO

When fourteen-year-old Artemis had had a moment to consider things, sometime in between scaling pylons and outwitting murderous Extinctionists, he realized that there were a lot of unanswered questions about his mother's illness. *He* had supposedly given her Spelltropy, but who had passed it to him? Holly's magic had permeated his body in the past, but she herself was hale and hearty. Why wasn't she sick? Or, for that matter, how did Butler escape infection? He had been healed so many times that he must be half fairy by now.

And, of *all* the thousands of humans healed, mesmerized or wiped every year, *his* mother was the one to fall ill. The mother of the only human on Earth who could do something about it. Very coincidental. Too coincidental by far.

So. Either someone had deliberately infected his mother, or the symptoms were being magically duplicated. Either way, the result was the same: Artemis would travel back in time to find the antidote. The lemur, Jayjay.

And who would want Jayjay found as much as Artemis did? The answer to that question lay in the past. Opal Koboi, of course. The little primate was the last ingredient in her magical cocktail. With his brain fluid in her bloodstream she would be literally the most powerful person on the planet. And if Opal couldn't nab Jayjay in her own time, she would get him in the future. Whatever it took. She must have followed them back through the time stream, jumped out early and organized this whole affair. Presumably, once she had Jayjay's brain fluid, navigating her way back would not be a problem.

It was confusing even for Artemis. Opal wouldn't even be in his present if he hadn't gone back in time. And *he* only went back in time because of a situation she created. It was Artemis's own attempts to cure his mother which had led Opal to infect her.

But one thing he now felt sure of was that Opal was behind this. She was behind them and in front of them. Chasing their group into her own clutches. A time paradox.

⊕⊞▢•⬡⚶⊕♌♭Ɛ ⟐•◉⚶⟐⊍▢⊖♭Ɛ☊•◉

There are two Opals in this equation, thought Artemis. *I think there should continue to be two Artemis Fowls.*

And so a plan had taken shape in his mind.

Once the young Artemis had been apprised of all the details and convinced of their accuracy, he at once agreed to accompany them to the future, in spite of Butler's vocal objection.

'It's my mother, Butler,' he said simply. 'I must save her. Now I charge you to stay by her side until I return. Anyway, how could they hope to succeed without me?'

'How indeed,' Holly Short had wondered, then taken more pleasure than was necessary in watching that arrogance drain from the boy's features when the time stream opened in front of them, like the maw of some great computer-generated serpent.

'Chin up, Mud Boy,' she'd said as Artemis the younger watched his arm dissolve. 'And watch out for quantum zombies.'

The time stream had been difficult for Artemis the elder. Any other human would have been torn apart by such repeated exposure to its particular radiation, but Artemis held himself together by sheer willpower. He focused on the high end of his intellect, solving unprovable theorems with large cardinals and composing an ending for Schubert's unfinished Symphony $N^o 8$.

As he worked, Artemis sensed the odd derisive comment from his younger self.

$\int \partial \delta \? \cdot \partial \omega \ell \cdot \Box \partial \delta \? \cdot \otimes \ell \Theta \S \? \rightarrow \cdot \ell \cdot \odot \bigcirc \otimes$

More B minor? Do you really think so?

Had he always been this obnoxious? How tiresome. Little wonder people in general did not like him.

FOWL MANOR, THE PRESENT

Back in his own time, in his own house, Artemis the elder paused only to grab some clothes from the wardrobe before quickly exiting his study, warning Foaly and N°1 to keep silent with a simple *shhh*. He moved quickly along the corridor towards the dumb-waiter shaft adjacent to the second-floor tea room. This was not the most direct route to the security centre, in fact the route was circuitous and awkward, but it was the only way to pass through the house undetected.

Butler believed he had every square inch of the manor, apart from the Fowl's private chambers, under surveillance, but Artemis had long since worked how to travel through the house without being picked up on camera. This route involved hiding in corners, walking on furniture, travelling in dumb waiters and tilting a full-length mirror to just the right angle.

It was possible, of course, that a hostile could figure out the same pathways, co-ordinates and trajectories, and also move about the house undetected. Possible, but highly improbable, not without an intimate knowledge of nooks and crannies that did not exist on any plans.

Artemis followed a zigzag pattern down the hallway, a second behind a security camera's sweep, then ducked quickly inside the dumb-waiter shaft. Luckily, the box was on this floor, or he would have been forced to shin down the cable and *shinning* was not one of his strong suits. Artemis reached outside and pressed the ground-floor button, whipping his hand back in before the descending box caught his wrist. While it was true that security would register the dumb waiter descending, it would not set off any red lights.

Once at kitchen level, Artemis rolled on to the floor, opening the fridge door to shield his movement into the pantry. Deep shadows concealed him until the camera swung away from the doorway allowing him to climb on top of the table and jump outside.

All the time thinking. Plotting.

Assume the worst. Little Artemis is helpless and Holly and Number One are already incapacitated. Quite possible if someone like Butler were mesmerized and doing the incapacitating. Opal is somewhere near the command centre, manipulating my mother. It was Opal who could see the magic inside me. Not Mother. She peeled away the spell I had cast over my parents.

And: *Of course B minor. If one starts in B minor, one finishes in B minor. Any fool knows that.*

A suit of medieval armour stood in the main lobby. The same armour that Butler had put on to do battle with a troll during the Fowl Manor seige five years earlier. Artemis approached it slowly, his back flat against an abstract grey-black tapestry that camouflaged him almost perfectly. Once concealed behind the suit of armour, he nudged the base of an adjacent mirror until it reflected a spotlight's beam directly into the lens of the lobby camera.

Now his path to the security centre was clear. Artemis strode purposefully towards the booth. This was where Opal would be, he was certain of it. From there she could monitor the entire house and it was directly below Angeline's bedroom. If Opal was indeed controlling his mother, closer was better.

It was clear from several metres away that he was right. Artemis could hear Opal ranting from a distance.

'There is another one. Here somewhere, another Artemis Fowl.'

Either the penny had dropped, or young Artemis had been forced to reveal their plan. 'Find him,' shrieked Opal. 'Find him immediately. At once.'

Artemis stepped quietly into the security control booth – a boxroom off the main lobby that had served in its time as a cloakroom, weapons lock-up and holding cell for prisoners. Now, it housed a computer desk, similar to those found in editing suites, and stacks of monitors displaying live feeds of the manor and grounds.

Huddled before the monitor bank was Opal, dressed in Holly's LEP gear. She had wasted no time in stealing the fairy suit. It was mere minutes since Artemis had locked it in the safe.

The little pixie was multi-tasking furiously, scanning the monitors while maintaining remote control over Artemis's mother. Her dark hair was sweat-slicked and her childlike limbs shook with the effort.

Artemis sneaked into the room, quickly punching the code into the weapons locker.

'When this is over, I am going to destroy this entire estate just for spite. And then, when I return to the past, I shall —'

Opal froze. Something had made a clicking noise. She turned to find Artemis Fowl pointing a weapon of some kind at her. She immediately abandoned all other spells, throwing her efforts into a desperate *mesmer*.

'Drop that gun,' she intoned. 'You are my slave.'

Artemis felt instantly woozy, but he had already pressed the trigger and a dart loaded with a *Butler special* concoction of muscle relaxants and sedatives buried its long needle in Opal's neck, where there was no protection from the suit. This was a shot in a million, since Artemis was not proficient with firearms. As Butler put it: *Artemis, a genius you may be, but leave the shooting to me, because you couldn't hit the backside of a stationary elephant.*

Opal concentrated furiously on the puncture wound, dousing it with magical sparks, but it was too late. The drug was already entering her brain, loosening her control on the magic inside her.

She began to sway and flicker, alternating between her real pixie self and Miss Book.

Miss Book, thought Artemis. *My suspicions were correct. The only stranger in the equation.*

Intermittently, Opal disappeared altogether, shield buzzing in and out. Magical bolts shot from her fingers, frying the monitors before Artemis could get a look at what was going on upstairs.

'*Now* I can do the bolts,' she slurred. 'I've been trying to focus enough magic all week.'

The magic shifted and swirled, finally etching a picture in the air. It was a rough picture of Foaly, and he was laughing.

'I hate you, centaur!' screamed Opal, lunging towards and through the insubstantial image. Then her eyes rolled back in her head, and she collapsed snoring on the floor.

Artemis straightened his tie.

Freud, he felt certain, *would have a field day with that.*

Artemis hurried upstairs to his parents' room. The rug was coated in a pool of lumpy fat. Two sets of fairy footprints led from the turgid pearlescent puddle into the en suite wetroom. Artemis heard the power shower drilling against the tiles.

Opal used animal fat to suppress Number One's magic. How despicable. How horrible.

Young Artemis was studying the spreading mass of goo.

'Look,' he said, noticing his older self. 'Opal used animal fat to suppress Number One's magic. How ingenious.'

Under the noise of the shower were the sounds of retching and complaining. Butler was hosing down Holly and N°1 and they were not happy or healthy.

But alive. Both alive.

◉ • ◭ | ⚸ ◍ • ⚘ ⚭ ✢ ⚮ ◍ • ⚲ • ⚞ ◯ ◯ ⚟ • ⚭ ◉ • ⚇

Angeline lay on her bed, wrapped in a goosedown duvet. She was pale and dazed, but was it Artemis's imagination or had just a tinge of colour crept back into her cheeks? She coughed gently and immediately both Artemises were at her side.

Artemis the elder raised an eyebrow at his younger self.

'You can see how this might be awkward,' he said pointedly.

'I can indeed,' conceded the ten-year-old. 'Why don't I have a poke around in your . . . in my study. See what I come up with.'

This is a problem, Artemis realized. *My own inquisitiveness. Perhaps I should not have promised not to mind-wipe my younger self. Something will have to be done.*

Angeline opened her eyes. They were blue and calm, peering out from tired dark sockets.

'Artemis,' she said, her voice the rasp of fingers on tree bark. 'I dreamed I was flying. And there was a monkey . . .'

Artemis shook with relief. She was safe; he had saved her.

'It was a lemur, Mother. Mum.'

Angeline smiled wanly, reaching up to stroke his cheek. 'Mum. I have waited so long to hear you say that. So long.'

And with that smile on her face Angeline lay back and drifted off into deep natural sleep.

Just as well, Artemis realized. *Or she may have noticed the fairies in the bathroom, or the contents of a fat barrel on the rug. Or a second Artemis lurking shiftily by the bookcase.*

⊕⊠⟩ᘯ•⚇⊗Ѕᕔ•⟁⟓ᚹᎦ•⊜ᐃ⚹ᐃᏫ•ⵔ♭ᵡ

Butler emerged from the wetroom dripping wet, shirt-less, paddle marks scorched into his skin. He was paler than usual, and had to lean against the doorframe for support.

'Welcome back,' he said to Artemis the elder. 'This little one is quite a chip off the old block. Gave me one hell of a jump-start.'

'He *is* the old block,' said Artemis wryly.

Butler jerked a thumb over his shoulder. 'Those two didn't enjoy their dip in the barrel.'

'Animal fat is poison to fairies,' explained Artemis. 'Blocks the magical flow. Turns their own power rancid.'

A shadow settled on Butler's brow. 'Opal made me do it. She . . . Miss Book approached me at the main gates as I left for the airport. I was trapped in my own skull.'

Artemis laid a gentle hand on his bodyguard's forearm. 'I know. No apologies are necessary.'

Butler remembered that he did not have his weapon, and he remembered who did have it. 'What did you do with Schalke? Knockout dart?'

'No. Our paths did not cross.'

Butler staggered to the bedroom door, Artemis hot on his heels. 'Opal is controlling him, though he's making her work for it. We need to secure them both right now.'

It took them several minutes to reach the security booth, Butler pulling himself along the walls, and by that time Opal was already gone. Artemis ran to the window just in time to see the blocky rear end of a vintage Mercedes take the bend in the driveway. A small figure bounced on the back seat. Two bounces, the first time it was Opal, the second Miss Imogen Book.

Already her power returns, realized Artemis.

Butler loomed above him, panting.

'This isn't over yet,' he said.

Artemis did not respond to the comment; Butler was simply stating the patently obvious.

Then the engine noise increased in volume and pitch.

'Gear change,' said Butler. 'She's coming back.'

Artemis felt a chill pass over his heart, though he had been expecting it.

Of course she's coming back, he thought. *She will never have another chance like this one. Butler can barely walk. Holly and Number One will be diminished for hours and I am a mere human. If she retreats now, Jayjay will be free of her forever. Soon Foaly's squad will arrive from Tara and whisk the little lemur underground. For perhaps five minutes, Opal has the upper hand.*

Artemis planned quickly. 'I need to take Jayjay away from here. So long as he is in the manor, everyone is in danger. Opal will kill us all to cover her tracks.'

Butler nodded, sweat running in rivulets through the lines on his face. 'Yes. We can make it to the Cessna.'

'*I* can make it to the Cessna, old friend,' corrected Artemis. 'I am charging you with the protection of my mother and friends, not to mention keeping my younger self off the Internet. He is as dangerous as Opal.'

It was a sensible tactic and Butler knew it was coming

before Artemis said it. He was in such bad shape that he would slow Artemis down. Not only that but the manor would be wide open for any of Opal's thralls to stroll in and exact her revenge.

'Very well. Don't take her over three thousand metres and watch the flaps – they're a bit sticky.'

Artemis nodded as if he didn't know. Giving instructions comforted Butler.

'Three thousand. Flaps. Got it.'

'Would you like a gun? I have a neat Beretta.'

Artemis shook his head. 'No guns. My aim is so bad that even with Holly's eye to help me I would probably only succeed in shooting off a toe or two. No, all I need is the bait.' He paused. 'And my sunglasses.'

CHAPTER 15: MURDER MOST FOWL

 THE Fowl family currently had three aircraft. A Learjet and a Sikorsky helicopter, were hangared at the nearby airport, and a small Cessna, which lived in a small garage workshop beside the high meadow on the northern border of the estate. The Cessna was several years old and would have been recycled some time ago had Artemis not taken it on as a project. His aim was to make it carbon-neutral *and* cost-effective, a goal which his father heartily approved of.

'I have forty scientists working on the same problem, but my money is on you,' he had confided to his son.

And so Artemis coated the entire body of the craft with lightweight super-efficient solar panels, like NASA's prototype flying wing, the Helios. Unlike the Helios, Artemis's Cessna could still fly at its normal speeds *and* take passengers. This was because Artemis had removed the single engine and installed smaller ones to turn the main propeller, the four extra props on the wings and the landing gear.

333

Most of the metal in the skeleton had been stripped out and replaced with a lightweight polymer. Where the fuel tank had been now sat a small battery.

There were still a few adjustments to make, but Artemis believed his ship was skyworthy. He hoped so. There was a lot riding on the soundness of the little craft. He sprinted from the kitchen door across the courtyard and towards the high meadow. With any luck Opal would not realize he was gone until she saw the plane taking off. Of course *then* he wanted her to see him. Hopefully, he could draw her away long enough for LEP reinforcements to arrive.

Artemis felt the tiredness in his legs before he had gone a hundred metres. He had never been the athletic type and the recent time-stream jaunts had done nothing for his physique, even though he had concentrated hard on his muscles during the trips. Willing himself to tone up. A little mind-over-matter experiment that sadly had not yielded any results.

The old farm gate to the meadow was closed, so Artemis scaled it rather than struggle with the heavy bolt. He could feel the heat from the simian's body high inside his jacket and its little hands were tight on his neck.

Jayjay must be safe, he thought. *He must be saved.*

The garage doors were sturdier than they looked and protected with a keypad entry system. Artemis tapped in the code and threw the doors wide, flooding the interior with the deep orange rays of the early-evening sun. Inside, nestled in a horseshoe of benches and tool trolleys, was the modified Cessna, hooked up to a supplementary power cable. Artemis snapped the cable from its socket on the fuselage and clambered into the cockpit. He strapped himself into the pilot's seat, remembering briefly when he had first flown this plane solo.

Nine years old. I needed a booster seat.

The engines started immediately and virtually silently. The only noise came from the whirring of the propellers and the clicks of switches as Artemis ran through his preflight check.

The news was generally good. Eighty per cent power. That gave the small plane a range of several hundred miles. Easily enough to lead Opal on a merry dance along the Irish coast. But the flaps were sticky and the seals were old.

Don't take her over three thousand metres.

'We're going to be fine,' he said to the passenger inside his jacket. 'Absolutely fine.'

Was this the truth? He could not be certain.

The high meadow was wide and long and sloped gently upwards to the estate wall. Artemis nudged the Cessna from her hangar, swinging the nose in a tight turn to give himself maximum runway. Under ideal circumstances, the five-hundred-metre stretch of grass was more than ample for a take-off. But there was a tailwind and the grass was a few centimetres longer than it should be.

Despite these considerations, we should be OK. I have flown in worse conditions than these.

The take-off was textbook. Artemis pulled back on the nosewheel at the three-hundred-metre mark and comfortably cleared the north wall. Even at this low altitude he could see the Irish Sea to the east, black with scimitars of sunlight slicing across the wave tips.

He was tempted, for the merest fraction of a moment, just to flee, but he didn't.

Have I changed utterly? Artemis asked himself. He realized that he was running out of palatable crimes. Not so long ago, nearly all crime had been acceptable to him.

No, he decided. There were still people who deserved to be stolen from, or exposed, or dropped in deep jungle with only flip-flops and a spoon. He would just have to put more effort into finding them.

Artemis activated the wing cameras. There was one such person on the avenue below. A megalomaniac, cold-hearted pixie. Opal Koboi. Artemis could see her striding towards the manor, jamming Holly's helmet down over her ears.

I was afraid of that. She thought to take the helmet. A most valuable tool.

Still, he had no alternative but to attract her attention. The lives of his family and friends were at stake. Artemis took the Cessna down thirty metres, following Opal's path to the manor. She may not hear the engine, but the sensors in Holly's helmet would throw up a dozen red lights.

On cue, Opal stopped in her tracks, throwing her gaze skywards, capturing the small plane in her sights.

Come on, Opal, thought Artemis. *Take the bait. Run a thermal.*

*

⚬⚬⚬⚬⚬⚬⚬⚬⚬⚬⚬⚬⚬⚬⚬⚬⚬⚬⚬⚬⚬⚬⚬⚬⚬

Opal strode purposefully towards the manor until she snagged the toe of one LEP boot under the heel of another.

Stupid tall elf, she thought furiously, righting herself. *When I am queen – no – when I am empress, all tall fairies will have their legs modified. Or, better still, I will have a human pituitary gland grafted to my brain so that I shall be the tall one. A giant among fairies, physically and mentally.*

She had other plans too: an Opalesque cosmetic face mould that could give any of her adoring fans the Koboi look in seconds. A homeopathic hoverchair covered in massage bars and mood sensors that would read her humour and spray whatever scents were needed to cheer her up.

But those plans could wait until she was empress. For now the lemur was her priority. Without its brain fluid, it could take years to accomplish her plans. Plus magic was so much easier than science.

Opal slotted Holly's helmet on to her head. Pads inside the helmet automatically inflated to cradle her skull. There was some coded security, which she contemptuously hacked with a series of blinks and hand movements. These LEP helmets were not half as advanced as the models in her R&D department.

Once the hemet's functions were open to her, the visor's display crystals fizzled and turned scarlet. Red alert! Something was closing in. A 3D radar sweep revealed a small craft overhead, and recognition software quickly pegged it as a human-built Cessna.

She quickly selected the command sequence for a thermal

scan and the helmet infra-red detector analysed the electro-magnetic radiation coming from inside the aircraft. There was some waffle from the solar panels but the scan isolated an orange blob in the pilot's seat. One passenger only. The helmet's biometric reader conveniently identified the pilot as Artemis Fowl, and dropped a 3D icon over his fuzzy figure.

'One passenger,' murmured Opal. 'Are you trying to decoy me away from the house, Artemis Fowl? Is that why you fly so low?'

But Artemis Fowl knew technology, he would anticipate thermal-imaging.

'What do you have up your sleeve?' wondered the pixie. 'Or perhaps up your shirt.'

She magnified Artemis's heart and discovered a second heat source superimposed over the first, distinguishable only by a slightly cooler shade of red.

Even at that desperate moment, Opal could not help but admire this young human, who had attempted to mask the lemur's heat signature with his own.

'Clever. But not ingenious.'

And he would need to be ingenious to defeat Opal Koboi. Bringing back the second Artemis had been a neat trick, but she should have caught it.

I was defeated by my own arrogance, she realized. *That will not happen again.*

The helmet automatically tuned into the Cessna's radio frequency and so Opal sent Artemis a little message.

'I am coming for the lemur, boy,' she said, a pulse of

magic setting the suit's wings a flutter. 'And this time there will be no *you* to save you.'

Artemis could not feel or see the various waves that probed the Cessna, but he guessed that Opal would use the helmet's thermal imager to see how many hot bodies were on the plane. Perhaps she would try X-ray too. It would seem as though he was trying to hide Jayjay's heat signature with his own, but that was a transparent ploy and should not fool Opal for more than a heartbeat. When the pixie was satisfied that her prize was escaping, then how could she not follow?

Artemis banked starboard, to keep Opal in the camera eye, and was satisfied to see a set of wings sliding from the slots in Holly's suit.

The chase was on.

Time for the bait to pretend it was trying to escape.

Artemis peeled away from the estate, heading for the deep purple sea, opening the throttle wide, satisfied by the plane's smooth acceleration. The batteries were channelling a steady supply of power to the engines without releasing one gram of carbon dioxide into the atmosphere.

He checked the tail camera view and was not totally surprised to find the flying pixie in his monitor.

Her control over the magic is addled by sedative, he guessed. *Opal may have had barely enough power to jump-start the suit. But soon the dart's after-effects will peter out and then there may be lightning bolts flaring across my wing.*

◻•⌐△⅃⅄∿•⋆∿⊗•⌐⅂⊗∫∿⊗∿•⊗△•∿⅄

Artemis turned south, following the jagged coast. The clamour and bustle of Dublin's high-rise apartment blocks, belching chimneys and swarm of buzzing helicopters gave way to long stretches of grey rock shadowed by the north–south railtrack. The sea pushed against the shore, folding its million fingers over sand, scrub and shale.

Fishing boats chugged from buoy to buoy, trailing white sea-serpent wakes, sailors snagging lobster pots with long-handled gaffs. Fat clouds hung ponderously at four thousand metres, rain brewing in their bellies.

A peaceful evening, so long as no one looks up.

Though at this altitude, Opal's blurred flying form could be mistaken for an eagle.

Artemis's plan went smoothly for longer than he'd hoped. He made sixty miles without interference from Opal. Artemis allowed himself a glimmer of hope.

Soon, he thought. *The LEP reinforcements will come soon.*

Then his radio crackled into life.

'Artemis? Are you there, Artemis?'

Butler. He sounded extremely calm, which he always did before he explained just how serious a situation was.

'Butler, old friend, I'm here. Tell me the good news.'

The bodyguard sighed into his microphone, a breaking wave of static.

'They're not coming after the Cessna. You are not the priority.'

'Number One is,' said Artemis. 'They need to get him below ground. I understand.'

'Yes. Him and —'

'Say no more, old friend,' said Artemis sharply. 'Opal is listening.'

'The LEP are here, Artemis. I want you to turn round and fly back.'

'No,' said Artemis firmly. 'I will not put Mother at risk again.'

Artemis heard a strange creaking sound and surmised that Butler was strangling the microphone stalk.

'OK. Another location then. Somewhere we can dig ourselves in.'

'Very well, I am on a southerly heading anyway, so why not —'

Artemis never completed his veiled suggestion as his channel was blocked by a deafening burst of white noise. The squawk left a droning aftershock in his ears, and for a moment he allowed the Cessna to drift.

No sooner had he regained control than a thudding blow to the fuselage caused him to lose it again.

Several red lights flashed on the display-plane solar-panel icon. At least ten panels had been shattered by the impact.

Artemis spared half a second to check the rear camera. Opal was no longer trailing behind. No surprise there.

The pixie's voice burst through the radio speakers, sharp with petulance and evil intent.

'I am strong now, Mud Boy,' she said. 'Your poison is gone, flushed from my system. My power grows and I am hungry for more.'

Artemis did not engage in conversation. All his skill and quick thinking would be needed to pilot the Cessna.

Opal struck again on the port wing, smashing her forearms into the solar panels, breaking them as a child would break sheets of ice in a pool, windmilling her arms gleefully, wings buzzing to keep pace. The plane bucked and yawed and Artemis fought the stick to pull the craft level.

She's insane, thought Artemis. *Utterly insane.*

And:

Those panels are unique. And she calls herself a scientist.

Opal scampered along the wing, punching an armoured fist into the fuselage itself. More panels were obliterated and tiny fist-sized dents buckled the polymer over Artemis's shoulder. Tiny cracks ran along the dents, slit by the wind.

Opal's voice was loud in the speaker. 'Land, Fowl. Land and I may not return to the manor when I have finished with you. Land! Land!'

Each order to *land* was emphasized by another blow on the cockpit. The windscreen exploded inwards, showering Artemis with jagged chunks of plexiglass.

'Land! Land!'

You have the product, Artemis reminded himself. *So you have the power. Opal cannot afford to kill Jayjay.*

The wind screamed in Artemis's face, and the readings from his flight instruments made no sense unless Opal was scrambling them with the LEP suit's field. But Artemis still had a chance. There was fight left in this Fowl.

He pointed the nose downwards, banking sharply left. Opal kept pace easily, tearing strips from the fuselage. She was a destructive shadow in the dimming dusk light.

Artemis could smell the sea.

He was too low. Too soon.

More red lights on the instrument panel. The power supply had been cut. The batteries were breached. The altimeter whirred and beeped.

Opal was at the side window. Artemis could see her tiny teeth grinning at him. She was saying something. Shouting. But the radio was not operational any more. Just as well probably.

She is having the time of her life, he realized. *Fun, fun, fun.*

Artemis struggled with the controls. The sticky flaps were the least of his worries now. If Opal decided to snip a few cables, then he would lose whatever say he had over the plane. Though it was too early, Artemis lowered the tricycle landing gear. If Opal sabotaged the mechanism now, the wheels should stay down.

They plummeted earthwards, locked together. A sparrow on an eagle's back. Opal smashed her armoured head through the door window's plexiglass, still shouting inside the helmet, spittle spraying the visor. Issuing orders that Artemis could not hear and could not spare enough time to lip-read. He could see that her eyes glowed red with magic and it was clear from her manic expression that any threads connecting her to rationality had been severed.

343

More shouting. Muffled behind the visor. Artemis cast a sardonic gaze at the radio, which sat dead and dark in its cradle.

Opal caught the look and raised her visor, shouting over the wind, too impatient for the helmet PA.

'Give me the lemur and I will save you,' she said, her voice mesmerizing. 'You have my —'

Artemis avoided her gaze and pulled the emergency flare gun from under the seat, sticking it in her face.

'You leave me no choice but to shoot you,' he said, voice cold and certain. This was not a threat, it was a statement of fact.

Opal knew the truth when she heard it and for one second her resolve wavered. She pulled back, but not quickly enough to prevent Artemis from firing the flare into her helmet, then reaching up to flick down the visor.

Opal spun away from the Cessna, trailing black smoke, red sparks swarming round her head like angry wasps. Her wing smashed into the Cessna's, and neither survived intact. Solar-cell splinters flashed like stardust and tail feathers from Opal's flying rig helicoptered slowly earthwards. The aeroplane yawed to starboard, moaning like a wounded animal.

I need to land. Now.

Artemis didn't feel guilty about what he'd done. Flare burns would not hinder a being of Opal's regenerative power for long. Already the magic would be repairing her skin damage. At best he had bought himself a few minutes' reprieve.

344

When Opal comes back, she will be beyond furious. A true maniac. Perhaps her judgement will be clouded.

Artemis smiled grimly, and for a moment he felt like his old conniving self, before Holly and his mother had introduced him to their pesky moral codes.

Good. Clouded judgement may give me the advantage I need.

Artemis levelled the craft as much as he could, slowing his descent. Wind slapped his face, tugging his skin. Shielding his eyes with a forearm, he peered downwards through the blur of propeller spin.

Hook Head peninsula jutted into the blackness of the sea below him like a slate-grey arrowhead. A cluster of lights winked on the eastern curve. This was the village of Duncade, where Butler had awaited his young charge's return from Limbo. A magical inlet which had once sheltered the demon isle of Hybras. The entire area was a magical hotspot and would set LEP spectrometers buzzing.

Dark blue night was falling quickly, and it was difficult to tell hard ground from soft. Artemis knew that a carpet of meadow ran from Duncade to the Hook Head light-house, but could only see the grass strip once every five seconds when it flashed emerald in the tower's beam.

My runway, thought Artemis.

He dragged the Cessna into the best possible approach line, descending in uneven, stomach-lurching swoops. Solar panels frittered away from the nose and wings, streaming behind the craft.

Still no sign of Opal.

She's coming. Make no mistake about it.

With each flash of green, the hard earth rushed up to meet him.

Too fast, thought Artemis. *I am coming in too fast. I will never get my legal pilot's licence flying like this.*

He clenched his jaws and held the stick tightly. Touchdown was going to be rough.

And it was, though not bone-shatteringly so. Not the first time. It was on the second bounce that Artemis was shunted forward into the console and heard the left side of his collarbone snap. A horrible sound that brought bile to his throat.

No pain yet. Just cold. I am going into shock.

The Cessna's wheels skidded on the long grass, which was coated with sea-spray and slicker than ice. Artemis scowled, not because of his injuries but because his fate was in the hands of chance now; he had no control. Opal would be coming for Jayjay and he must do his utmost to distract her.

The outside world continued to intrude most violently on Artemis's thoughts. The front wheel strut glanced off a sharp rock, shearing away completely. For several seconds the wheel continued to roll alongside the plane, until it veered off into the darkness.

Another bump and the Cessna collapsed on to its nose, propeller ploughing furrows in the earth. Sheaves of grass fanned the air and clods of muck rained through the holes in the windscreen.

Artemis tasted earth and thought, *I don't see what Mulch*

makes all the fuss about. It's not exactly lobster mousse.

Then he was out of the plane and stumbling towards the rocky shoreline. Artemis did not call for help and none would have come if he had. The rocks were black, treacherous and deserted. The sea was loud and the wind blew high. Even if the lighthouse beam had pinned the falling plane's image to the sky, it would be a long while before unarmed, unsuspecting villagers arrived to offer assistance. And by then it would be too late.

Artemis stumbled on, his left arm hanging low. His good hand cupped the furry head poking from the front of his jacket.

'Almost there,' he panted.

A pair of sea stacks jutted from the waters like the last teeth from the gums of a tobacco chewer. Thirty-metre-high hard-rock columns that had resisted the erosive power of wind and wave. The locals called them The Nuns because of their sisterly appearance. Head-to-toe habits.

The Nuns were quite the local attraction and sturdy rope bridges spanned the chasms from shore to Little Sister and on to Mother Superior. Butler once told Artemis that he had spent many lonely nights on the second sea stack with night-vision binoculars, glassing the ocean for a sign of Hybras.

Artemis stepped on to the first span of the bridge. It rippled and creaked slightly under his feet, but held firm. He saw the sea far below through the slats, flat rocks pushing through the surface like mushrooms through clay. The body of an unlucky dog lay splayed on one of the lower rocks, a stark reminder of what could happen if you lost your footing on The Nuns.

I am hurrying towards a dead end, he told himself. *Once I reach the second stack, there is nowhere to go but down.*

But there was no choice. A quick glance over his shoulder told him that Opal was coming. He did not even need his shield-filtered sunglasses to see her. The pixie had no magic to spare for invisibility. She lurched zombie-like across the meadow, a red haze of magic lighting her face inside the helmet, fists clenched balls at her side. Her wings were outstretched, but tattered and battered. She would not be flying anywhere on those. Only the power of Jayjay could save Opal now. He was her last hope for victory. If she did not inject his brain fluid soon, then surely the LEP would arrive to protect the endangered lemur.

Artemis walked across the bridge, careful not to bash his dangling arm against the railing. Miraculously, he was in little constant pain, but every footstep sent a throb of white-hot agony flashing across his upper chest.

Distract her a while longer. Then the cavalry will surely arrive. The winged, invisible cavalry. They wouldn't abandon him, would they?

'Fowl!' the shriek came from behind him. Closer than he expected. 'Give me the monkey!'

The voice was layered with wasted magic. No eye contact. No *mesmer*.

Monkey, thought Artemis, smirking. *Ha ha.*

Further across the chasm. Blackness above and below,

star points in the sky and sea. Waves growling like tigers. Hungry.

Artemis stumbled towards the first Nun. Little Sister. Stepping out on to a rock plateau worn treacherous. His foot slipped on the surface and he spun across the diameter of the summit like a ballroom dancer with an unseen partner.

He heard Opal's shriek. For Jayjay to die now would be disaster, as she would be stuck in this time with the entire LEP on her trail and no ultimate powers.

Artemis did not look back, though he ached to. He could hear Opal clanking across the boards, swearing with each breath. The words sounded almost comical in her childlike pixie voice.

Nowhere to go but forward. Artemis almost fell on to the second span of bridge, pulling himself along the rope rail until he arrived at Mother Superior. Locals said that if you stood at the right point on the coastline at sunrise, and squinted a little, then you could just make out stern features on the Mother Superior's face.

The rock felt stern now. Bleak and unforgiving. Even one false step would not be tolerated.

Artemis dropped to his knees on the mushroom curve of the plateau, cupping his left elbow in his right palm.

Soon, shock and pain will overcome me. Not yet, genius. Focus.

Artemis glanced down to the V of his jacket. The furry head was gone.

Dropped on Little Sister. Waiting for Opal.

This was confirmed by a sudden shriek of delight from

behind. Artemis turned slowly and with great effort to face his enemy. It seemed as though he had been fighting her forever.

The pixie stood atop the sea stack, almost dancing with delight. Artemis could see a small furry figure splayed on the plateau.

'I have him,' Opal cackled. 'With all your genius! With your big bursting brain! You dropped him! You simply dropped him!'

Artemis felt the throb build in his shoulder. In a minute, there would be worse coming, he was certain of it.

Opal stretched two hands towards her prize.

'He is mine,' she said reverentially, and Artemis swore he heard thunder in the distance. 'The ultimate magic is mine. I have the lemur.'

Artemis spoke clearly, so his words would carry across the divide.

'It's not a lemur,' he said. 'It's a monkey.'

Opal's smile froze, all tiny teeth, and she grabbed what she had thought was Jayjay. The figure was soft in her hands.

'A toy!' she gasped. 'This is a toy.'

Artemis's triumph was dulled by pain and exhaustion. 'Opal, meet Professor Primate. My brother's plaything.'

'A toy,' repeated Opal dully. 'But there were two heat sources. I saw them.'

'Microwave gel pack stuffed inside the foam,' explained Artemis. 'It's over, Opal. Jayjay is in Haven by now. You can't get him. Turn yourself in and I won't have to hurt you.'

⊕◑൫•൫◔⊹◊⅄⊕⊖♋ß℧•◉◊♋໑•⅄♋◑）

Opal's features were twisted with rage.

'Hurt me! Hurt *me*?' She dashed the toy monkey against the rock surface over and over again until the dented works fell out. A metallic voice issued from the speaker.

'History will remember this day . . . History will . . . History will remember this day.'

Opal screamed and red sparks boiled round her fingertips.

'I cannot fly and I cannot shoot lightning, but I have enough magic to boil your brain.'

Opal's dreams of supreme power were forgotten. At that moment all she wanted to do was kill Artemis Fowl. She stepped on to the second span with murder in her heart.

Artemis stood wearily, reaching into his pocket.

'Your armour should save you,' he said to Opal, his voice calm. 'It will be terrifying, but the LEP will dig you out.'

Opal scoffed. 'More tactics. Bluff and double bluff. Not this time, Artemis.'

'Don't make me do this, Opal,' Artemis pleaded. 'Just sit down and wait for the LEP. No one needs to get hurt.'

'Oh, I think someone needs to get hurt,' said Opal.

Artemis took a modified laser pointer from his pocket, activating the narrow beam and aiming it at the base of Little Sister.

'What are you going to do with that thing? It would take a hundred years to saw through this rock.'

'I'm not trying to saw through it,' said Artemis, keeping the beam steady. 'And it's not a rock.'

Opal raised her hands, sparks laced like barbed wire round her fingers.

No more talk.

Artemis's laser beam cut deep into the base of Little Sister, until it pierced the outer shell and reached the vast pocket of methane beneath.

Little Sister was not a rock. It was the seventh kraken, attracted by the magical resonance of Hybras. Artemis had been studying it for years. Not even Foaly knew it was there.

The explosion was huge, shooting a column of fire fifteen metres into the air. The outer shell collapsed under Opal, engulfing her in a blizzard of shrapnel.

Artemis heard the dull twang of her LEP armour flexing to take the shock.

Foaly's armour should save her.

He threw himself flat on the sea stack, suffering the rain of rock, weed and even fish on his back and legs.

Luck will save me now. Only luck.

And luck did save him. The plateau was hammered with several sizeable missiles but none struck Artemis. He was hailed with smaller objects and would have a hundred bruises and cuts to add to his list of injuries, but not a single bone was broken.

When the world felt as though it had stopped vibrating, Artemis crawled to the lip of the sea stack and gazed down at the bubbling sea below. A pyramid of rubble steamed gently in the waves where the kraken had been. The great beast would be moving away silently now, to find another magical hotspot. Of Opal there was no sign.

The LEP will find her.

Artemis turned over on his back and watched the stars. He did this often, and the sight usually caused him to wonder how he could reach the planets orbiting those pinpricks of light, and what he would find there. On this evening, the stars just made him feel tiny and insignificant. Nature was vast and mighty and would eventually swallow him, even the memory of him. He lay there cold and alone on the plateau, waiting for a feeling of triumph that he realized would never arrive, and listening to the distant shouts of the villagers as they made their way across the long meadow.

Holly arrived before the villagers, gliding in from the north, touching down soundlessly on the sea stack.

'You're flying,' said Artemis, as though he had never seen this before.

'I borrowed a suit from Number One's bodyguards. Well, I say borrowed . . .'

'How did you find me?' asked Artemis, though he could guess.

'Oh, I saw a huge explosion and wondered, *Now who could that be?*'

'Hmm,' said Artemis. 'A bit of a giveaway.'

'Also, I followed my old suit's radiation trail. I'm still following it.' Holly touched a finger to her visor and the filter changed. 'That's quite a pile of rocks you dumped on Opal. It's going to take a Retrieval team some time to dig her out. She's cursing like a tunnel dwarf down there. What did you do to her?'

'The seventh kraken,' explained Artemis. 'The one Foaly missed because it was tubular rather than conical, I would guess. I picked it up on a weather satellite.'

Holly placed a finger on Artemis's forehead. 'Typical Artemis Fowl. Beaten to a pulp and still he delivers a lecture.'

Magical sparks flowed from Holly's fingertip, engulfing Artemis like a cocoon. He felt comforted and peaceful, like a baby in its blanket. His pains were wiped away and his shattered collarbone liquefied, then solidified whole.

'Nice trick,' he said, smiling, his eyes glassy.

'I'm here till Tuesday,' said Holly, smiling back. 'Number One filled my tank.'

Artemis gazed up at his friend through a red haze. 'I'm sorry I lied to you, Holly. Truly. You've done so much.'

Holly's eyes were distant. 'Maybe you made the wrong decision; maybe I would have made that decision myself. We're from different worlds, Artemis. We will always have doubts about each other. Let's just carry on and leave the past in the past, where it should be.'

Artemis nodded. That was as good as he was going to get, and better than he deserved.

Holly pulled a tether from her belt, looping it under Artemis's arms. 'Now, let's get you home before the villagers start building a gallows.'

'Good idea,' mumbled Artemis, drowsy with the after-effects of his magical makeover.

'Yes, believe it or not, other people do have those occasionally.'

'Occasionally,' agreed Artemis, then his head lolled back and he was asleep.

Holly reset her wings for the added weight and launched them both off the lip of the sea stack, flying low to avoid the torch beams of the locals that strobed the night sky like searchlights.

Foaly tuned into Holly's helmet frequency while she was airborne.

'The seventh kraken, I'm guessing. Of course I had my suspicions . . .' He paused. 'This would be a good opportunity to mind-wipe Artemis,' he said. 'Save ourselves a lot of grief in the future.'

'Foaly!' said Holly, horrified. 'We don't wipe our friends. Artemis brought Jayjay back to us. Who knows how many cures lie in that lemur's brain.'

'I'm kidding. I'm kidding. And, guess what, we won't even have to ask Jayjay to donate some brain fluid. Number One synthesized it while he was waiting for the shuttle. That kid is one of a kind.'

'I seem to run into a lot of those. By the way, we need to send a team in for Opal.'

'They're en route. I think you're in for another rake over the coals from IA when you get back here.'

Holly snorted. 'What's new?'

Foaly fell silent, waiting for Holly to share the details of her adventures. Eventually he could wait no more.

'OK, you win. I'll ask. What happened back then – eight years ago? My gods, it must have been mayhem.'

Holly felt a phantom tingle on her lips where she had kissed Artemis.

'Nothing. Nothing happened. We went, we got the lemur, we came back. A couple of glitches, but obviously nothing we couldn't handle.'

Foaly didn't press for details. Holly would tell him when she had processed it herself.

'Do you ever think you might like to go to work and then just come home? No drama.'

Holly watched the ocean flash by below her and felt the weight of Artemis Fowl in her arms.

'No,' she said. 'I never think that.'

𝔄𝔅𝔇𝔢 • 𝔢𝔧𝔦𝔬𝔦 • 𝔦𝔞𝔰𝔢 • 𝔞𝔅 • 𝔞𝔬𝔅𝔦𝔞𝔲

CHAPTER 16: A TEAM OF HAIRDRESSERS

 LESS than an hour later they landed at Fowl Manor. Artemis woke up just as Holly's heels hit the gravel and was instantly alert.

'Magic is wonderful stuff,' he said, pinwheeling his left arm.

'You should have held on to yours,' quipped Holly.

'Ironically, if I had not attempted to cure Mother, Opal would have allowed her to recover. It was my journey into the past that gave Opal the basis for her plan, which she instigated by following us to her future.'

'I liked you better asleep,' said Holly, retrieving her tether. 'My head hurt less.'

'It's the big time paradox. If I had done nothing, then nothing would have needed to be done.'

Holly touched her helmet. 'Let me get Foaly on the com. You two could both talk at the same time.'

The exterior lights cast a soft glow on the gravel, setting the stones shimmering like gems. Lofty evergreen trees swayed in the gentle breeze, rustling with life. Like Tolkien's creatures.

Artemis watched Holly stride towards the main doors. *If only*, he thought. *If only*.

N°1 sat on the front step, flanked by a squad of LEP officers bristling with the latest weaponry. Artemis knew that his DNA was coded into their guns and all they had to do was select his icon from a list and there would be no escape. Jayjay had wrapped himself around the demon's crown like a hunting cap and seemed most comfortable there. He roused himself when he saw Artemis, leaping into the boy's arms. A dozen LEP rifles instantly beeped, and Artemis guessed that his icon was being selected.

'Hello there, little fellow. How do you like the present?'

N°1 answered for the lemur. 'He likes it fine. Especially now that no one will be sticking any needles in his head.'

Artemis nodded. 'You duplicated the fluid. I thought that might be an option. Where is Doctor Schalke?'

'He collapsed once Opal departed. Butler put him in a guest room.'

'And Artemis Junior?'

'Technically, you are Artemis Junior,' replied N°1. 'But I know what you are trying to ask me. Your younger self has been transported back to his own time. I sent a Retrieval captain and stayed here as a marker. I thought you would want him out of the way as soon as possible, what with your father and the twins on their way home.'

Artemis tickled Jayjay under the chin. 'It might have proved awkward.'

Holly was troubled. 'I know we promised not to wipe him, but I'm not particularly thrilled that there's a little Fowl running around with fairy knowledge in his devious skull.'

Artemis raised an eyebrow. 'Devious skull? Charming.'

'Hey, if the flap fits . . .'

N°1 was a little pale. With a flex of his tail, he lifted his squat rump from the step.

'About this no mind-wiping promise. The thing is, nobody told me.'

Holly stared at him. 'So you wiped him?'

N°1 nodded. 'And Schalke. I also left a residual spell in young Artemis's eyeballs so Butler will get it too. Nothing fancy, just a blanket memory loss. Their brains will fill in the gaps, invent believable memories.'

Holly shuddered. 'You left a spell in his eyeballs. That is revolting.'

'Revolting but ingenious,' said Artemis.

Holly was surprised. 'You don't seem too indignant. I was expecting a speech. Rolling eyes, flapping arms, the whole Fowl thing.'

Artemis shrugged. 'I knew it would happen. I didn't remember anything, so I must have been wiped, therefore we must have won.'

'You always knew.'

'I didn't know what the cost would be.'

⊖⏀⏀Ᏺᖇ·⅁⅃)⊛·◻)⅃ᏺᏒᏴⓄ⊛⅃ℓ·ᏒᏴᔆ)⅃⊛

Nº1 sighed. 'So I'm off the hook, as you humans say?'

'Absolutely,' said Holly, clapping him on the shoulder. 'I feel a lot better now.'

'On the positive side, I bolstered your atomic structure. Your atoms were a bit rattled by the time stream. I'm amazed you are still in one piece. I can only imagine how hard you were forced to concentrate.'

'Well, you *had* bolstered my atoms, and I have to beg one more favour,' said Artemis. 'I need you to send a note back in time.'

'I've been ordered not to open the time stream again, but maybe we can squeeze back one more thing,' said Nº1.

Artemis nodded. 'That's what I thought.'

'When and where?'

'Holly knows. You can do it from Tara.'

'How do you spell *stupendous*?' said Holly, smiling.

Artemis stepped back, craning his neck to peer upwards at the front window of his parents' room. Jayjay mimicked the action, climbing on to Artemis's shoulders and tilting his tiny head back.

'I'm afraid to go up, for some reason.'

He noticed himself wringing his fingers, and stuffed both hands in his jacket pockets.

'What she must have been through, all because of my meddling. What she must have —'

'Don't forget us,' interjected Nº1. 'We were submerged in animal fat. You have no idea how gross that is. Eyeball spells are the epitome of good taste compared to animal fat.'

'I was turned into an adolescent,' said Holly, winking at Artemis. 'Now *that* was gross.'

Artemis's smile was forced. 'Strangely, all this guilt tripping is not making me feel any better. The DNA cannons aren't helping either.'

Holly gestured at the LEP squad to stand down, then tilted her head slightly as a message came through.

'There's a chopper coming in. Your father. We've got to fly.'

N°1 wagged a finger. 'And that's not just a figure of speech. We actually have to fly. I know humans use that expression even when they don't intend to actually fly, so just to avoid confusion –'

'I get it, Number One,' said Artemis softly.

Holly raised her forearm, and Jayjay jumped on to it. 'He will be safer with us.'

'I know.'

He turned to Holly, meeting her gaze. Blue and hazel eyes.

She gazed back for a second, then activated her wings, rising a little from the surface.

'In another time,' she said, and kissed him on the cheek.

He was at the front door before Holly called to him.

'You know something, Fowl? You did a good thing here. For its own sake. Not one penny of profit.'

Artemis grimaced. 'I know. I'm appalled.'

He looked down at his feet, composing a pithy remark,

but when he looked up again the avenue was empty.

'Goodbye, my friends,' he said. 'Take care of Jayjay.'

Artemis could hear helicopter rotors in the distance by the time he reached his mother's bedroom. He would have some explaining to do, but he had a feeling that Artemis Senior would not press him for details once he saw Angeline in good health.

Artemis flexed his fingers, summoning his courage, then pushed through into the bedchamber. The bed was empty. His mother sat at her dresser, despairing at the state of her hair.

'Oh dear, Arty,' she said in mock horror on spotting her son in the mirror. 'Look at me. I need a team of hairdressers flown in immediately from London.'

'You look fine, Mother . . . Mum. Wonderful.'

Angeline ran a pearl-handled brush through her long hair, the lustre returning with each stroke. 'Considering what I have been through.'

'Yes. You were ill. But you are better now.'

Angeline turned on her dresser stool, reaching out her arms.

'Come here, my hero. Hug your mother.'

Artemis was happy to do as he was told.

A thought struck him. *Hero. Why did she call him a hero?*

Generally, victims of the *mesmer* remembered nothing of their ordeal. But Butler had remembered what Opal had done to him; he had even described the experience to

Artemis. Schalke had been wiped. But what of Mother?

Angeline held him tightly. 'You have done so much, Arty. Risked everything.'

The rotors were loud now, rattling the windows. His father was home.

'I didn't do so much, Mum. What any son would do.'

Angeline's hand cradled his head. He could feel her tears on his cheek. 'I know everything, Arty. Everything. That creature left me her memories. I tried to fight her, but she was too strong.'

'What creature, Mother? It was the fever. You had a hallucination, that's all.'

Angeline held him at arm's length. 'I was in the diseased hell of that pixie's brain, Artemis. Don't you dare lie to me and say that I wasn't. I saw your friends almost die to help you. I saw Butler's heart stop. I saw you save us all. Look me in the eye and tell me these things did not happen.'

Artemis found it difficult to meet his mother's stare and, when he did, it was impossible to lie.

'They happened. All of them. And more.'

Angeline frowned. 'You have a brown eye. Why did I not notice that?'

'I put a spell on you,' said Artemis miserably.

'And on your father?'

'Him too.'

Below, the front door crashed open. His father's footsteps raced across the lobby, then on to the stairway.

'You saved me, Artemis,' said his mother hurriedly. 'But

I have a feeling that all your spell-casting in some way put us in this situation. So I want to know everything. Everything. Do you understand?'

Artemis nodded. He couldn't see how to escape this. He was in a dead end and the only way out was complete honesty.

'Now we will give your father and the twins time to hug me and kiss me, then you and I are going to have a talk. It will be our secret. Understood?'

'Understood.'

Artemis sat on the bed. He felt six years old again, when he had been caught hacking into the school computers to make the test questions a little more challenging.

His father was on the landing now. Artemis knew that his secret life ended today. As soon as his mother got him alone he would be explaining himself. Starting at the beginning. Abductions, uprisings, time jaunts, goblin revolutions. Everything.

Complete honesty, he thought.

Artemis Fowl shuddered.

Some hours later, the master bedroom had been transformed by the whirlwind known as Beckett Fowl. There were pizza boxes on the night table and tomato-sauce finger paintings on the wall. Beckett had stripped off his own clothes and dressed himself in one of his father's T-shirts, which he had belted round his waist. He had applied a mascara moustache and lipstick scars to his face and was currently fencing with an invisible enemy using one of his father's old prosthetic legs as a sword.

Artemis was finishing his explanation of Angeline's miraculous recovery. 'And then I realized that Mother had somehow contracted Glover's Fever, which is usually confined to Madagascar, so I synthesized the natural cure preferred by the locals and administered it. Relief was immediate.'

Beckett noticed that Artemis had stopped talking and heaved a dramatic sigh of relief. He rode an imaginary horse across the room and poked Myles with the prosthetic leg.

'Good story?' he asked his twin.

Myles climbed down from the bed and placed his mouth beside Beckett's ear.

'Artemis simple-toon,' he confided.

EPILOGUE

HOOK HEAD, IRELAND

COMMANDER Trouble Kelp led the Retrieval team to dig Opal Koboi out of the rubble himself. They inflated a distortion bubble over the work zone, so they could fire up the shuttle's lasers without fear of discovery.

'Hurry up, Furty,' Trouble called over an open channel. 'We have one hour until sunrise. Let's get that megalomaniacal pixie out of there and back into her own time.'

They were lucky to have a dwarf on the team. Normally dwarfs were extremely reluctant to work with the authorities, but this one had agreed so long as he didn't have to work any of the hundred and ninety-odd dwarf holy days, and if the LEP paid his exorbitant consultant's fees.

In a situation like this one, dwarfs were invaluable. They could work rubble like no other species. If you wanted to dig something out alive, then dwarfs were the ones to do it. All they needed to do was let their beard hairs play over a surface, and they could tell you more about what was going on under that surface than any amount of seismic or geological equipment.

Currently Trouble was monitoring Furty Pullchain's progress through the kraken debris on the feed from his helmet cam. The dwarf's limbs were a shade paler than usual in the night-vision filter. One hand directed a nozzle of support foam that coated the tunnel wall at stress points, and the other reached in under his beard to rehinge his jaw.

'OK, *Commander*,' he said, managing to make the rank seem like a insult. 'I made it to the spot. It's a miracle I'm alive. This thing is as steady as a house of cards in a hurricane.'

'Yeah, whatever, Furty. You're a marvel. Now, pull her out and let's get below ground. I have a captain I need to discipline.'

'Keep yer acorns on, Commander. I'm readin' the beacon loud and clear.'

Trouble fumed silently. Maybe Holly Short was not the only one who would have to be disciplined.

He followed the live feed. Watching Furty scoop aside the rock, weed and shell fragments covering Holly's suit. Except there was no suit. Just a helmet with its flashing tracer beacon.

'I come all this way for a helmet?' said Furty, aggrieved. 'Ain't no pixie here, just the smell of one.'

Trouble sat up straight. 'Are you sure? Could you be in the wrong spot?'

Furty snorted. 'Yep. I'm at the *other* buried LEP helmet. Course I'm sure.'

She was gone. Opal had disappeared.

'Impossible. How could she escape?'

'Beats me,' said Furty. 'Maybe she squeezed through a natural tunnel. Them pixies are slippery little creatures. I remember one time when I was a sprog. Me and Kherb, my cousin, broke into a –'

Trouble cut him off. This was serious. Opal Koboi was loose in the world. He put a video call in to Foaly in Police Plaza.

'Don't tell me,' said the centaur, running a hand down his long face.

'She's gone. She left the helmet so the beacon would draw us in. Any vitals from her suit?'

Foaly checked his monitor. 'Nothing. It was loud and clear until five minutes ago. I thought it was a suit malfunction.'

Trouble took a breath. 'Put out an alert. Priority one. I want the guard tripled on *our* Koboi in Atlantis. It would be just like Opal to bust herself out.'

Foaly got to it. One Opal Koboi had almost managed to take over the world. Two would probably shoot for the entire galaxy.

'And call Holly,' continued Commander Kelp. 'Inform the captain that her weekend leave is cancelled.'

Fowl Manor, almost eight years ago

Artemis Fowl awoke in his own bed, and for a moment red sparks danced before his eyes. They sparkled and twinkled hypnotically before chasing their own tails out of existence.

Red sparks, he thought. *Unusual. I have seen stars before, but never sparks.*

The ten-year-old boy stretched, grabbing handfuls of his own duvet. For some reason he felt more content than usual.

I feel safe and happy.

Artemis sat bolt upright.

Happy? I feel happy?

He couldn't remember feeling truly happy since his father had disappeared, but on this morning his mood was bordering on cheerful.

Perhaps it was the deal with the Extinctionists. My first major chunk of profit.

No. That wasn't it. That particular transaction had left Artemis feeling sick to the pit of his stomach. So much so that he couldn't think about it and would probably never dwell on the past few days again.

So what could account for this feeling of optimism? Something from the dream he'd been having. A plan. A new scheme that would bring enough profit to fund a hundred Arctic expeditions.

That was it. The dream. What had it been about?

ᘓꙶꙨ • ◻ ᘖᘔᘖ꙰꙰ ➔ • ᔕᘓᔕ ➔ • ◌ᘝᘝ • ꙥᘔꙞᘔ⚛ • ⊕

It was just out of reach. The images already fading.
A crafty smile twitched at the corner of his mouth.
Fairies. Something about fairies.

THE END

You want MORE
fairy action and adventure?

LEPrecon

BY
EOIN COLFER

You got it . . .

For Finn. Artemis's best friend

Captain Holly Short is known by everyone under the world as one of the key members of the LEPrecon Squad. But the daring young elf's job wasn't always so exciting. Like all Recon officers, she began her career in Traffic. This is the story of her initiation as a Recon captain, and how she became the first female officer to serve under Commander Julius Root.

CHAPTER 1: ALONG CAME A SPIDER

'**THE** thing about pain, Major Evergreen,' said the old elf, laying a small wooden case on the table, 'is that it hurts.'

Evergreen was still too groggy for jokes. Whatever the stranger had put in the dart was taking its time leaving his system. 'What are you . . .? Why am I . . .?' Full sentences wouldn't come. He couldn't pluck one from his addled brain.

'Quiet, Major,' advised his captor. 'Don't fight the serum. You will make yourself ill.'

'Serum?' gasped the major.

'A very personal concoction. Since I don't have my magic any more, I have had to rely on nature's gifts. This particular serum is concocted from equal parts ground Ping Ping flower and cobra venom. Not lethal in small doses, but quite an effective sedative.'

Fear was piercing the LEP officer's daze now, like a hot poker through snow. 'Who are you?'

A child's scowl twisted the stranger's ancient face.

'You may address me as Captain. Don't you know me, Major? From before today? Cast your mind back to your first years in the LEP. Centuries ago, I know, but try. The fairy People often think that they can forget me completely. But I'm never far away, not really.'

The major wanted to say, *yes I know you*, but something told him that lying would be even more dangerous than telling the truth. And the truth was that he couldn't remember seeing this old elf before in his life. Not until today when he had assaulted him on the docks. Evergreen had tracked a runaway-gnome signal to this hut, and the next thing he knew this old elf had stung him with a syringe gun and was asking to be addressed as Captain. And now he was tied to a chair, being given a lecture about pain.

The old elf flipped two brass clasps on his case and lifted the lid reverentially. Major Evergreen caught a glimpse of a velvet lining. Red as blood.

'Now, my boy, I need information. Information only an LEP major would know.' The captain lifted a leather pouch from the box. There was another box of some kind inside the bag, its edges pressing into the leather.

Evergreen's breath came in short gasps. 'I'll tell you nothing.'

The old elf undid the bag's leather tie with one hand.

The box shone from inside the bag, casting a sickly glow on the old elf's pallor. The wrinkles around his eyes were thrown into deep shadow. The eyes themselves were feverish.

'Now, Major. The moment of truth. Question time.'

'Do yourself a favour and close the bag, Captain,' said Major Evergreen, with more bravado than he felt. 'I am LEP: you can't harm me and hope to escape.'

The captain sighed. 'I cannot close the bag. What is inside yearns to come out, to be free and do its work. And don't think anyone is coming to save you. I have jacked into your helmet and sent a malfunction message. Police Plaza thinks your communications are on the blink. They won't be worried for hours.'

The old elf pulled a steel object from the leather bag. The object was a mesh cage, and inside was a tiny silver spider with claws so sharp, the tips seemed to disappear. He held up the cage before Evergreen's nose. Inside, the spider slashed its claws in a starving frenzy, an inch from the major's nose.

'Sharp enough to cut air,' said the captain. And indeed the claws seemed to leave short-lived rents where they passed.

The mere act of revealing the spider seemed to change the old elf. He had power now and seemed taller. Twin red dots sparked in his eyes though there was no light source in the hut. The ruffles of an old-style LEP dress uniform poked from beneath his overcoat.

'Now, my young elf, I will ask but once. Answer promptly or bear my wrath.'

Major Evergreen shivered from fear and cold, but he kept his mouth tightly closed.

The captain caressed the major's chin with his cage. 'Now, here is your question: where is Commander Root's next Recon initiation site?'

The major blinked sweat from his eyes. 'Initiation site? Honestly, Captain, I don't know. I'm new on the squad.'

The captain held the cage even closer to Evergreen's face. The silver spider lunged forward, clawing the major's cheek.

'Julius's site!' roared the captain. 'Out with it!'

'No,' said the major through gritted teeth. 'You will not break me.'

The captain's voice grew shrill with madness. 'Do you see how I live? In the human world, I grow old.'

Poor Major Evergreen steeled himself for death. This entire assignment had been a trap.

'Julius robbed me of Haven,' raved the captain. 'Evicted me like a common traitor. Exiled me to this foul cesspool of the human world. When he brings the next corporal for initiation, I will be waiting – along with a few old friends. If we cannot have Haven, then we will have our revenge.'

The captain stopped his rant. He had said too much already and time was against him. He must finish this.

'You came here to search for a missing gnome: there was no gnome. We manipulated the satellite images to trap an LEP officer. I have waited two years for Julius to send a major.'

It made sense. Only a major would know the locations of LEP initiations.

'And now that I have you in my clutches, you will tell me what I need to know.'

The elderly elf pinched Major Evergreen's nose until he was forced to draw breath through his mouth. In a flash the captain jammed the mesh cage between Evergreen's teeth and flipped the gate. The silver spider was down the young elf's gullet in a shining blur.

The captain tossed the cage to one side. 'Now, Major,' he said. 'You are dead.'

Evergreen spasmed as the silver spider's claws went to work on the lining of his stomach.

'That feels bad: internal injuries always hurt the most,' commented the old elf. 'But your magic will heal you for a while. In minutes, however, your power will dry up, and then my little pet will claw her way out.'

Evergreen knew it was true. The spider was a Tunnel Blue. The creature actually used its claws as teeth, pulping its meat before sucking it between its gums. Their favourite method of destruction was from the inside. A nest of these little monsters could take down a troll. One was more than enough to kill an elf.

'I can help you,' said the captain. 'If you agree to help me.'

Evergreen gasped in pain. Whenever the spider clawed

him, the magic sealed the wound, but already the healing was slowing.

'No. You'll get nothing from me.'

'Fine. You die, and I will ask the next officer they send. Of course, he may refuse to cooperate too. Ah well, I have plenty of spiders.'

Evergreen tried to think. He had to get out of this alive, to warn the commander. And there was only one way to do that.

'Very well. Kill the spider.'

The captain grabbed Evergreen's chin. 'First, my answer. Where is the next initiation? And do not lie, I will know.'

'The Tern Islands,' moaned the major.

The old elf's face glowed with demented triumph. 'I know them. When?'

Evergreen mumbled the words, shamefacedly. 'A week from today.'

The captain clapped his captive on the shoulder. 'Well done. You have chosen wisely. No doubt hoping to live through this ordeal and warn my brother.'

Alarm cut through Evergreen's pain. Brother? This was Commander Root's brother? He had heard the story; everyone had.

The captain smiled. 'Now you know my secret. I am the disgraced Captain Turnball Root. Julius hunted his own brother. And now I shall hunt him.'

Evergreen winced as a dozen tiny gashes were opened in his stomach. 'Kill the insect,' he pleaded.

Turnball Root drew a small flask from his pocket. 'Oh, very well. But don't think you'll be warning anyone. There was an amnesiac in the dart I gave you: in five minutes this entire incident will be a dream floating beyond your grasp.'

Captain Root opened the flask, and Evergreen was relieved to smell the pungent aroma of strong coffee. The Tunnel Blue was a hyperactive finely tuned creature with a hair-trigger heart. When the coffee entered its blood-stream, it should trigger a fatal heart attack.

Turnball Root poured the scalding brew down Evergreen's throat. The major gagged, but swallowed it down. After a few seconds, the spider began to thrash in his stomach, then the vicious activity ceased.

Evergreen sighed in relief, then closed his eyes, focusing on what had happened.

'Oh, very good,' chuckled Captain Root. 'You are trying to reinforce the memories so they can be brought out under hypnosis. I wouldn't bother. What I gave you wasn't exactly regulation. You'll be lucky if you remember what colour the sky is.'

Evergreen hung his head. He had betrayed his commander, and all for nothing. In one week's time, Julius Root would walk into a trap on the Tern Islands. A location that he had revealed.

Turnball did up his overcoat, hiding the uniform below. 'Farewell, Major. And thank you for your help. You may find it difficult to concentrate for the next while, but by the time your resolve returns, those straps should have dissolved.'

Captain Root opened the hut door, stepping out into the night. Evergreen watched him go, and a moment later he could not have sworn that the captain had ever been there at all.

CHAPTER 2: SOMETHING FISHY

THE BOULEVARD OF KINGS, HAVEN CITY, THE LOWER ELEMENTS, ONE WEEK LATER . . .

 CORPORAL Holly Short was on traffic detail on the Boulevard of Kings. Lower Elements Police officers were supposed to travel in pairs, but there was a league crunchball match being played across the river, so her partner was patrolling the sidelines in Westside Stadium.

Holly strolled down the Boulevard, resplendent in her computerized traffic suit. The suit was more or less a walking road sign, which could display all the common commands, plus up to eight lines of text, across her chest plate. The suit was also coded to her voice, so if Holly ordered a driver to stop, the command would also appear in yellow lights across her chest.

Being a walking road sign was not exactly what Holly had in mind when she signed up for the Lower Elements

Police Academy, but every corporal had to put in a stint in Traffic before he or she was allowed to specialize. Holly had been on the streets for over six months, and sometimes it seemed as though she was never going to get her chance at Reconnaissance. If the brass did give her a shot, and if she did pass the initiation, then she would be the first female ever to make it into Recon. This fact did not daunt Holly Short, in fact it appealed to her stubborn nature. Not only would she pass the initiation, but she intended to smash the score set by Captain Trouble Kelp.

The Boulevard was quiet this afternoon. Everyone was over in Westside enjoying vegetable fries and mushroom burgers. Everyone except her, a few dozen public servants and the owner of a camper shuttle that was illegally parked across a restaurant's loading bay.

Holly scanned the purple camper's barcode by running her glove's sensor across the bumper plate. Seconds later, the LEP central server sent the vehicle's file to her helmet. It belonged to a Mister E. Phyber, a sprite with a history of traffic violation.

Holly tore back a Velcro strip covering the computer screen on her wrist. She opened the parking-fine program, sending one to Mister Phyber's account. The fact that giving someone a ticket made her feel good told Holly that it was high time she got out of Traffic.

Something moved inside the camper. Something big. The entire vehicle swayed on its axles.

Holly rapped on the blacked-out windows. 'Step out of the vehicle, Mister Phyber.'

There was no reply from inside the camper, just more pronounced swaying. There was something inside. Something a lot bigger than a sprite.

'Mister Phyber. Open up, or I will conduct a search.'

Holly tried to peer through the tinted windows, with no luck: her street helmet did not have the filters to penetrate. It felt as though there was some kind of animal in there. This was a serious crime. Transporting animals in a private vehicle was strictly forbidden. Not to mention cruel. The fairy People may eat certain animals, but they certainly did not keep them as pets. If this person was smuggling animals of some kind, it was quite possible that he was buying them direct from the surface.

Holly placed both hands on the side panel, pushing as hard as she could. Immediately the camper began to buck and vibrate, almost tipping over on one rail.

Holly stepped back. She would have to call this in.

'Ah . . . Is there a problem, Officer?'

There was a sprite hovering beside her. Sprites hovered when they were nervous.

'Is this your vehicle, sir?'

The sprite's wings beat even faster, lifting him another six inches off the sidewalk.

'Yes, Officer. Eloe Phyber. I am the registered owner.'

Holly raised her visor. 'Please land, sir. Flying is restricted on the Boulevard. There are signs.'

Phyber touched down gently. 'Of course, Officer. Pardon me.'

Holly studied Phyber's face for signs of guilt. The sprite's pale-green skin was slick with perspiration.

'Are you worried about something, Mister Phyber?'

Phyber smiled a watery smile. 'No. Worried? No, nothing. I'm running a bit late, that's all. Modern life, you know, always on a timetable.'

The camper bounced on its axles.

'What have you got in there?' asked Holly.

Phyber's smile froze. 'Nothing. Just some flat-packed shelving. One of the units must have fallen over.'

He was lying. Holly was certain of it. 'Oh, really? There must be quite a few units in there, because that's the fifth one that's fallen over. Open it up, please.'

The sprite's wings began pumping up. 'I don't think I have to. Don't you need a warrant?'

'No. I need probable cause. And I have reason to believe that you are illegally transporting animals.'

'Animals? Ridiculous. Anyway, I can't open the camper, I appear to have lost the chip.'

Holly drew an Omnitool from her belt, placing the sensor against the camper's rear door. 'Very well. Be advised that I am opening this vehicle to investigate the possible presence of animals.'

'Shouldn't we wait for a lawyer?'

'No. The animals could die of old age.'

Phyber moved back a yard. 'I really wouldn't do that.'

'No. I'm sure you wouldn't.'

The Omnitool beeped, and the rear door swung open. Holly was confronted by a huge, wobbling cube of orange jelly. It was hydrogel, used to safely transport injured sea life. The creatures could still breathe, but were spared travel bumps. A shoal of mackerel was struggling to swim inside the lined interior of the camper. They were no doubt destined for an illegal fish restaurant.

The gel might have held its shape if the shoal hadn't decided to head for the light. Their combined efforts dragged the cuboid of gel out of the camper and into thin air. Gravity took hold and the blob exploded all over Holly. She was instantly submerged in a tidal wave of fish-flavoured gel and actual fish. The gel found holes in her uniform that she never knew were there.

'D'Arvit!' swore Holly, falling on her backside. Unfortunately this was the moment that her suit shorted out, and a call came through from Police Plaza informing her that Commander Julius Root wanted to see her immediately.

POLICE PLAZA, THE LOWER ELEMENTS

Holly dropped Phyber off at the booking desk, then darted straight across the courtyard to Julius Root's office. If the LEPrecon commander wanted to see her, she had no intention of keeping him waiting. This could be her initiation. At last.

There were already people in the office. Holly could see bobbing heads through the frosted glass. 'Corporal Short to see Commander Root,' she said breathlessly to the secretary.

The secretary, a middle-aged pixie with an outrageous pink perm, glanced up briefly, then stopped work completely, giving Holly her undivided attention. 'You want to go in to the commander looking like that?'

Holly brushed a few blobs of hydrogel from her suit. 'Yes. It's only gel. I've been on the job. The commander will understand.'

'You're sure?'

'Positive. I can't miss this meeting.'

The secretary's smile was tinged with nastiness. 'Well, all right then. Go on in.'

On any other day, Holly would have known that something was wrong, but on that day it slipped past. And so did she, right into Julius Root's office.

There were two people in the office before her. Julius Root himself, a broad-chested elf with buzz cut hair, and a fungus cigar screwed into the corner of his mouth. Holly also recognized Captain Trouble Kelp, one of Recon's brightest stars. A legend in the police bars with more than a dozen successful recons under his belt in less than a year.

Root froze, staring at Holly. 'Yes? What is it? Is there some kind of plumbing emergency?'

'N-No,' stammered Holly. 'Corporal Holly Short, reporting as requested, sir.'

Root stood, red spots burning on his cheeks. The commander was not a happy elf.

'Short. You're a girl?'

'Yessir. Guilty as charged.'

Root did not appreciate humour. 'We're not on a date, Short. Keep the witticisms to yourself.'

'Yessir. No jokes.'

'Good. I assumed you were male because of your pilot test scores. We've never had a female score that highly before.'

'So I believe, sir.'

The commander sat on the edge of his desk. 'You are the eightieth female to have made it as far as the initiation. So far none have passed. The equal-rights office is screaming sexism, so I'm going to handle your initiation personally.'

Holly swallowed. 'Personally?'

Root smiled. 'That's right, Corporal. Just you and me on a little adventure. How do you feel about that?'

'Great, sir. My privilege.'

'Good girl. That's the spirit.' Root sniffed the air. 'What's that smell?'

'I was on traffic duty, sir. I had a tangle with a fish smuggler.'

Root sniffed the air again. 'I guessed fish were involved. Your uniform appears to be orange.'

Holly picked at a blob of gel on her arm. 'Hydrogel, sir. The smuggler was using it to transport the fish.'

390

Root rose from the desk. 'You do know what Recon officers actually do, Short?'

'Yessir. A Recon officer tracks runaway fairies to the surface, sir.'

'The surface, Short. Where the humans live. We have to be inconspicuous, blend in. Do you think you can do that?'

'Yes, Commander. I think I can.'

Root spat his cigar into a recycler. 'I wish I could believe that. And maybe I would, if it wasn't for that.' Root pointed a stiff finger at Holly's chest.

Holly looked down. Surely the commander wasn't upset about a few blobs of gel and the smell of fish.

He wasn't.

The text bar on her chest displayed one word in block capitals. It was the same word that she had shouted just as the hydrogel had frozen the text display: 'D'Arvit,' swore Holly, under her breath, which coincidentally was the same word frozen on her chest.

E1

The trio proceeded directly to E1: a pressure chute that emerged in Tara, Ireland. The corporals were not given any personal time to prepare, because they would not have any if they managed to graduate to Recon. Rogue fairies did not escape to the surface at a time prearranged with the police. They took off whenever it suited them, and a Recon officer had to be ready to follow.

They took an LEP shuttle up the chute to the surface. Holly had not been given any weaponry and her helmet had been confiscated. She had also been drained of magic by a pinprick to the thumb. The tack was left in until every drop of magic had been used to heal the wound.

Captain Trouble Kelp explained the logic to her as he used his own magic to seal the corporal's tiny wound. 'Sometimes you get stuck on the surface with nothing: no weapon, no communications, no magic. And you still have to track down a runner, who's probably trying to track you down. If you can't accomplish that, then you won't make it in Recon.'

Holly had expected this. They had all heard the initiation stories from other veterans. She wondered what kind of hellhole they would be dropped in, and what they would have to hunt.

Through the shuttle portholes, she watched the chute flash by. The chutes were vast subterranean magma vents that spiralled from the Earth's core to the surface. The fairy People had excavated several of these tunnels worldwide and built shuttle ports at both ends. As human technology grew more sophisticated, many of these stations had to be destroyed or abandoned. If the Mud People ever found a fairy port, they would have a direct line to Haven.

In times of emergency, Recon officers rode the magma

flares that scoured these tunnels in titanium eggs. This was the fastest way to cover the five thousand miles to the surface. Today they were travelling as a group in an LEP shuttle at the relatively slow speed of eight hundred miles an hour. Root set the autopilot and came back to brief Holly.

'We are headed for the Tern Islands,' Commander Root said, activating a holographic map above the conference table. 'A small archipelago off the east coast of Ireland. To be more precise we are headed for Tern Mór – the main island. There is only one inhabitant: Kieran Ross, a conservationist. Ross travels to Dublin once a month to make his report to the Department of the Environment. He generally stays over in the Morrison Hotel, and takes in a show at the Abbey Theatre. Our technical people have confirmed that he is booked into the hotel, so we have a thirty-six-hour window.'

Holly nodded. The last thing they needed was humans butting into their exercise. Realistic exercises were one thing, but not at the expense of the entire fairy nation.

Root stepped into the hologram, pointing at a spot on the map. 'We land here, at Seal Bay. The shuttle will drop you and Captain Kelp off on the beach. I will be deposited at another location. After that it's simple: you hunt me and I hunt you. Captain Kelp will record your progress for review. Once the exercise has been completed, I will evaluate your disk and see if you have what it takes to make it into Recon. Initiates are generally tagged half a dozen times over the course of the exercise, so don't worry about that. What's important is how difficult you make it for me.'

Root took a paintball pistol from a rack on the wall and tossed it to Holly. 'Of course, there is one way to get round the review and straight into the programme. You tag me before I tag you, and you're in. No questions asked. But don't get your hopes up. I have centuries of above-ground experience, I'm running hot with magic and I have a shuttle full of weapons at my disposal.'

Holly was glad that she was already sitting down. She had spent hundreds of hours on simulators, but had only actually visited the surface twice. Once on a school tour of South American rainforests, and another time on a family holiday to Stonehenge. Her third visit was going to be a bit more exciting.

CHAPTER 3: THE ISLAND OF BROKEN DREAMS

TERN MÓR

 THE sun scorched away the morning mist and Tern Mór gradually appeared off the Irish coast like a ghost island. One minute there was nothing there but cloudbanks, and the next the crags of Tern Mór cut through the haze.

Holly studied it through the porthole. 'Cheery place,' she noted.

Root chewed on his cigar. 'Sorry about that, Corporal. We keep asking the runaways to hide somewhere warm, but darned if they don't keep suiting themselves.'

The commander returned to the cockpit: it was time to switch back over to manual for the landing.

The island looked like something from a horror film. Dark cliffs reared from the ocean, spumes of foam slapping at the waterline. A line of greenery hung on desperately, flopping untidily over the edge like an unruly fringe of hair.

Nothing good is going to happen here, thought Holly.

Trouble Kelp slapped her on the shoulder, breaking through the gloom. 'Cheer up, Short. At least you got this far. A couple of days on the surface is worth any price. This place has air like you wouldn't believe. Sweet as heaven.'

Holly tried to smile, but she was too nervous. 'Does the commander usually handle initiations himself?'

'All the time. This is the first one-to-one though. Usually he tracks a half dozen or so, to keep himself amused. But you get him all to yourself, 'cause of the female thing. When you fail, Julius doesn't want the equal-rights office to have any reason to complain.'

Holly bristled. 'When I fail?'

Trouble winked at her. 'Did I say when? I meant if. Of course, if.'

Holly felt the tips of her pointed ears quiver. Was this entire trip a charade? Did the commander already have her report written?

They touched down on Seal Bay, which was remarkably devoid of seals or sand. The shuttle had a second skin of plasma screens that projected the surroundings on to the craft's outer plates. To the casual observer, when Trouble Kelp popped the hatch, it would seem like a door in the sky.

Holly and Trouble hopped out on to the pebbles, scurrying forward to avoid the jet wash.

Root opened a porthole. 'You've got twenty minutes to cry or say your prayers or whatever it is you females do, then I'm comin' a callin'.'

Holly's eyes were fierce. 'Yessir. I'm going to start crying presently. Soon as you're over the horizon.'

Root half smiled, half scowled. 'I hope your skills can pay the cheques your mouth is writing.'

Holly had no idea what a cheque was, but she decided that now was not the time to say that.

Root gunned the engine, taking off over the hillside in a low, looping arc. All that was visible of the craft was a faint translucent shimmer.

Holly found that she was suddenly cold. Haven was completely air-conditioned, and her traffic suit did not have heating coils. She noticed Captain Kelp adjusting the thermostat on his computer.

'Hey,' Trouble said. 'No need for two of us to be uncomfortable. I've already passed my initiation.'

'How many times did you get tagged?' Holly asked.

Trouble grimaced ruefully. 'Eight. And I was the best in the group. Commander Root moves quickly for an oldtimer, plus he has a couple of million ingots' worth of hardware at his disposal.'

Holly turned up her collar against the Atlantic wind. 'Any handy hints?'

'I'm afraid not. And once this camera starts rolling, I can't even talk to you any more.' Captain Kelp touched a button on his helmet, and a red light winked at Holly. 'The only thing I can say is that if I were you, I'd get moving. Julius won't waste any time, so neither should you.'

Holly looked around. *Make use of your environment*, the manuals said. *Use what nature provides.* That maxim wasn't much good to her here. The pebble beach was bordered by a steep rock face on two sides, with a steep mudslide incline on the third. It was the only way out, and she'd better take it before the commander had time to set himself up at the top. She double-timed it towards the slope, determined to make it out of this exercise with her self-respect intact.

Something shimmered in the corner of Holly's eye. She stopped in her tracks.

'That's hardly fair,' she said, pointing to the spot.

Trouble looked across the pebble beach. 'What?' he asked, even though he was not supposed to talk.

'Look there. A sheet of cam foil. Someone is hiding on the beach. Do you have a little back-up in case the corporal proves a bit quick for the old-timers?'

Trouble instantly realized the seriousness of the situation. 'D'Arvit,' he growled, reaching for his sidearm.

Captain Kelp was quick on the draw. He actually managed to get his weapon out of its holster before a sniper's rifle pulsed beneath the cam foil, catching him high on the shoulder, spinning him across the wet stones.

Holly darted right, zigzagging through the rocks. If she kept moving, the sniper might not be able to get a lock on her. Her fingers were actually digging into the mud slope when a second sniper reared up from the earth, shrugging off a sheet of cam foil.

The newcomer, a stocky dwarf, was holding the biggest rifle Holly had ever seen. 'Surprise,' he grinned, teeth crooked and yellowing.

He fired and the laser pulse hit Holly in the gut like a sledgehammer. That's the thing about Neutrino weapons: they don't kill, but they hurt worse than a bucket of hang-nails.

Holly came to, and immediately wished she hadn't. She leaned forward on the oversized chair she was tied to, and threw up all over her boots. Beside her, Trouble Kelp was involved in the same activity. What was going on here? Laser weapons were not supposed to have side effects, unless you were allergic, which she wasn't.

Glancing around, Holly caught her breath. They were in a small roughly plastered room, dominated by a huge table. A huge table or a human-sized table? They were in a human residence? That explained the sickness. Entering human residences without permission was expressly forbidden. The price for ignoring this edict was loss of magic, and nausea.

The details of their predicament sparked in Holly's memory. She had been on her initiation when a couple of fairies had ambushed them on the beach. Could this be some kind of extreme test? She looked across at Captain Kelp's drooping head. That was pretty realistic for a test.

A huge door creaked open and a grinning elf stepped

through. 'Oh, you are unwell. Sorcery sickness, or Book Barfing as I believe the younger fairies call it. Don't worry, it will soon pass.'

The elf looked older than any fairy Holly knew, and was wearing a yellowed LEP dress uniform. It was like something out of a period movie.

The elf caught Holly's glance. 'Ah, yes,' he said, plumping up his ruffles. 'My finery fades. It is the curse of living without magic. Everything fades, and not just the clothing. To look in my eyes you would never guess that I am barely a century older than my brother.'

Holly looked in his eyes. 'Brother?'

Beside her, Trouble stirred, spat and raised his head. Holly heard a sharp intake of breath. 'Oh gods. Turnball Root.'

Holly's mind spun. Root? Brother. This was the commander's brother.

Turnball was delighted. 'Finally, someone remembers. I was beginning to think I was forgotten.'

'I majored in Ancient History,' said Trouble. 'You got your own page in the Criminally Insane section.'

Turnball tried to appear casual, but he was interested. 'Tell me, what did this page say?'

'It said that you were a traitorous captain who tried to flood a section of Haven just to wipe out a competitor who was muscling in on your illegal mining scheme. It said that if your brother had not stopped you with your finger on the button, then half the city could have been lost.'

'Ridiculous,' tutted Turnball. 'I had engineers study my plans. There would have been no chain reaction. A few hundred would have died, no more.'

'How did you escape from prison?' asked Holly.

Turnball's chest puffed up. 'I have never spent a day in prison. I am not a common criminal. Luckily, Julius lacked the gumption to kill me, and so I managed to escape. He has hunted me ever since. But that ends today.'

'So that's what this is all about: revenge?'

'Partly,' admitted Turnball. 'But also freedom. Julius is like a dog with a bone. He will not let go. I need a chance to finish my Martinis without looking over my shoulder. I have had ninety-six residences in the past five centuries. I lived in a fabulous villa near Nice in the seventeen hundreds.' The old elf's eyes grew misty. 'I was so happy there. I can still smell the ocean. I had to burn that house to the ground because of Julius.'

Holly was rotating her wrists slowly, trying to loosen the knots. Turnball noticed the motion.

'Don't bother, my dear. I have been tying people up for centuries. It is one of the first skills you learn as a fugitive. And well done, by the way. A female at an initiation. I bet my little brother doesn't like that. He was always a bit on the sexist side.'

'Yes,' said Holly. 'Whereas you are a real gentlefairy.'

'Touché,' said Turnball. 'As I used to say in France.'

Trouble's face had lost the green tinge. 'Whatever your plan is, don't expect any help from me.'

Turnball stood before Holly, lifting her chin with a curved nail. 'I don't expect help from you, Captain. I expect help from the pretty one. All I expect from you is a little screaming before you die.'

Turnball had two accomplices: a sullen dwarf and an Earthbound sprite. Commander Root's brother called them into the room for a round of introductions.

The dwarf's name was Bobb, and he wore a wide-brimmed sombrero to keep the sun off his delicate dwarf skin.

'Bobb is the best burglar in the business after Mulch Diggums,' explained Turnball, draping an arm round the squat dwarf's massive shoulders. 'However, unlike the canny Diggums, he doesn't plan so well. Bobb made his big mistake when he dug into a community centre during a police fund-raiser. He's been hiding out on the surface since then. We make a good team: I plan, he steals.' He turned to the sprite, spinning him round. Where the sprite's wings should be, there were two bulbous knobs of scar tissue.

'Unix here got in a fight with a troll and lost. He was clinically dead when I found him. I gave him the last shot of magic I had to bring him back, and to this day I don't know if he loves me or hates me for it. Loyal though. This fairy here would walk into the Earth's core for me.'

The sprite's green features were impassive, and his eyes were as empty as wiped disks. These two fairies were the ones who had picked off Holly and Trouble on the pebble beach.

Turnball ripped Holly's nametag from her chest. 'Now, here's the plan. We are going to use Corporal Short here to lure Julius in. If you try to warn him, then the captain dies in terrible agony. I have a Tunnel Blue spider in my bag that will rip his insides apart in seconds. And having entered a human dwelling, he won't have a drop of magic to ease that pain. For your part, all you have to do is sit in a clearing and wait for Julius to come and get you. When he does, then we get him. It's that simple. Unix and Bobb will accompany you. I will wait here for the happy moment when Julius is dragged through that door.'

Unix cut selected straps, hauling Holly from the chair. He propelled her through the giant doorway, into the morning sunlight. Holly breathed deeply. The air was sweet here, but there wasn't a moment to pause and enjoy it.

'Why don't you run, Officer?' said Unix, his voice alternately high and low, as though half broken. 'Run and see what happens.'

'Yeah,' taunted Bobb. 'See what happens.'

Holly could guess what would happen. She would get another laser burst, this time in the back. She would not run. Not yet. What she would do was think and plan.

They dragged and prodded Holly across two fields that sloped southwards to the cliffs. The grass was sparse and rough, like clumps of missed beard after a shave. Flocks of gulls, terns and cormorants appeared over the cliff line like fighter jets climbing to cruising altitude. Down past a thicket rampant with wildlife, Bobb stopped beside a low rock erupting through the earth. Just big enough to shelter one fairy from an easterly approach.

'Down you go,' he grunted, pushing Holly on to her knees.

Once she was down, Unix clamped a manacle round her leg, hammering the spike on the other end into the earth.

'This way, you can't just take off,' he explained, grinning. 'If we see you playing with your chain, then we knock you out for a while.' He patted the scope on the rifle strapped across his chest. 'We'll be watching.'

The rogue fairies retraced their steps across the field, settling down in to two hollows. They pulled sheets of cam foil from their packs, draping them over their frames. In seconds all that could be seen were two black-eyed gun barrels poking from beneath the sheets.

It was a simple plan. But extremely clever. If the commander found Holly, it would seem as though she were setting herself up for an ambush. Just not a very good one. The second he showed himself, Unix and Bobb could nail him with rifle fire.

There must be some way to warn the commander without endangering Trouble. Holly chewed it over. *Use what nature provides*. Nature was providing plenty, but unfortunately she couldn't reach any of it. If she even tried, then

Bobb and Unix would stun her with a low-level charge, without having to alter the basic structure of their plan. There was nothing much on her own person either. Unix had searched her from head to toe, even confiscating the digi-pen in her pocket in case she used it as a weapon. The only thing they missed was the wafer-thin computer on her wrist, which was shorted out anyway.

Holly lowered her arm behind the rock, peeling back the Velcro patch that protected her computer from the elements. She flipped the tiny instrument over. It seemed as though hydrogel had seeped into the seal, shorting out the electrics. She slid off the battery panel, checking the circuit board inside. A tiny drop of gel was sitting on the board, straddling several switches, making connections where there shouldn't be any. Holly plucked a blade of coarse grass, using it to scoop up the drop. In less than a minute the remaining film of gel had evaporated and the tiny computer hummed into action. Holly quickly blacked out the panel on her chest, in case Bobb or Unix spotted the flashing cursor.

So, now she had a computer. If she only had her helmet then she could send the commander an e-mail. As it was, all she could do was run some text across her chest.

CHAPTER 4: BROTHERS WITH ARMS

TERN MÓR, NORTHERN PENINSULA

 JULIUS Root was surprised to find that he was breathing hard. There was a time when he could have run all day without breaking a sweat, and now his heart was battering his ribcage after a mere two-mile jog. He had parked the shuttle on a foggy cliff top on the island's northern peak. Of course, the fog was artificial, generated by a compressor bolted on to the shuttle's exhaust. The shuttle's projection shield was still in operation, the fog was merely a back-up.

Root ran low, bent almost double. A hunter's run. As he moved he felt the primal joy that only surface air could bring. The sea crashed on all sides; an ever-present behemoth, a reminder of the Earth's power. Commander Julius Root was never happier than when he was on the hunt above ground. Strictly speaking, he could have delegated these initiations, but he wouldn't give up these excursions until the first rookie beat him. It hadn't happened yet.

Nearly two hours later the commander paused, taking a deep swallow from a canteen. This hunt would have been much easier with a pair of mechanical wings, but in the name of fair play he had left the wings on their rack in the shuttle. He would not have anyone claim that he had beaten them with superior equipment.

Root had searched all the obvious sites, and had yet to find Corporal Short. Holly had not been on the beach, or in the old quarry. Neither had she been perched in a treetop in the evergreen wood. Perhaps she was smarter than the average cadet. She would need to be. For a female to survive in Recon, she would have to rise above a lot of suspicion and prejudice. Not that the commander was tempted to cut her any slack. He would treat her with the same brash disdain that all his subordinates got. Until they earned something better.

Root continued his search, senses alert to any change in his surroundings that could indicate he himself was being tracked. The two hundred or so species of birds that nested on Tern Mór's crags were unusually active. Gulls screeched at him from overhead, crows followed his movements, and Julius even spotted an eagle spying at him from the heavens. All this noise made it more difficult for him to concentrate, but the distraction would be even worse for Corporal Short.

Root jogged up a shallow incline towards the human

dwelling. Short could not be inside the actual dwelling itself, but she could be using it for cover. The commander hugged the thicket, his dull green LEP jumpsuit blending with the foliage.

Julius heard something up ahead. An irregular scraping. The noise of material against rock. He froze, then slowly twisted his way into the foliage itself. A disgruntled rabbit turned tail, wriggling deeper into the hedgerow. Root ignored the brambles dragging at his elbows, inching forward towards the source of the noise. It could be nothing, but on the other hand it could be everything.

It turned out to be everything. From his shelter inside the thicket, Root could clearly see Holly hunkered behind a large rock. It wasn't a particularly clever hiding place. She was sheltered from an easterly approach, but otherwise she was wide open. Captain Kelp was not visible, possibly filming from a raised vantage point.

Root sighed. He was surprised to find that he was disappointed. It would have been nice to have a girl around the place. Someone new to shout at.

Julius drew his paintball pistol, poking the barrel through spirals of briar branches. He would tag her a couple of times just to make an impression. Short had better wake up and do better if she ever wanted the Recon insignia on her lapel.

There was no need for Root to use the sights on his helmet. It was an easy shot, barely six metres. And even if it hadn't been, Root would not have used his visor. Short didn't have electronic sights, so he wouldn't use them either. This would give him even more to shout about after the failed initiation.

Then Holly turned in the direction of the thicket. She still couldn't see him, but he could see her. And even more importantly, he could read the words scrolling across her chest.

TURNBALL + 2.

Commander Root drew his gun barrel back into the thicket, retreating into the blackness of the overgrowth.

Root battled to contain his emotions. Turnball was back. And he was here. How was it possible? All the old feelings quickly resurfaced, lodging in the commander's stomach. Turnball was his brother, and a nub of affection for him still remained. But the overriding emotion was sadness. Turnball had betrayed the People, and had been willing to see many of them die for his own profit. He had allowed his brother to escape once before, he would not let it happen again.

Root wiggled backwards through the thicket, then activated his helmet. He tried establishing a link with Police Plaza, but all he got on the helmet radio was white noise. Turnball must have detonated a jammer.

Turnball may control the airwaves, but he could not control the air itself. And any living thing would heat the air. Root lowered a thermal filter on his visor and began a slow grid search of the area behind Corporal Short.

The commander's search did not take too long. Two red slits shone like beacons among the pale pink of insect and rodent life teeming under the field's surface. The slits were probably caused by a body-heat leakage from underneath two sheets of cam foil. Snipers. Lying in wait for him. These fairies were not professional. If they had been, they would have kept their gun barrels beneath the sheet until they were needed, thus eliminating the overspill.

Root holstered his paintball pistol, drawing instead a Neutrino 500. Usually in combat situations he carried a tri-barrelled water-cooled blaster, but he hadn't been expecting combat. He berated himself silently. Idiot. Combat does not arrange itself around schedules.

The commander circled round behind the snipers, then put two bursts into them from a distance. This may not be the most sporting course of action, but it was definitely the most prudent. By the time the snipers regained consciousness they would be shackled to each other in the back of a police shuttle. If by some chance he had stunned two innocents, then there would be no lasting after effects.

Commander Root trotted to the first hide, drawing back the sheet of cam foil. There was a dwarf in the hollow beneath. An ugly little spud. Root recognized him from his Wanted sheet. Bobb Ragby. A nasty character. Just the kind of dim-witted felon Turnball would recruit to his cause. Root kneeled by the dwarf, disarming him and zipping plasti-cuffs round his wrists and ankles.

He quickly crossed the fifty metres to the second sniper-hide. Another well-known fugitive: Unix B'Lob. The grounded sprite. He had been Turnball's right-hand fairy for decades now. Root grinned tightly as he bound the unconscious sprite. Even these two would be a good day's work. But the day wasn't over yet.

Holly was surreptitiously worming the spike from the ground when Root arrived.

'Can I give you a hand with that?' asked Julius.

'Get down, Commander,' hissed Holly. 'There are two rifles trained on you right now.'

Root patted the guns slung over his shoulder. 'You mean these rifles. I got your text. Well done.' He wrapped his fingers round the chain, yanking it from the earth. 'The parameters of your assignment have changed.'

You don't say, thought Holly.

Root used an Omnitool to pop open the shackle. 'This is no longer an exercise. We are now in a combat situation, with a hostile and presumably armed opponent.'

Holly rubbed her ankle where the shackle had chafed. 'Your brother, Turnball, has Captain Kelp in the human dwelling. He has threatened to feed him a Tunnel Blue spider if anything goes wrong with the plan.'

Root sighed, leaning against the rock. 'We can't go inside the dwelling. If we do, not only are we disorientated, but the arrest won't be legal. Turnball is clever. Even if we did outsmart his goons, we couldn't take the house.'

'We could use laser sights and knock out the target,'

suggested Holly. 'Then Captain Kelp could walk out himself.'

If the target had been anyone else besides his own brother, Root would have smiled. 'Yes, Corporal Short. We could do that.'

Root and Holly double-timed to a ridge overlooking the human dwelling. The cottage was in a hollow, surrounded by silver birch trees.

The commander scratched his chin. 'We have to get closer. I need to get a clean shot through one of the windows. One chance may be all we get.'

'Should I take one rifle, sir?' asked Holly.

'No. You're not licensed for weapons. Captain Kelp's life is at stake here, so I need steady fingers on the trigger. And even if you did bag Turnball, it would blow our entire case.'

'So what can I do?'

Root checked the load in both weapons. 'Stay here. If Turnball gets me, then go back to the shuttle and activate the distress signal. If help doesn't arrive and you see Turnball coming, then set the self-destruct.'

'But I can fly the shuttle,' protested Holly. 'I have hundreds of hours on the simulators.'

'And no pilot's licence,' added the commander. 'If you fly that thing, you may as well kiss your career goodbye. Set the self-destruct, then wait for the Retrieval Squad.' He handed Holly the starter chip, which doubled as a locator. 'That's a direct order, Short, so take that insolent look off your face, it's making me nervous. And when I get nervous I tend to fire people. Get the message?'

'Yessir. Message understood, sir.'

'Good.'

Holly squatted behind the ridge while her commander threaded his way through the trees towards the house itself. Halfway down the hill, he buzzed up his shield, becoming all but invisible to the naked eye. When a fairy shielded, he vibrated so quickly that the eyes could not capture an image of him. Of course, Root would have to turn off his shield to take the shot at his brother, but that need not be until the last moment.

Root could taste metal filings in the air, doubtless left over from the radio jammer that Turnball had detonated earlier. He stepped carefully over the uneven terrain until the front windows of the house were clearly visible. The curtains were open, but there was no sign of Turnball or Captain Kelp. Round the back then.

Hugging the wall, the commander crept along the cracked flagstone path to the rear of the cottage. Trees lined both sides of a narrow unkempt yard. And there, perched on a stool on the flagstone patio, was his brother, Turnball, face lifted to the morning sun without a care in the world.

Root's breath caught and his step faltered. His only brother. Flesh of his flesh. For a single moment, the commander imagined what it would be like to embrace his brother and wash away the past, but the moment quickly passed. It was too late for reconciliation. Fairies had almost died, and still could.

Root raised his weapon, training the barrel on his brother. It was a ridiculously easy shot for even a mediocre marksman. He could not believe that his brother had been stupid enough to expose himself in this way. As he crept closer, Julius was saddened by how old Turnball looked. There was barely a century between them, and yet his older brother looked as though he had barely enough energy to stand. Longevity was part of fairy magic, and without magic, time had taken a premature hold on Turnball.

'Hello, Julius, I can hear you there,' said Turnball, without opening his eyes. 'The sun is glorious, is she not? How can you live without her? Why don't you unshield? I haven't seen your face for so long.'

Root relaxed his shield and fought to keep his aim steady. 'Shut up, Turnball. Just don't speak to me. You're a convict-to-be, that's all. Nothing more.'

Turnball opened his eyes. 'Ah, little brother. You don't look well. High blood pressure. No doubt brought on by hunting for me.'

Julius couldn't help being drawn into conversation. 'Look who's talking. You look like a rug that's been beaten once too often. And still wearing the old LEP uniform, I see. We don't have ruffled collars any more, Turnball. If you were still a captain, you'd know that.'

Turnball fluffed his collar. 'Is that really what you want to talk to me about, Julius? Uniforms? After all this time.'

'We'll have plenty of time to talk when I visit you in prison.'

Turnball extended his wrists dramatically. 'Very well, Commander. Take me away.'

Julius was suspicious. 'Just like that? What are you up to?'

'I'm tired,' sighed his brother. 'I'm tired of life among the Mud People. They are such barbarians. I want to go home, even if it is to a cell. You have obviously dispatched my helpers, so what choice do I have?'

Root's soldier's intuition was pounding like a bell clapper inside his skull. He dropped the thermal filter in his visor and saw that there was only one other fairy in the dwelling. Someone tied in a sitting position. That must be Captain Kelp.

'And where is the delightful Corporal Short?' asked Turnball casually.

Root decided to leave himself an ace in the hole, in case he needed it. 'Dead,' he spat. 'Your dwarf shot her when she warned me. That's another charge you will have to answer for.'

'What's another charge? I only have one life to spend in captivity. You'd better hurry up and arrest me, Julius. Because if you don't, I may go back inside the house.'

Julius had to think quickly. It was obvious that Turnball had something planned. And he would probably make his move when Julius zipped on the cuffs. Then again he couldn't make a move if he was unconscious.

Without a word of warning, the commander hit his brother with a low-level charge. Just enough to knock him out for a few moments. Turnball slumped backwards, a surprised look on his face.

Root holstered his Neutrino and hurried towards his brother. He wanted Turnball trussed like a solstice turkey when he came to. Julius took three steps, then he didn't feel so well. A pounding headache landed on him like a lead weight from a height. Sweat popped from every pore and his sinuses were instantly blocked. What was going on here? Root dropped to his knees, then all fours. He felt like throwing up, then sleeping for eight hours. His bones had turned to jelly and his head weighed a tonne. Every breath sounded amplified and distant.

The commander stayed in that position for over a minute, completely helpless. A kitten could have knocked him over and stolen his wallet. He could only watch as Turnball regained consciousness, shook his head to dislodge the after-buzz, then began to smile slowly.

Turnball rose, towering above his helpless brother. 'Who is the smart one?' he shouted at his stricken brother. 'Who has always been the smart one?'

Root could not answer. All he could do was try to marshal his thoughts. It was too late for his body: that had betrayed him.

'Jealousy,' proclaimed Turnball, spreading his arms. 'This has always been about jealousy. I am better than you in every way, and you can't handle it.' The madness was in his eyes now, and flecks of spittle spattered on to his chin and cheeks.

Root managed two words: 'You're insane.'

'No,' said Turnball. 'What I am is fed up. I am fed up of running away from my own brother. The whole thing is too melodramatic. So, much as it pains me to do it, I am going to take your edge away from you. I am going to take your magic. Then you will be like me. I've already started, would you like to know how?'

Turnball took a tiny remote control from the pocket of his great coat. He pressed a button, and glass walls shimmered into view all round the brothers. They were no longer outside in the garden, they were inside a conservatory. Root had entered through open double doors.

'Naughty, Commander,' admonished Turnball. 'You entered a human dwelling without an invitation. That is against the rules of our religion. You do that a few more times, and your magic will be gone forever.'

Root's head hung lower. He had waltzed into Turnball's trap, like a raw recruit two days out of the Academy. His brother had rigged a few sheets of cam foil and some projectors to disguise the conservatory, and he had fallen for it. His only hope now was Holly Short. And if Turnball had outwitted Captain Kelp and himself, what chance did a girl have?

Turnball grabbed Root by the scruff of the neck, dragging him towards the house. 'You don't look so well,' he said, his voice loaded with false concern. 'We'd better get you inside.'

CHAPTER 5: CAREER OR COMRADES?

HOLLY watched the commander's capture from the ridge. When Root went down, she jumped to her feet and sprinted down the hillside, fully prepared to disobey her orders and go to the commander's aid. Then the conservatory shimmered into view, stopping Holly in her tracks. She would be of no use inside the house boundaries, unless she could somehow save the commander by vomiting. There had to be another way.

Holly turned, crawling back uphill on all fours, digging her fingers into the earth, dragging herself towards the wood. Once undercover, she activated the locator in the shuttle's starter chip. Her orders were to return to the craft and send a distress signal. Eventually it would penetrate the jammer's waffle. Though by then, it would probably be too late.

She ran across the wild fields, scutch grass grabbing at her boots. Birds circled overhead, their desperate cackling somehow echoing her own mood. The wind pushed in her face, slowing her pace. Even nature seemed to be against the LEP on this day.

The locator beep led her across a thigh-high stream. The freezing waters slashed through gaps in Holly's suit, pouring over her legs. She ignored it, and a trout the size of her arm who seemed very interested in the material of her suit. She battled on, over a human-sized stile and up a steep hill. Low-lying fog sat on the hilltop like whipped cream on a wedge of cake.

Holly could smell the fog before she reached it. It was chemical. Manufactured. The shuttle was obviously inside the cloud bank.

With the last vestiges of her strength, Holly batted aside sheets of clinging fake fog, remote activating the shuttle door. She collapsed inside, lying prone on the bay doors for a brief moment, drawing in huge breaths. Then she clambered to her feet and slapped the emergency button on the dash, activating the emergency beam.

The beam icon winked on, followed by a huge anti-climax. All Holly could do was sit there watching failure messages flash on to the plasma screen. Here she was, sitting on millions of ingots' worth of technology, and her orders were to do nothing.

Captain Kelp and Commander Root were in mortal danger, and her orders were to twiddle her thumbs. If she flew the shuttle she would be in breach of a direct order, and her career in Recon was over before it began. But if she didn't fly it, then her comrades were dead. Which was more important, career or comrades?

Holly stuffed the starter chip into the ignition slot, and strapped herself in.

Turnball Root was enjoying himself immensely. Finally the moment he had dreamed about for so many decades had arrived. His baby brother was at his mercy.

'I thought I might keep you here for the next twenty-four hours until your magic is completely gone. Then we will become true brothers again. A real team. Perhaps you will decide to join me. If not, you certainly won't be leading the chase. The LEP do not employ personnel without magic.'

Root was curled up in a ball on the floor, his face greener than a sprite's behind. 'Dream on,' he grunted. 'You're no brother of mine.'

Turnball pinched his cheek. 'You'll warm to me, little brother. It's amazing who a fairy turns to in times of desperation. Believe me, I know.'

'In your dreams.'

Turnball sighed. 'Still obstinate. You are probably entertaining notions of escape. Or perhaps you believe that in the end, I could never hurt my baby brother. Is that it? You believe that I have a heart? Perhaps a small demonstration . . .'

Turnball lifted Captain Kelp's head from his chest. Trouble was barely conscious. He had been in the house for too long. He would never run at a hundred per cent of his magical potential again. Not without an infusion from a team of warlocks. And soon.

Turnball held a small cage up to Trouble's face. Inside, a Tunnel Blue spider scratched at the mesh.

'I like these creatures,' said Turnball gently. 'They will go through anything to survive. They remind me of myself. This little one will make short work of the captain here.'

Root tried to raise a hand. 'Turnball, don't.'

'I must,' said Turnball. 'Think of it as already done. There is nothing you can do.'

'Turnball. It's murder.'

'Murder is a word. Just another word.'

Turnball Root began wiggling the tiny bolt. Barely an inch of metal was left to hold the hatch, when a spearlike communications spike punctured the roof, embedding itself in the floorboards. Holly's amplified voice boomed from the speaker in the shaft, shaking the entire house.

'Turnball Root,' said the voice. 'Release your prisoners and surrender.'

Turnball reset the bolt, pocketing the cage. 'The girl is dead, eh? When are you going to stop lying to me, Julius?'

Julius was too weak to respond. The world had become a bad dream. He was breathing treacle.

Turnball turned his attention to the com spike. He knew that the instrument would broadcast his words to the shuttle above.

'The pretty corporal, alive and well. Ah well, no matter. You cannot come in, and I will not go out. If you do enter,

I will go free. Not only that, but I will have gained a shuttle. If you try to detain me when I am ready to leave, then my arrest will be illegal and my lawyer will carve you up like a whale in a human boat.'

'I will blast that house to kingdom come,' warned Holly, through the com spike.

Turnball spread his arms. 'Blast away. You will put me out of my misery. But when the first bolt hits, I will feed my spider to the commander. The Root brothers will not be surviving this assault. Face it, Corporal. You cannot win as long as this house stands.'

Overhead in the shuttle, Holly realized that Turnball had all the angles covered. He knew the LEP rulebook better than she did. Even though she was the one with the aircraft, Turnball was the one with the upper hand. If she broke the rules, then he simply walked away and took off in his own shuttle, which was no doubt concealed somewhere close by.

You cannot win as long as this house stands.

He was right. She couldn't win as long as a human dwelling surrounded her fellow LEP officers. But what if there were no dwelling?

Holly quickly checked the shuttle's specs. It had the standard docking clamps prow and aft. The clamps allowed the shuttle to be reeled in for landing on uneven terrain, but could also be used to tow vehicles, or possibly for other more unconventional operations.

You cannot win as long as this house stands.

Holly felt sweat break out in the nape of her neck. Was she crazy? Could what she had planned ever stand up in court? It didn't matter, she decided. Lives were at stake.

She flipped the safety covers from the prow clamps, angling the shuttle so that the nose was pointing at the fisherman's cottage.

'Final warning, Turnball,' Holly said into the com spike. 'Are you coming out?'

'Not just yet, my dear,' came the cheerful reply. 'But do feel free to come in and join us.'

Holly did not bother with more conversation. She deployed the prow clamps with the flick of a switch. The clamps on this particular model were operated by opposing magnetic fields, and there was a slight pulse in the readouts as the two cylindrical clamps rocketed from the belly of the shuttle and straight through the roof of the cottage.

Holly set the cable for twenty metres so the clamps would not reach head height. Gripper claws extended from the clamps, grasping wooden joists, floorboards and plaster. Holly retracted the clamps, discarding the detritus. Most of the roof was gone, and the south wall teetered dangerously. Holly took a quick photo and ran it through the computer for analysis.

'Computer,' she said. 'Verbal query.'

'Proceed,' said the computer in the tones of Foaly, the LEP's technical wizard.

'Locate load-bearing points.'

'Locating.'

In seconds the computer had reduced the photograph to a 3D line representation. Four red dots pulsed gently on the drawing. If she could hit any one, the entire house would collapse. Holly looked closer. Demolition had been one of her favourite classes at the Academy, and she could see that if she took out the first-floor crossbeam on the gable end, then what was left of the house would collapse outwards.

Turnball was ranting into the com spike. 'What are you playing at?' he roared. 'You can't do this. It's against regulations. Even if you tear off the roof, you can't come into this house.'

'What house?' said Holly, and fired the third clamp.

The clamp grabbed the beam and ripped it right out of the brickwork. The house groaned like a mortally wounded giant, then shuddered and collapsed. It was almost comical in its suddenness, and barely a brick fell inwards. Turnball Root was left with nowhere to hide.

Holly put a laser dot on Turnball's chest. 'Take one step,' she said, 'and I will blast you into the ocean.'

'You can't shoot me,' Turnball retorted. 'You're not certified for combat.'

'No,' said a voice beside him. 'But I am.'

Trouble Kelp was on his feet, dragging the enormous chair behind him. He launched himself at Turnball Root, and they went down in a tangle of wooden and flesh-and-bone legs.

Overhead in the shuttle, Holly slapped the dash. She had been quite prepared to knock out Turnball Root with a laser sting; after all, it was a little late to start worrying about regulations. She piloted the shuttle to a safe distance, and swooped in for landing.

In the cottage ruins, Commander Root's strength was slowly returning. Now that the human dwelling was effectively destroyed, the magic sickness was receding fast. He coughed, shook his head and climbed to his knees.

Trouble was fighting with Turnball in the rubble. Fighting and losing. Turnball may be older, but he was possessed and lucid. He smashed blow after blow into the captain's face.

Julius picked up a rifle from the floor. 'Give it up, Turnball,' he said tiredly. 'It's over.'

Turnball's shoulders sagged, and he turned slowly. 'Ah, Julius. Little brother. It's come to this, once more. Brother against brother.'

'Stop talking, please. Lie flat on the ground with your hands behind your head. You know the position.'

Turnball did not lie down, instead he stood slowly, talking seductively all the time. 'This doesn't have to be the end. Just let me go. I'll be out of your life forever. You'll never hear from me again, I swear it. This whole thing was a mistake, I see that now. I regret it, sincerely.'

Root's energy was returning, bolstering his resolve. 'Shut up, Turnball, or so help me I will blast you where you stand.'

Turnball smiled easily. 'You can't kill me: we're family.'

'I don't have to kill you, just knock you out. Now look into my eyes and tell me I wouldn't do that.'

Turnball searched his brother's eyes and found the truth there.

'I can't go to prison, brother. I'm not a common criminal. Prison would make me run of the mill.'

In a flash, Turnball reached into his pocket for the tiny mesh cage. He released the bolt and swallowed the spider. 'There was an old man who swallowed a spider,' he said, and then: 'Goodbye, brother.'

Root crossed the ruined kitchen in three paces. He ripped open a fallen cupboard searching among the foodstuffs. He grabbed a jar of instant coffee and spun the lid off. In two more paces he was kneeling beside his fallen brother, forcing handfuls of coffee grains down his throat.

'It's not going to be that easy, Turnball. You are a common criminal, and you will go to jail like one.'

After a moment Turnball stopped jerking. The spider was dead. The old elf was hurt, but alive. Root quickly zipped him up in a pair of cuffs, then hurried to Trouble's side.

The captain was already sitting up. 'No offence, Commander, but your brother hits like a pixie.'

Root nearly smiled. 'Lucky for you, Captain.'

Holly rushed down the garden path, through what had once been a parlour, and into the kitchen.

'Is everything all right?'

Root had had an unusually stressful day, and unfortunately Holly caught some of the overspill.

'No, Short, everything is not all right,' he barked, brushing dust from his lapels. 'My exercise has been hijacked by a notorious criminal, my captain has allowed himself to be tied up like a prize pig, and you have disobeyed a direct order and flown a shuttle. This means that our entire case is blown.'

'Just this case,' said Trouble. 'He still has several lifetimes to serve for past crimes.'

'That is beside the point,' continued Root, unrelenting. 'I cannot trust you, Short. You saved us, it's true, but Recon is all about stealth, and you are not a stealthy person. It might seem unreasonable after all you've done, but I'm afraid there is no place for you in my squad.'

'Commander,' objected Trouble. 'You can't flunk the girl after all this. If it wasn't for her I'd be biodegrading right now.'

'This is not your decision, Captain. Nor is it your fight. This squadron is all about trust, and Corporal Short did not earn mine.'

Trouble was flabbergasted. 'Pardon me, sir, but you haven't given her a fair chance.'

Root glanced sharply at his officer. Trouble was one of his best fairies, and he was putting his neck on the block for this girl.

'Very well, Short. If you can do anything to change my mind, now is your chance. Your only chance. Well, can you do anything?'

Holly looked at Trouble, and she could have sworn that

he winked at her. This gave her the courage to do something unthinkable, ridiculously impertinent and insubordinate given the circumstances.

'Just this, Commander,' she said.

Holly drew her paintball pistol and shot Commander Julius Root three times in the chest. The impact knocked him back a step.

'You tag me before I tag you, and you're in,' mumbled Holly. 'No questions asked.'

Trouble laughed until he threw up. Literally. The magic sickness had left him nauseous. 'Oh gods,' he panted. 'She got you there, Julius. That's what you said. That's what you've been saying for the past hundred years.'

Root ran a finger through the congealing paint on his chest plate.

Holly stared at her toes, convinced that she was about to be slung out of the force altogether. To the left, Turnball was calling for his lawyer. Flocks of protected birds were whirling overhead, and out in the fields Unix and Bobb would be wondering what had hit them.

Holly finally risked an upward glance. The commander's features were twisted with conflicting emotions. Anger was in there, and disbelief too. And maybe, just maybe, a touch of admiration.

'You did tag me,' he said finally.

'That's right,' agreed Trouble. 'She did.'

'And I did say . . .'

'You certainly did.'

Root rounded on Trouble. 'What are you? A parrot? Will you shut your trap, I'm trying to swallow my pride here.'

Trouble locked his lips, throwing away the imaginary key.

'This is going to cost the department a fortune, Short. We're going to have to rebuild here, or generate a localized tidal wave to cover the damage. That's six months of my budget right there.'

'I know, sir,' said Holly humbly. 'Sorry, sir.'

Root drew out his wallet, taking a set of silver acorns from a compartment. He tossed them to Holly, who almost missed the catch in her surprise.

'Put them on. Welcome to Recon.'

'Thank you, sir,' said Holly, clipping the insignia to her lapel. It caught the rising sun and flashed like a satellite.

'The first female in Recon,' groaned the commander.

Holly lowered her face to hide a grin that she couldn't contain.

'You're going to wash out in six months,' continued Root, 'and probably cost me a fortune.'

He was wrong about the first, but right about the second.

SOMETHING IS SERIOUSLY WRONG WITH ARTEMIS FOWL.

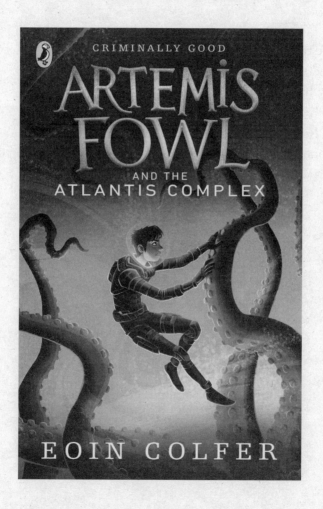

CRIMINALLY GOOD

ARTEMIS FOWL
AND THE
ATLANTIS COMPLEX

EOIN COLFER

Find out what afflicts the child genius in the
seventh book in the Artemis Fowl series
– turn the page for an extract . . .

VATNAJÖKULL, ICELAND

 VATNAJÖKULL is the biggest glacier in Europe with an area of more than five thousand stark blue-white miles. It is for the most part uninhabited and desolate, and, for scientific reasons, the perfect place for Artemis Fowl to demonstrate to the fairy People how exactly he planned to save the world. Also, a little dramatic scenery never hurts a presentation.

One part of Vatnajökull that does see human traffic is the Great Skua restaurant on the shores of the glacier lagoon, which caters to groups of ice tourists from May to August. Artemis had arranged to meet the proprietor at this *closed for the season* establishment very early on the morning of September first. His fifteenth birthday.

Artemis steered his rented snowmobile along the lagoon's rippling coastline where the glacier sloped into a black pool dotted with a crazy-paving pattern of broken ice plates. The wind roared around his head like an excited crowd in a stadium, carrying with it arrowheads of sleet that peppered his nose and mouth. The space was vast and unforgiving, and Artemis knew that to be injured alone on this tundra would lead to a quick and painful death – or at the very least abject humiliation before the popping flashes of the tourist season's tail end, which was slightly less painful than painful death but lasted longer.

The Great Skua's owner, a burly Icelander in proud possession of both a walrus moustache with the wingspan of a fair-sized cormorant and the unlikely name of Adam Adamsson, stood in the restaurant's porch, popping his fingers and stamping his feet to the rhythm in his head and also finding the time to chuckle at Artemis's erratic progress along the lagoon's frozen shore.

'That was a mighty display,' said Adamsson when Artemis finally managed to ram the snowmobile into the restaurant's decking. 'Hell, *harður maður*. I haven't laughed that hard since my dog tried to eat his reflection.'

Artemis smiled dourly, aware that the restaurateur was poking fun at his driving skills, or lack thereof. 'Hmmph,' he grunted, dismounting the ski-doo as stiffly as a cowboy after three days on a cattle drive, whose horse had died, forcing him to ride the broadest cow in the herd.

The old man actually cackled. 'Now you even sound like my dog.'

It was not Artemis Fowl's habit to make undignified entrances, but, without his bodyguard Butler on hand, he had been forced to rely on his own motor skills, which were famously unsophisticated. One of the sixth-year wits at St Bartleby's School, the heir to a hotel fortune, had nicknamed Artemis *Left Foot Fowl*, as in he had two left feet and couldn't kick a football with either of them. Artemis had tolerated this ribbing for about a week and then bought out the young heir's hotel chain. This choked the teasing off abruptly.

'Everything is ready, I trust?' said Artemis, flexing fingers inside his patented sola-gloves. He noticed that one hand was uncomfortably warm; the thermostat must have taken a knock when he'd clipped an ice obelisk half a mile down the coast. He tugged out the power wire with his teeth; there was not much danger of hypothermia as the autumn temperature hovered just below zero.

'And hello to you,' said Adamsson. 'Nice to finally meet you face to face, if not eye to eye.'

Artemis did not rise to the *forge a relationship* lure that Adamsson had tossed out. He did not have room in his life at the moment for yet another friend that he didn't trust.

'I do not intend to ask you for your daughter's hand in marriage, Mr Adamsson, so I think we can skip over any ice-breakers you may feel obliged to offer. Is everything ready?'

Adam Adamsson's pre-prepared ice-breakers melted in his throat and he nodded half a dozen times.

'All ready. Your crate is round the back. I have supplied a vegetarian buffet and goodie bags from the Blue Lagoon Spa.

A few seats have been laid out too, as bluntly requested in your terse e-mail. None of your party turned up, though – nobody but you – after all my labours.'

Artemis lifted an aluminium briefcase from the ski-doo's luggage box. 'Don't you worry about that, Mr Adamsson. Why don't you head back to Reykjavik and spend some of that extortionate fee you charged me for a couple of hours' usage of your frankly third-rate restaurant and perhaps find a friendless tree stump to listen to your woes?'

A couple of hours. Third-rate. Two plus three equals five. Good.

Now it was Adamsson's turn to grunt and the tips of his walrus moustache quivered slightly.

'No need for the attitude, young Fowl. We are both men, are we not? Men are entitled to a little respect.'

'Oh, really? Perhaps we should ask the whales? Or perhaps the mink?'

Adamsson scowled, his wind-burnt face creasing like a prune. 'OK, OK. I get the message. No need to hold me responsible for the crimes of man. You teenagers are all the same. Let's see if your generation does any better with the planet.'

Artemis clicked the briefcase's lock snap precisely twenty times before striding into the restaurant.

'Believe me, we teenagers are not all the same,' he said as he passed Adamsson. 'And I intend to do quite a bit better.'

There were more than a dozen tables inside the restaurant, all with chairs stacked on top, except for one, which had been dressed with a linen cloth and laden with bottled glacier water and spa bags for each of the five places.

Five, thought Artemis. *A good number. Solid. Predictable. Four fives are twenty.*

Artemis had decided lately that five was his number. Good things happened when five was in the mix. The logician in him knew that this was ridiculous, but he couldn't ignore the fact that the tragedies in his life had occurred in years not divisible by five: his father had disappeared and been mutilated, his old friend Commander Julius Root of the LEP had been murdered by the notorious pixie Opal Koboi, both in years with no five. He was five feet five inches tall and weighed fifty-five kilos. If he touched something five times or a multiple of that, then that thing stayed reliable. A door would remain closed, for example, or a keepsake would protect that doorway, as it was supposed to.

Today the signs were good. He was fifteen years old. Three times five. And his hotel room in Reykjavik had been number forty-five. Even the ski-doo that had got him this far unscathed had a registration which was a multiple of five, and boasted a 50 cc engine to boot. All good. There were only four guests coming to the meeting, but including him that made five. So no need to panic.

A part of Artemis was horrified by his newfound superstition about numbers.

Get a grip on yourself. You are a Fowl. We do not rely on luck — abandon these ridiculous obsessions and compulsions.

ᚻᚻ•ᚢᚫᚦ→•ᚦᚪᚫᚾᚷᚦ•ᚦᚦ•ᚢᚦᚷᚦᚫᚦᚷᚦᚻ

Artemis clicked the case's latch to appease the number gods – twenty times, four fives – and felt his heart slow down.

I will break my habits tomorrow, when this job is done.

He loitered at the maître d's podium until Adamsson and his snow tractor had disappeared over a curved ridge of snow that could have been a whale's spine, then waited a further minute until the vehicle's rumbling had faded to an old smoker's cough.

Very well. Time to do some business.

Artemis descended the five wooden steps to the main restaurant floor (*excellent, good omen*), threading a series of columns hung with replicas of the Stora-Borg mask until he arrived at the head of the laid table. The seats were angled to face him and a slight shimmer, like a heat haze, flickered over the table top.

'Good morning, friends,' said Artemis in Gnommish, forcing himself to pronounce the fairy words in confident, almost jovial, tones. 'Today's the day we save the world.'

The heat haze seemed more electrical now with crackles of neon-white interference running through it and faces swimming in its depths like ghosts from a dream. The faces solidified and grew torsos and limbs. Small figures, like children, appeared. Like children, but not the same. These were representatives of the fairy People and among them perhaps the only friends Artemis had.

'Save the world?' said Captain Holly Short of the LEPrecon. 'Same old Artemis Fowl, and I say that sarcastically as *saving the world* is not like you at all.'

Artemis knew he should smile, but he could not, so instead he found fault, something that would not seem out of character.

'You need a new shield amplifier, Foaly,' he said to a centaur who was balanced awkwardly on a chair designed for humans. 'I could see the shimmer from the front porch. Call yourself a technical expert? How old is the one you're using?'

Foaly stamped a hoof, which was an irritated tic of his and the reason he never won at cards. 'Nice to see you too, Mud Boy.'

'How old?'

'I don't know. Maybe four years.'

'Four. There, you see. What sort of number is that?'

Foaly stuck out his bottom lip. 'What *sort* of number? There are *types* now, Artemis? That amplifier is good for another hundred years. Maybe it could do with a little tuning, but that's all.'

Holly stood and walked lightly to the head of the table.

'Do you two have to start with the sparring right away? Isn't that getting a little clichéd after all these years? You're like a couple of mutts marking territory.' She laid two slim fingers on Artemis's forearm. 'Lay off him, Artemis. You know how sensitive centaurs are.'

Artemis could not meet her eyes. Inside his left snow boot, he counted off twenty toe-taps.

'Very well. Let's change the subject.'

'Please do,' said the third fairy in the room. 'We've come

across from Russia for this, Fowl. So if the subject could be changed to what we came here to discuss . . .'

Commander Raine Vinyáya was obviously not happy being so far from her beloved Police Plaza. She had assumed command of LEP general some years previously and prided herself on keeping a finger in every ongoing mission. 'I have operations to get back to, Artemis. The pixies are rioting, calling for Opal Koboi's release from prison, and the swear-toad epidemic has flared up again. Please do us the courtesy of getting on with it.'

Artemis nodded. Vinyáya was being openly antagonistic and that was an emotion that could be trusted, unless of course it was a bluff and the commander was a secret fan of his, unless it was a double bluff and she really did feel antagonistic.

That sounds insane, Artemis realized. *Even to me.*

Though she was barely a metre tall, Commander Vinyáya was a formidable presence and someone that Artemis never intended to underestimate. While the commander was almost four hundred years old in fairy terms, she was barely middle-aged and in any terms she was a striking figure: lean and sallow, with the reactive feline pupils occasionally found in elfin eyes, but even that rarity was not her most distinctive physical characteristic. Raine Vinyáya had a mane of silver hair that seemed to trap any available light and send it rippling along her shoulders.

Artemis cleared his throat and switched his focus from numbers to the project, or, as he liked to think of it, *THE*

PROJECT. In the end, when it came down to it, this was the only plan that mattered.

Holly punched his shoulder gently.

'You look pale. Even paler than usual. You OK, birthday boy?'

Artemis finally succeeded in meeting her eyes – one hazel, one blue – framed by a wide brow and a slash of auburn fringe that Holly had grown out from her usual crew-cut.

'Fifteen years old today,' muttered Artemis. 'Three fives. That's a good thing.'

Holly blinked.

Artemis Fowl muttering? And no mention of her new hairstyle – usually Artemis picked up on physical changes straight away.

'I . . . ah . . . I suppose so. Where's Butler? Scouting the perimeter?'

'No. No, I sent him away. Juliet needed him.'

'Nothing too serious?'

'Not serious but necessary. Family business. He trusts you to look after me.'

Holly's lips tightened as though she had tasted something sour.

'He trusts somebody else to shepherd his principal? Are you sure this is Butler we're talking about?'

'Of course. And, anyway, it's better that he's not here. Whenever my plans go awry, he's close at hand. It's vital, *imperative*, that this meeting goes ahead and that nothing goes wrong.'

Holly's jaw actually dropped in shock. It was almost comical to see. If she understood Artemis correctly, he was *blaming* Butler for the failure of previous schemes. Butler? His staunchest ally.

'Good idea. Let's go ahead, then. The four of us should get this show on the road.'

This from Foaly who had spoken the dreaded number with no thought for the consequences.

Four. Very bad number. The absolute worst. Chinese people hate the number four because it sounds like their word for death.

Almost worse than saying the number four was the fact that there were only four people in the room. Commander Trouble Kelp had apparently not been able to make it. In spite of their historic dislike for each other, Artemis wished the commander were here now.

'Where is Commander Kelp, Holly? I thought he was attending today. We could use the protection.'

Holly stood at the table, ramrod straight in her blue jumpsuit, acorn cluster glittering on her chest.

'Trouble . . . Commander Kelp has enough to deal with in Police Plaza, but don't worry. There's an entire squadron of LEPtactical hovering overhead in a shielded shuttle. Not even a snow fox could make it in here without a singed tail.'

Artemis shucked off his snow jacket and gloves. 'Thank you, Captain. I am encouraged by your thoroughness. As a matter of interest, how many fairies are there in an LEP squadron? Exactly?'

'Fourteen,' replied Holly, one jagged eyebrow raised.

'Fourteen. Hmm. That is not so . . .' Then a light-bulb moment. 'And a pilot, I presume?'

'Fourteen *including* the pilot. That's enough to take on any human squadron you care to throw at them.'

For a moment it seemed as though Artemis Fowl would turn round and flee the meeting that he himself had requested. A tendon tugged at his neck and one forefinger tapped the chair's wooden headrest. Then Artemis swallowed and nodded with a nervousness that escaped from him like a canary from a cat's mouth before being swallowed back down.

'Very well. Fourteen will have to do. Please, Holly, sit. Let me tell you about the project.'

Holly backed up slowly, searching Artemis's face for the cockiness that usually dwelled in his smirk lines. It was not there.

Whatever this project is, she thought, *it's big.*

THE FINAL BOOK IN THE
ARTEMIS FOWL SERIES . . .

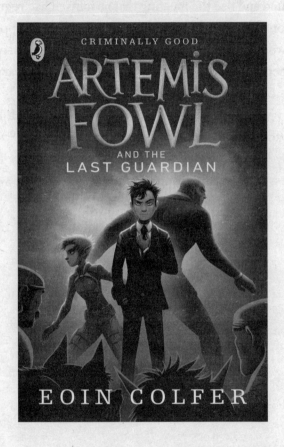

CRIMINALLY GOOD

ARTEMIS FOWL
AND THE
LAST GUARDIAN

EOIN COLFER

Opal Koboi is back, and up to no good. Her plan:
to release an ancient spell that will wipe out all human life.

Artemis and his friends must make a final stand against
the power-crazed pixie. But who will be willing to
make the ultimate sacrifice?

The People – A Spotter's Guide

There are many different types of fairy and, with each one, it's important to know what you are dealing with. This is just some of the information collected by Artemis Fowl during his adventures. It is confidential and must *not* fall into the wrong hands. The future of the People depends on it.

Elves

Distinguishing features: About one metre tall. Pointy ears. Brown skin. Red hair.
Character: Intelligent. Strong sense of right and wrong. Very loyal. Sarcastic sense of humour, although that might just be a particular female LEP officer.
Loves: Flying, either in a craft or with wings.
Situations to avoid: They really don't like it if you kidnap them and take their gold.

Dwarfs

Distinguishing features: Short, round and hairy. Large tombstone teeth – good for grinding . . . well, anything really. Unhingable jaws enabling them to excavate tunnels. Sensitive beard hair. Skin capable of acting like suction cups when dehydrated. Smelly.
Character: Sensitive. Intelligent. Criminal tendencies.
Loves: Gold and precious gems. Tunnelling. The dark.
Situations to avoid: Being in a confined space with them when they have been tunnelling and have a build-up of trapped air. If they reach for the bum flap on their trousers, get out of there . . .

Trolls

Distinguishing features: Huge – as big as an elephant. Light-sensitive eyes. Hate noise. Hairy with dreadlocks. Retractable claws. Teeth! – lots and lots of teeth. Tusks like a wild boar (a really wild boar). Green tongue. Exceptionally strong. Weak point at the base of the skull.
Character: Very, very stupid – the troll has a tiny brain. Mean and bad-tempered.
Loves: Eating – anything. A couple of cows would make a light snack.
Situations to avoid: Are you joking? If you even think a troll is near, run like the wind.

GOBLINS
Distinguishing features:
Scaly. Lidless eyes – they lick their eyeballs to keep them moist. Able to throw fireballs. They go on all fours when speed is important. Forked tongue. Less than a metre tall. Slimy, fireproof skin.
Character: Not clever, but cunning. Argumentative. Ambitious. Power-hungry.
Loves: Fire. A good argument. Power.
Situations to avoid: Don't get in the way if they're throwing a fireball.

SPRITES
Distinguishing features:
About one metre tall. Pointy ears. Green skin. Wings.
Character: Average intelligence. Generally happy-go-lucky attitude.
Loves: Flying – more than anything else under or above the Earth.
Situations to avoid: Watch out for low-flying sprites – they don't always look where they're going.

CENTAURS
Distinguishing features:
Half-man, half-pony. Hairy – obviously! Hooves can get very dry.
Character: Extremely intelligent. Vain. Paranoid. Kind. Computer geeks.
Loves: Showing off. Inventing.
Situations to avoid: They aren't very dangerous physically, but they will sulk if you criticize their latest invention, mess with their hard drive or borrow their hoof moisturizer.

PIXIES
Distinguishing features:
About one metre tall. Pointy ears. Apart from their ears and their height, pixies look almost human.
Character: Extremely intelligent. No morals. Cunning. Ambitious. Greedy.
Loves: Power and money. Chocolate.
Situations to avoid: Never get on the wrong side of a pixie, especially one as clever and ruthless as Opal Koboi, unless you are as brilliant as Artemis Fowl, of course.

ARTEMIS FOWL:
HUMAN-FAIRY HYBRID

Butler and I will be observing closely the extent and form of my
new powers, and how they may affect me.

Distinguishing features:
14 years old. Criminal mastermind (see IQ rating).
One magic eye (hazel) and one human eye (blue).

Does this mean telepathic connection with Holly Short?
Do I have mesmer skills?

Blue sparks emitted from fingertips. Healing powers.
To be continued ...

Any other magic?

IQ rating

145–164	165–179	180–199	200+
Genius	High Genius	Highest Recorded Genius	Artemis Fowl

DEMONS

Distinguishing features: Are
born imps and stay that way
until they reach puberty, when
they warp into demons.
Demons have an armoured hide
which nothing can penetrate.
Razor-sharp talons and
curved horns.
Character: Loud.
Confrontational. Aggressive.

Loves: Hunting. Butchering.
Fighting. Howling.
Situations to avoid: Any
involving a demon. They are
the most human-hating
species known to man.
Exception to all of the above:
Warlocks. These are demons
with magical powers and fewer
anger issues.

Gnommish Alphabet

Never-seen-before fairy symbols

The World

Unknown

The Book

King of the Fairies

Unknown

Unknown

Unknown

Unknown

FOALY'S TOP-SECRET GADGETS

Titanium pod

Capable of carrying LEP officers to the Earth's
surface, either powered by its own motor
or able to ride on currents of hot gas released
by magma flares.

External camera

Retractable stabilizing fin

Harness

Instrument panels

Fender

Exhaust ports

Joystick

Clamp

Equipment for a member of the LEP Retrieval Squad

Locator

LCD locator screen

Locator
sensitivity
controls

Interface
ports

Wristband

Control joystick

Wings
('Dragonfly' model)

Counter-beat
wing stabilizers

Super-strength
polymer wings

Exhaust ports

Air intake

Helmet

20 mega-pixel camera

200 watt lamps

Anti-glare visor

Control buttons

Detachable
Oxygen/pollution
mask

THE BEGINNING

Wait – you didn't think that was it, did you?

Puffin has **LOADS** more stories for you to discover.

Find your next adventure at **puffin.co.uk**, along with:

- **Quizzes, games and apps starring your favourite characters**
- **Videos, podcasts and audiobook extracts**
- **The chance to check out brand-new books before anybody else!**

puffin.co.uk

Psst! You can also find Puffin on PopJam